Hell's Half-Acre

CALGARY PUBLIC LIBRARY

APR   2016

Also by Nicholas Nicastro

Antigone's Wake
The Isle of Stone
Empire of Ashes
Between Two Fires
The Eighteenth Captain
Circumference

Hell's Half-Acre

A Novel

NICHOLAS NICASTRO

WITNESS
IMPULSE
An Imprint of HarperCollinsPublishers

This is a work of fiction. Names, characters, places, and incidents are products of the author's imagination or are used fictitiously and are not to be construed as real. Any resemblance to actual events, locales, organizations, or persons, living or dead, is entirely coincidental.

Cover photo by Precious Posh Photography.

HELL'S HALF-ACRE. Copyright © 2015 by Nicholas Nicastro. All rights reserved under International and Pan-American Copyright Conventions. By payment of the required fees, you have been granted the nonexclusive, nontransferable right to access and read the text of this e-book on screen. No part of this text may be reproduced, transmitted, downloaded, decompiled, reverse-engineered, or stored in or introduced into any information storage and retrieval system, in any form or by any means, whether electronic or mechanical, now known or hereafter invented, without the express written permission of HarperCollins e-books.

EPub Edition NOVEMBER 2015 ISBN: 9780062422552
Print Edition ISBN: 9780062422569

10 9 8 7 6 5 4 3 2 1

Dedicated to M.J.O.

Help your brother's boat across the river,
and your own will reach the shore.
—Hindu proverb

Let Kansas bleed, if she has a fancy for it . . . Blood is a very common fluid. It is worth very little. A man is killed, it does not matter much; it is really a matter of small consequence to him, to his family, or to the country.

SENATOR LOUIS TREZEVANT WIGFALL
(D-TEXAS), 1858

Prologue

Anteroom

THE MAN AWOKE, nostrils plugged with slate dust as if he had become mineral. Half animate, he felt, but could not comprehend, that his right eyeball had been lying against the stone, rendering it misshapen. Blinking, his eyelid would not close over the flat-sided bulb. He tried to rise but found the impulse would not direct his limbs but only drifted toward his extremities like a handful of dirt settling in a still pond. When his fingers flexed, they traced tremulous ant trails in the slate.

A scratching pierced the stone man's scab of deafness. To turn his head toward the sound seemed as impossible as twisting a tree stump rooted in the ground. The effort wrung from him a groan, but more ancient, like the croak of the first fish to lift its scaly head from the water.

His wits coalesced. The slate that dusted him was the surface of some cellar floor. The closeness of the air around him, and the way sound fell dead nearby, suggested he lay in a tiny space, little more than a generously proportioned grave. In the vault of this peculiar oblivion, there were lines of flickering light, like a lamp shining through the seams of a rudely constructed door. Formless shadows broke the light that, by their shadows moving, seemed cast by living figures. The obscurities flitted, paused, whispered to each other. Thoughts freed from self-consciousness, a buried Narcissus, he believed everything they said must be about him. He was correct.

Instead of pain, he felt an ache that pierced him like a bad memory. The tears shed from his eyes rolled into tiny balls of mud as they coursed down his dusty cheek. Somewhere beyond his brow, far away, a more consequential wetness worried him, but the effort to feel the crown of his head was monumental. He felt split, rent, and discarded. He remembered a dream he'd had as a child, of shrinking so small he could enter a gopher's lodge, slipping down its passages as soil and stone brushed his lips. It was not a nightmare, but it broke his heart. His father would drop torches in the burrows and brain the creatures with a spade as they rose to escape the smoke. On his father's lips, the purse of satisfaction he made at a stockyard bargain.

If he was sure of anything in this pit, as he shed from his brow some vital essence that he could not name, it was of the pure inconsequence of his existence. If one pebble had tumbled from the back of another in the most obscure corner of the darkest valley in the back of the moon, it would matter as much as him to his fellow men. In his abjectness he became a supernova of self-pity. Imagining himself posted in the sky like Orion, he was visible to brokenhearted mothers everywhere, in broad daylight. They would come out of their dugouts and soddies, these women of the Kansas plains, and point with their lye-scorched forefingers at the abandoned boy in the sky, prone and smashed and forever beyond their arms to embrace.

He wanted his mother now. He wanted her so much he shed tears that drained down those channels of moon dust, down those lonely untracked lunar valleys to the place where sadness collected on this most doleful of worlds. He cried as he had not since he was first laid on his mother's glistening belly, a purple-faced infant. Like that babe, he could not utter the name of his beloved.

The sky opened with a rusty squeak. From beyond, light from a linen wick shone, as brilliant to his frozen pupils as the gaze of the Almighty. Three figures stood above, looking at him by lamplight, squinting as if his form offended their eyes. This mute gaping went on for some minutes, until a fourth figure appeared: smaller, more slender than the others, shining with a certain warmness that suggested she wore no clothes.

In his state of disassembly this did not seem strange to him. Nor was he surprised when she leapt into the pit in a single, pantherish bound. She was indeed naked, round limbs caressed by tendrils of light and gloom, loosed breasts casting shadows down to a maidenly tapered waist. She was regarding him with eyes half lidded, an appraising frown on her face.

Cleaved in two, some part of his brain still perceived the girl's handsomeness. Her face was perfectly ovoid, with a high, unblemished forehead and brows plucked into neat, downy arches. Her hair was thick and shining like pistol metal in the lamplight, yet adorned with a girlish bow. The only flaw: the thin, tight mouth that seemed to ripple with tension, as when she had conversed with him at the table, eons before.

Perceiving the girl's handsomeness, the man responded to it. Senses unspooling, dusty nostrils scraping the ground, his mouth found feminine toes mashed and tapered by years crammed in pointed boots. He could neither speak nor think, but by some convolution of mashed nerves, his sense of smell was heightened. He detected on those toes an odor he knew from the whorehouses of Dodge City, that particular combination of perfume and leather and sweat of women disrobed for pleasure. It made him want to form his lips into a gesture that should have been familiar to him but whose name was gone now, stolen. Instead, when he placed his rounded mouth on her foot, he drooled blood and spit on her toes.

"By the Lord, a pig even now!" the girl declared, voice clear but fluttering in his ears like a scream launched in the teeth of a prairie wind.

"*Schnitt ihm*," someone said from above. "*Jetzt.*"

Shaking her foot free, she disappeared behind him. Then the stone man felt himself rising, leaving his little nest of bodily humors. Stooping, she had hold of him now, grasping him by the strip of his undamaged pate. He moaned with the exertion of being so handled. And as she pulled him higher, he felt he might speak, might produce some kind of protest, until his attention was drawn to a sharp new insult to the left point of his jaw.

They froze there together for a moment, her breath caressing his upturned forehead, the image of the girl's face across the table. Suggesting, promising. The very prettiness of her! Caught in those lusty emanations, he forgot his meal. Her smile delivered up small, sharp, white teeth.

Just then, when he was about to make some indecent suggestion, the girl pushed the tip of the blade through his jugular and drew it across his neck like a fiddler bowing the final note of the reel. He sprayed forth, the stream spattering the walls.

The work done, she lowered him back into place with what, in his final thought, seemed great gentleness. And then he was done.

Chapter One

What Remains

APRIL, 1873

ON A WET morning, grim-faced men gathered with picks and shovels. They collected in a spot midway between the Bender cabin and the claim's makeshift stable, making small talk as they smoked and picked at the ground and waited for Leroy Dick, the town trustee, to arrive from Harmony Grove.

In any other gathering of the township's citizens there would have been a degree of high spirits, that good-natured joking they indulged no matter what the occasion, be it a wedding or funeral, just because they were men, and liked to believe they were impervious to mere circumstances. But there was little mirth this time—except for the Irishman, John Moneyhon, who grinned when the name of pretty Kate Bender came up, and made an obscene gesture with his cigarette that drew knowing smiles from the others. But the smiles were thin, and brief.

A steady rain the night before had softened the roads, delaying the trustee's arrival until after nine. When he came, Dick was driving the little runabout he took on supply runs to Cherryvale or Parsons. Beside him sat Billy Toles, a neighboring rancher who, the previous afternoon, had first noticed the strange condition of the Bender place and run to straight to the magistrate.

"You shouldn't be up there without someone official," Dick had told him. "They'd be within their rights to shoot you."

"There ain't nobody up there for days, I tell you," replied Toles, who observed a pitiful lowing from the vicinity of the Benders' corral while rounding up a cow from the perimeter of the property.

Dick listened to his story and kept his suspicions to himself.

"I found the calf tied up. He was a long way dead, maybe four or five days," Toles said. "And the heifer was not ten feet away, penned up, where she couldn't get to the calf. Udders split like old melons. The stink of it, I tell you. And the flies, and the look of the poor beast, still screaming after she watched her baby starve before her eyes. Who does an animal that way? What kind of monster?" And Toles wagged his head slowly and profoundly in disbelief. "Right before her eyes," he repeated.

"I don't know," Dick said after a long silence. "I'll get word to everyone around. We'll meet tomorrow morning around nine—and do this thing legal and proper."

The inquiry commenced as Dick stepped down from his runabout and announced, "Here we are, then." With a heavy sigh of a man about to embark on matters of unfathomed complexity, he led the good citizens of northwestern Labette County to the front door of the Bender cabin.

The first thing they noticed was that the sign formerly posted over the door—GROCERY—was gone. The condition of the nail holes suggested that it had been wrested away in a hurry.

The door was not locked. It swung open silently on leather hinges, its swing checked by an apple box filled with twists of grass and old corn cobs. The interior of the cabin, furnished with a table, a few chairs, bedstead, and some meager scraps of merchandise, seemed forlorn but orderly. There was a fine layer of dust on the floor and the furniture innocent of finger- or footprints. Yet the pendulum of the eight-day clock was still in motion.

Though their cabin was soundly built, the Benders had never bothered to construct a proper ceiling for it, nor covered the plank walls with anything. This was not unusual—most settlers in the vicinity had other priorities than caulking and papering, and indeed prided themselves on their sturdy plainness. Instead of any formal partition, the space was divided only by a square of duck canvas, grade heavy number 3, that had been taken from the roof of a wagon and stretched along a line of joists that bisected the room more or less in the center. Morning light from the cabin's back window shone through the material; at the very center of it, partly obscuring the light, was a greasy splotch, as if something had exploded upon the canvas. The magistrate looked at the stain carefully but could see neither color nor consistency in it.

Nothing was necessarily unusual, except for the feel of the place, which had always struck visitors as exceedingly odd, as if the doing of perverse things had impressed itself on the general atmosphere. It made grown men nervous under normal circumstances. Their disquiet was relieved only with the appearance of the daughter, coming forth with an open fearlessness that aroused and confounded them. Kate, with eyes that laughed or ridiculed. Kate, who swore like a man, whose hair blazed like whiskey held up to the sun. If the men said they were not hoping they would come upon a disrobed Kate on their uninvited tour, they'd have been lying.

The contents of the place were more or less in place, except for one detail: there were virtually no personal items. No clothing on the drying rope, no linens on the bed. No dirty dishes in the washtub. Not so much as a dirty sock on the floor. Sifting the ashes in the stove, John Moneyhon reported them cold through and through. The planks on the wall were unclad—but not undecorated. On the wall behind the clock, there were odd things carved in the wood. Nudging the clock aside, Dick uncovered carvings of roughly human shape. The homunculus was more or less true to life, except that certain body parts—like the head and the male genitalia—were exaggerated in size. Through the arms, head, torso, and penis there were carved rough *X*'s.

Checking under the stove, Moneyhon found three hammers of varying size. These were not clumsy mallets but the kind of iron tools used by cobblers or farriers. These were not suspicious in themselves, but only puzzling in their method of disposal. What man kept his tools under a stove? And if they were supposed to be hidden, why not find a better place to conceal them?

Billy Toles fetched a book from under the table. It was Old Man Bender's German Bible—the one he was often seen poring over. "Wasn't this always at the end of his arm?" asked Billy, holding the book up by its corner like some putrid fish.

"They've absquatulated," declared George Mortimer. He was a farmer who had responded to Dick's summons to investigate strange goings-on at the Bender place by bringing his plow. What he expected to plow up with it, everyone wondered but no one would say.

Then someone noticed something under a leg of the table. "Look! There's something there!"

All eyes fell on the outline of an opening in the floor—a trapdoor flush against the planks except for a short length of boot leather nailed there as a handle. In a flash the table was lifted away, the door swung open. But light from the windows seemed loath to penetrate the space beneath.

"Fetch a lantern," Dick ordered.

Toles was on his way down, using some rude bits of rock stuck in the surface of the passage as handholds. The floor of the cellar was only six feet below, and covered with a large square of undressed stone the Benders had brought in from somewhere. Though Billy credited his own bravery for being first in, a sense of futility struck him as he stood there in the gloom, unable to report anything about his surroundings.

"I can't see a thing. But it smells," he said.

"Smells how?"

"Queer."

They passed a lantern down to him. Now he could see that the dugout was about eight feet square, with the sandstone monolith on the floor running to within six inches of the walls. From one side, the north, a crawl space had been excavated, with daylight showing through the cracks of the double doors at the far end. Kneeling, Toles brought the light down to the surface of the stone. Dark stains meandered over its pitted surface.

"It's old blood," said Leroy Dick, who had lain on his belly to test the air in the passage.

He pulled back to let John Moneyhon drop into the pit. "There must be some poor soul buried under this rock," the Irishman declared. With the heavy work hammer he'd found under the stove, he commenced to pound on the sandstone, trying to break off a piece. With three swings he dislodged a chunk. But when he lifted it away, the soil underneath seemed dry, undisturbed.

"It's not coming from underneath," said Billy. "It's *here*."

He was sniffing around the loose dirt beyond the edge of the stone, near the wall. Something wet the soil there, giving it a faintly shiny appearance, as if it had been sugared.

"Here, use this," said someone out of the glare above, holding out an iron rod for Billy to take. It was the kind of probe used to test the depth of topsoil in fields. Grasping it, heart pounding now, Billy stuck the end into the discolored ground. The rod sank down with virtually with no resistance, as if penetrating the cream on a pie. There was a faint squish as the tip disappeared, and a slight pull from below, as if a vacuum had formed from its entry. And then the smell hit him.

"Oh my Lord!" he cried. A redoubled stench, the stinging odor of concentrated decay, hit him full in the face, making his eyes suddenly pour tears. "Oh my goodness."

"What is it?" Dick cried. He moved to stick his head back into the hole but was shoved back as Billy Toles scrambled out. The boy was frantic, crazed with fright from the rot and darkness and confinement. He didn't stop until he was outside. Pacing, he took great gulps of fresh air, alternately slinging his arms around himself and pumping them, as if his body were a bellows.

Moneyhon scoffed from the cellar. He took up the probe, saying, "Leave it to me, boys. This mess don't bother me!"

"Well, if you're sure . . ." said Dick.

Moneyhon had the rod in the mire again, shoving it down

until it stopped, then stirring it around as if he were churning some pot of pure corruption. The layer of adulterated dirt went deep, almost half a yard. But despite his vigorous efforts, he found no victims buried there. And indeed, nothing solid at all. Instead, Moneyhon found the limits of even an Irishman's strong stomach. Gut rolling and heaving, he abandoned the iron and the Bender hammer behind him. Presently he was outside with Billy Toles, gasping.

They gathered back at the magistrate's runabout to confer on what to do next. To be sure, they had already learned much in their investigation, but the trustee felt a sense that he was being rushed by circumstances, tested against a wave of expectations already crashing upon him. What would that pushy senator from Independence who had lost his brother—Colonel York—do when he learned the Benders had lit out? How soon before the same howls for vengeance went up, the headlong rush to visit retribution on the Benders and anyone in the way, which had so thoroughly bloodied Kansas earth before the war? How many hours before the same furies of self-righteousness stalked their land again?

Looking up, Leroy Dick could already see dozens of people—a veritable crowd on those parts—converge on the Bender claim. They came from all directions, on horseback, by wheeled conveyance, on foot. All the neighbors, except for Brockman and Ern, who lived less than two miles away. He made a little mental note of that, the incuriousness of that pair, as his eyes swept the horizon, settling finally on the little orchard behind the cabin— the orchard where the Benders were often seen at work, patiently, meticulously grading and regrading. And then he saw it.

From the modest height of his carriage there was a rectangle of discolored soil among the apple trees. With the runoff from the night's rain, the edges of the patch had been deepened, leaving the outline of a shallow mound about six feet long and two feet wide.

"Men, get your shovels," Dick said, a hollow thrum of regret in his voice. "I think I see a grave."

Chapter Two

Borrowed Rooms

JULY, 1857

KATE LEARNED YOUNG how to sleep in borrowed rooms. In the summer she would be in bed no later than six, with the sun still mockingly high in the southwest, blowing its hot breath across the careworn white muslin that seemed to dress every window in every hotel west of Chicago. Wide awake, she would watch it tremble, appearing to swell and retreat as the distant giant breathed across the dusty plains until, at dusk, a steady breeze rose in the east, propelling the material inward like a ghostly hand reaching toward her in the twilight. Only then, safe and tight in the bedclothes, would she feel the urge to close her eyes.

But not yet to sleep. For with day's end came the clatter of dishes through the thin floorboards, as dinner was served the guests impatient for the night's real business to begin. Before the games, before the losses, all the guests were in high spirits, doling out deep-voiced innuendoes and hearty helpings of comradely laughter. The good humor stopped when the dishes were cleared away, and the liquor, smokes, and cards came out. In her mind she could picture them, if only in her child's terms—large unshaven men intently bent to their game, muttering to themselves just as she did when she arranged her dolls.

With this image in her mind, of all those giants at play, and of her father sitting among them all, rolling the butt of his cigar along his lips as he did when absorbed in a task, drowsiness would finally overcome her. And when she awoke in the morning, he would always be there, still in the clothes he wore the night before, saying something inscrutably poetic such as—

> Be not afraid, dear gumdrop: the isle is full of noises,
> Sounds and sweet airs, that give delight, and n'er hurt.
> Sometimes a thousand twangling instruments
> Will hum about my ears; and sometime voices,
> That, if I then had waked after long sleep,
> Will make me sleep again: and then, in dreaming,
> The clouds I thought would open and show riches
> Ready to drop upon me; that, when I waked
> I cried to dream again.

They were words that, by their music, fetched her from the far shore, but also caused her unease, making her cry out, "Papa, what are you saying?" But as often as she asked, she never got an answer. Instead, he would just smile in his mysterious way, the whiteness of his teeth rivaling in brilliance his diamond stickpin.

And soon after the fruits of his night's labor would arrive:

breakfasts delivered to their room on polished silver trays. Eggs and steaks and biscuits of buttermilk. Blackberry jam in crystal bowls, and Seville marmalade in jars with labels from New Orleans, New York, San Francisco. Potatoes in cream and plums stewed in their own juice. And for him, pots of black coffee, thick and smelling of the woodstove, with a potency she imagined worthy only of full-grown men.

When the eating was done, and if the night was particularly profitable, a parcel would come, dressed with fancy string. Inside would be a new dress for her, suitable for a promenade down the dusty, manure-strewn streets of whatever camp hosted them. On his arm she would cling in her fresh stiff finery, mindful of all the adult girls who did the same for their "daddies." And how they would scowl at her behind her father's back! Contempt mixed with disbelief at this youth, this six-year-old with her powder-free glow, her unpainted lips like plump, reclining bloodworms. She learned to perceive their contempt, hidden so flimsily beneath their cries of "Oh, just look at the little darling!" until her father had turned away and their faces hardened.

She perceived it, and learned to return it, raising her pert little chin in their directions and closing her downy eyelids at the sight of them, "the broken-down provincial whores," as her father called them. She would repeat this phrase herself as best she could, "the broke-down purple wars," like a magic formula to protect herself from their spite.

This perpetual holiday was her life. From town to gambling town they would travel by train, or by coach to the less connected camps, like boon companions. He shared his hopes and his frustrations as he would to any partner, in frank and vivid language. He scratched himself in intimate places in her presence and laughed about it. He'd given the girl her first sip of beer at the age of three and her first nip of champagne at five. He taught her curse-words in German, the language of his parents, and laughed when she unleashed Teutonic abuse on tardy waiters.

In St. Louis he won big at the faro tables and bought her her first pony. It was a sorrel with a four-pointed star that she loved right away. She called him Nickers because he was a smart pony who would always nicker when they arrived at a new place, as she was led off to the hotel and he to the livery. These partings pained her because she never knew how long it would be before she rode him again—a day, a week, or many weeks. It all depended on how the cards treated them.

But mostly there were the books. For a man of her father's vocation, the investment of time with his opponents was as important as the investment of money. He therefore left her with much time alone, for which he tried to compensate by steering every manner of printed matter into her hands—newspapers and pamphlets and circulars and catalogs—but mostly just books. The hotels always had a few on hand, usually moldering in some corner case. Presented with them, she would feel their weight, turn the pages, wave aside the dust, and laugh, "But I'm just a kid. I can't read!" To which he would laugh his avuncular, never paternal laugh, and remark like some barbershop wag to his buddies, "No time like the present, Katie!"

Though she sensed, even with her child's intuition, her father's impropriety, it had one healthy effect: she wished never to disappoint his exaggerated faith in her abilities. No one had ever sat down to teach her to read. None of the books she found in hotel lobbies was appropriate for the task. But for the length of many idle afternoons, and sometimes evenings, she would sit with these masses of incomprehensible symbols, puzzling them out. Sometimes she was so frustrated she would throw the books away, or kick them along the floor with her little high-button shoes. More often, she tried so hard that sweat stood out on her forehead, and she would have to buttonhole drunks and bellhops to ask, "Good sir, can you tell me what this word means?" And though half of them lacked either the education or the sobriety to answer, she asked again and again, and again still more, until the words made a kind of sense.

In this way she made slow progress—and familiarity with a strange collection of subjects. She was one of the rare six-year-olds familiar with the works of Sir Walter Scott, albeit more with the names of the characters than the stories. She had dipped into Washington Irving and the liberal philosophers Burke and Montesquieu, especially the latter's discussion of the renal glands, but not any of his theories of government. She sampled the dialogues of Plato but disliked them because they had no pictures. Much more to her taste was a book of demonology called *The Lesser Key of Solomon*, which she found in a lobby in Evanston, Illinois. The first section ("Shemhamphorash") included a list of seventy-two demons known to King Solomon, with descriptions of their powers and, best of all, pictures.

In essence this was nothing more than a catalog, much like those that sold harvesting equipment and ladies' underwear through the mail—except much more absorbing. She spent hours poring over the parade of demons, examining their attributes, deciding which were her favorites. Among her champions was the noble Stolas, who appeared as an owl with a crown and the legs of a stork, and who taught knowledge of the Heavens. And there was King Balam, who taught invisibility and rhetoric and had three heads, one human, one bull, and one ram. She was also impressed that King Balam rode on a bear—probably a Rocky Mountain grizzly. These were "good" demons who made her feel that her world made sense. She dreaded the "bad" ones with equal passion, particularly Andras, who rode a wolf and fed on the discord of others, and the cruel Focalor, who drowned men in their ships.

One day her father gave her a ream of plain paper and a box of sketching pencils. This inspired her to carefully trace the image of every one of the seventy-two, cut them out, and arrange the paper armies on her bedspread. Each demon duke and demon king got his chance at the forefront of his familiars. At her signal, they would charge up the little hill of woolen fabric to contend at the summit. And when they met, she could hear the rumble of their clash shake the bowels of the earth—though to the guests in the other rooms, it was just the half perceptible murmuring of a lonely girl.

She was playing this very game—matching the wily Zepar against the valorous Purson—when her father came to her that last time. It was early one morning in Denver, and from his undisturbed bed she could tell he had been playing all night. This in itself wasn't unusual—such stints actually tended to be the most profitable for him, resulting in extra gifts for her. But this time all the blood seemed to have drained from his cheeks, and his eyes were filled with a fear she had never seen before.

"Get up now," he said. *"Es ist an der Zeit, dich anzuziehen."*

"What's the matter?"

"We have to leave."

She dressed, less to please him than to calm herself by her obedience. As she did so, he cracked his trunk abruptly, tossing his clothes into it in a manner that, to older eyes, would have seemed a combination of haste and resignation. He said nothing and did not look at her. Unlike every other time he came back from a night of pokering, he did not go to the dresser to remove his ivory cuff links—the ones backed with gold, which he'd won in a game before she was born—because they were gone.

With the disappearance of those cuff links, and a child's natural sensitivity to the mood of her parent, she became alarmed. But she was also uncomprehending, confused by the presence of a threat made more terrible for being unknown. Unlike the bad demons in her book, this terror had no name.

When she was packed and had donned her coat of navy wool, and the little hat trimmed with lace designed for a woman four times her age, he laid his hand on her shoulder. He did not push her but with a shuffling of his feet crowded her out of the room with his body. His gaze remained fixed over her head, never dropping it to meet hers.

There was a man waiting for them in the hallway. His eyes were blue and shone with the icy glint of an axe blade left in the snow. She backed up against her father as he tried to shut the door.

"You pullin' foot on me?" the man asked.

"You could have set downstairs."

"Is this it?" The man turned the cold blue light of his gaze down on her. This, and the way he referred to her as "it," propelled her backward, against the unyielding bulk of her father.

"To hell with you, Clarrity, if you won't let me talk to her first."

With a casually indolent shifting of his weight, the man removed his shoulder from the wall and stood up straight. For the first time she noticed how his free arm crooked at the elbow and disappeared under his coat, where a butt of gun metal shone. In all her time around saloons and gamblers, Kate had never before seen a man place his hand on a firearm.

With a look of faint accusation, but saying nothing, the man retreated down the stairs. The heavy tread of his boots, the *clop, clop . . . clop . . . clop*, descended with increasing slowness, like a dying heartbeat. At the foot of the stairs there was a creaky floorboard she knew well because she liked to jump on it on her way down to the dining room. The board groaned as he paused on it.

"Who's that man, Papa?"

He swallowed with the expression of a man forced to drink poison.

"Look here, gumdrop. This man is called Clarrity, and we have this little deal going. For it to work I'm going to need you to play along. Can you do that for me?"

She smiled. "What's our play?"

"He thinks he won himself a little girl in our card game, and you're gonna go off with him and do what he says. OK?"

"It's OK. When will you come get me?"

"Soon. Real soon."

They went outside. Nickers rocked his head when Kate appeared at the door, stepping with anticipation as her little carpetbag was loaded on his back. The sky was a cloudless, severe blue, the mountains clear even miles away. A little crowd had gathered for some reason to watch her go—she didn't know why. And there was Clarrity, mounted and waiting on a big black, half turned around with the grip of his pistol still showing under his coat.

Her father boosted her into her saddle. The sorrel was small enough that Kate's eye level was barely above his when she was mounted. Looking to him for reassurance, she got nothing but averted eyes and a faint, pained smile on his face.

"Play along," he whispered.

He handed the lead rope to Clarrity, who started them down the street. And though she didn't want to fail her father, Kate felt her stomach flutter and her knuckles ache as she grasped the reins.

Some of the women she'd seen around town were outside the hotel, watching her go. These were the same "broke-down purple wars" she'd met in a hundred other places, always with a sneer on their faces as they inspected her miniature, unmerited finery. Out of unthinking habit, she looked down on them coldly—until she saw that this time they weren't sneering. Instead, they seemed sad, as if someone had run over a dog in the street. Their feathered heads turned together, following her as she departed, the regret of their forsworn maternities pouring from the pits of their blackened eyes.

Chapter Three

Clarrity

> To attempt a portrayal of that era and that land, and leave out
> the blood and the carnage, would be like portraying Mormon-
> ism and leaving out polygamy... The deference that was paid
> to a desperado of wide reputation, and who "kept his private
> graveyard," as the phrase went, was marked, and cheerfully
> accorded.
>
> —**Mark Twain,** *Roughing It*

THEY RODE IN silence for the next two hours. Clarrity never
looked back to check if she was still there, and Kate never called
on him to slow down. The gambler and the girl, evenly matched
in their stubbornness, traveled together as if willing themselves
separate, save only for a sense of proprietary entitlement on the
man's part, which kept his ears attuned to the pony's hoofbeats
behind him. When they sounded too far behind, he pulled up and
waited, resuming before she caught up. Kate, who would scarcely
let her eyes rest on the man's wool-clad back, did nothing to stop

Nickers from turning aside on the trail to browse. Here, she used the opportunity to turn in her saddle, scanning the distance for her father. For he was surely out there somewhere, tracking them. He would know when it was time to end their game.

Shortly after noon they reached an ugly peak clad in broken cobbles. A black pipe clung to the low angle of the hill's flank, tail buried in a gathering of haphazard, tar-papered shacks, pouring out smoke from its summit. Closer, and mud-caked byways appeared, zigging and zagging through the mining camp as if some of the buildings were impatient to cross the thoroughfare. The uneven street lines made it impossible to judge at a glance how many people were out—with each turn of a corner, more hatted figures appeared, each greeting the appearance of Kate and her companion with a quick appraisal of her pony and fancy rig. But by the time she was abreast of them, they seemed to have forgotten her existence, resuming some inward totaling of imaginary fortunes.

Clarrity dismounted at what looked like a livery, except that the proprietor was wearing a bloody smock and he was butchering fresh meat on a block. The men conferred in low tones, the proprietor stroking his chin hairs. The question occurred to her of what they might be negotiating, but only as a matter of idle curiosity, for what had this man Clarrity's business to do with her? Preferring not to give him the satisfaction of asking, she looked down to straighten the laces of her fancy French riding gloves—the ones her father had bought in New Orleans.

When she looked up, he was next to her. "Get down," he said.

"Why?"

"Because I told ya, that's why."

Before the next question left her lips, he yanked her tiny boot heels out of their sterling silver stirrups, pulled her off her saddle of tooled red leather, and planted her with a *squish* in the mud. He motioned to the man in the smock, who seized Nickers by the bit to lead him away. And the pony, after a moment's hesitation and a widening of his eyes, followed.

"You rascal, did you just sell my pony?"

Clarrity was already standing by his horse. The way he stood, motioning for her to join him on his mount, was answer enough.

Though it was hard to see from one end of the thoroughfare to the next, no one in the camp could fail to hear the riot that followed. Kate screamed, threw handfuls of mud, and cussed Clarrity and his mother in the manner she'd learned sleeping for a thousand nights above saloons from Ohio to Colorado. She called him a brute and pug ugly. She declared she would kill him "graveyard dead" for what he'd done. She discarded all the restraint she'd summoned when she left her father, lest she disappoint him—for the sake of Nickers.

Clarrity just stood and watched at first, as if he might outlast the eruption. But soon the effects of her words on passersby, the blast of hot abuse that would torch the manhood of tougher men, had its effect. Witnesses were startled . . . and then they laughed at him.

He charged at her so fast her tirade died mid-sentence. Then she was off her feet and being carried like a sack of meal by his side. He had her up on his mount and halfway out of town before she could think of another insult.

"Who do you think you are, you—you—" she sputtered. She was seated just behind the saddle horn, her back against him, with his arms encircling her in a mockery of fatherly care as he grasped the reins. Closer to him now, she could smell his detestable odors—the sweat and leather and staleness of his phlegmy, unwashed mouth. Disgusted, she needled back at him with her elbows.

"Stop that," he said. And when she jabbed him again, he twisted her ear so hard she cried out. Then he slipped his hand down the length of her belly, down to her crotch, and grasped her there.

Kate was too surprised to speak or breathe. This was a shame that was beyond her experience, beyond all comprehension. Shocked, she felt his breath on her ear.

"You little cunny, what makes you think you count for anything?"

She was left to consider this question for several strides of his horse, until it occurred to him to say something else and he was back at her other ear: "Yer just lucky I don't like 'em in the bud. But I cain't speak for the next man . . ."

He released her from that humiliating grip. Kate, feeling utterly bereft, scanned the horizon again for her father. For surely he would never stand for her to be treated this way.

"My father will shoot you in the face."

Silent, he drove them into a zone of cleared land, picking his way around felled trees and piles of half-planed lumber for the houses newly rich miners would build on the edge of camp. Beyond that, a forest stretched deep and trackless. As it swallowed them, she felt the temperature drop, until she hunched shivering against Clarrity's detestable form. Resenting every bit of heat shared between them, she tried to sit apart. This drew another twist of her earlobe, which he applied this time without warning. Defeated, she could only sit with spine straight, making herself as unyielding a burden as possible, willing her hatred to emanate from every pore of her back.

Another half day of this left her cold and exhausted, fatigue robbing her eyes of focus. She heard, but hardly saw, the stream they crossed, its waters stained by mud and stinking of some chemical that burned the inside of her nose. The horse, irritated, shook its head, setting her insides ajar in a way that increased her misery but not her wakefulness. Though vexed and insulted, she still took refuge in that insulating unconsciousness that children often adopted on long journeys. She adopted it—with the difference that her young dreams were full of profanities and the ugly fates people like Clarrity would find in this world.

They arrived at some new habitation. Perking up, she beheld a place that made the previous camp look like a proper metropolis. Instead of a chaotic agglomeration of roofs, this one was a mass of canvas tents stretched by lines that crissed and crossed like some insane spiderweb in argument with itself. As they stepped through the tortured mud on the edge of camp, Kate saw a full-grown man come out of his tent and squat. Bent at the knees, he absently held his pants away from his ankles, regarding her with what seemed like philosophic calm, if that book on the pagan philosophers she had once read was any guide to such things. Then, in full view of God and everyone, his bowels let go a torrent of loose material that was the ultimate product of a bellyful of whiskey and a crust of rotten bread. When he caught her staring, he winked.

"Why are we stopping here?" she asked Clarrity. "There is surely no decent hotel."

His only response was a guttural rumble that sounded somewhere between amused and self-satisfied. As they found their way through the jumble of rope cords, it seemed not only Clarrity but his horse knew where they were going. They had been here many times before, and their arrival was not a matter of chance.

They came to a gray tent sagging in a hollow. It was in a less favored position, far from the line in the forest where the loggers were working and distant from the creek that supplied the camp's fresh water. On the ground, frequent spring rains had left the tent in a permanent morass. As the horse trudged to the flap, stepping high to extract its hooves from the mud, Clarrity gave a clicking sound with his tongue that served as some signal.

Summoned from within was a not-young woman. She wore a dirty smock, streaked with the guts of pickling fruits, over a gingham dress so stripped and worn that it seemed ready to split into tendrils. Her arms, ropy and soap-blasted, were exposed to the elbow. Her features told of nothing—neither past beauty nor ugliness, but only of cares. Her hair, on the other hand, was almost handsome, fair and sprinkled with flecks of gold. But gray was already spreading from the part, beginning its inevitable conquest.

"*Du,*" is all she said.

"With the package," he replied, dismounting first.

And the two of them stood together, akimbo and appraising her in the saddle as she glared back at them with an ingenue's contempt.

"*Ganz richtig sieht sie nicht aus.*"

"She's close enough," answered Clarrity. "And how would they know anyway?"

"True," came the reply. "You! Get down."

THE CAMP—THE BUSINESS of which she had never learned—became her new home. Clarrity stayed in the tent with them for three days, sharing the woman's bed, while Kate slept behind a canvas partition. The trappings of her former life were quietly withdrawn, to be replaced by those of another girl who had somehow disappeared. Whenever Kate demanded information about her, the woman answered only in German. She reserved her English for commands, such as "Git into these cloths" and "Eat this."

She was not mistreated at first. Compared to life on the trail with Clarrity, it was almost pleasant, with plenty to eat and almost nothing expected of her. As ordeals went, it was tolerable—at least until her father decided that she need not play along anymore. She imagined he was very close now, perhaps in the next tent over, biding his time until he saw his opening for a rescue. For the moment, she studied the book of demonology she had spirited under her pillow, where the woman wouldn't find it. Like a player dealt two weak pair in a game of seven card stud, she trusted that her full house would come.

Clarrity disappeared on the morning of the fourth day. As much as she hated him, she was sorry to see his black mount—her sole conveyance back to her former life—go with him.

That afternoon, two strangers came to the tent. The woman called her out to be examined by them. Standing under a light drizzle of sickly yellow sunset, she could see their marshals' badges shining through the mist, their interrogating eyes staring from under the brims of their hats. They seemed very interested in her particular whereabouts for the last two months.

"Are you about to swear before God now that this is your daughter, Almira?"

"*Mein Gott,* what a question! Who else's girl would she be?" replied Almira, striking her brow with thespian effect. And as she did this, her eyes fixed on Kate in a warning that needed no stage-craft: *fail me now and you will pay.*

She need not have bothered with threats. Her father had taught her never to cooperate with the law unless there was some clear profit in it. And if the marshals took her away, how would her father find her?

The first marshal turned to the second and shrugged in capitulation. The other doffed his hat, pouring rain from the brim. And with that, the lawmen went back to their wet, miserable horses, who had been pushing their noses into the dead ground, blowing air into the mud in apparent frustration at the lack of fodder.

Later, as she tucked into a plate of beans and broken hoecakes, she was surprised to notice Almira sitting across the board, smiling at her. She placed a plump, ripe apple on the table. In the gray world of the camp, the apple's redness seemed almost to pulsate, like the beating heart of some strong, slaughtered tree. Kate stopped eating.

"You are the smart girl," said the woman. "Maybe the smartest yet."

"I want my father."

"Maybe you trust me, and we find him. *Ser gut?*"

Kate chewed for a while, wondering what to do with the credit she had earned.

"Who was the girl they were looking for?" she asked.

Almira's smile vanished. She rose to take her plate to the washtub.

"Was she your daughter? What happened to her? Why did you need someone to pretend to be her?"

Almira turned and pointed a dirty ladle at her. "You ask these questions, you maybe not so smart," she said. And then, as if seeing Kate's discomfort, her face softened until light spread into the creases and the dead weight lifted from her eyes, and she seemed for a moment not so very far from what Kate imagined was a mother.

"You stay here, you ask me later. Now eat."

Chapter Four

Hauling Varnish

APRIL, 1870

THE 440 "AMERICAN" rose from the Mississippi Valley spitting ember-flecked fumes. As the train had pulled out of Davenport, the late season storm merely toyed with her, giving her a confetti send-off of plump, happily dancing flakes. But somewhere along the main line to Iowa City, the sky's mood soured. It unfurled great bales of rolling whiteness that smothered the smoke and sparks and seemed to demand more. By the twenty mile marker, the cowcatcher plowed a furrow through drifts that rose twelve inches an hour. Looking out of their windows, the passengers watched the train's wake rise and curl into the adjoining corn-fields, as if they all rode on a steamship.

The farmers in the neighborhood could tell from the blackening smoke that the engine was in trouble. Inside a firebox caked with slag, the "American" strained to burn arm-sized boughs of waterlogged wood as the engineer—heedless of the signs—cracked open the throttle. The farmers watched with remote pity as the train lost momentum in the snow. As she dragged, she pulled less air through her flues, making her burn still less efficiently, until the old engine seemed to stagger on her trucks. Three more desultory thrusts of the drive arm and she'd had enough. With a tired wheeze, she ground to a halt.

Behind the tender and two mail cars, the five newly varnished wooden passenger carriages shone slick in the blizzard's twilight. Unscheduled stops were not unusual on this line, but this pause felt different: windows slid open and covered heads stuck through, scanning the pastures for explanation. The cattle, belly deep in powder and likewise immobile, stared back.

Heads turned downward at a figure manifesting in the crystalline swirl. The train's brakeman, suspenders swinging by his oily flanks, ambled with a tender-footed gait along the tracks. Sticking in the immediate lee of the train, he ignored the questions and throat-clearings that descended on him. To his mind, professional aloofness was answer enough: in a trade full of necessary evils, passengers were the biggest evil and the least necessary.

When he reached the engine, he found the fireman looking down from the cab with a blank expression that sought to dissociate him from the engineer. The latter, unembarrassed in what should have been his moment of shame, cast his eyes to the east with an interrogative flick:

"How long?"

The brakeman checked his watch. There was less than an hour until the 1:38 out of Davenport came through on the same line. And all three stood in silence, seeming to chew over the implications of their arrest.

By 2:00 P.M. they were still alone on the track. Glancing at his watch, the conductor sucked his upper lip and supposed that the next train had been held at the station as the storm worsened. Outside, the sky was the gunmetal gray of a prairie blizzard that had installed itself, with obstinate malevolence, right above them. With the drifts building in front, there would be no question of resuming their run. They would have to be rescued.

The interior of the first car blazed with the heat of bored, frustrated passengers. When the conductor appeared, all eyes fixed on him, as if he were the overdue keeper visiting a cage of unfed animals. Their predicament seemed still worse as the windows, humid with the breath of fifty bodies, were fogged whiter than the scene they concealed.

The train was filled with the usual collection of mutually uncomprehending types. The businessmen in their suits and ties, on the short run to their franchises or bank branches or partners elsewhere in the great state of Iowa, grasping their briefcases with gloveless hands, fretting over dinners grown cold for them in their fine town houses. The westering families, their expressions charged with anxious, determined optimism, wearing every stitch of decent clothing they owned, weighed down by hatboxes and hobbyhorses and the other detritus of their former lives. And the wayfarers, the itinerant drunks and drifters, the people of indefinite means, the whores, the crooks one step ahead of the law, the absconded fathers, filling in the spaces between the commuters and the immigrants.

"You already know as much as any of us," the conductor announced without sympathy or preliminaries. "There's no headway against this. The stoves will stay lit as long as there's fuel—women and children get priority. Best break out those warm clothes."

With that, he proceeded down the aisle to the next car. His face remained impassive as he was peppered with questions. How long will we remain here? Is rescue on the way? Does anybody know where we are? And he thought: how presumptuous of them all to believe information was so easily come by, so without consequences to dispense! What little regard they had for facts, that they expected them to come free!

He occupied himself with such thoughts as he proceeded down the length of the crowded car, passing without notice a female passenger sitting alone on a seat designed for three. The girl's solitariness was not explained by her general appearance, dressed as she was in a humble checked skirt, the plain pleats of her white blouse exposed beneath unbuttoned woolen coat. On her head, a pillbox hat of black straw barely covered a head of ginger hair, lustrous in hue and extent, loosely curled and faceted with drops of water condensed from the snow.

No, it was her beauty that warded them off: a face of precise, enameled exquisiteness, unblemished as an infant's, fanned by long black lashes, unlined in its fearsome symmetry, sealed from her surroundings as if on display in a vitrine. Her mouth, though red-lipped, was not the rosy flower bud of contemporary calendars and matchboxes, but a tense line that seemed to bend slightly under some unseen pressure. Her eyes, black and elusive, were a prize sought by admirers, but when caught made them all regret. Eyes like blades clad in velvet, soft by all appearances, yet suddenly, with an instant unsheathing, sharp enough to cut the souls of men.

On the way from Davenport, Kate had barely seemed to register her surroundings, preferring to gaze toward the breath-smeared window to her left. Her body was still, but the way she grasped the black lace handkerchief in her lap, compulsively squeezing and releasing it, flicking at its tortured folds with lacquered fingertips, betrayed the energy coursing through her. When the conductor confirmed their emergency, she turned from the window for the first time, watching him sidelong and coldly.

She reached into her scuffed leather satchel. From it she pulled a small wood box. Opening it, she produced an oblong object, wrapped in purple satin and tied with a silk drawstring. Before touching the fastenings, she brought the parcel to her lips and, in a gesture both perfunctory and practiced, kissed it.

Soon, the passengers were puzzled to hear a new sound coming from that formerly silent corner of the carriage: the click and slap of fresh playing cards dealt out, one by one, on a wicker seat bottom. And on Kate's face there was a new expression for those who dared peek—a relaxed, inviting readiness. She was open for business.

The gamblers amongst her neighbors craned their necks at the prospect of some well-timed diversion. They soon turned away in disgust, for the cards she dealt were not of the proper, money-dividing kind, but that dandified, Gypsy sort with funny pictures and suits of cups, swords, wands, and coins. One elder fellow, wearing a bowler with a piece of the brim missing as if from a wolf bite, muttered, "What does she think this is, a French bordello?" Some of the other women looked on with mild curiosity, but dared not penetrate the zone of freezing exclusivity around the dealer. She distributed the cards facedown in a series of patterns—crosses, horseshoes, circles, and vees—occasionally turning one up and reflecting on it, as if totaling up a long line of figures in her head.

By four-thirty the light outside was failing. Snow still descended, with the drift on the windward side of the train now brushing the lower edges of the windows. The fireman, with nothing to do in the cab, went through distributing armfuls of wood gleaned from the tender, which the conductor used in the small stoves at the head of each carriage. Seated closest to the fire, the girl with the tarot cards continued her lonely reading, the vaguely medieval devices on her cards seeming yet more archaic by the flutter of flames.

Her first customer approached as the last frosty gleam drained from the carriage. In the gloom, the woman's bulk could be felt more than seen; she was only half again as tall as she was wide, clad in material as humble and care-stained as sackcloth, topped by a tasseled bonnet. Her eyes and the corners of her mouth were lost in the shadows of fleshy craters. As she moved, she seemed to wobble, as if rolling on mismatched wheels.

The young woman did not bother to look as the other filled the seat opposite. "Good evening, ma'am," she said. "I am Professor Kate."

"Almira," said the other.

"Our prospects in the coming season may be read in the cards . . . if we attend," Kate continued.

Her cue given, the old woman held out her right hand. In it, a sweaty and tarnished dollar coin.

"Thank you, madam. And now to your question, which we may properly apprehend using the following arrangement . . ."

As the night deepened, eyes turned to the pool of firelight at the head of the car, toward the two figures peering at the spread of cards beneath them. Necks craned. Expertly, as curiosity rose around them, the young woman's voice, which projected so theatrically at the outset of the reading, became softer, drawing her audience closer.

By the conductor's next trip through the carriage, there was a small crowd gathered around the tarotist and her patron. The former, in the midst of explaining the significance of the seven of cups in the number eight position of the Celtic cross, glanced at the conductor as he passed, as if expecting him to object. But the conductor said nothing. Knowing as he did the number of empty hours that stretched ahead of them all, with the snow still falling and the line paralyzed through ten counties, of what significance was this small, harmless fraud? Two cars down, a large, occasionally raucous poker game between armed men had been under way for two hours. As long as it didn't end in gunplay, he was prepared to allow Satan himself to climb up through the cross ties to practice his sorcery.

Boredom worked in Professor Kate's favor. As the night dragged on, with most of the passengers stuck upright in their seats and unable to sleep, they drifted forward. Almira, as if forgetting her assigned role, refused to move but sat with eyes closed and hands crossed, like an obstinate cat staking out her favorite corner of the sofa. But her stillness was an illusion: if one was alert, and had the dark-adapted eyes of an owl, one would see that it was not Professor Kate herself but the old woman who collected the fees, snatching up the dollar coins with thick fingers and slipping them into her purse.

For years it had been this way. Kate had grown and refined her skills at cards and beguiling of souls, and Almira, recognizing that Clarrity had gifted her with a prodigy, stood by and relieved her of the need to deal with the baser functions of their trade. Though Almira's nature would not allow her to reflect an emotion as useless as *awe*, she felt it for this girl. Only a few months after she had arrived in that camp—she had already forgotten the territory—she had realized the futility of beating her, as it only hardened the girl's pride into something diamondlike, more precious and inaccessibly buried. The spirit in her stayed her hand in a way her own daughter never did. Kate came to share her bed on cold nights and got the best cuts of the meat when meat was to be had. There was no more lace and silk, but there was gingham and the standing promise of cakes, sweet and enticing in the imagination of a girl. Almira's forbearance had allowed the girl to become haughty, yes. But also profitable.

AT MIDNIGHT, POCKET watches throughout the carriage sounded the hour. Owners roused, the chink of latches sprung as they checked the time, sighed, and clicked the covers shut. To the casual ear, so used to the cacophony of creaks and groans that accompanied train travel, the snow-swaddled silence came not as a relief but as something disquieting, ominous. Yearning for a sign of civilization, a light in the gloom, the anxious watchers saw a jet of bronze sparks arc into the night, like a flare launched from a stricken ship. Backsides rose and spines unreeled—were they rescued at last? But it was only a fellow passenger between the cars, discarding his spent cheroot into the snow. Reentering the car, he rubbed his frozen hands, confronted a gallery of disappointed faces, and asked, "What?"

By 3:00 A.M. not even their discomfort prevented the travelers from drifting off to sleep. Professor Kate's clientele thinned out. With a parting kiss, the cards went back in their satin wrapping. Almira counted out eight dollars, careful not to let the coins clink together lest the partnership be too obvious. Kate, the flinty hardness back on her face, shook her head slowly, holding up ten fingers. The eyes of the other inquired. Kate kept showing both hands, palms first this time, as if this were a more imperative gesture.

Upon delivering more fuel to the stoves, the conductor retired to the caboose for a few hours' shut-eye. At first light he jerked awake with a curse on his lips. He stared at himself in the small mirror over the washbasin for some moments and, with a faintly aesthetic disdain on his face, took up his lathering cup to shave. He undertook this task with precise deliberateness, aiming his razor at every stray follicle, rinsing the blade with every stroke, like a man with nothing else to do but stroll the decks on a trans-Atlantic passage. He was in no rush to confront the passengers again after their long night upright in their seats. Yet despite this care, he still ended up with a drop of blood on his collar that could not be concealed by his jacket.

Making his way toward the engine, he found the poker game still under way in the third carriage. The four players were scattered, knocked down like bowling pins, their arms so listless they could barely hold their cards above their belts. The dealer, who was clad in a suit of green worsted with a houndstooth waistcoat, sat with one hand full of cards and the other resting on the bulge of the liquor flask on his breast pocket. As he passed, the conductor's nose twitched—the unwashed odor of these men was powerful, especially in contrast to the aroma of shaving lather still adhering to his upper lip. By his watch, their one-hundred-minute run to Iowa City had now taken eighteen hours.

The conductor could never be mistaken for a sensitive man; for personal instance, he never let sentiment for a lonely wife and neglected son disturb his professional rounds. Yet even he could sense that the mood on the train had passed from mere annoyance through resignation to something more ominous. In the air, a suspension not only of ordinary life and its soothing routine, but of ordinary civilization, arrested and gradually more in question. The pressure of eyes on his back had become perceptible, a faintly hostile burrowing beneath his skin in search of some nugget of reassurance that would spare neither his flesh nor his bones. He became urgently conscious of the blot of blood on his collar. A Union Pacific conductor had been beaten almost to death by indignant customers trapped for five days on a snowbound train in Nebraska territory—an eventuality whose only consolation was the fact that his attackers soon turned on each other over scraps of food. The injured man was rescued by his brakeman, who had rifled the baggage for boxes of fancy biscuits to distract the passengers. The railroad, innocent of sentiment, charged the cost of the biscuits against the salary of the injured man.

In the foremost car, Professor Kate was back in her accustomed attitude, wrists resting on crossed knee, equally oblivious to her fellow passengers and their predicament. But her aloofness now had company: in addition to Almira, two new figures sat. The first was a young man, perhaps no older than twenty but dressed respectably in black overcoat and stickpin in his tie, lip adorned with a moustache he had clearly taken great pains to cultivate. Silent but with eyes open and receptive, he glanced at the conductor as he passed, nodding in acknowledgment of a comradely solidarity that was entirely in his own mind.

The other newcomer was a hirsute lump of a man, bulk magnified by fringes of beard, eyebrow, ear hair, and unkempt mane streaked with gray. His face, such as could be seen, was split by deep clefts that were not laugh lines or frown lines, but corresponded with no known human expression. He was not so much sitting on the seat as grown upon it, a sloping mountain of flesh with no head, just a headlike peak conjoined with rocky shoulders. He acknowledged the conductor no more than a mountain would acknowledge the passage of an insect along its base.

The women had, in fact, noted well the arrival of the two. Sure of his charms, the younger man had looked Kate in the eye with the same presumption he showed the conductor. But the message was different: not just mere agreeableness, but a gleam and a look of shared understanding, punctuated by a glance at her deck of cards that suggested amusement. No, he didn't want a reading. No, he didn't want to part her skirts. He and his partner, the human rock pile, were presenting their services. Kate eyed him, sizing up his suitability.

"Kansas?" she asked.

His eyes sparkled like a well-rested child, promised a morning of play. "That would do," he replied.

With that, and no further negotiations necessary, the deal was struck. They all sat together for the next two hours, exchanging hushed words while the old woman embroidered a handkerchief that seemed more antique than herself. At one point the conductor came through, and although he never listened to the conversations of the passengers, he inadvertently heard Junior holding forth:

"They come down that trail with cash. A regular bankful of coin every single day."

"It can't be that easy," Almira responded, emphasizing the *can't* in a theatrical manner she had once seen among a troupe of variety players from Chicago.

"It can . . ."

But now they had noticed the conductor lingering in earshot. Four pairs of eyes turned on him, their repulsive force so powerful the hairs on the back of his neck stood on end. Indeed, for a man in his line of work overheard many things, and none of it was of any importance whatsoever next to what he might hear the very next moment, between businessmen and gamblers and lovers and families in the carriage beyond. Instead, he warded off their unspoken indignation with his one infallible defense—the bland, professional equanimity of a man paid to take interest in nothing.

And indeed, to mere laypersons, to the great multitude of ordinary citizens and nongrifters, the four seemed like nothing more than a collection of mismatched fellow travelers. The full value of their arrangement was only theoretical at this point. Its advantages would manifest only later, after the sound of a distant whistle perked up the passengers, and a passenger from the foremost carriage charged through, crying, "The rotary! The rotary!"

They heard it before they saw it—a deep, steady whooshing noise, like a wave breaking forever on a beach. Next, an arcing cascade of snow appeared over treetops, casting an icy penumbra that clothed the sun in crystalline sparks. The great, black, flat-nosed beast slipped from behind the trees, and the passengers, heedless of the cold, threw open the windows to hang from the casements, whooping and pounding the sides of the carriages.

Their salvation was a massive machine—a converted locomotive with cowcatcher removed and a set of fanlike circular blades fitted to the smoke box. The blades spun in the great metallic maw, devouring the drifts ahead and tossing aside the leavings. Like a great slug hesitating as it contemplated a meal it could never engulf, the snow plow slowed to a creep as it neared the train. When it finally stopped, the whirling blades were just twelve inches from the nose of the locomotive.

The engineers, bundled to their ears against the cold, came

down from their cabs and met in the middle, shaking hands like two polar explorers congratulating each other. Unhurried by disaster or adulation, they stood thigh deep in the snow, exchanging lights, the blue haze of their celebratory cigars rising and mingling with the trickle of steam from the idling engines. By the ingenuity of man, another obstacle of nature had been conquered.

But in their satisfaction, it did not occur to them that the stoves in the cars had gone out. With the windows temporarily opened, temperatures in the carriages plunged to below freezing. When they all finally got under way for Iowa City, the rotary leading the way in reverse, the passengers began to truly suffer.

"Where is that *blanked* conductor?" they all demanded of each other. "Where is the heat?" But the conductor was too far away to hear, reluctantly stationed at the back of the rotary to warn for collisions. In his own discomfort, he did not think it urgent to ask someone else to deliver wood to the stoves.

To those who suffered through it, this was the worst part of the ordeal, the four hour crawl behind the low-geared snow plow, which they had all cheered at first but now cursed for its cruel slowness. Moisture of their exhalations froze on beards, lapels, seat backs, and windows. In this fresh misery, all propriety banished, unattached males and females huddling together for warmth, and the men too stupefied by cold to take advantage of the women forced into their arms.

Kate, for her part, did not huddle and did not shiver. Enduring in proud self-sufficiency, she seemed to drain of all color, her lips purpling over like dried blood, her skin becoming paler and more glassy. Her fingers succumbed by withdrawing into her small, hard fists. If anything, she was even more beautiful—beautiful and terrible and scarcely human except when, with uncharacteristic curiosity, she cast looks at the old woman beside her. For her part, the latter sat with expression set and eyes half lidded, like some old dray horse enduring the cold solely through dumb, unquestionable instinct.

The train reached Iowa City station at six in the evening. It was thirty-two hours late. At the far end of the platform a table had been set up with pots of coffee and rolls, tended by wives and daughters of the local railroad men. Passengers stumbling off the carriages, lips blue and eyes hollowed, were led to this bounty gently, as if pushed too hard they would snap. Steaming tin cups were pushed into their stiff fingers, warming them so abruptly that it caused some little cries of pain. Those who so proved their power of speech were approached by a young man in mismatched plaid suit, bearing a pad and pencil in fingerless wool gloves, the handlebars on his lip decorated not with icicles but the oily sheen of the finest Parisian pomade. In his eyes, that combination of pity and idle curiosity common on the frontier, whenever complacence stared into the eyes of misfortune.

"Care to tell your story?" the reporter asked everyone and no one, eyes sweeping the crowd with indiscriminate attentiveness. "Care to talk to *The Iowa City Plainsman & Heartland Advertiser*?" When no one answered, he narrowed his appeal, focusing on a young, strikingly beautiful redhead who was, at that very moment, taking her first sip of hot coffee. At the sight of her, his words stuck momentarily in his throat, and he simply stared as she tilted the cup to her pursed lips.

"Want to tell the people what happened?" he asked, his voice hushed in amorous reverence.

Kate seemed to consider answering him—but then, as if remembering her circumstances, looked to her male companions to speak for her. The young man stepped forward, hat placed over his breast.

"I will," he began. "Much have I had occasion to ride these rails, but never to encounter such ill use. They were more prepared to convey cattle than their fellow men. Women and children and the elderly, exposed to the elements in this way—were quite certainly to have perished had there been any more delay. Most of our baggage, I tell you, was inaccessible. Not a stick of warmth to be had—a long, cruel night with nothing but idle vices to occupy us. Thrown upon our own resources—wind and cold—indifference and perfidy—if not for my father's Bible—sustaining—in that wilderness—"

The old man, as if activated by the mere mention of the word, raised his Bible in mute testimony. But he added nothing to the account. Instead, the young man went on, utterances breaking and scattering in the wake of his racing mind. And the reporter listened, his pencil poised above his pad but not writing yet, wondering if the young man's wits were addled by the cold—until professional instinct asserted itself.

"And may I ask, what is your name?"

"John Bender, Junior. This is my father, John Bender, Senior—mother, Almira—and sister—" Gesturing at each member of his new family, the hurtling wreck of his thoughts drew to a halt as he introduced Kate—and realized he had run out of lies. He suffered a fit of panic. But Kate, who could not remember an occasion when she was at a loss for words, merely gifted the reporter with the merest token of coquetry—a half wink over the rim of her cup.

With that, the reporter's loins melted, and he forgot his curiosity at a "brother" who could not put a name to his "sister."

"So . . . do your father and mother speak?"

"As it happens, in German only."

"*Sag' ihm, wir sind gerade eingetroffe.*" said the old man in a weary voice, prompting the old woman to interject, "*Sag' ihm, er soll' uns alleine lassen, der frechen Hund!*"

This having demonstrated the old couple's uselessness to him, the reporter pursued the interview as if they'd ceased to exist. Looking at John Junior—but drinking Kate in sidelong—he asked, "From where may I say the Bender family has traveled, and to what destination and purpose?"

Thus came the christening of this heretofore putative thing, "the Bender family." On John Junior's face, the faint glow of triumph at the success of their first deception, and his natural volubility, gave a singsong lilt to his answer:

"From Cook County, Illinois, we hail, traveling to the state of Kansas with the intention of making our mark upon the land."

Chapter Five

Sixteen by Twenty-four

NOVEMBER, 1870

THE PRAIRIE STRETCHED beyond the brims of their hats to a listless horizon, pouring its way to infinity. For miles in every direction there were no trees or shrubs to relieve the eye, except
along the streams that snaked down the imperceptible slopes,
their entourages of shrubs on meandering paths to no place. To
the newcomer used to the conveniences of scale offered by eastern
landscapes—those houses and barns and fence lines that testified
to human endeavor—the prairie offered nothing by which to measure its indifference. Only here and there lay some hump of soil
topped with a treelet, stunted as if with astonishment at its strange
elevation. These gestures at topography left the prairie monoto-
nous but lumpen, a tablecloth spread over rotting secrets.

To the old-timer, by contrast, the place would have looked un-
characteristically lush. Since the end of the war it had rained more

than usual in southeastern Kansas. This fostered new growth, fattened the streams, tamed the summer bush fires. The locusts, as if party to the conspiracy with the railroads and retailers and professional boomers drawing newcomers westward, kept a temporarily low profile. The only disadvantage to all that wet was a profusion of gnats breeding in the thickened backwaters. But what was a gnat compared to the prospect of a comfortable, independent life on one's own clod of earth?

The corn just leaps out of the ground, says the Boomer, invariably over a mug he's purchased for you at some neighborhood saloon. *Just jumps up for you to take it. The soil's charmed, I tell ya—laid down in the times of Adam and never planted since. Put a pint of Kansas dirt in a glass and leave it covered for a week and you know what you'll have? No, not biscuits—not at first. Green shoots. Eatable green shoots. No seeds necessary. Now tell me, friend, if the soil is that fertile, imagine what she'll do with modern methods, done the modern way? It's a scientific fact that rain clouds follow cultivated earth. Somethin' about breaking ground alters the hydro-tautological cycle. Rain follows the plow, my friend.*

The trail from Fort Scott drove like a frown line down the face of the prairie. Traced from the most distant horizon, the furrow seemed to flirt with the eye, disappearing now and then as it was hidden by the carpet of rusty autumn blooms. Closer, it resolved itself at last into twin wheel ruts. Between them ran a path of forlorn earth, trampled by untold pairs of boot heels.

The Bender men, John Senior and Junior, walked the trail from the east in their black woolen suits and city shoes. Between them a solitary mule trod with eyes half closed, pulling an ancient army wagon piled with supplies. Having already ridden and walked for many days together, they proceeded in silence, eyes sweeping the

landscape but never meeting. For today they were not trail companions, liable to small talk and the little complaints prerogative
of travelers. Today they were shoppers. And the prairie was not an
oppressive emptiness, not the Great American Desert it was called
back East, but a great emporium of opportunities.

Searching for them, John Junior's eyes blazed with happy
anticipation. His enthusiasm so energized his step that he often
strayed into the ruts, causing himself to stumble, yet without any
effect on his jaunty mood. What John Senior's eyes burned with,
deep in their fleshy sockets, no one could say.

*Saw me a family that came back for the brother's wedding in
Ohio, and ya know what? Hale and plump, every one of them. Even
the damn young'uns. Had to order yards 'n' yards of new material
from Ward's to make 'em new clothes. With that kind of produc-
tion, you work as you please, friend. You're beholden to none. Now
tell me, how much is that worth to you?*

At a spot some days from Fort Scott but well short of Independence, they stopped to confer. Though there was no one to over-
hear them for miles, they spoke in such hushed tones that, even
in the stillness of the evening, one could not hear them over the
murmuring of insects in the turf. Now and again they peeked out
at the scene around them, as if to confirm in their minds that yes,
this was the place.

There was nothing on the surface to explain how suited it was
to their purpose. The earth lay as flat and brown as anywhere else.
But it had two key advantages. First, the spot afforded a clear view
of the trail in every direction, from where it emerged between two
mounds in the northeast to its disappearance southwest, toward
the village of Cherryvale. From there, the approach of any traveler
on those wastes could be spied for a good thirty minutes. And

second, it was splendidly isolated, with no other buildings visible a few windowless roofs miles away. It was, in fact, the ideal place to build what was not intended to be acknowledged at all.

As the sky frowned and lowered after them, as if impatient to drive them to shelter, John Junior marked the spot with a cairn of pebbles. Then they resumed their journey southwest.

They arrived before sundown at a cabin a few miles short of Cherryvale. The house was small and unkempt, its boards apparently salvaged from other structures that had suffered through their share of winters and summers. There was a single window, covered with greased paper, and a door, set high above ground level in anticipation of a set of steps that had never been installed. Above, the words GUT STORES were painted on a board.

Two men stepped outside, eyes questioning but not vigorously, mouths too full to speak, the bibs from their interrupted dinner still stuck in their shirtfronts.

"*Guten Abend,*" John Junior hailed them, having discerned from their wariness that these were fellow Germans. "*N'Abend,*" came the reply, somewhat uncertainly. For eyeing the newcomers and their rig, Rudolph Brockman was troubled by certain signs. The wagon, being an ancient one that had seen action in the war in Tennessee and Kentucky, was a wreck, with sides patched rudely and a replaced rear axle wider than the front. Its load, though, was entirely store-bought and new, as if the newcomers were tenderfoots with no experience surviving on the frontier, and worse still, competitors in the supply trade. "Might we trouble you to camp on your property this evening?" Junior asked, punctuating his words with a small laugh that was meant to suggest he was harmless, but instead gave the impression he was simple.

Brockman turned to look to his cabin mate, Augustus Ern. The latter's eyes, blasted almost opaque by ten thousand days of squinting through the prairie sun, signaled no objection.

"Ye may stay. But we beg ye to come in first to eat. If ye eat beans, that is."

"We do," replied Junior, who laughed again.

And so began the strange sojourn of the Benders with Brockman and Ern. That night and for three more, the visitors slept on blankets spread under the wagon, fully clothed in their city blacks. In the morning, Ern came outside to serve them breakfast of dried carrot coffee and biscuits from a dainty serving platter engraved with paisleys. This had once belonged to a young wife who, in her despair, had abandoned her westering husband and all her belongings on the side of the trail. Brockman had found many such useful items on his trips to and from Fort Scott—including his porcelain chamber pot, a concertina, a trousseau of women's undergarments—and the coffeepot itself. For as much as the prairie was an unforgiving mistress, mankind was profligate in his giving, and would provide much to those who let themselves become as spare in character, as patient and mutely unchanging, as the prairie itself.

Brockman was still a young man, only in his late twenties. Multiple seasons on the plains had told on his health, however. Hair made sparse with labor and care, his scalp was cracked and burnt like an old buggy seat. The cold of winter made his joints ache. The heat of summer, exacerbated by his woolen clothes, filled him like some creeping venom, addling his brains. He dreaded the sun even in November; when he took the Bender men out to look at claims available in the neighborhood, he wore a linen cloth under his hat, which hung down to shade his neck. He had fashioned this himself out of cut-up women's nightclothes from the abandoned trousseau.

The Benders obliged by going along on these excursions. To the virtues and disadvantages of each parcel, John Junior would nod, perhaps adding some inane question, such as, "Would you say this is good country for emu?" John Senior sat in silence next to him in the wagon, expressing with the lean of his glowering bulk the urge to be as far as possible from his "son." To direct questions, he would answer *ja* and *nein,* even if the questions were not "yes or no" ones. Brockman, perceiving them to be an odd pair, showed them every property except the one bordering his. Though he preferred German-speaking neighbors, these were not normal men. Most of all, he had learned to dread the sickly giggle of the younger one—that sound, a titter from Hell itself, was so irritating he believed he would hear it from miles away.

The newcomers showed no interest in any of the places they saw, including ones with year-round water and the right amount of timber. At a claim five miles north, when informed, *"Ich hatte einen Rutengänger hier im letzten Sommer. Die Wuenschelrute sprang ihm aus seinen Händen!"* they showed not a flicker of reaction, except when Junior pointed at a patch of fennel and asked if it could be brewed up into a tolerable tea.

Just as Brockman feared, they at last perked up at the place adjoining his to the northeast, though there was nothing to recommend it especially except proximity to the trail and a ragged stream a quarter mile away. Junior jumped out of his shirt with excitement. He kicked over a cairn of stones someone had built, which was common practice to prevent another claimant from establishing priority. The way he seemed to have prior knowledge it was there, however, set Brockman to thinking he had built it himself.

That they wanted to situate themselves beside the trail was all the proof he needed: the Benders had come to compete for his business. Worse, any store they set up would be encountered first by travelers coming west from Fort Scott.

It was a quiet half hour's ride back to "Gut Stores," with Brockman keeping his thoughts to himself and Junior at last realizing the virtue of silence. When Ern saw them coming up, and Brockman fixed him with a confirming look, Ern smiled. The Benders would be neighbors after all. "You owe me a nickel, then!" Ern declared, rubbing his hands together.

That evening—the Benders' last before they trekked to Humboldt to register their claim—their hosts invited them inside to sup. The Germans had put a board between two flour barrels as a table, and stoked up the cooking fire to drive out the evening chill. Junior, who seemed delighted to be allowed into the inner sanctum at last, perched on an apple box and chirped excitedly. John Senior, by contrast, sat quietly, blinking, as if half blinded by the brightness of the lime wash on the walls.

After supper—beans and a joint of pork—Ern at last got the question out in the open: "So what are you intending with that land?"

To which Junior assaulted their ears with that damnable laugh, and launched into a description of a thousand implausible schemes about patent medicine farms and ostrich meat ranches and stages for observation balloons against the Indians. John Senior listened as he scooped his food into the toothy cleft between his beard hairs, palming his spoon like a child. He seemed particularly engaged by this question, his eyes threatening some unwonted eruption. Breathless with the rarity of it, Brockman and Ern watched it gather. Then the spoon lowered and the great cleft split:

"We'll be in the murderin' business," he declared.

English. And that voice, like the scrape of a sinking hulk against the rim of a submarine canyon. Brockman and Ern were so surprised by this articulate croak, they barely registered its content.

But Junior did. Leaping from his apple box, he jabbered, "My father's English is poor. He simply meant the butchery of animals all farmers must. *Ja, vater?*"

But the old man was already far away, tonguing his empty spoon for whatever sheen of pork grease was stuck to its underside. The temperature in the cabin, meanwhile, had seemed to drop five degrees.

Brockman lost patience. No use, he thought inwardly, of sticking oneself between one man who was pointlessly talkative and another who was cryptically silent. He brought out cigars, but smoked his quickly, without enjoyment. He offered no brandy to his guests.

Soon the Benders were back outside, under their wagon for the night. And Brockman was digging deep in the little box where he kept his spare buttons, needles, and U.S. currency.

After much rummaging, he found a nickel. Handing it over to Ern, he declared, "I think those two shall cost us far more than this."

On the prairie, everyone is a rich man, says the Boomer. *Just pick yer spot, build a little on it, and in five years the whole blinkin' lot is yours. Don't believe me on this, friend: believe the Congress of the whole United States. Just a little cabin, maybe a chicken coop, an' someplace to keep hay for your horse. Free hay, that is, that you reap on your own property. Beholden to no man, like I said. Free an' clear an' yours.* And he drinks, winking over the froth in his cup, while out of his breast pocket peeks the schedule of the trains for the railroad that will take you there. For the price of a ticket, of course.

Chapter Six

Horse High, Bull Strong, Pig Tight

THE BENDER MEN returned from Humboldt a week later, wagon laden with building supplies. With the land conveyance done, and with it all necessity for further human contact, John Senior emerged from his torpor to take command of construction.

In less than a morning the two of them had leveled a sixteen-by-twenty-four-foot spot fifty paces to the south of the trail. Next day, they dug the small cellar with their new, store-bought shovels, and a well that struck water just twelve feet down. They rigged out a stable from green saplings and a roof of sheaved grass. The afternoon after, they explored the big mound to the southeast, where Brockman said decent stone was available. In the glancing sunbeams, they spied a slab of yellow sandstone half exposed in the scree, gleaming. They wrangled the seven-foot-square monolith into the wagon by themselves. Four hours later it was in place as the floor of their cellar, under the spot where they intended to build a trapdoor.

Just then, as he beheld the rock of sand on which they would erect their temple, the old man was moved to fetch his Bible. He opened it to a well-creased page:

> Now it came to pass after these things that God tested Abraham, and said to him, "Abraham!"
>   And he said, "Here I am."
>   Then He said, "Take now your son, your only son Isaac, whom you love, and go to the land of Moriah, and offer him there as a burnt offering on one of the mountains of which I shall tell you . . ."

He wet a finger and turned the leaf.

> And Abraham called the name of that place Jehovah-jireh: as it is said to this day, In the mount of the LORD it shall be seen.

The cabin was framed out in just two days, the old man fashioning joists with sure swings of the hammer. There was something about the knotty musculature of his right arm that made it seem incomplete without an implement at the end of it. Rudolph Brockman, watching from a distance, was impressed with the work, and heartened that perhaps his new neighbors were not so hapless after all.

The rest of the neighborhood was watching too. And when the newcomers had gotten as far as two men working alone should, a team of volunteers showed up for the final, labor-intensive steps. For the closure of a new habitation was not just a private matter in the Great American Desert—it was a sacrament of human enterprise, a shaking of a collective fist against the mute brutality of the elements. No invitation was necessary for it, and no compensation was expected.

They showed up at the Bender claim on a cold November morning. At the forefront was Leroy Dick, who introduced himself as "city trustee." It was a lofty-sounding title, yet he carried it with the same ease as he wore his old bison-hide jacket. Shaking John Junior's hand with real warmth, the magistrate examined the newcomer with gray eyes naturally averse to snap judgment. Junior did his best to invite one anyway, quailing in the elder man's grasp as if half crazed by the gravity of his personage. Yet Dick was barely his senior—he was just twenty-eight years old, and two years younger than his wife Mary Anne.

It was the virtue of a gentleman to avert one's eyes from the weakness of another. Instead, Dick looked to the old man. The latter, already half turned away, would only acknowledge him with a faint grumble.

"We are sorely in need of baritones for our choir," said Dick, bright and unfazed. "Should God will it, what a blessing you would be down in Harmony Grove Sunday next!"

To which the old man turned away completely, growling, *"Wenn Gott es will."*

Dick introduced them all in turn—his brother Temple, whose work belt was already around his waist (nodding); John Moneyhon, a smooth-cheeked Irishman (hat tip); George Majors, Justice of the Peace (head bob); Minister Dienst, who had exchanged his starched collar for overalls (smile); Silas Toles and his brother Billy, who ran cattle on the prairie (nodding); and of course Brockman and Ern, who were there only to avoid the shame of revealing their real indifference to the newcomers (no gesture). And there were other names—Mortimer and McCrumb, Hornback and Swingle—which Junior heard and repeated with exaggeration, rolling the syllables around his mouth as if preparing for some future address to Congress.

The work left to be done was to complete the cabin's roof and clad the walls with boards snuggly fit to keep out the winter winds. The menfolk of Osage Township went about these tasks in the same manner they had a dozen times before—with high spirits, good humor, and an unspoken awareness of their collective generosity.

The Benders, however, seemed ill-at-ease with this amiable invasion. Junior just wrung his hands, hardly driving a single nail. John Senior was all but overtly hostile—hoarding the implements for himself, he elbowed the other men aside and redid their work when he considered it beneath his standard. When Billy Toles tried to take a shingle from his pile, the old man whirled and growled at him. At midday, when the canteens of beer and applejack came out, he didn't join them but went on hammering.

Those who came near to him later told their wives about his smell. At one end, the deathly stink of gums pitted with rotting food. At the other, the stench of an orifice that had barely known cloth or water in months. It was hard to offend the nostrils of men like this, used to the odors that came with long hours of honest labor. But even they learned fast to stay upwind of John Bender, Senior.

By end of day the sun peeked under the roof of overcast, lighting up the newly finished Bender cabin with hardy crimson beams. The workmen stood in a semicircle around the north end, silently regarding what they had wrought together. A rude horse stall, fashioned from saplings, had been freshly roofed with prairie grass, and the bright, unweathered posts of the chicken coop were planted, waiting for fresh wire to be stretched between them. The little spread, incarnadined by the dying daylight, lay on the prairie like some unwashed, newborn thing, its future both bright and shadowed by possibility.

Later, after everyone had gone and the old man was asleep, Junior stood admiring the sign he had painted on an old board pried from the side of the wagon. With jerky, slashing strokes that made the letters seem almost Chinese, he'd stabbed out in wheel grease: *Grocry*.

Satisfied, he went off to fetch a nail and one of the shoe hammers his partner had brought from Germany—a coarse, angular, wooden-handled thing from the shop of some long-dead Alsatian cobbler. Its business end, crudely flattened, had already suffered untold strokes and was fit to strike many more.

Chapter Seven

Pink Pills for Pale People

> When I first came to town,
> They called me the roving jewel;
> Now they've changed their tune,
> They call me Katie Cruel,
> Oh, diddle, lully day,
> Oh de little lioday.
>
> —"Katie Cruel," traditional Scottish folk ballad

DECEMBER, 1870

ONE DAY, SOMEONE with a godlike vantage would look down on eastern Kansas and see a land stitched tightly together by steel. Remote Labette County would be amply served by three railroads: the St. Louis & San Francisco; the Southern Kansas; and Kansas City, Fort Scott & Gulf lines. Beyond the county spun the Atchison, Topeka & Santa Fe; the St. Louis, Fort Scott & Wichita; the Missouri, Kansas & Tulsa—roads whose ever-shifting names, in consecutive topographical order, promised unbroken access to ever more far-flung locales. Before century's end the little village of Cherryvale would become the confluence of three lines that formed a great asterisk on the prairie. And indeed, in 1927 a mortal with just such a godlike vantage, Charles Lindbergh, would use the great, five-pointed star to get his bearings as he flew solo from San Diego to St. Louis.

But in 1870 there was just Leavenworth, Lawrence & Galveston, reaching down from the Kansas River Valley as it raced two other roads to link cities in the north with the Oklahoma Territory. It crossed three county lines, then skirted the upper waters of the Neosho River, before it ground to a formal halt at the little town of Humboldt. Beyond, the grading and track-laying was well under way to extend it to the equally obscure towns of Neosho, Thayer, and Morehead, any or all of which might perish as communities if the executives back in Chicago or New York suddenly decided, on some brandy-induced whim, to move the rail bed a few miles east or west. Like the seasons and the growth of crops in their fields, the locals checked the progress of construction with quiet, low-grade anxiety—except that the railroad was more important that the seasons or the crop in any single year. Those other things, after all, were transient. The railroad would define the shape of their homes forever.

In mid-December the Bender men were at the LL&G station in Ottawa, Kansas, one hundred miles north of their claim. Junior waited by the tracks—there was no platform—with a cigarette stuck so deep in his mouth he risked burning his lips. Pacing at a fast walk, he periodically stopped short when he thought he heard a distant rumble, peering out over the short-grass prairie.

By noon there was a smudge in the sky where the line of the tracks met the horizon. Flitting back to the wagon, he found John Senior sitting there, studying his German Bible.

"They're coming!"

"*Ja*."

The train came on fast, stack smoke unfurling like a banner. It flew full throttle, as if reluctant to shorten steam until the last minute. The pause in Ottawa was accompanied by a bright metallic squeal that, for some peculiar reason, made Junior's teeth hurt.

Male passengers jumped off before the carriages halted, clutching trunks whose momentum made them tumble as they hit the ground. Though Ottawa was a sizable settlement, not many got off there in the middle of a typical day. The train paused for the full three minutes of a neat stop—no water, no fuel—before the engineer blew the whistle again. The iron links of the couplers groaned as the carriages were yanked forward.

The riders who had jumped off early dusted themselves off, regarded their destination with pained, embarrassed grins, and resumed lugging their trunks. Junior stared at the absence before him with rising anxiety. He turned back to John Senior, shrugged. No women at all had debarked. Had there been some mistake?

A flash of skirts at the back of the last carriage. Before Junior could take two steps forward, two female figures seemed to flee from the train. One was young and thin, well-dressed in a buff-colored dress and hat tied with a lavender scarf, moving with a loping poise that alighted easily from the moving carriage. The other was a great round globule of a woman, clothed indifferently but in identical hat and scarf, who bounced awkwardly as her feet hit the ground.

"It's them," Junior said.

Rushing forward, he greeted them with kisses so forceful they felt like assaults. Then he took their carpetbags.

Kate was puffy-eyed, as if she had gotten no sleep; Almira was wearing her stone face, and not looking in Kate's direction at all.

"Somethin' eatin' your corn?" Junior asked.

Almira stood mute. Kate seemed about to say something, but only managed to mutter, "This *creature* . . ." before giving up. For what purpose was there to recount yet another squabble with this miserable woman, who had adopted her as her child so long before yet never made the slightest effort to understand her? There had been a thousand times in the years since she had intended to abandon her. And yet—when there was a mark on the hook, and profit to be made, they worked together as if driven by a single mind. She often had occasion to wonder: was there any amount of money that would be enough for her to strike out on her own?

Her gaze shifted to Junior. There she saw his urgent, almost canine devotion, his eyes that seemed to pull her inward to some core of affection for which she had no use. As a female unattached, she had long become used to the ways men gazed at her, from the sybarite's frank lust to the aesthete's appraisal to the soft invitation of those caught in the grip of a romantic illusion. Of all these, the latter, the silent bid for marriage in the eyes of an unsuitable man, was the most contemptible. Stomaching it wearied her more than the journey from Kansas City.

From the station, the Benders proceeded to the shops to buy what their "grocry" lacked.

The wagon presently swayed on its springs with the weight of a cast-iron stove, lumber for store shelving, and a bedstead big enough for two, disassembled. There was a calendar clock for sale at the hardware for two dollars, and an Empire dining table with four wolf-paw feet. At the dry goods store, they procured a small cask of flour, another of cornmeal. On the way out, Almira spied a set of four table knives with long, triangular profiles and ivory-clad handles fastened with three rivets. She lofted one, feeling its balance.

Finally, a stop at the druggist for some patent medicines—Pink Pills for Pale People, Mentho Goose Grease, Seelye's Wusa Tusa. Idly perusing the labels, Kate read that Gombault's Caustic Balsam was a veterinary treatment for "wind galls, distemper, poll evil, founder, capped hock & collar boils." For "dyspepsia due to hyperacidity," there was nothing better than Green's August Flower, while the key ingredient in St. Jacob's Oil—a liniment—was a goodly amount of chloroform. And of course everyone stocked Lydia E. Pinkham's Vegetable Compound ("a positive cure for all those painful Complaints and Weaknesses so common to our best female population"), whose efficacy was guaranteed by containing twenty percent ethyl alcohol.

Displaying a flair for decorating, Almira also selected sprigs of dried herbs—sandhill sage, bee balm—for them to stock. Long experience running shops from Ohio to Colorado had taught her that such herbs were as useful for freshening an establishment as they were as merchandise.

"*Wir hätten in Humboldt einkaufen sollen,*" said the old man, impatient.

"There are no decent shops in Humboldt," Almira answered.

"*Sie wollte nicht den vollen Preis bezahlen.*"

"We're alone here, you ape," she snapped. "You can speak English."

John Senior shrugged. "You know what I say."

THE QUALITY OF the shops in Ottawa was poor compensation for
the journey that followed. The trip to their claim took a week of
rocking and shaking in the back of the wagon, under scudding
late autumn skies that too often opened up with frosty down-
pours that soaked through the patchwork Indian blanket Junior
had traded for a half pouch of cigarette tobacco. As they pushed
deeper into the desert, the women were chilled by the loneliness of
the expanse, which seemed as forlorn as anything they had seen in
their collective years on the frontier. From that modest elevation,
they peered miles into the heart of a land stunted by the years of
strife and neglect that had come to be known, the nation over, as
Bleeding Kansas.

This was the time from the passage of the Kansas-Nebraska Act
to the opening of the Civil War, when the future of the territory,
slave or free, still hung in the balance. "bushwhackers" defending
that peculiar institution and "jayhawkers" against it ranged the
Missouri borderlands, committing acts of butchery so foul that
reporters shrank from describing them. Settlers who dared try to
prove out their claims, or even set a cooking fire for all to see, were
rooted out by one side or the other, and sometimes both in turn.
Others contemplating the effort were dissuaded by rumors of out-
rages by knife and fire made more heinous for their lack of details.
In the process, the laying of the nation's railroads and telegraph
ground to a halt—something not even the Rocky Mountains accomplished. For years, as development skirted north, south, and
west, the contested lands were hollowed out by the cycle of attack
and reprisal, the delivery of bloody "messages" to the other side
that were never heeded but never forgotten.

The wagon swayed for mile after desolate mile, bringing more
charred barns and tangles of wrecked fencing into view. In the

empty miles between the shallow-rooted towns, farms stood half built but abandoned; newly planted fruit trees grew up buried in weeds, and feral horses watched from the streambeds. Rolling on, they saw a schoolhouse, lovingly built and endowed by its community, abandoned to a mother skunk and her litter, who trooped inside as if lessons were about to resume. A discarded stove and rusty iron bedstead reclined in the grass like beached hulks. A little farther on, a dead calf, the leathery remains of its skin stretched tentlike over crumbling bones, sockets eyeless but staring.

When the sun grazed the bottom of the sky, and the journey was finally done for the day, the men unhitched the mule. Hobbling it, they set it loose to graze as they pitched camp. Blankets were spread under the wagon and an iron stand unfolded for the cook pot, as Kate and Almira came down to gather the only fuel at hand: pats of dried cattle dung. Kate hated this chore, the searching and stooping and picking at the revolting deposits with her fingers. The choicest of these "meadow muffins," as Almira called them, were at least a foot around and a few days old—too old to attract flies, but fresh enough to retain some of their moisture, which helped them burn a little longer. The old woman instructed her to carry them in the hollow of her apron. Kate held her share of the flat, stinking things up and away from her skirts, fearing their odious substance would spoil them by mere proximity.

Night came as a relief, as the darkness poured itself widely and evenly over the sea of grass, hiding its interminable extent from their eyes. The old man made coffee by folding the beans in a canvas seat cover, beating it with the hammer he kept hung on his belt and boiling the blasted shards in stream water. The typical supper—dollops of fried corn mush, slabs of unctuous matter that passed for bacon—was consumed as the moon rose, and Kate retired some distance away to watch it. Here at last, after hours of creaking, clanging progress in the ancient wagon, a moment of peace. Here, she cast her eyes out over the desert and, with a deliberate effort of misperception, saw a distant figure in the moonlight, biding his time until the rescue she knew must come.

There was no sign of rain that evening, so there was no need for them to sleep under the wagon. Lying out on the open prairie, her nostrils filled with semisweet rot of the summer's growth. Later, wrapped in the warm oblivion of her blankets, and with unbidden slip of memory, Kate was back in the tent camps of her childhood, soon after Clarrity had abandoned her with Almira.

Going to sleep among the sounds of eventide, she heard a distant fiddle wheeze as it was rosined. The clank of pans being washed, and the guttural utterances of a man decanting into a whore. A muffled gurgling sound—but this time coming not from somewhere beyond the canvas, but within her tent.

The seven year-old Kate got up, and peeking around the blanket separating her space from Almira's, saw a man lying on his back in her bed. He was bearded amply, and hairy in every other place, down to the wiry thatch between his legs. She stared at this first, compelled and disgusted, until her eyes swept upward and she saw the leather thong twisted around his neck. His coal-smudged face was black, but his lips were blue. His eyes did not blink.

Almira stood nearby, arms crossed and cigarette burning in her fingers. She was as naked as the dead man. And in her eyes, not disapproval at Kate's intrusion, but the patience of an instructress. She was silent as she raised the man's open purse to the lamplight, patiently removing the last of his money. Kate stood starting for some minutes, expecting to be ordered back to her bed. But the order never came. In time the spectacle became unremarkable; Kate yawned.

The next morning the body was gone. Kate thought it best not to ask about it—until the impulse struck her ten years later, on the train, as they traveled to meet the Bender men in Ottawa. Tired of looking out at the expanse of gray winter prairie, she had turned to Almira.

"So did you do your real daughter the same as that miner in the tent?"

The other, who had expressed not a hint of emotion at the time, was suddenly indignant: "How dare you ask me that!"

Kate, surprised at this reaction, resorted to her first instinct—self-pity. "If you didn't want to be asked, why were you so careless, leaving such a thing in front of a child?"

Almira, sneering—"You are the smart girl. But you are a little foolish too, yes?"

"I hate you."

"Good. You learn."

They had endured the rest of the trip in silence.

ON THEIR SIXTH day in the wagon they glimpsed the mounds from afar. Compared to the hills of Ohio or Indiana, or indeed anywhere she could think of, they were low, begrudging things, barely worth being called "topography." But to Kate, in this expanse, these sweeping bottoms of vanished seas, the mounds might as well have been lofty mountain peaks. Their appearance meant rest at last, though in what quarters she could only imagine. The Bender men had told them nothing of the home they had built. Her only knowledge of them was from what they lacked, based on the supplies they had brought in the wagon.

Hurrying over the last few miles in the gathering dusk, they saw the cabin just as the quarter moon rose. The faint silvery gleam shone off the tin stovepipe like a landward beacon. As they approached the structure, sitting foursquare and alone, the mule pulled up, ears swiveling, murmuring with anxiety. Junior fumbled to light a lantern. John Senior, sensing they were not alone, reached behind his seat, drawing forth his hammer.

Suddenly Kate glimpsed a lean, scissor-sharp form emerge from the shadows, striking out for open ground. As it passed, she saw a wolf looking back at her, eyes aglow like smoldering coals. She shuddered as if someone had poured ice water on her open heart. The wolf was the familiar of one of the most dreaded of demons in the *Lesser Key*—old Amon, who anchored the left of her dark army, ever on watch to cast down Barbatos the Archer.

"Where is it going?" she asked Junior. "What bearing?"

"Northwest."

"Northwest," she repeated, sitting back in relief, as if the direction were of supreme significance.

Junior eyed the tool in the old man's hand, "A lot of good a shoe hammer will do you against the likes of *that*."

"You don't know what good it can do," the old man replied. Then he laid it beside his hip, in easy reach as always.

Junior's feeble lamp threw more shadows than light. Exhausted from the trail, they spread their bedrolls on the floor of the cabin and went to sleep without supper.

The next morning Junior awoke to find Kate standing in the middle of the room, hands on her hips, appraising the walls. The way her hair was unclasped and cascading down her back inspired him to prop himself up on his elbow and stare.

"This will not do," she said, pointing with her chin at the

newsprint—from *The Thayer Searchlight*—the men had waxed to the walls.

"It's done," replied Junior, meaning to say "it is *customary*" but also implying "it is accomplished, so don't touch it."

Kate peeled off the paper, balling the pages up and dropping them on the floor. The noise woke Almira, and finally the old man, who cursed in German and buried his head.

"Why are you doing that?" asked Almira.

"We'll need this space, for the carving."

"The what?"

"The glyphs," said Kate with an ingenuous smile, as if she were a little girl keeping secrets. But when Junior opened his mouth to question her further, her face hardened and he kept his peace.

She found somewhat more practical work to do when she got outside. Upon seeing Junior's sign, *Grocry,* she took a broom and knocked the hat off his head.

"What kind of oaf are you, to spell that way?"

He regarded the sign. "Seems right to me."

"It would to an ape, wouldn't it? Now if you'd get me a brush and paint, I'll try to stop them laughing at us."

Chapter Eight

The Watching Chair

THE SNOW CAME about when it should have. One morning after the New Year the gloom of night didn't lift by morning, but kept the sun at bay. A swath of thick overcast, so heavy the weight could be felt from the ground, covered the sky from horizon to horizon. When the first flakes fell they were small. Only later did the storm begin in earnest, speckling the prairie like the surface of some world-sized egg.

The relative warmth of the trail kept it free of snow for a while. The old man sat in the "watching chair" he'd moved outside, turning the pages of his Bible as he eyed the thoroughfare. At noon the Fort Scott–Independence stage came through, an occurrence that barely merited his attention. He was looking instead for traffic of a particular kind—the well-equipped, solitary, minimally armed kind. The traveler must also be separated enough from any others that no one else should be visible for as far as the eye could see. The criteria were very specific, for the four Benders had spent much time discussing it in the weeks they had settled into their new home.

In his zeal to encounter this traffic, Old Man Bender was prepared to sit for all the hours of the day, moving so little that the snowflakes accumulated in his beard and great gristly mass of his hair, making him seem like some mythic monster from the caves of Sind.

His dedication paid off as the afternoon faded and a lone figure on horseback appeared between the mounds. As he approached at a slow walk, no other travelers followed or intruded from the other direction. The visitor was still a half mile off when the old man, believing he could wait no longer, cried out, *"Hier!"*

"I see him," came the reply from the window. For after the days' washing was done and food prepared, there was not much for Kate to do but sit, laying out her tarot in various patterns that might tell her how their enterprise might fare. Gathering up her cards, she looked to Almira, who retreated to the back of the cabin to warm up the savories that would lure their visitor in.

The skinny mare was no bigger than a pony, stepping gingerly over the trail as if feeling her way over a frozen lake. Her rider was likewise thin, with gangling arms and legs draped over her flanks and a sparse growth of beard clinging to his face. With the snow falling harder now, he was peering up from under the brim of his hat as he neared the cabin. His soft eyes and air of pensive loneliness marked him for a boy, despite the bulge of the side holster under his buckskin jacket. His face ventured out from under his hat as he saw Kate standing alone in front of the cabin. The more he saw of her, staring back at him, the wider his mouth hung open.

"Hello, good sir!" she hailed him. "Seems we're getting some weather today."

"Seems."

Wary. Hand close to his hip.

"Where are you bound, traveler?"

"Tucson. Independence for now."

"Then you've got a ways to go! You'd be welcome to break your trip here, if you like. We have food, a fire. A warm place to bed down too, should you chose to sojourn . . ."

Kate made no overt promises with the prospect of "bedding down," but what man needed them when offered shelter by a pretty woman? The typical man supplied all the promises himself. And to punctuate the suggestion, she gave him a smile of such calculated sweetness she was aware of how false it should seem. And yet—

"All right," replied the rider.

Like actors awaiting their cue, Junior and the old man came out to play their respective roles. Junior, with a genial nod, led the horse to the stable. As their guest entered the cabin, the old man arranged the furniture, planting the back of a chair against the line of naked joists dividing the room and the table in front of it. The slashing rapidity of his movements was odd. It gave the stranger pause, but Kate was right beside him, laying a warm hand on his arm. With her touch, his doubts lapsed long enough for him to take the proffered seat.

"Smells good, what's cooking?" he said.

"My mother keeps the best stew pot in east Kansas. What's your name?"

"John. John Jesperson."

She stayed close to him as he sat, keeping his eyes fixed on hers through a magnetism she had never understood but somehow knew how to control. And it was just as well, for the old man was already standing behind the curtain of joists, looking at the back of their guest's head as he rehearsed swings of the hammer. Almira, alarmed, laid a hand on his arm to restrain him. The other angrily shook her off, looking to Kate for a signal. She gave him a freezing glance.

"Warten."

She entertained Jesperson, serving him water in a mug of polished brass, until Junior finally returned from the stable. His examination of the boy's rig was promising—a fine saddle, brand new bridle and martingale, quality equipment in his bags. No cash money, of course, as any sane man would carry that close to his person.

He looked to Kate, who made no response. She was a sphinx now, testing her wayfarer with riddles of desire and possibility. The way she had loosed her hair—was that a signal? Women were not rare in this part of the frontier, but a roadside encounter with a young, conversable one, who brazenly displayed the lack of a ring on her left hand, was not a pleasure typically enjoyed by a young man on the trail. Not unless this was like the stories he had heard, among those dirty-minded boys his age, of women who plied a certain trade in the remoteness and anonymity of the open range, with the active connivance of their parents. After all, did he not have money? And she was sitting adjacent to him, the top buttons at her neck undone, throat softly plunging to frontiers that beckoned, swell of maidenly bosom resting upon an arm bared to the elbow. She smiled, tilted her head, fingertips caressing spiral locks beside her ear—the ear that seemed open only to him, to his halting attempts at conversation.

"So what awaits in Tucson?" she was asking him.

"An uncle got a claim on some copper near to. He died. There's a lawyer there, but my paw can't get away just now . . ."

"Do you have any relations in these parts . . . someone who might be interested in your passing through?"

"We are Illinois folk going back to my grandfather."

"I see," she replied. And she went on presenting the smell of her, of candle wax and vanilla and burnt corncob. His stomach rumbled for Almira's stew, and the impress of the young woman's red lips, which he imagined were as smooth and hard as those of his sisters' porcelain dolls he had once stolen and kissed. Seated, hypnotized, semi-erect, he watched her eyes laugh at him until they flitted above and behind him, indicating some kind of signal. For him? For he was hungry indeed.

And yet—tremulous now on the threshold of a different sort of fate—the Benders hesitated. John Senior stood behind, leaning against the hot stovepipe, hammer in left hand, right laid across his mouth in a tableau of personal reflection. John Junior hid in the corner, and Almira ambled forth with a bowl of stew. Scowling, she placed it in front of their guest like she was presenting an invoice, and Jesperson tore his eyes off Kate long enough to look up and shudder at her homeliness. Almira didn't take it personal—she never did.

The old man launched himself, taking a long windup with his weapon that cast a swooping shadow across the rest of the cabin. Unfortunately for him, his hurtling reflection was visible in the polished surface of Jesperson's water cup. The boy ducked. The butt of the hammer missed his head clean, striking his shoulder instead with a muffled thud. The blow broke his collarbone.

But the pain only seemed to accelerate him. Rolling off his

chair, he glanced off Kate's lap and onto the floor. The old man, thwarted by the joists, was out of reach now, while Kate, who was both surprised by the boy's quickness and annoyed at her partner's clumsiness, did nothing but watch.

Jesperson was fumbling under his overcoat for his gun. Before he could draw, John Junior was at his arm—not with any particular violence, but almost discreetly, as if directing him to his proper seat at the theater. "Let's have none of *that*, now," he said, a chiding tone in his voice. "We'd just as well get on with our business."

"To hell with you," replied the other, still fumbling, until the old man caught up and with a mighty swipe laid his hammer athwart the boy's temple. His skull there opened up with a crack, spurting blood that caught Junior in the mouth and splashed Kate's apron. "For God's sake!" cried the boy, and then again, "For God's sake!"

With a twist he was free, retreating to the far corner of the cabin beside the bottles of patent medicine. Astonishment at his wounding made him forget his gun; he reached up to touch his face as his contents ran loose and pink over his nose and into his mouth, his face going white as he tasted his mortality.

"You have murdered me."

"*Steh still und lass mich dich töten!*"

John Senior struck again. The blow stove in the dome of the boy's forehead, dislodging fragments of hair-fringed skull and driving them into the matter beneath. This time, and without further comment, John Jesperson collapsed in an invertebrate heap.

The four of them stood there for what felt like minutes but was only a few moments. Kate was the first to rouse from their collective shock. She stood up to inspect the blaze of red on her apron, then tore it off before the stain spread to her dress. Junior, giving the body wide berth, looked out the window to confirm that no one else was around—the trail, disappearing now under the deepening snow, was deserted.

As they had earlier agreed, their first step was to get the body out of sight. Junior dumped it in the space beneath the trapdoor. He followed it down with one of the ivory-handled carving knives to cut the boy's throat. The deed done, he stayed down there, contemplating for some time the slow seep of dead blood on the stone, as if unwilling to accept that Jesperson's demise was final.

It was almost as an afterthought that he searched the victim's pockets. Coming up, he laid their loot on the table: $530 in notes from the Commercial National Bank of St. Louis, neatly stacked and tied with a piece of linen. Beside them were ten twenty-dollar gold eagles in a small burlap sack and a silver locket on a neck chain. Inside the locket, Kate found a lock of smooth, straight blond hair, lovingly bound with a piece of pink hemp ribbon.

Almira, with a sweeping movement of her forearm, deposited the coin and folding money in an old cracker tin. Then she placed the tin on a shelf in plain sight, next to others containing flints and old nails.

"Best throw that in the fire," she said, indicating the lock of hair. But to Kate, something about the delicacy of its tiny bow made it unfit for burning. She crumpled it in her fist, intending to find a more fitting end for it later.

"Did you get his iron?" Almira asked Junior, after the trapdoor had already been closed and the table slid over it.

Junior, hissing with annoyance, went back to fetch the gun he had forgotten.

The inauguration of the Benders' plan did not go as well as they'd hoped. Thanks to John Senior's looming reflection, the victim's instinct had almost redeemed his life. Only a sticky holster stood between success and disaster. Serving from different drinkware was one obvious change in their operation—but it could not be the only one. There had to be a better way for the approach to be made than simply sneaking up from behind. Some way for the strike delivered in utter security, against which there was no defense.

It was Almira who hit on the solution. The back of the army wagon was ribbed, with a canvas cover that could be stretched or rolled according to the weather. When they stripped off this cover and nailed it to the joists in the cabin, they found that it was a perfect fit from floor to rafters. Best of all, the canvas was a translucent divider, with the lamp in the front section casting sharp shadows. From the vantage of the back room, the outline of anyone seated at the table was projected as clearly as a paper silhouette.

"*Here* is our fortune," proclaimed Almira, proud of herself as she regarded the image of John Junior's naked head through the screen. She flicked at it with a forefinger, making Junior's head jerk forward. "*Können Sie es tun?*" she challenged the old man.

"Watch me."

"If they all go as hard as that one, there'll be no more," Kate told them. "It is not what was promised." Paroxysms of violence—and a lap full of blood—was not what she had come to expect from their collaboration. In her mind, the men coming down the trail were nothing more than gunmen and gamblers and grasping land speculators, the kind she had seen a thousand times at cards with her father or waiting patiently at the perfumed tent flaps of soiled doves. They tipped their caps at her but devoured her with their eyes. They thought their money entitled them to everything. For their sins, they should fall drily, silently, like pinned insects.

Indeed, quickly. But not like this—not a boy slathered in the same humors from which his mother had borne him, begging for his life.

"So the princess is afraid of a little blood," Almira laughed at her. "She wants only the easy money!"

"I want what was promised."

"These isn't playing at cards, *kleines Mädchen*. This is the business."

"Without me, there is no business."

"You will do as you are told," Almira said, eyes flitting at the old man with his hammer.

"No!" the head said from behind the canvas. It was Junior, with an urgency that compelled the women's attention. He stood up, an erect man-shadow speaking to them:

"She's right. It is not as it will be. I promise."

The surprising severity in his voice, and the fact that he was just a silhouette and not so obviously Junior, made them keep their silence.

Chapter Nine

Harmony Grove

SABBATH SERVICES WERE held at the Harmony Grove school-house at eight o'clock. Early in the morning, the deacons, including Leroy Dick and Justice of the Peace George Majors, stacked the children's desks in the storeroom at the back of the school. With care lest they disturb the books left open there, they nudged the teacher's desk against the windowless north wall and put out flowers gathered by the neighborhood children—random and exuberant clutches of mallow and plains violet in the spring, hollyhock and phlox in the summer, aster and lady's tresses and lobelia in autumn. There were no wildflowers to relieve the severity of the whitewashed room in winter, but there was a stove to light, and the topping up of the school's supply of fuel with wood from their own piles.

In all seasons, Dick had a final task: on the blackboard, in a round, sinuous cursive festooned with precious curls and bits of calligraphic business that struck folks as charming in such a serious man, he wrote chapter and verse of the day's Reading. Under that, in a different color of chalk, he inscribed the title of the morning's Lesson. This was dispatched to him by Minister Dienst late each Saturday night in the hands of his nine-year-old nephew, who turned up breathless from the mile run from the minister's house, but also from anticipation over the cakes and sweet cream Mary Ann Dick would reward him for his trouble. This Sunday the boy delivered a scrap of paper with the question, "How may we inquire after news not as Athenians, but as Christians?"

The two dozen or so residents of Osage Township parked their vehicles—buggies and buckboards for the better-off, pony carts for the less so—right on the road. There was no need to leave space for vehicles to pass, because everyone who belonged there was already present, and there was no other conceivable destination for anyone to go but church.

Services lasted two hours and were endured on hard benches. And when the last strains of the processional faded, and the people filed outside to exchange neighborly greetings, they would gather at tables piled with cakes and pies baked by the wives, accompanied by fresh tea in the summer or hot coffee in the cooler months. As the boys organized games of baseball in the schoolyard, and the girls gathered mulberries and jumped rope, the adults gathered in loose cohorts of gossips, flirts, or—in the case of the married men—to stand with hands thoughtfully in pockets, exchanging hard-won bits of settler intelligence on well-cladding and fence-posting and privy-digging and livestock. When the menfolk were done talking, they left the grass behind them stained with the slick, foamy black of their tobacco spit.

A small group stayed behind for several hours more—the church choir under the direction of Leroy Dick. The magistrate played no instrument, but consoled himself with the thought that the voices of his neighbors were nobler and more glorious than any fiddle or whistle. He spent untoward sums on new hymnals from back East, and took pride in training his female brethren, who, as their voices rose in praise of the Most High, looked back at him with pure, unspiritual pleasure. For women liked Leroy Dick. They were assured by the casualness of his masculinity, of his dark good looks that neither proclaimed themselves nor insisted upon their attentions. His dignity was not like a tower, loudly proclaiming itself and casting others in shadow. Instead, it was like the sun, serenely shining upon all without discrimination. When Dick stayed behind after practice to put the children's desks back in order, he often had more than enough lady volunteers to help.

So went an ordinary Sabbath morning. Matters changed that Sunday in early January when Kate and John Junior first came for services. They arrived late, driving through a light snow in their army wagon; they took seats at the very back, picking up their hymnals and joining the singing as if they'd attended Harmony Grove Church all their lives. Junior was in a clean black suit, his hair parted and shining with French pomade. Kate wore a dress of buttercup yellow, lace gloves on her hands, hair demurely pinned under a hat that matched her dress, but with select strands allowed to escape and play around the nape of her neck. When other parishioners turned to look over their shoulders at her, or peek over the edges of their hymnals, she would fearlessly meet their eyes. Minister Dienst lost his train of thought in mid-preach as he became ensnared in her gaze.

After services the new pair was welcomed to the area by each and every member of the community. The men—who didn't withdraw to chew and talk this time—seemed anxious for the opportunity to shake Junior's hand, albeit only when his sister was standing beside him. "Very pleased to make your acquaintance! *Dee*-lighted!" Junior proclaimed, pumping their fists. Kate stood by with a polite smile on her face, her eyes lightly lidded, as if—all of the sudden—she was shy.

Rudolph Brockman came up to reintroduce himself, having not bothered to visit the Benders since the men had first appeared at his cabin months before. Now he behaved as if no subject in the world was more important to him than the welfare of his new neighbors. "Come by sometime and I'll lend ye a proper post driver!" he said, eyes flitting toward Kate. She seemed not to focus on anything, but allowed a slight smile to curl the edges of her lips. Brockman's cabin mate Augustus Ern, meanwhile, bid Junior only the most cursory of welcomes, and pointedly failed to acknowledge Kate at all.

For their part, the ladies of Harmony Grove spread their goodwill more evenly. Junior seemed like a decent sort of young man to them, showing the proper respect for the matrons. The girl was pretty, and seemed not to notice the clumsy flirtations of their husbands and sons. Yet she also showed a certain semibored blandness before the sisterhood of frontier women. After all, these were lifelines of practical wisdom to a newcomer on the plains; anyone beginning the rest of her life there would be wise to cultivate their favor. Kate, instead, seemed to show only as much enthusiasm as absolutely necessary, as if she were playing for a draw right from the start.

When Mary Ann Dick approached her, armed with a pumpkin pie, Kate hesitated before accepting it. Mrs. Dick, a tall, wide-faced woman, was neither threatened nor hostile to Kate's beauty. She had, after all, outsmarted and outcompeted more convention-ally pretty women all her life—most famously for the hand of her husband. Instead, she thought she detected in Kate a heart with a wide-open hole in it. A hole that, at least at that moment, only a fresh pumpkin pie could fill.

"Did you find your stock?" she asked. When Kate and Junior looked at her blankly, she explained, "That was the devil's own tempest the other day, but I happened to be at my window around noon, and thought I saw your rig out on the road." She indicated the Benders' wagon with the mismatched wheels parked thereby. "I asked Leroy about it, and he said you must be out looking for some lost animal."

"Terrible blow to be out and about in," opined Mrs. Dienst.

"The calf . . . in the snow . . . yes!" stammered Junior, who had indeed accompanied the old man out in the blizzard.

The storm was supposed to give them cover as they dumped the body of John Jesperson in Drum Creek, at what they thought was a safe distance from the cabin. They hadn't counted on anyone seeing them in such a storm.

"It was hard, yes. Tracks got filled in right away in that snow-fall. Couldn't tell you how long it took to bring it to heel."

"It can't be helped," Mrs. Dick said. "A calf parted from the herd is as good as lost in these parts, with all these beasts." And she gestured broadly, as if the vicinity was that very moment crowded with hungry wolves.

"So we understand," replied Junior, looking sidelong to Kate for her interjection. For she always seemed to be dissatisfied with the way he handled these situations. Sure enough, she spoke:

"They went out in that storm for me. She was my favorite . . . the calf," she said, keeping her eyes averted.

Mrs. Dick laid a hand on Kate's forearm. "Of course, child. It can't be helped."

Later, Mrs. Dick whispered to Mrs. Dienst, who thought Kate haughty, "The poor girl, she was overwhelmed. You might give her another chance."

"Showing up to church in *that* dress is all I needed to see."

"They have queer ideas in Iowa," replied Mrs. Dick, who had somehow gotten the impression the Benders were from the Hawkeye State.

It wasn't until the magistrate and the pastor had finished putting the school back in order that they went out to greet the Benders formally. Minister Dienst paid his respects to the girl first, paternally taking both her hands in his as he bade her welcome. Kate continued to play the ingenue, looking up as if in awe before the very spectacle of him. But her fingers were cold in Dienst's grasp, and if he'd had the insight to perceive her true feelings, he would have seen that she could barely contain an impulse to flee. For ever since she had begun her study of *The Lesser Key of Solomon,* she had a visceral reaction against priests, ministers— all those purpled hypocrites, those purported men of God. Where this aversion had come from, she could not say for sure, for the book itself taught nothing of the kind. It was something she just assumed she should feel.

But a different sensation came over her when Leroy Dick paid his respects. When he took her hand, the frigid fingertips abruptly thawed.

"Our little convocation is surely not as splendid as you are used to, but we think it godly enough."

He spoke in the kind of gentle, unrushed tones one used with a child. Yet somehow, she seemed to taste his words with her tongue, not hear them with her ears. "I rejoiced in His presence," she replied.

"That's all we can ask. And are you in good voice, my dear? Can you join our little choir?"

"You will see me again."

Chapter Ten

Being Right with the Goose

"It was not worthwhile to fix up a nice house to live in and then have it all burned by the border ruffians."

—Francis H. Snow (1840–1908)
Chancellor, University of Kansas

AUGUST, 1856

CORNELIUS DICK, LEROY's father, staked his first 160-acre claim on the south bank of the Kansas River just after passage of the Kansas-Nebraska Act. The substance of the new law—that the disposition of the future state, slave or free, would be decided by plebiscite—brought many new settlers to the area, as eastern abolitionists and southern slaveholders rushed in to tilt the voting in their favor. But Cornelius and Florence Dick had not come to Kansas to make territorial policy. They came from upstate New Hampshire for cheap land and a shot at prosperity in a place where, they had heard, corn need not be cultivated, but sprung out of the soil by its own accord, like a weed.

The elder Dick had his opinions on the institution of slavery. As he broke his back on the rocky New England uplands, he considered the possibility of doing it with the additional disadvantage of competing against slave labor—and shuddered. Something about the institution of owning black men offended the dignity of the poor whites, whose sweat was cheapened by its discomfiting closeness to the occupations of the slave. Dick would declare to his startled sons: "Let the fat southern aristocrats sow their own fields! Let that codfish aristocracy pick that noxious crop with their own soft hands! Then let us then see the size of their spreads!" By his reckoning, slavery changed the very ground on which it was instituted, infesting and altering it in favor of the entitled slaveholder and his stock of bovine, dependent Negroes—and against independent free whites like Cornelius Dick.

These were his thoughts. If called upon to vote on the great burning question of the day, he would cast it to keep Kansas soil free. But this was far from his first concern as he drove his family over fifteen hundred miles from Concord to Lawrence. As they went west, he told those inquiring about their destination that they were going to the Territory, but "not because of *that infernal business.*" In Missouri, where the suspicions of proslavery men burned white hot, he was quizzed regularly on "how he stood on the Goose" ("the Goose" being how Missourians perceived the prospect of extending slavery into Kansas, like an unexpected prize). On a steamboat landing on the Missouri River, a man in a white suit and slouch hat, sporting a Louisiana drawl, tried to bait him into saying the word "cow" The logic was that if a newcomer pronounced it like a southerner, "kow," he could be trusted to vote "correctly" in the great referendum. But if he said it like a New Englander, "keow," he was most likely one of those "dogs of abolitionists," and best rethink his intentions.

Dick, who had read of this ploy in the Illinois papers, refused to gratify the man but said "stock" instead. Thereafter, he instructed his two sons, Leroy and Temple, not to speak to strangers at all, but if they did, to declare their destination lay in Nebraska, not Kansas.

Crossing the border at Westport, they proceeded upriver to a spot about midway between Lawrence—then little more than a handful of log cabins—and Lecompton—which was even smaller. Their claim was on a rise south of the river, with good timber in the streambeds and sweet water less than twenty feet below the ground. The Dicks' first house was a dugout excavated into a south-facing hillside. With the help of his two boys and his wife, he lined the one-room chamber with four-inch logs sealed with mud. Smoke from the cast-iron stove was let out through a pipe forged out of old coffee tins. The floor remained of beaten earth for as long as they lived there, covered only with straw at first, then with a rug as their fortunes improved. Their only privacy lay behind a wool curtain Florence had traded for in Lawrence against Leroy's old cradle. She had no use for the latter because she had suffered much in the birth of her younger son and could have no further children.

Leroy hated the dugout, for it was a gloomy place whose structure was too delicate to contain two active boys. Any sort of rough-housing loosened the mud that kept water from seeping into the house during the spring rains. Running on the ground above tended to dust the furniture below with dirt, as the flimsy "ceiling" shook under their feet. Too often Cornelius would be inside in the early evenings, reading by lamplight, as one of the boys ran over the top of the dugout, soiling his newspaper with a clumps of fine Kansas loam. "Leroy!" he would cry, at which Leroy would know to make himself scarce, because if he went inside to answer for his misbehavior, his backside would be greeted by the sting of Cornelius's belt.

It took two years for them to finish the first stage of a proper house. This was just a two-room structure, with door holes cut in the walls for wings that would be added later. Leroy and Temple got the loft above, which had a window and seemed like a palace compared to the dingy gopher lodge they were used to. Below, there was space at last for the furniture the family had brought from New Hampshire and kept stored under canvas for two long winters. When her husband brought in the heavy oak dining table she had inherited from her parents, Florence Dick wept.

The situation in his fields soon gave Dick his own reason to cry. The corn did not come up spontaneously after all. In his ignorance, he had plowed as if he were still farming in the East, turning up deep riverine soil. This gave him a good crop the first few years. After that, the precious loam washed into the river, stripping him down to sterile, sandy stuff that begrudged any decent yield. Cornelius was forced to experiment with various crop rotation schemes, dividing up his spread into test fields. He finally hit on planting cold-resistant rye (*Secale cereale*) after corn harvesting. This grew through the winter, even in the snow, and offered shelter for other winter crops like clover, turnips, and radishes, which restored the vitality of the soil. The rye he plowed under as mulch for his corn crop the next summer. The turnips, moreover, were good for fodder, and the radishes for sale to the burgeoning hotel trade in Lawrence and Lecompton. With this formula, Cornelius gradually prospered, enabling him to acquire another forty acres along the river, and a strip of forty more on the top of the ridge behind the farm.

Of equal benefit to their fortunes, he managed to avoid getting caught up one way or another in the increasingly bitter political divisions in the Territory. Calls came from Lawrence for free-soil partisans to gather for this or that worthy cause, but Dick usually found other matters to detain him. When a land dispute led to a fatal altercation between a squatter and a member of the Free State militia a train of events followed that culminated in the so-called Wakarusa War—the siege of Lawrence by two thousand proslavery Missourians. The proslavery men were soon opposed by a similar number of free-soilers, who poured into the town and turned it into an armed camp. Seven-foot-high redoubts were erected on Massachusetts Street, with enfilades devised to trap the "invaders." Every household became a barracks, feeding and housing the defenders as the women and girls worked far into the night, making cartridges. When the women and children did sleep, their dreams were disturbed by tales of rape and plunder that would await them if the Border Ruffians broke into the town. The besiegers, meanwhile, lit cheery fires and drank until dawn, toasting the courage they would soon have occasion to display against the "damned slaves of the nigger." A howitzer was dragged in from Westport and positioned in clear view of the defenders, with crates conspicuously marked as INCENDIARIES.

Alas, the "war" ended without a shot fired, in a settlement brokered by the governor. But nobody was content with this outcome, which only seemed to swell the stock of venom accumulating on both sides. And in the general indignation, few noticed Cornelius

Dick had arrived too late, with his son Leroy at his side and his shotgun across his lap—unloaded.

The conflict soon arrived at the Dick claim in a form that could not be so easily avoided. Leroy remembered the late summer day in '56, with the air over the cornstalks fluttering with the heat of a true plains scorcher, and the atmosphere in the house so heavy it seemed to droop like a wet curtain. It was one of those days when the crickets were so calamitously loud one despaired of opening the windows. Leroy was alone with his mother, bored enough to be diverted by watching her fold laundry, when there came a knock on the back door.

Opening up, the boy found a tall, thin figure waiting there.

"Hello there, young sir," the Negro said.

As those of his kind were expected to, he stood a few feet back, off the doorstep, and had adopted the usual posture of deliberate inoffensiveness, with head down and hands empty and plainly visible at his belt. A portmanteau thick with contents lay on the grass beside him. He appeared very young, no more than twenty, with hair cropped very close. On his broad, smooth face a spray of black freckles—and a smile.

"My name is Ernest Calvin Tubbs Junior. May I ask yours?"

"What do you want? And hello," replied Leroy, who had little experience talking with Negroes, and didn't quite know what manner to adopt.

"Would it be a terrible imposition for me to speak with your father?"

"He's away. But my maw's here."

"Alone? Hmm," he said, evidently troubled by the prospect of having to importune a white woman.

"Who is it, Leroy? Don't just let him stand out there in the sun . . ." Florence Dick approached from behind. For it was her practice to show nothing but indiscriminate hospitality to anyone who knocked on her door. And when she laid eyes on their visitor, her expression did not waver, though her eyes did sweep over him, and noting his scrupulous neatness, seemed satisfied.

"Would you like something to drink, young man?"

"To that I would be most obliged."

She sent Leroy to fetch a ladle from the keg of good water they kept by the stove. As he came back, striding carefully lest it spill, he heard his mother and Tubbs conversing with an ease that worried him. For their words struck his ears as somehow transgressive, as something that naturally called for watchfulness, like the tracks of one of those big cats not seen in twenty years but looming large in prairie legend. This vigilance was not something he had been taught by anyone. It was something he learned from the subtle stiffness in his father's back whenever a black man approached his family—a wariness, like any other sort of parental fear, that was more powerful for never being acknowledged.

" . . . then I thank you kindly, ma'am, and wish you a good evening," the Negro was saying, to which his mother said, "I will send the boy with beddings and something to eat."

Mr. Tubbs took the dipper, and with a wink at Leroy, drank. Then he picked up his portmanteau and headed in the direction of the old dugout.

"He will be staying the night out there," his mother told him after she closed the door.

"Staying? You mean, for the night?"

"Yes! What's wrong with you, Leroy? Since when do when turn away a traveler in need?"

"Don't you think we should ask Paw?"

"Your father would do no different," she snapped as she retrieved two heavy blankets from the linens chest. "The poor man has been walking for a week. Would we have him spend the night on the ground, with a storm coming?"

"No ma'am. But—"

"Take these to him," she ordered. "Tell him you'll bring him his supper presently. And never begrudge proper Christian charity again—or else your father *will* hear about it."

Cornelius and Leroy's elder brother Temple came home just before dark. Florence waited until they were at the supper table to tell them about their guest. As his father absorbed the news, it seemed to slow him down bodily, as if he were settling into a tub of molasses. This reaction annoyed her.

"You too? For what are we spending our Sundays in church, then, if this is the example you intend to set for your sons?"

"Now Fla, I never said that."

"I think you're saying a lot, by the way you are!"

"All I'm saying," he went on, wearily, "is that these things can be more complicated than that, and that we need consider how we set before having the vanity to think we can help."

"What vanity can there be in simple charity?"

"Much, I'd say."

Temple, who was busy with geometric doodlings with the gravy at the bottom of his bowl, spoke up: "What kind of things could happen, Paw?"

Cornelius kept silent for a moment, as Florence cast an interrogative eye on him.

"I don't know," he finally said. "We know nothing about him."

"If you listened to him speak, you'd know he's not what you're thinking. There's nothing about the plantation about him. He's a gentle, free soul from back East."

"So he says," replied Cornelius, taking up his spoon and leaning over his bowl in a manner that said the conversation was finished. Until he added: "His free soul will be on its way tomorrow. That is the last of it."

As typical on the plains, the day's heat was the silent, tormenting harbinger of what was to come. Steel-gray clouds built up in the west, mounting up to the very vault of heaven. Their flanks caught the gleam of the setting sun as barbs of incandescence stabbed their bases. The Dicks knew to seal the shutters when they smelled that close odor approaching, that moist exhalation of foreign essences, as if air had been sucked off some distant swamp and expelled across the plains.

The breeze soon picked up, and then a steady wind. By midnight the rain came on, assaulting the roof, lashing the wooden shingles, then shifting around from the east to seek a fresh angle of attack. Listening to it from their bed, Cornelius jerked awake with every creak of the house, which was still in the process of settling on its foundations. He assumed Florence was asleep beside him. But she was awake and thinking too, of the misery of many a rainy night she had spent in the dugout, the roof inevitably leaking as it saturated.

"He'll be soaked through," she whispered.

"Better there than open ground."

By morning the storm had passed. Rising to collect the morning's eggs from the coop, Leroy found the world transformed. The heat had broken. The rain had refreshed the appearance of plants and out-buildings, as if some giant painter had come in the night, touching it all up with more vibrant colors. Redoubled in intensity were the smells of the grass and the soil and the manure stinking sweetly from the pastures. These impressions were impossible to ignore, making Leroy conscious of his sensual surrounds in a way he feared was unmanly. For other boys his age never smelled flowers from yards away, never knew when they were just about to drop from their stems, as he did.

He was absently pondering these things, this sensitivity and the imperative to hide it, when he rounded the barn—and saw riders approaching.

The four of them were coming from the east, at a trot and riding abreast. It was too far to see their faces, but Leroy could already discern their clothing: waistcoats of dingy blue, knee-length boots, red bandannas tied on their heads. The stocks of their guns, carbines, rose at their right hands from their cavalry holsters, and the hilts of their sabers shone in the dawn. The kits he had seen many times before, in Lecompton and elsewhere—the unofficial uniforms of proslavery bushwhackers.

"Paw," he said, too low at first to be heard. Then he cried "Paw!" more loudly, and ran back to the house.

The visitors slowed as they approached the cabin, eyes sweeping. Stepping down, they left their long guns, but kept their right hands empty and resting in relaxed fashion close to their hips. Through a crack in the window curtain, Leroy and Temple watched them file up the front path—wary, but striving to step casually, as if they were on the most innocent of errands.

"You two, come out of there!" hissed their mother.

"They're coming!"

"Boys, come away," Cornelius ordered. "I'll be answering . . ."

He opened up, and was face-to-face with a bushwhacker with a youthful face. He was perhaps no more than a couple of years older than Temple, with the kind of beard that a young man would envision and aspire and coax from his chin with each glance in the looking glass. It was still so thin his acne was visible through its fine hairs. He removed his hat, exposing the crimson of his bandanna, and laid it with all evident sincerity against his chest. The three behind him followed suit, but more slowly.

"Good morning, sir," he said.

"Good morning," said Cornelius.

"Allow me to introduce myself: I am Captain Robert Givan Davis, representing the Third Kansas Brigade for the Preservation of Public Safety in Douglas County. And these gentlemen"—he gestured over his shoulder—"are my associates."

"The Brigade of Public Safety is it? Would that be of Douglas County Kansas, or Douglas County *Missouri*, young man?"

"That would be of Kansas, sir," replied Davis.

"And how might we help you today, Captain?"

"We've had word that a runaway has been seen hereabouts. We are checking all the farms on behalf of his lawful owners. The nigger goes by the name of Tubbs, but his real name is Trail."

"His lawful owners, where?"

"Out of Territory, sir."

"St. Louis? Gallatin?"

"Out of Territory."

Cornelius turned to give his wife a glance—a glare, actually, of the kind that a spouse gives when he means to tell her that what he so clearly warned against has come to pass. "We haven't seen any runaways round here," Dick said.

"Trail was off in this direction, yesterday noon. He was seen."

"I think we have answered your question, young man. Would you care for a drop before riding out?"

Captain Davis looked at him coolly, expression shading into bemused disbelief. He had, after all, been lied to before, especially in the abolitionist environs of Lawrence. But he would not come on a man's property and declare him a liar—at least at first.

"All right, then," he said. "We will take some water, if you don't mind."

Leroy went to the keg, just as he had for Tubbs (or Trail) when he first arrived. And as Davis and his men each took their dutiful sips, the Dick family stood and watched them, just as the bush-whacker regarded them back over the lip of the ladle.

"Just so's you know, hiding a runaway is a crime against property in this Territory."

To which Cornelius Dick replied, "By the lights at Shawnee Mission, that is true," leaving perhaps too plain his contempt for the laws passed by the proslavery legislature meeting in that distant, minor place on the Missouri border.

When the visitors had gone, Cornelius and the boys went to the dugout to see if Tubbs was still there. They found the door shut and the contents exactly as they had been when their guest arrived. As Florence had feared, there was a puddle under the place where the roof leaked. But there were no unfamiliar belongings.

"He is gone, then," said Cornelius, with some relief.

Soon Florence was calling him in the voice he knew meant that she had found something that wouldn't please him. Coming out, he found her at the privy, arms akimbo. And then he knew.

"He hid in here when he heard their voices," she explained, perceiving the suspicion in her husband's face. Looking into the privy, Cornelius saw the thin figure standing by the commode, dressed for the road, the pale palms of hands turned toward him and a look of contrition on his face. The expression, though understandable, was maddening. Cornelius did not feel like exchanging pleasantries with him.

"Did they see you?"

"Most definitely not," the Negro replied. "And let me say that I am most obliged that you sent them away, for whatever they told you about me is very certainly false."

Cornelius stared at him, his face showing equal parts pity, contempt, and mistrust. But to Leroy, at his age, only the contempt showed through—a quality the boy duly emulated, casting repugnant looks. This seemed to redouble the Negro's urge to defend himself.

"My name is Tubbs," he declared. "I was born a free man in the city of Cambridge, Massachusetts, on August the twelfth, 1833. I was educated at Miss Stemple's Free Colored Academy, where I not only learned my letters, but became conversant in the language of the Caesars. *Accusare nemo se debit, nisi coram Deo*, yes? *Lex non distinguitur nos non distinguere debemus.* Upon my graduation, I was privileged to use my education in business establishments in Hartford, Connecticut, and New York City. I am not a slave. No one in my family has ever been enslaved."

"Do you know those men?"

"No! No, not personally . . . in fact, only by hearsay . . . rumors of Defensives are not unknown in this territory, as you must know."

Cornelius, glowering, rumbled: "Don't tell me what I know, boy."

"He sure doesn't sound the slave," said Florence.

"That is nothing to do with us. They know about him somehow, and they know he's here. Woman, your imprudence has put us all in danger."

Like a jab to the gut, the declaration hit her physically. Her eyes flitted at the boys, who stared up at her in that half-disbelieving way children do at the transgressions of parents. But the granite foundation beneath her act did not shift.

"The Lord will judge me. Not you, Cornelius Dick," she said.

Cornelius turned back to the Negro. "You—Tubbs, Trail, or whatever your name is: the Defensives have not left. They are over that hill, watching anyone who leaves this place. Go back to the dugout and stay there."

Tubbs was about to give his thanks, and the next in a series of eloquent apologies. But Dick quashed them: "Stay away from the door. Stay away from the windows. And if you light a fire, I'll turn you over to them myself!"

Then he turned to Leroy and Temple. "You boys. You can't be seen running back and forth. Get the cart and load it with enough water and supplies for a week. Everything a body can need. Do it now. And don't earn a whipping by forgetting something!"

The boys ran to fetch the market rig, and Florence, moving to follow, paused. "Thank you," she said to Cornelius. "The Lord will bless you."

"Can't very well have him live in the privy until them boys get bored, can we?"

Captain Davis and Company were indeed watching the property. The glow of their fire showed over the hill the very first night, where their neighbor, the widow Crocker, allowed them to camp. The widow was a staunch abolitionist—sprung from one of the oldest Quaker families in Ohio—but on this part of the frontier, her politics did not entitle her to deny the privilege due to peaceable travelers. The Defensives revealed themselves sometimes up on the ridge, single and double figures spindly and black against the sky. Sometimes they would point and sweep the landscape with their arms, as if describing a military campaign that had happened in the past. Or was yet to come.

Tubbs, to his credit, was nothing more than a phantom, a rumor of a presence. Indeed, in the next few days Leroy would catch himself genuinely forgetting there was a man hiding in the dugout, running across the top of it as he did in those days when it was new, no doubt dislodging clumps of dirt on its occupant that he once did on his parents. But then he would catch a glimpse of his worried mother looking out toward the refuge—and he would remember.

The standoff went on for four more days until Davis reappeared at their door. This time he had only one other man with him, with the others posted some distance back on horseback, their rifles resting in the crooks of their arms.

"How may I help you this morning, Captain?" said Cornelius, coffee mug in hand.

"Good morning, sir. I am here, alas, on the same business. Perhaps you would be willing to assist us now?"

"I'm not sure what you mean, son."

Davis lifted his cap on his head and reset it. "I mean, sir, that there is someone living in the dugout behind your house. We've seen evidence of it. So I ask again—are you prepared to fulfill your duty under territorial law? Or do you oblige me to take direct action?"

Florence and the boys, listening from their places at the table, neither moved nor breathed. In an attempt to appear indifferent, Cornelius took a sip from his cup—but he pulled at it a little too hard, gulping the scalding liquid. The Defensive eyed his discomfort without speaking or blinking, while the man behind him, as if in delayed emulation, doffed and reset his cap too.

"What evidence have you seen, Captain, that would make you believe such a thing?"

"Trail is here. That is the only fact we need agree upon."

"I do not agree."

"Then, sir, I am obliged to call you a liar."

So there it was. Cornelius searched the eyes of the other, plumbing the depth of his resolve. Then he shrugged. "That much is obvious! But it alters nothing—the body you seek is not here. And so I bid you a good morning, and ask you to remove yourself and your men from my property."

Davis smiled, shook his head. "I don't know what possesses good white folk in these circumstances to play the *nigger-lover*," he said, and drew out the last two words as if he were unsheathing a dagger. "I warn you, sir, we need no further authorization to secure the property rights of your neighbors."

"And I warn you, Captain, that this kind of talk might impress the pukes, but will not stand here."

With that, he shut the door in the Defensive's face. He turned and went back to his porridge without further comment, wearing the kind of expression one had after some dull obligation had been discharged, like spreading slop for the hogs. And yet, Leroy perceived a stiffness in his father's step—a stiffness that belied an awareness of imminent consequences, such as the door being kicked in, or a hail of bullets plunging through it. But as the minutes crept by, and it became clear that Davis had not yet decided to take "direct action," something like normalcy resumed at their breakfast table. Then Cornelius, as he spooned more molasses into his bowl, cleared his throat as if he intended to speak. The others watched him as the words seemed to wander together in his head, linking up at their own deliberate pace.

"Temple, I will need you to be watchful today. Do you remember what I taught you about the Sharps?"

"Yes, paw."

"I want you to give Leroy a lesson today. And be sure to clean and oil the action, like I showed you."

"Yes, Paw."

"Where are you going?" Florence asked.

"I'll go to town as I always do. I'll be damned if that bunch keeps me from my business."

Cornelius did go to Lawrence later that morning, and as he drove the wagon past Davis's camp he took the opportunity to stare long and hard at the bushwhackers. The latter attempted to stare back with matching determination, but were in fact temporarily stymied by Cornelius's departure. While their peculiar sense of honor entitled them to any sort of mischief, from torchings to lynchings to draggings, it would not allow them to invade a farm defended only by a white woman and two young boys.

Cornelius returned half an hour before sunset, wagon empty, a frown on his face. He said nothing to Florence until after she'd fed him and he leaned back in his chair with his pipe.

"I couldn't find a single body in Lawrence to come out here," he said. "They don't see us as good enough allies in the cause . . ." And he laugh a little bit at that, at his threadbare reputation as an abolitionist, even as he hid what was reputed to be a runaway slave in his dugout.

"We could look further off," she said. "There are good people farther east, or in Iowa."

"There won't be time for that," he said. "You and the boys need to understand. We may need to give him up."

"Don't say that."

"Without help, there's nothing for it."

Florence bristled. "We won't. I won't." And when he laid down his pipe in that way he did when he was able to give her a lecturing, she got up and left before he could speak. Alone, he picked it up again and declared "We may!" before putting the stem back in his mouth.

Their situation looked worse the next morning. When Leroy ran in from feeding the hogs, he found that one of their draught horses had escaped its paddock. Upon examining the fence, Cornelius could see the damage was no act of God— the posts and beams had been deliberately hacked with a sharp implement. The horse, alas, had not strayed far; as Leroy held the lead rope and Cornelius trudged behind with the rifle, the Defensives watched in attitudes of deliberate repose. Davis had a cup of coffee in his hand.

"Good morning, Mr. Dick! Trouble with your stock today?" he asked, smiling, as the rest of them lay about and sniggered.

Cornelius did not answer because he knew whatever came out of his mouth might worsen matters.

"Should you ever find yourself in need again, call on us!" the Defensive said, tipping his cap. And then he added, "Should it ever happen again."

Back at the house, Leroy went up to the loft to lie in his bed and listen to his parents' inevitable confrontation.

"They have given notice of their intentions," said his father below. "And this is only the beginning of the mischief they can do."

"What is a fence against the life of a man? Is this what we have become, that we may put mere things on the scales against the value of a human soul?"

"I swear, woman, it's *our* souls that are at risk here too. Do you think us so rich that we may stand on principles we can't afford?"

"*I will not have your profanity in this house,*" his mother replied. And though Leroy could not see her from his bed, he knew she was pointing as she rebuked him. "This is not one of your St. Louis doggeries, Cornelius Dick, where your kind more properly belong!"

"And I think you not a proper mother at all, for all the strife you bring upon us. Your boys should be your first concern, should they not? Not some wandering—"

"Don't say it!" she cried. "Let *them* say the word, but not us!"

There was a pause, as Leroy imagined his father taking his mother's trembling hand.

"Listen here, Fla: this is only the beginning. They seem prepared to be patient, and we have a lot of property to sacrifice. That is a game we cannot win."

With that, there was another lull, and the rustle of skirts as his mother fled the table. When she closed the bedroom door, she did it not with a dramatic slam, but an eerie reticence, merely clicking it shut.

They next day they found the pigs' water trough smashed. The day after that, they had to rig a rude fishing pole to remove a dead goat from their well. Davis came to the door again around sundown, issuing the same demands and the same dark warnings. Cornelius again shut the door in his face. The Defensives retreated back to their camp on Crocker land, no doubt to plot their next stroke of mischief.

The following morning, Leroy was breakfasting at the table with his father, who was reading the newspaper. Florence was feeding kindling into the stove when she remarked, "Where is that boy?"—meaning Temple, who often retired to his room after morning chores to read his chapter books. Leroy was about to say something like "the usual place," when a loud *pop* sounded from the loft. Then they heard Temple—not exactly screaming, but delivering a deep and despairing moan, as if all his hopes had suddenly gone for naught.

Cornelius shot up the ladder with Leroy just behind. They found Temple lying in his bed with his hands covering his face. Blood ran from between his clenched fingers. The bed, which was directly under the small window, was glittered with fragments of broken glass. Cornelius tried to pull his hands from his face but Temple would not budge them, as his father pried and begged and shouted at him to be a man and let himself be tended to. Temple relented—and revealed the spray of shards that had embedded themselves in his face. Looking closer, Leroy could see that one dagger—about an inch long—had lodged in his shut eyelid and penetrated an unknowable distance into his eye.

"What is it?" Florence cried from below.

"Leroy, take the cart and fetch the yarb."

"What is it!"

"For the Lord's sake woman!" Cornelius cried.

There were no book doctors within a day's ride in those days. There was a "rubbing doctor" or herbalist named Mann just a half mile away, and he came at once. When the man saw Temple's face, he issued a hiss of disapproval, as if all this was the result of some free and foolish choice.

Cornelius inspected the window; it had been blown in from

outside by some firearm. The shot had shattered the wooden cross-tree, shivering all four panes of glass and sending them cascading inward. Looking out, he could see the bushwhacker encampment on its low hill, almost at eye level. The Defensives were hunched around their fire in poses that seemed unusually subdued, as if they had noted the arrival of the doctor and understood the consequences of what they had done. But Cornelius, in his fury, envisioned the sly and petulant smiles that hid behind their glowing cheroots. When Florence understood why her baby had been disfigured, she rounded furiously on Cornelius. "Why is that nigger still here? Why did you let him stay? Why couldn't you be a man and get rid of him?" She lapsed into sobs, but when he touched her, she whipped her arm away. "Get away from me! How could you let this happen?" she screeched. "If those bastards want him, give him to them! *Give him to them!*"

With that, Cornelius flew down the ladder, donned his hat and coat over his sleeping clothes—for he had not had a chance to dress that morning—and seized his rifle. After checking that it was loaded, he left the house without shutting the door.

"See after him," Florence ordered Leroy.

His father strode with the kind of stomping determination that Leroy had seen before, in one of his incandescent rages. A mood, he had learned, where it was not wise to appear anywhere in his sight, but to follow discreetly. To his relief, Cornelius did not stride toward a final reckoning with the bushwhackers, but instead made for the dugout. But before he reached the door, he rounded on Leroy.

"You, back to the house! Don't test me, boy."

Leroy stopped—and as his father's eyes blazed at him, he started to drift back from where he had come. But when Cornelius turned back to the dugout, Leroy stopped. His mother, after all, had commanded him to do the exact opposite.

It took a while for the next thing to happen. Leroy, bored, sat down on the prairie and picked at a rudbeckia blossom, separating the petals from the head and then pulling the head apart. When that was done, he stripped another, and then another after that, losing himself in the idle dismantling in the way he found comforting in times of strife. His lap was covered with yellow rudbeckia petals when he heard the door of the dugout open.

Mr. Ernest Calvin Tubbs Junior came out first, grasping his portmanteau, the tails of his shirt loose and flapping in the breeze. His father came out after, not exactly escorting the Negro by the arm but close enough, rifle poised on his arm not exactly pointing at his guest but near enough to make his point. If he listened closely, Leroy could hear a disconnected word or two of what Tubbs was saying: "near an imposition as I dared . . . fairly upon the rights of man . . . an educated citizen . . ." But his father only nodded at him, eyes half lidded and stubborn as he propelled Tubbs onward.

The flower petals tumbled to Leroy's feet as he stood up to watch their progress over the hill. His father was ejecting Tubbs in a southwesterly direction, away from the Defensives camped on the other side of his property. Yet the way Tubbs moved, with shoulders rounded and head pulled down, testified to his vulnerability. With nothing but gently sloping ground between him and Captain Davis's party, the Negro was an absurdly exposed figure on that expanse.

Leroy watched him grow smaller and smaller until he was startled by his father's voice right beside him.

"Say nothing to your mother," he said.

There was no bite in his tone now, no reproach. Instead, there was a horrified look on his face, as if he had witnessed the crimes of some other person. As they walked back to the house together, Cornelius placed his hand on the back of Leroy's neck, squeezing it gently over and over, as if he could pump away his guilt by repetitive acts of affection. For his part, Leroy would not have known what to say to his mother anyway.

Tubbs was forgotten as the yarb wrapped Temple's face in spiderweb dressings soaked in turpentine. The howls of agony this drew were, to the conventional thinking, therapeutic. Mann came down from the loft to give his report: the cuts to Temple's face were extensive, though with careful tending some of them would not leave scars and most of the rest would be subtle marks. The jagged glass in his eye had penetrated as far as the white matter around his eyeball, the sclera, but removing it had caused no further damage. The wound would look ugly for a while, but would heal more completely than the cuts to his cheek and forehead.

With word that her son would not be blinded or greatly disfigured, Florence collapsed into her chair with relief. Though it was only ten in the morning, Cornelius broke out the brandy and offered Doc Mann a cup. In the general celebration, even Leroy got a nip.

Leroy never saw the bushwhackers depart; he only noticed they were gone when he led the doctor's horse out from his paddock hours later. Davis and his men had gone after Tubbs so hastily the embers of their morning fire were left smoldering. A thin column of smoke rose from their camp, drifted upward until it met a breeze high above the ground, and rushed to the southwest.

Chapter Eleven

A Pearl of Great Price

MARCH, 1871

KATE AND JOHN Junior mounted the wagon before dawn. There was a coating of frost on the seat, which Kate swept away with her gloved hand before sitting. Her backside was insulated by her flannel drawers, petticoat, skirt, and heavy wool overcoat, but it was only moments before the frigidity penetrated all those layers. For months she had been so cold that she thought with a proper shake her bones might shatter. It was an affliction on everyone in that season—a dull, constant body-cold that never seemed to go away, even in heated rooms—that wore on every soul, like a collective, untreated toothache. As they began their trip to Cherryvale that morning, and the sun seemed to drag itself reluctantly over the far hills, Kate looked into her glove. The frost, which had temporarily melted when she wiped the seat, had frozen again in her palm.

Being new to the territory, they had only the haziest notion how long winter might last in southeast Kansas. Some ladies at Harmony Grove told her to expect the warm-up when the first shoots of green appeared on the horse apple tree. Others dismissed that as unscientific superstition and swore by the date of the first appearance of the spring peepers: after their songs began, there would be *exactly* three more killing frosts before the beginning of spring proper. Rudolph Brockman said it could happen anytime between March and May—there was no sure way to tell year-to-year—but in his experience when the turkey buzzards appeared there would be no more frosts. The question was of more than academic interest to the Benders: in winter, traffic on the Osage slowed to a trickle, and that was bad for the family business.

They had an appointment with the neighbors that morning. After rolling and jerking through frozen ruts for twenty minutes, they neared the Brockman place in its little hollow out of the wind. Rudolph, as usual, hailed them straightaway. His partner Ern rarely came out, and when he did he stayed away, watching from a distance as he leaned and smoked a cigarette.

"*Morgen*, Kate," Rudolph said, eyes twinkling, and then to John Junior, as an afterthought, "And ye too, Johnny."

"Good morning to you, Rudolph," she replied, with the merest smile necessary to charm him. Junior, for his part, was never insulted by his invisibility. It was only reasonable that men would pay tribute to Kate.

"And this is it?" Brockman nodded at their latest delivery. It was a saddle, all but new, finely tooled and oiled. Pulling it toward him, he noted its quality, as well as its only flaw: the roughed-up spot on the fender where Johnny had wrenched off the plate inscribed with the name of its owner. The silver stirrups on their leathers scrapped along the boards of the wagon as Brockman lifted the rig to examine the underside.

"A pretty thing for a customer to leave behind."

"Presented in lieu of payment. You would be surprised to know how few of them will part with cash."

"*Ja*, we find that," said the other as he finished his inspection. Then he pronounced, "There's a man in Thayer who might take it. But best not rip the plate off next time—it can be engraved again."

"We're off to Cherryvale," Kate said brightly. "Can you guess why?"

"No. But I'd be delighted for ye to tell me."

"I have a job!"

"Is that a fact?"

"There's a situation at the Cherryvale Hotel that might suit her," said John Junior.

"Oh *pshaw* on 'might' . . . it *will* suit, and it will be gay!"

"That will be as temporary as the job, I think."

Kate put forth a hand to give his cheek a playful shove. And Brockman, smoldering with lust for her girlish vivacity, wished it were his cheek that was being shoved instead.

"Well, it's a good bet they pay ye in coin instead of tack," he declared.

Bidding Rudolph Brockman a good day, they struck out for Cherryvale, six and a half miles to the southwest. Out on open range the cold deepened and the breath of their horse was like the snort of a locomotive, vaporous plumes spraying forth as the wagon humped and tipped and its occupants huddled, not speaking. Over their left shoulders there was a glow beyond the overcast that hinted of a cheery, warm yellowness. But it was only a promise, and by the time they reached the outskirts of town it had not been redeemed.

Before the railroad, Cherryvale was a one-lane settlement with a well, a livery, and a general store. On the claim of Mr. Thomas Whelan, the LL&G had kept a tented work camp where supplies were stored and prepared for the extension of the railroad into Montgomery County. Through the early part of '71 the railroad's surveyors were seen all over the area, laying out an extensive network of streets. But to any of the one dozen or so permanent residents of the area, there never seemed to be anybody in the camp. Instead, the workmen were all at the town's four saloons, situated along the thoroughfare in easy staggering distance from each other. Between them sprung up buildings that were one step up from the rude temporary structures that bloomed first on virgin ground—each two or three stories, carpentered just enough to assure they would last more than a few seasons. Their slab frontages had none of the decorative elements, the architraves and wooden-hewn scrollwork and dentils, that lent an air of permanence. Instead, they seemed to regard each other across the street half embarrassed by their ongoing existence, as if fully expecting to be demolished and improved at any moment.

The avenue was mud. The freeze had at least turned its grotesque rills and craters rock hard, precluding the boards that usually stretched across it and were now piled loosely along the covered sidewalks. Junior had Kate's arm as they stepped across them and through the hotel's doors, scuffed with the marks of steel-toed boots as years of travelers kicked their way onto the premises. Junior led the way until they gained the planked, unvarnished lobby, but Kate shot ahead of him to greet the proprietor, Mr. Jeremiah Babcock Moore. The latter seemed to know she was there even before he looked up. Junior had the uncomfortable impression Moore had been spying on their approach while they were still in the street.

"My dear," he pronounced as he put down the pen. Mr. Moore's bare pate, which was like a pale bull's-eye encircled by a very long, waxed bolt of hair, flashed red as Kate laid hands on it, searching the contours.

"Truly an expressive cranium!" she exclaimed, "Such a testament of character to one trained in the proper art!"

Blushing to the roots of his lashes, Moore looked through them at Junior.

"And this must be the celebrated brother."

"He is indeed," he replied with artificial jocularity. "Here to serve the mistress."

"As you all must," she declared.

"Well, we thank you for delivering her fresh. And if I might steal her now . . . ?"

"Gladly purloined," said Junior with a sort of gallant presentation, mispronouncing the word and leaving thinly lettered Mr. Moore to wonder if it really should sound like "*pure* loined."

With nothing much else to do, Junior stayed to watch Kate work her first day as a waitress in the Cherryvale Hotel dining room. She was coached in the trade not by the smitten Mr. Moore but by Alice Acres, a tall, plain woman who needed spectacles only when she read yet squinted at all other times. She seemed to size Kate up at a glance, saying, "A small thing, aren't you? I doubt we have an apron for your kind of little . . ."

To which Kate dropped her facade of girlish haplessness and returned to the steely determination of her road days. Emulating Alice Acres to the very nuance, she learned how to take and remember orders; she learned how to communicate orders to the cook, who tended to deafness if the proper jargon was not used; she learned how to loft trays full of china brimming with meats and boiled potatoes and gravies, and deliver them with the minimum of steps to the table. She also learned how to dodge wandering hands that made for her ankles and bottom.

As Brockman had predicted, the buzzards returned early that year and brought spring with them. There were more travelers from the East, and as they came into the hotel from streets of boot-sucking muck, they were pleased to be attended by Kate the serving girl. Men would rush to claim a seat at one of her tables; the few women who came through also found her fine features a relief from the menagerie of hairy masculine mugs to which they were daily exposed.

For all her bloody-mindedness, Kate was pragmatic. She disliked the drudgery but valued the freedom to move among her neighbors in a context less guarded than the church at Harmony Grove. After those initial stares and gropes, she became all but invisible as she did her rounds. Moving among her customers, she overheard their problems, hopes, fears, and regrets. She learned all about the parents worried about the marriages of their daughters, or the lack of marriages, and the farmer who thought he bought a healthy cow but got one with foot rot, and the hilltop claim near Independence that turned out to be bottomland prone to flooding, and the lack of tooth powder at the dry goods store. There were ample rumors about the direction the railroad would be built, and sometimes mutually exclusive ones at neighboring tables at the same moment.

But for all the flavors of their small concerns, underneath there was the same groan of offended pride. She had lived on the frontier all her life, but it was only here, amid the tinkling glassware and dusty bison heads of this minor hotel well beyond the main line, that she glimpsed the hidden truth. Behind the eyes of all of them, from the hardest gambler to the most cloistered frontier wife, lurked the identical plaint—that their neighbors, the seed companies, the railroads, the banks, and especially the government, were together and severally out to get them. Everyone saw himself as an underdog; all shared the conviction the cosmos owed them a debt of decent luck. Meanwhile, all the other louts who also saw themselves as underdogs were really just fakes—fat cats and bullies, scheming the ruin of the ordinary, honest folk. Everyone imagined he was his own master, and was proud of it. But with the freedom there came terror that it was just one short step above slavery. And the joy of the one never seemed to temper fear of the other.

She would smile as she noted these things. Smile and serve, and smile some more, the comely one with the spotless apron and empty head, bringing the bowl of salt and a whiff of rosewater and "May she please bring a new napkin for the gentleman's shirt-front?" She served until her feet throbbed and smiled until her cheeks ached.

For her own part, for all the pip cards life had dealt her, she felt no injury. To perceive oneself as cheated one needed to have expectations of her fellow men, of which she had none. Instead, she was conscious only of opportunities ripening and the urgency of her need to exploit them. For somewhere out there, probably in a better place than Kansas, her father was still searching for her. Not always actively, of course—a player has to pause and replenish his bankroll from time to time. But just as she never forgot him, so must he never have forgotten about her. Now that she was grown, the search must succeed because they could find each other. Every dollar she earned, by hook or by crook, must bring them closer.

And so one day, a couple of months after hiring her, Mr. Moore looked up and saw Kate handing a lady customer a handbill. Later, she handed out another, and still another from a stash she kept folded in her apron. Curious, he waited until she had gone to the kitchen, then retrieved one that had been left behind on a table. Lips rounded to a pensive pout, he read:

Prof. Miss KATIE BENDER

Can heal all sorts of diseases; can cure blindness, fits, palsies and all such diseases.

Also dumbness and sickness of spirit.

Residence, 14 miles east of Independence, on the road from Independence to Osage Mission, one and a half miles South East of Norahead Station

---

KATE'S SHIFT ENDED around four o'clock, after the family dinner crowd was gone but before the poker and faro players showed up. John Junior waited for her in the lobby, rocking on his feet, turning the brim of his hat around in his fingers. She did not greet him but gave only the merest gesture, an arching of an eyebrow as she passed. He followed her out to the army wagon parked in the street. Like a proper boulevardier, he lifted her skirts for her as she stepped through the mire.

Almira didn't like Kate's new job. When she was informed of

it, after the fact, she remained silent in such a manner as to express she had much to say on the matter. Kate waited for the inevitable outburst.

"You put us in danger, with these comings and goings about! You think you are the smart one, but one day will prove you wrong! I've seen it and it will come!"

"You should see her there," said Junior from the window, where he monitored the trail. "She's some pumpkins, I tell you. She reigns over all of them."

"*Acht,* you are a fool. She *will* say something, in her pride. You don't know her like I do."

"You don't understand," sighed Kate, the frustrated pedant. "It's the opposite of what you say. We must be out there, being seen, lest suspicion fall on us sooner. It is easy to accuse what you don't know."

"The wisdom of all your years?" Almira sneered. "Don't listen to me, then, with all the time I've had at this. *Sie!*" she shouted at Pa. "What is it you say?"

John Senior was smoking in the corner with his Bible in his lap, ensnared in a knot of smoky blue tendrils. He took the pipe stem from his mouth as if about to say something—but then he smacked his lips and put it back.

"Worthless!" Almira threw up her hands. "I am beset by fools and fools of fools, and it will end in blood, I tell you!"

"Theirs, I'd wager," remarked Kate.

"Yours, I swear to you, if you give us away!"

Thrown by so bald a threat, it took a moment for Kate to respond. But Junior preempted her:

"Rider!" he cried, pulling back from the curtain. And at the word, with the automatic efficiency of a well-drilled army unit, the Benders scrambled to their assigned places—John Senior and Almira behind the canvas, Junior at the counter, hunching over as if hoping he might seem invisible. Kate stood front and center, hands at her waist, palming down the creases in her skirts. Like an actress at her makeup, but without a mirror, she precisely wetted an auburn strand with her spit and guided it over her brow to its station above her eye.

They heard footsteps crunching on the icy stubble and a pregnant silence as their visitor paused beyond the door—perhaps to straighten his hat, perhaps to pry manure from a boot. Then, after what seemed like cruel delay, the knock came.

"Evening, traveler," Kate said as she opened up and the lamplight fell across his face. This one was older than the last—not a boy, but a man of some years, perhaps twenty-five. He wore a billycock with an oilskin cover, the brim bent down over his eyes. The suit peeking from beneath his wet duster was assembled from madly clashing patterns—pinstripes on his trousers, spinning paisleys on his vest. When he lifted his chin to answer, he revealed gray eyes, smoky but moist from the evening chill.

"Sorry to come at your shutting in," he said. "Must have misjudged the distance from St. Paul. Mought I trouble you?"

"It is impossible for you do so, sir, because it is our pleasure."

Stepping inside, he stood back on his heels and took in what they presented: a spare interior somewhat overwarmed by the stove, Junior staring at him from before a wall of dusty patent medicine boxes, and Kate in her muslin apron, arms crossed behind her back as if concealing a gift.

"If you'd set at the table, we'll show you why we're famous in these parts."

Unbuttoning, he sat. The act released Junior to go out and see to his horse.

Upon Kate's gentle questioning, he disclosed his name was Hiram; he was traveling east, to his family in Missouri, where he was to be married.

"Are there no girls of Kansas you fancy?" she asked.

"I am to be sealed to the godly Constance Adare of Jackson County, that we may be together through eternity, as is provided by Heavenly Father."

"I see."

Kate cast down her eyes, perceiving the situation and making an inward adjustment. She had read of Hiram's faith—at first in-stance, when someone had deposited *The Pearl of Great Price* in a hotel lobby in Casper, Wyoming. And there were other occasions later, such as in newspaper accounts of their tribulations and tri-umphs in settling in Utah, though these were not always sympa-thetic. It was no more or less a matter of indifference to her—the hypocrisy of such clerics, no matter what doctrine stuffed their wooly heads, was equally deplorable. But they could be useful in keeping a body preoccupied:

"Were not those of your stripe roused out of Jackson County, years ago?"

"Not all of us," he replied, smiling.

"What do you mean, 'sealed'?"

"It is the belief of the true heirs of Christ that men and women are meant to dwell together not only in this life, but abide all the phases of our Father's plan through all eternity. 'I give unto you power, that whatsoever ye shall seal on earth shall be sealed in Heaven, and whatsoever ye shall loose on earth shall be loosed in

Heaven; and thus shall ye have power among this people.' Hela-
man 10:7. But only if they are sealed according to ordinance."

"His plan?"

"The Scripture says: 'I rejoice in the day when my mortal
shall put on immortality, and shall stand before him; then shall
I see his face with pleasure, and he will say unto me: "Come
unto me, ye blessed, there is a place prepared for you in the
mansions of my Father."' Enos 1:27. It is our fate to be judged
for our choices, which will tell our path through Heaven, or
Spirit Prison, as the case may be, to our proper station among
the Three Spheres . . ."

There was trail-weariness in his voice that belied the Good
News. She joined him at the table, elbow resting and chin in hand,
attentiveness shining on her face.

"But do you really want to talk about this?" he asked, developing a smile to mirror hers.

"I find nothing more fascinating."

" 'How beautiful upon the mountains are the feet of him that
publisheth salvation,' Isaiah 52:7."

With that, he unfolded his duster, which he had draped neatly
upon the table, and extracted a book that was tucked in a pocket.

"I see you have yours . . ." he said, gesturing at John Senior's
German Bible resting on a chair. "But have you seen mine?"

His *Book of Mormon* was leather-bound and ribboned, its
spine limber from a thousand openings and closings. He cracked
it, and in her mind she imagined the long and strenuous hours
of his reciting and committing the passages to memory, all for
an opportunity like this—to present his benefaction, his pearl of
great price, to a fair and receptive stranger. In her current state it
seemed to her such a pleasant preoccupation that she allowed her-

self to be swept up in it, to momentarily see the world through the pleasant mist of his enthusiasm. He was turning the pages for her, running his fingers down the serried lines, as deliberate as a salesman showing off his traveling case full of jewels. The gracefulness of his fingertips hypnotized her, and for that minute she wanted to be what he perceived, a high plains bumpkin who had rarely glimpsed the orderly intricacies of the printed page.

"I cannot help but believe I am called to some great labor in this land," she heard him say, distantly.

"What does it say about prophecy?" she asked, voice slowed to a contented purr.

"The one from Tarsus said it best: 'Charity never faileth: but whether there be prophecies, they shall fail; whether there be tongues, they shall cease; whether there be knowledge, it shall vanish away.'"

"I don't like that."

Silenced by this response, he moved aside for Almira, who was standing with the bowl of stew and a spoon, towel draped over her arm. She laid the meal before the spot on the canvas still stained with John Jesperson's blood. Hiram obliged by sliding to the bowl, laying the book next to him as if it deserved a place setting. Kate, looking up, perceived the impatient glare in Almira's eyes: *Get on with it.*

"You say you have a mission. What are your plans after you are married?"

"After the sealing I will bring my family west. There we will instruct by example the ways of a godly life."

"Do you have any friends or relations near-abouts, who might help you?"

He swallowed, and with the light of his certainty shining

through his eyes like an oncoming train, said, "I am but a stranger in Egypt."

John Junior had returned from quartering Hiram's horse. He nodded, cleared his throat significantly. The guttural noise irritated Kate, for without turning around she could somehow hear him nodding behind her, could sense the vector of this man's fate without the need for its utterance. The knowledge of it filled her with unspeakable awe, is if she were some angel winging high above the earth, looking down and seeing not only the trails mortal men had laid down in their lives, but the paths ahead of them. The path of the man before her, the one attending so closely to the stew before his nose, would dead-end right here, in the next moment. She was sure the terrible power of this could be read in her eyes. Averting them, she began to tremble.

She startled at a sudden scratching noise behind the canvas, as if a boot heel were dragged along the boards.

"Are you all right?" Hiram asked.

She could not summon an answer, and in the clumsy silence the moment seemed to telescope, yawning before and disheartening her because she had run out of words for this man. Why does he not strike? she thought as she covered her eyes and felt a pinpricking warmth as she flushed from brow to breast. She had heard John Senior back there, heaving his clumsy bulk. Let it be done! she screamed inwardly, and again, Do it now! Still the man across from her sat alive, picking idly with his spoon for strands of meat in his bowl, and looking up at her with his decency, his indiscriminate Christianity. Lips shaping fulsome pieties, teeth stuck with inches of pork tendon, he poured forth hypocrisies syrupy and ancient, appalling and aggrieving her. And now her face was naked too, and she could stand it no longer.

"*Töte ihn! Mach' schon!*" someone cried.

"Pardon?"

Like a carpenter measuring twice to cut once, John Senior took his time. At last he swung, plunging the head of the Alsatian hammer through the screen at the round shadow beyond. And again his aim was off—the blow struck the man not on the crown of the head but glanced off his right temple.

Hiram pitched forward, his jaw striking the rim of his bowl and upending it. Then he straightened, an expression on his face like a man who had been bothered by an untoward fly. There was no blood yet, and apparently no pain, until the rip in his skin parted under the weight of torn flesh. Kate watched as a great fold of skin, including the man's entire ear, slowly pulled free, flopping down like the page of a book left open in a breeze.

Chapter Twelve

A-jayhawkin'

SEPTEMBER, 1856

LEROY DICK NEXT saw Ernest Tubbs Junior three weeks later, when he was on the way back from school. The trail led through some woods surrounding the district schoolhouse and into a stretch of unclaimed prairie split by wheel ruts. There he spied a knot of boys dancing with excitement over something. The four of them took turns rushing off to a spot on the ground a hundred yards from the trail, where each would come up short, loiter on jangly legs for a moment with hands in pockets, then dash back to the group.

Closer, one of the boys called to Leroy: "You! C'mere an' see somethin'!" And the others summoned him in the same peculiar way, with excitement but also a hint of dread, as if what they showed forced them to implicate as many witnesses as they could. And when Leroy approached slowly, eyes sweeping the grass for hints of mischief, the ringleader stamped his bare feet in the dirt and hung his arms at his sides and asked, "So c'mon Dick whatsamatter with ya are ya *yella*?"

"No," he replied, for yella he wasn't, but had an inkling that this something would not be pleasant. Following the pointing fingers, he found his way off the trail, to a spot beside a straggling tree. It was a locust, boughs splayed just a foot or two above his extended arms, fringed with wreaths of red, inch-long spikes. There was a loop of rope tied to one of the branches, running down only a few inches to where it was hacked with a dull knife. And below that lay a sack of skin with a roughly human outline.

He stared at the body for quite some time without summoning much reaction. The time for disgust had long passed, for this was no longer a corpse but some kind of curio, like a mummy. The body was naked, the skin split where the edges of bones had begun to push through. It was darkened by decay, blue like a bruise, except for the ivory of the teeth exposed by the retracting lips, and the buttery yellow of the vitrified eyes. Between them was a scatter of freckles that, with a constriction of his gut, Leroy recognized.

The abdomen was opened, gaping like a rifled knapsack. Yet it did not stink in the round, effusive way he'd encountered before, as when he and his father had discovered stock freshly killed on the range by coyotes. The blood was old now, soaking and searching deep into the soil. The stench of earth corrupted, like an unspeakable curse, or the soil itself in despair. It was an odor he would not encounter again until seventeen years later, in the pit under the Bender cabin.

In the evening, with the western sky foiling the roofs with gold and salmon-tinted shadows, he invited his father out for a private conversation. The discretion made him feel like a man, as did the effect his news had on Cornelius, whose bemusement at his youngest son's grave demeanor soon tumbled.

"Are you sure?" he asked.

"I am."

His father removed the pipe from his mouth and turned it about as if seeing it for the first time.

"Then I suppose we'll have to go out there tomorrow," he said.

They left the house the next morning before his mother or Temple were up. Leroy was particularly gratified that his elder brother was not included in their secret. Instead, they went out side by side in the market wagon, picks and shovels clanging in the bed as they bumped and rolled.

When they reached the spot, Cornelius looked at the remains with a ruefulness that refused to rise to the level of empathy. The Negro had, after all, come uninvited into his life, and left it with a decent chance at escape, if he'd had the sense to use it properly. He might have made for the river and stayed hidden in the brush until nightfall. From there he could have slipped away to Lawrence, where Davis and his men would never have shown their faces. From there he could have taken a stage north to Nebraska, or Colorado Territory. What tragedy befell him was his own fault as much as anyone else's. Why he expected heroics from a man with a family to defend was beyond comprehending.

And yet.

"We'll take him a ways off the trail," he said.

They used the shovels to collect the remains, which disarticulated and scattered and unfurled wreaths of centipedes. As they rolled south, Leroy could not help but swivel in his seat and look back at the lump wrapped in canvas in the wagon bed, which until recently had been a living man. Laying a hand on his arm, his father gave him an admonishing glance as if to say "best not look back."

And so Leroy kept eyes forward as they rolled on, gliding along on ground flatter and gentler than the trail, scaring up plumes of sparrows and surprising the white-tailed deer at their morning graze. They went some distance, seeking the lowest stretch of ground they could, until they reached a spot near the river where a solitary willow tree stood in a field of Queen Anne's lace. There they stopped and together attacked the turf, until they had a gash that was roughly oval and three feet deep. Cornelius gently pushed Leroy aside and worked to deepen and straighten the hole until it was something like a proper grave.

He was slick with sweat when he dropped the shovel. They shared the corners of the bundled canvas as they slid it from the wagon—though they didn't have to—and laid it at the bottom. Then Cornelius brought out the Bible he had brought in a rucksack. Wetting his fingers, he turned to a passage he had apparently considered beforehand, and began to read in a voice that was clear but subdued, as if he was afraid of being overheard.

"And Jacob went out from Beersheba, and went toward Haran.

And he lighted upon a certain place, and tarried there all night, because the sun was set; and he took of the stones of that place, and put [them for] his pillows, and lay down in that place to sleep.

And he dreamed, and behold a ladder set up on the earth, and the top of it reached to heaven: and behold the angels of God ascending and descending on it.

And, behold, the Lord stood above it, and said, I am the Lord God of Abraham thy father, and the God of Isaac: the land whereon thou liest, to thee will I give it, and to thy seed;

And thy seed shall be as the dust of the earth, and thou shalt spread abroad to the west, and to the east, and to the north, and to the south: and in thee and in thy seed shall all the families of the earth be blessed . . ."

Leroy often found himself numbed by the recitation of Scripture. Looking around, he gathered a bouquet of lacy white blossoms, with their solitary purple flowers in the center, and twisted one of the stems around the bundle to keep it from falling apart. And as his father came to the end of the passage, reading, " 'And he was afraid, and said, How dreadful is this place! this is none other but the house of God, and this [is] the gate of Heaven,' " he tossed the bouquet into the hole. Cornelius laid the book on the seat of the wagon and took up his shovel. Leroy did the same, and reversing the blades, they backfilled the grave.

They sat in silence on the trip home, until they could see their fence line. Cornelius instructed him to gather a hammer and some nails to straighten one of the boards that had sagged, and then became silent again.

The Tubbs incident had its effect on all the Dicks. Despite the assurances of the doctor, Temple's face was left permanently scarred, spoiling his good looks. His poxy appearance did little for his prospects in the local marriage market, which embittered him and made him blame Tubbs and his entire race for bringing misfortune on him. When the war came, he joined up with Jim Lane to hunt Defensives, but also bullied and robbed free blacks whenever he could. When Leroy questioned this apparent contradiction, Temple quoted Lane himself: "We are not fighting to free black men but to free white men."

Florence Dick implored her Lord for the reason why her compassion had been so cruelly repaid. As the answer could never be some flaw in His design, she reasoned that her own vanity was to blame. In penance, she stopped indulging her appearance, stopped shaving herself and bathing, and entered into conjugal relations with Cornelius only out of sullen, joyless duty. She took to wearing a chemise made of sackcloth. Christmas was no longer kept, and sweets like cakes and pies were unknown in the Dick house, which became infamous in the neighborhood for its dreariness.

Yet with every abnegation, every stingy choice, she became not more secure in her state of grace, but less. It seemed the Lord had in mind only to punish her and take her peace. Her sons forgot the last time they saw a smile on her face. Grinding to a pensive halt at her laundry boiler, she ruminated over the years of futility before her. Sometimes, she fondly imagined ending her life.

For every time Cornelius assured himself that he was not to blame, the suspicion grew that he was only fooling himself. Though any father would surely have taken strict measures had a child been injured, it might have occurred to him to escort the Negro safely to Lawrence. In his fury, he knew he had been impulsive, and in his impulsiveness he had been weak. The thought afflicted him every time he looked at Leroy, who had been forced to bear witness to his error. To keep his son from seeing the self-loathing in his face, he avoided looking at him at all, which Leroy noticed and wondered if he had somehow done wrong in bringing the discovery of the body to Cornelius's attention. And minute by silent minute, stone by stone, the wall of mutual incomprehension rose up between father and son.

Leroy grew up withdrawn and pensive, aware of the deep wrong that had been done his family and nursing this conviction like a secret love. Under most circumstances these qualities read as gravitas—he was frequently astonished when he was roused from his daydreams to find that he was being nominated for some position of leadership in the schoolroom, or being admired by girls who took his quietude as a challenge. More often his mother, exasperated by his remoteness, accused him of being simple.

When the war came, he was eighteen years old, with a good horse to ride and an old Colt Paterson .36 revolver nearly as long as his forearm. He had bought the latter in secret in Lawrence— and regretted the purchase right away when he learned that the pistol had to be partly disassembled each time it was loaded. To add insult to ignorance, a chamber blew out the first time he tested it. Instead of buying a new cylinder, he opted to turn the weapon into a four-shooter by never loading the defective chamber. After all, the fighting he had in mind would be no occasion for long exchanges of gunfire. For it was his intention that he would do his part for the Union by going a-jayhawking along the Kansas River.

This pastime, which usually involved armed gangs of abolitionists crossing the border into Missouri to deprive slaveholders of their slaves and other property, had by this time attained an almost mythic stature in Leroy's mind. Not only was it sweet retribution for the wrongs he had personally suffered, but it allowed him to exercise the sense of indignation he had nursed through boyhood, as he heard stories of Missouri men invading Kansas to stuff ballot boxes, reducing the Territory to a veritable colony. Cornelius's disapproval of any such ventures had held Leroy back.

But now that the proslavery men had declared for secession, and the stain on his family's honor was as obvious as the scars on Temple's face, he could no longer resist the call to go forth and, at long last, settle some hash.

Missouri itself was too far to go without rousing suspicion. Instead, he would ride in the other direction, toward Lecompton and the farms of Kansans who, if they didn't own slaves themselves, were proslavery in sympathies. He was going hunting, he told his folks, and would return in a few days. From behind his newspaper, Cornelius advised, "Better take one of the Sharps, then." And this Leroy delightedly did.

He was joined on the trip by two classmates he had known all his life. Nathan Bannerman was the only son of an older couple in Lawrence that had grown rich on remittances from an uncle who had gone to California in '49 and then, sadly, died of ague. Nathan had taken to dressing in the fashion of an East Coast slicker, in a green herringbone suit and a bowler. His gun—a Colt Walker—was nickel-plated. Out of town he rode a gray, lithe Arabian that high-stepped and cantered with its tail pertly upward, which caused some mirth among the ranch hands slumped on their mud-splattered quarter horses. There were other qualities that Leroy heard associated with Nathan's Jewishness that he did not credit, as long as he was a trustworthy partner in a scrap.

Daniel H.T. Woodeson, whom everyone called Fess, was a short-necked redhead with a face full of freckles like a bowl of black-eyed peas. His gear, from the sway-backed bay he rode to the rust-smudged Smith & Wesson .22 he carried, inspired little confidence. But he had a droll, sweet-natured disposition that was easy to take on the trail, combined with a volcanic hatred of bushwhackers that seemed to flare out of nowhere and vanish just as mysteriously. When he was asked, "Hey Fess, why do you hate them pukes so much?" that broad, gap-toothed smile would break over him like one of those sailor-take-warning sunrises, and he would reply something like, "Why you mought as well ask why a body hates locusts!" To the question, "So why do they call you Fess, anyway?" he would reply, "Can't rightly say, I do confess!"

The evening before they lit out they sat around, drinking applejack and arguing over a suitable name for their little gang. Any serious crew of jayhawkers, after all, had to have a handle, preferably terrifying but at least memorable to the string of victims they would leave in their train. Bannerman offered up "Lane's Right Hands," which Fess pretended not to understand:

"Why would Jim Lane have more than one right hand? And why wouldn't it be at the end of his right arm?"

"Ain't it typical of you to fuddle up what's perfectly clear?" replied Bannerman. "Leroy, tell him."

"I'm not sure he's far wrong."

Bannerman snorted and drank, and offered no objection to the choice they settled upon: they would ride into history as the Devil's Angels.

They struck out early one Monday morning under a clear cerulean dome, the rising sun warming their backs as it cast long snaking shadows ahead. It was a glorious morning to be eighteen and free and ennobled by a purpose. The horses' hooves threw up sprays of dew that wet Leroy's face and made the grass smell sweeter. In the side holster by his right leg, the carbine rested in its solid angularity, the scimitar like curve of its butt making him menacing and deadly and ready to do the Lord's work.

Their first destination was a farm outside Benecia where they had heard a secessionist flag was openly displayed. They found the place without trouble: a clapboard farmhouse standing in the center of a great oxbow abandoned by the Kansas River. From the south the crescent of water protected the farm like a moat, but from the river side the approach was flat and easy and covered by hedgerows. Taking up position behind one, they dismounted and ate a lunch of bread and hard cheese.

Bannerman took out his Montgomery Ward spyglass to study the target. When he was done, Leroy took his turn, squinting as he chewed until the magnified image sprang into focus. Beneath a curl of hearth smoke and a wheeling flight of turkey buzzards, the house stood solid and unexceptional, freshly washed bedding draped over the fence. Just behind and to the right was a rude staff made from a hewn sapling, and from it flew a peculiar flag.

To see it clearly, Leroy stuck his hunk of bread in his mouth and held the instrument with both hands. The flag was blood red, with a vertical cross of blue bars spangled with white stars and pairs of white objects—small from that distance—at the upper right and left corners. Try as he might, he couldn't make out those white blotches.

"Damn ugly thing."

"Let me see," demanded Fess.

Neither of his partners would speak up for the flag's aesthetic appeal, but there was nothing they could do about it in broad daylight. After watering the horses, they bivouacked a half mile away. Reclining in the grass, Leroy watched the crickets flit between the stalks above him, their murmur bringing on a pleasant lethargy that made the coming errand seem the business of a different person. Above his upturned eyes, the bugs traced parabolas as they pursued their unfathomable errands, arcing as if deflected by the earth's turning, the great cosmic swerve that comforted him as it joined all material things in their common mortality, until he let his eyelids droop and fell into a state of semiconsciousness that brought on an avalanche of thoughts that all seemed equally profound and equally forgettable.

Sometime in late afternoon Fess brought out a mouth harp and commenced a repetitive twanging that intruded on Leroy's repose. Sitting up, he sighted Fess crouching nearby with his boots off, pants rolled to the knees.

"If you're not going to play a tune on that thing, I'd just as soon see you lose it in the grass."

"Who's gonna?"

"Me."

"You and yer weight in wildcats."

Leroy extended a hand to take the instrument away, but Fess—a mulish curl on his upper lip—tucked it in his breast pocket.

When night at last filled up the hollows, the Devil's Angels rounded up their horses and returned to the homestead. A rising three-quarter moon revealed that the laundry had disappeared from the fence, but they saw no one in the yard or at the windows, and the treason flag was still flying from its jack.

"Snug and tight," remarked Bannerman. "So what's our play?"

'Fess laughed. "Play? We go down there and rip 'er down and they thank us for it, that's our play!"

"Like a strung trap, that mind of yours."

"Why don't you sit on them spurs?"

Bannerman looked to Leroy, who pulled out his Paterson and removed the barrel to confirm—for the third time in a quarter hour—that all the cylinders were loaded except the defective one.

"Off we go."

They went down three abreast and ten yards apart. Leroy's ears were bent with the effort to detect any threatening sound. Bannerman, meanwhile, made an unholy racket with those fancy steel spurs that gave a double click with each step.

The gate to the inner yard was open. As the others went through, Leroy watched the glow through the grease-papered window, looking for the telltale shadow of a head pausing in suspicion. But the place was inhabited only by ghosts. His foot brushed against something—a doll fashioned out of an old sock, coif spun of bedraggled yarn, button eyes shining in the moonlight like splatters of mercury. Worried by their brightness, he nudged the doll over on its belly.

They were standing under the staff now, looking up at the flag as it stirred and shrugged on the intermittent breeze.

"Now what?"

With an impatient snort, Bannerman placed one of his studded boots about three feet up the jack staff and pushed. Only a sapling, it bent somewhat, but not low enough for the top to be grabbed. Holstering his gun, Leroy reached up with both hands as Bannerman leaned with all his weight and Fess hooked an arm and pulled it down. After some moments' effort they manhandled it level enough for Leroy to get his fingers on the hem of the flag. The sapling popped and groaned in protest; Leroy kept a wary eye on the house as he ripped the cloth from its mount and threw it over his left shoulder. In a celebratory mood now, Fess let the sapling go, to whip upward with a fearsome *thwack*.

"Quiet, you fool!" Leroy hissed as the other did a little celebratory jig.

"Listen! What's that?" Bannerman breathed.

Under Fess's antics, Leroy had heard it—the slow creak of old hinges limbering. There was a door opening somewhere, and behind it a scratching like nails on a board. Or the claws of a frantic animal being restrained.

"Time to fly, boys!" Leroy cried.

They cleared the fence just as the snarling began. Wrapped in the treason flag as he ran, Leroy couldn't reach his gun. Bannerman, just ahead of him, whirled around and was illuminated as his barrel flicked red flame. Turning to see if the shot struck home, Leroy glimpsed a shadow bounding on four legs, features dark on a head that seemed as thick and square as a cobblestone. Its sound was the deep rumbling of some vengeful chthonic god. As it ran it rattled a chain of heavy forged links like those clanging between loaded railroad cars.

In that headlong rush, defenseless with his gun out of reach, Leroy felt panic stuff itself inside his brain, filling it up from the very pit of his skull. His flight took him over obstacles—hurtling over spare fence posts and dropped tools and other jetsam of settler life, but he was aware of nothing but a quaking and a shortness of breath that dried his throat as he gasped. He saw Bannerman turn again, present his Colt as if to fire but pull empty because he had forgotten to cock it first. With that failure, Bannerman's nerve broke and he flew with an abandon as wholehearted as it was shameless.

But just then, by some chance fall of the drapery on his body, Leroy found he could reach the grip of his pistol. With that sensation of smooth fatality, his senses all seemed to snap into focus; the molten coursing through his veins cooled, and some small part of his nerve asserted itself. Without really intending to, he grasped the Colt, withdrew it, and pulled back the hammer. Turning, he sighted the shadow twenty feet behind him as it bestrode the prone form of Fess, who was thrashing manfully with fists that seemed to worry the dog as much as the patter of raindrops. The margin of safety was close, but some part of Leroy, some resolute agency in the tissue of lizard brain he shared with a cornered snake, made a decision. He touched off the charge, lighting with an incandescent stab a tableau of flailing arms and flashing carnassials.

To Leroy, the sound of the shot was drowned out by the sudden silence that followed it. The shadow standing over Fess slumped sideways. There was a hearty pounding in his head as he stood, gun cocked for another shot as Bannerman suddenly appeared, stepping carefully at full height as he approached the toppled shadow.

Jaws frozen in mid-snarl, the mastiff gave a sigh like any dog settling down for a nap, and then a gurgling sound. It was two hundred pounds heavy.

Bannerman whistled. "That was some shot. Right through the heart, you got 'im."

"You OK?" Leroy asked, meaning Fess. The other was still on his back, sleeving from his face a splatter of mastiff blood.

"I swow, I saw the face of my Maker!" he exclaimed. And then he writhed in the grass, pumping his arms and legs like a pinned beetle as he whooped and cried, "Tell me that wasn't fun! Tell me boys!"

Their relief was cut short by the crack of someone else shooting from the house. Leroy heard a shot whistle by, close enough to tousle the hair over his ears. Looking back, he saw a figure at the door of the cabin, framed by the faint glow of a draped lantern. The form seemed to struggle to cock his rifle for a moment before raising it to his cheek—but Leroy, intending not to stumble in the dark, turned his attention to escape and saw nothing more.

They rode like the devil, north. Reaching the riverbank, they paused until first light, then forded the river at a place where the late summer drought had narrowed it to twenty yards. There was a meadow on the far side. Bone tired, they turned the horses loose and laid out their gear to dry on the short grass. Still fraught after the night's events, Leroy lay on his back and felt the morning sunshine strengthen on his face. There was not much talk; though their objective was achieved, none of them felt his conduct merited much glory. The flag they had stolen was puddled on the ground, forgotten. When Fess made a show of belting out a self-satisfied yawn, Bannerman told him to shut his trap.

Leroy had been dozing for a time—he couldn't tell how long—when he was nudged awake by Bannerman's boot.

"What is it?"

The other pointed with his chin across the river. Rising to his elbows, Leroy swept the far shore and then up the hill beyond it. There, at the crest, two riders in long, foul-weather coats stood silhouetted against the blue. Their faces were too far away to read but seemed set in their direction, as if appraising their defensive position. Rising to his feet now, Leroy watched another rider join them, and another after that. As the last rose from the far side of the hill, he could clearly see the red kerchief tied around his neck.

"Pukes," Bannerman said.

Leroy watched as the party opposing them swelled to six, seven, then nine mounted men. Though roving Defensives were not common this far from the borderlands, the developing logic of the situation was hard to dismiss: if the party was indifferent, retreat would do no harm. But if hostile, the Devil's Angels would have to give ground or get the worst of a fight.

"Get to your horses. But don't make it look like you're in a hurry."

The newcomers weren't fooled. The instant the three of them made as if to escape, the posse whipped their mounts and barreled down the slope. Leroy and company got a good head start, as the bushwhackers had to cross the river. But there was a bitter taste in his mouth as he realized he had left some important kit drying on the grass behind him: namely his boots, a good blanket lent by his father, and a certain other item of apparel.

"Say, Leroy, did you happen to know you're ridin' in yer union suit?" Fess yelled from behind.

"Long as he keeps the trapdoor shut it's nothing to me," chimed Bannerman.

Leroy stood up in his saddle and looked back just in time to see eighteen pairs of hooves rumble over his britches.

Breaking through the last of the tree cover, they struck out across the prairie as the sun buried itself in a stratum of bruise-colored clouds. These gathered its rays into great lancing columns of light that cut the dusty atmosphere and lit upon the Leavenworth line of the Union Pacific Railroad. In ten minutes of hard riding they reached the tracks, and for no other reason than to keep the glare out of their eyes, they turned to follow the roadbed west.

The double track ran straight and level through this corner of Kansas, creasing the gently undulating landscape like a suture. Miles ahead the buff of autumn prairie met the blue sky in a line precisely bisected by the railroad. On the featureless expanse they made for that point of convergence almost by geometric necessity, exhausting their horses as they chased the receding intersection.

As space stretched before him, time became foreshortened. He rode with a monomaniacal intensity, obliterating miles and spitting them back in the faces of his pursuit. Yet the landscape around him didn't change: the track still ran straight, the clouds stalled, the same fringe of switch-grass as if he were stationary before a short loop of theatrical backdrop. In what seemed like only a few minutes the sun was at the meridian. Waking from his trance, Leroy noticed his horse was lathered, the froth of its exertion flying back into his face. Soon he would have to choose between reining back or riding him to ground.

Meaning to signal his companions, he looked to Bannerman to his left and Fess to his right. The first was riding with one hand on the reins and the other grasping his side, like a man suffering a cramp. Fess was hunkered down in his saddle, trusting in mere solidity to keep him upright. The pounding of hooves—and a dryness in his throat from mouthfuls of trail dirt he had swallowed—made it impossible to get the attention of either.

He pulled up, wrestling with the pitching head of his horse until, as the trail of his dust caught up with him, he stopped. Surprised, the others went fifty yards farther on until they wheeled. Looking back, they saw Leroy turning in tight circles as his agitated mount danced with hot blood coursing through its legs. He had his weapon drawn and was peering back through the haze at the bushwhackers.

They were far behind—at least half a mile, perhaps more. And they were dismounted, standing with their horses loosed and grazing around them.

"Congratulations, boys!" declared Fess. "Looks like we rode 'em right out of the saddle!"

"And ourselves too."

"This is our chance, Leroy," Bannerman said. "If we can get enough ahead of 'em."

Dubious, foreseeing disaster, Leroy agreed to push on. Immediately, the bushwhackers rounded up their horses and resumed the chase. The parties went on like this a little farther, the landscape around them changing little except for the slow retraction of roadbed behind them. A sense of disorientation rose, making him feel he was riding not on the level ground but steadily upward, into the sky on a ladder composed of railroad ties. But in a short time, no longer than it took for the sun to proceed its own width in the sky, he heard a particular wheeze from his horse. It was a sound like a man attempting to breathe through a shallow pan of water.

"There's nothing for it," he cried out. "Got to stop."

He reined up, gun drawn. Yet just as he stopped, the posse did the same. Leroy then understood their true position: having ridden farther, the bushwhackers were in worse shape than they were. For the moment they meant only to prevent the three of them from escaping, and nothing more.

And so the antagonists stared up and down the line. They were out of earshot, out of pistol range, but close enough to monitor each other. The Bushwackers squatted on the gleaming rails, the tails of their dusters tenting in the breeze. They tilted canteens into the air; the Devil's Angels did the same.

Bannerman spat a mouthful into the weeds.

"Unless we run out of prairie, reckon they must have us."

"Looks like it," granted Leroy.

"We could split up."

"They would do the same."

"So we just sit here?"

Leroy laid back. "For now," he said, lacing his fingers behind his head and showing a grimace of contentment.

The interlude went on as the sun crossed the tracks and arced toward Colorado. As the wind freshened, a flotilla of cumuli floated above, casting first one party and then the other in shadow. The momentary coolness relieved the pounding in his head; he might have fallen asleep there, with his head against the rail and nostrils full of the odor of creosote, if the string of his cares did not suddenly pull taut. His eyes shot open to find Fess standing over him.

"Train's coming."

Leroy jerked erect. Where the westbound track met the eastern horizon, there was a gleam, flickering and ruddy like a candle reflected in bronze. It strengthened as he watched, becoming whiter and steadier as a high-pitched, faintly pneumatic roar rolled across the prairie. Closer, and the crown of gray smoke unfolded, almost translucent in the distance but gathering substance as it approached.

The bushwhackers wandered off the track, gathering on the north side as their coats whipped in the train's wake. Leroy, Fess, and Bannerman were standing on the south side; as the train approached at an oblique angle, it screened the two parties from each other. The bushwhackers were uncovered again when it was a hundred yards from them. At this, Fess lifted a fist to the sky, proclaiming, "The devil take 'em, I think I've got it!"

"What are you talking about, you jackass?"

"Tell me, is that or is it not a streambed down there?"

He gestured north to a line of scrub that seemed to march as long and straight as the track.

"Likely. And how does that help us, if they can plainly see us make for it?"

Fess winked. "You just get ready to move when I say!"

The train passed at forty miles an hour. It had six cars and no caboose, with a smoking platform on the end. Two figures stood on it: a gentleman in a stove-pipe hat and a woman in a lavender dress, elbow bent under mutton-chop sleeves as she dragged on a cigarette. Leroy caught her eye as she looked upon him blankly, like he was some nameless feature on the landscape. He imagined she forgot him a moment later. But under the strain of their desperate situation, her glance, delivered as it was from a place of gentility and perfect security, made a permanent impression on him. Her face came back to him for years after, when he thought on his misadventures during the war.

The boys had their first bite in twelve hours—stale biscuits from the Dicks' breakfast table two days previous—as they sat and waited to behold Fess's coup. The Defensives down the line made themselves a smoky fire out of grass and prairie muffins, and set up a stand to boil coffee. Fess was soon standing there with his nose in the air as if he could smell their brew. Bannerman laughed. "Thinking of joining them, you slanticular snake?"

"It may come to that," he replied, and resumed plucking his mouth harp. Leroy liked the sound no better than before, but under the circumstances, he preferred it to the desolate hiss of the breeze through the weeds. Weeds that, likely as not, would soon cradle his rotting bones.

It was well on toward sunset when their opportunity came at last. The next train appeared as evening rose on the eastern horizon, pure white headlamp piercing the dusk. As it neared the posse, Fess, who was keeping very still, murmured, "Don't move a muscle, but be ready to take horse."

After meditating on the angles and the timing, Bannerman vented a snort. "I think I see what he's cookin'," he said.

"Will it work?"

"How fast you gonna ride?"

When the train was abreast of them, the bushwhackers again shambled to the north. The locomotive, which let out a whistle either in salutation or warning, barreled through and interposed itself between the parties.

"It's now or never, boys!" Fess cried.

The three of them were mounted and running before they could get their boots in the stirrups. As they made for the stream, Fess led them on an oblique angle to the southwest, keeping them screened by the train as long as he could. Leroy hadn't ridden in such disarray since the first time he had galloped a horse. Already out of a pair of britches, he lost his hat and the gloves from his pocket too. When they finally reached the scrub he was almost out of his saddle, face buried in the mane but still on the daylight side of his horse.

The stream was little more than a rivulet this time of year, the bed barely low enough for a prone man to keep out of sight. Bannerman and Fess lay hatless on their bellies, peering at their pursuit. After tying his horse behind a screen of blackberry bushes, Leroy retrieved his Sharps and a bandolier. Then he scurried back, half running and half crawling, to join the others.

It took some time for their pursuers to register their absence when the train was gone. Their faces were too far away to see, but to Leroy they seemed to stand around in erect, attentive disbelief for a while—until the notion of giving chase came over them, though without much urgency as there was no sign of other riders for miles in every direction.

Fess punched Leroy in the arm. "You're more likely to catch a weasel asleep than outfox old Fess!"

"We're not in the clear yet," said Bannerman.

The Defensives trotted their horses down the roadbed, guns drawn as if they expected their quarry to leap suddenly from the earth. When they reached the spot where Leroy and Company had rested, they paused, circling as they read the ground. Leroy felt his gut lighten as he watched them pick up their trail and follow it. They were heading straight for their hiding place.

"Well, that was a nice try," said Bannerman as he turned over to extract a second Colt from under his jacket.

"So we make a stand here?"

"Do you want to keep running?"

They were closer now than they'd ever been. Bewhiskered, wind-chapped faces resolved as they approached, eyes flicking between the ground and the cover ahead. They wore a chance collection of duds salvaged from corpses—Union army jackets, gaiters, cattlemen's dusters, one or two breeches in Confederate brownish-gray. One of them had lieutenant's bars on his shoulders. No order was necessary for them to space themselves across their exposed front and hold their fire without a clear target. They were a hard, scary-looking crew.

Leroy swallowed. "Nathan, the three on the right?"

"I hope."

"Got the left," declared Fess.

Laying his Colt within easy reach in the grass, Leroy cocked and sighted along his Sharps. He had a bead on the one with the officer's bars when he looked into the man's eyes—and was chilled to see those eyes look straight back.

By some quirk of his attention he didn't register the rifle's kick, but he did hear the bullet pierce the man's breast, striking it like the open-palmed slap of a woman. A look of incredulity came over the man, for he was evidently one of those Defensives who never believed the wages of his crimes would ever be repaid. He stopped his horse, sorted his reins. Then he tumbled.

The gunfight erupted so fast that its exact progress was only clear to Leroy later, when they all had time to discuss it. Bannerman winged his first target in his nonshooting hand; the man shot back in haphazard fashion, pouring blue smoke from barrel and cylinder. Fess missed clean with his first shot, then hacked off four more with his eyes closed against the roar and the spit of powder. When he peeped over the rise again, he saw he had taken one man in the head and wounded the horse of another. The latter whirled in panic, its rider cursing and contorting himself to bring his gun to bear.

With the flight of the wounded horse, the bushwhackers' line broke. The seven still in their mounts scattered in a generally northeastern direction, shooting wildly into prairie and sky. None of their bullets came anywhere near them, but one severed the branch of a tree, which fluttered down upon Bannerman and rattled him so severely that he rolled over firing blind. Fess brayed with laughter.

"You go get 'em, gunfighter! You kill that tree dead!"

Leroy stood to watch the posse scatter. Euphoria, ballasted by relief, came over him as he watched their backs recede. At last, he had been measured against his heroic imaginings, and had not come up short. But his joy was brief, for there were two corpses left in the grass, and one of them, though just as certainly dead as the other, was still kicking its legs.

Leroy went to check on the horses. Climbing around, he found them with heads up, lips stained green, eyes whiteless and calm. Back on the turf, Fess and Bannerman stood over one of the Defensives. Kneeling, Fess extended the corpse's right hand and spread the fingers. Then he stood, cocked his Smith, and sighted along the barrel at the dead man's palm.

"Hey Daniel, what're you doing?"

So rarely was Fess called by his real name that he paused.

"Hey Leroy. Watch this."

The .22 cracked and kicked. The corpse's forearm whipped and twisted with the force of the shot, coming to rest at an oblique angle, as if the man were giving a companionable wave. A moment later Leroy heard something land in the weeds behind him.

"Didn't I just tell ya!"

"Well I'll be damned," marveled Bannerman.

"What're you apes talking about?"

"Look," said Fess, pointing with his gun. "Hit 'em in the lifeline and the fingers come off just as you please."

It was true: there were five clean, red, empty sockets where the Defensive's fingers had been. The digits were missing entirely, ejected in every direction.

Bannerman whistled, unholstered. "Let me try that."

"No you're not," Leroy said.

"What's it to you?"

"We don't do that, is all."

"Yeah? Well I don't take orders neither."

"Call it a strong suggestion, then."

He took out his Paterson and let it hang by his side.

"What is it to you, Leroy?" Fess repeated. And indeed, he would have been hard pressed to explain these sudden, unthinking qualms—except for the image, indelibly engraved in his memory, of Tubbs's similarly mutilated remains. The smell of it, the rank congealed finality, still lived in his nostrils. He trembled despite himself.

Bannerman stepped over the body to come within twelve inches of Leroy's nose.

"Ever been to Osawatomie?"

Leroy shrugged.

"They found six jayhawkers dead there last month. Hanging from trees. Guts split from collar to crotch. Any petikler thoughts on that, Leroy?"

"Wasn't me, if that's what you're thinking."

"Funny. Funny man."

After fixing him with a last glare, Bannerman stepped back and holstered his pistol. But then Fess piped up: "Now I've seen the elephant! Tough guy turns out to be a damn yella sheeny!"

"Shut up, Fess," Bannerman and Leroy said in unison.

"I wouldn't take that if I were you" Fess said. "Somebody might think I'm missing a load of sand."

"I said I'm warning you."

"Are you? Better ask Leroy before you do anything . . . sheeny."

In a flash of herringbone and flying nickel plate, Bannerman was on him. He cracked Fess across the jaw with his gun hand, hooking his lip with the trigger guard and ripping it to the gum line. Fess hit the ground unconscious. A stream of blood poured down his chin, over his neck, and into a pool in the dirt.

Bannerman massaged his hand.

"I told him," he said. "You heard me. I told him."

Chapter Thirteen

Sword, Wand, Chariot

SOME FOLKS TOOK well to the plains. For most of the men, who had occasion to travel to town to sell their crops or buy supplies, the unrelenting openness was an opportunity to test themselves, and if they measured up, to write their own fates. Its vistas were unsheltered, but at least they could see the paths before them, and the distance to their goals.

But their wives, unmarried sisters, widowed mothers and daughters found it harder to abide the solitude. Cloistered in their cabins, soddies and dugouts, the chasm of space between them and the horizon was as solid a prison as ever made out of stone and mortar. The poverty of faces and voices spawned loneliness akin to prisoners in solitary confinement. Some gazed for hours at drawings of human faces in Bibles, on pill bottles, and in mail-order catalogs. Others trekked for miles, to within sight of railway lines. There, if they were lucky, they might see a distant train pass, and wring from the chugging, whistling artifice some semblance of connection to the rest of the human race.

It was to these women that Kate tailored her services. As the days got warmer, she would collect her tarot, and a light meal in a basket, tie a sun-hat on her head, and strike out across the prairie. If Junior was home, he would come after her, offering to drive her wherever she wanted. But four months of winter trapped in a cabin with his simpering devotion was already too much for her to bear. She would turn away and walk for a quarter hour before peeking back to check if he followed. Often he would still be standing there—torturing himself with the sight of her receding back—until she dropped into the hollow near the Brockman place and was free.

With the mild temperatures and the surge of spring growth on the plain, her journeys were not unpleasant. Following the cow paths, she was well off the busier thoroughfares and seemed to have a broad green universe to herself. The fringe of her skirts dragged over the ground, raking the blossoms and enveloping her in their sweetly decaying scent. After the long winter she was desperate for the sun to thaw the cold, heavy core that weighed inside her. She removed her hat and unpinned her hair to warm across her shoulders. Ranchers watching from a distance stared, as did their wives at their wash lines and soap-making. Later, neighbors would meet up and ask if they had seen the vision that had manifested beyond their pastures. They would agree they had, and with a pensive glance downward, needed to say no more.

She had a regular customer, a settler's wife who had seen her handbill at the hotel. She lived three miles away on the trail to Parsons. When Kate arrived at her place late in the morning, Sarah

Mooney would greet her with a cup of tea brewed from sorrel or dandelion root and fresh cream she had skimmed that day. She had a small table set up outside, a tilt-top designed for card games, covered with a muslin cloth. There, after exchanging pleasantries about the weather, Kate would fetch her tarot from its ribboned box, touch it to her lips, and lay out the Celtic cross.

Interpreting the tarot was less like reading a story than writing one. Everything began with the proper kind of question—never a simple yes or no ("Will I go back East?")—but a question that offered room for elaboration ("How might I decide whether to go back East?"). The various cards, the Major Arcana with their persons and objects and principles, the Minor Arcana with their numbers and suits, each suggested many possible answers, all of which may be qualified in combination with other cards and their positions in the Cross. The Chariot could imply the questioner is on a quest—or seeking control over himself. In conjunction with Pentacles, it suggested an effort of self-discipline; with the Hanged Man, it implied grace in defeat. Death never meant only what it appeared to mean. With the Fool, it could mean a fresh start is in the offing, while Cups placed an emphasis on making a proper farewell, as in coping with grief. Performing a reading was an act of creation, calling for all of Kate's skills at association, of reading her client and her desires, of her surroundings, of the cards that served her well and those that hid in the deck, refusing to appear.

She turned up the Moon.

"The soul card appears in this position as the hidden factor. It suggests you suffer from certain dreams or yearnings at the root of your troubles."

Kate measured the impact of her words on Sarah's face. The

other perceived her looking, and hastened to agree, "Yes, I won't deny it."

Next, Knight of Cups. "In the position of receding influence, the seeker of sensation, of beauty . . ."

"Of love?"

"Of giving in to love."

"Oh dear Lord."

"Which corresponds with Two of Swords here, the card of thwarting, that testifies to something that is spoken but not heard . . ."

"As by a husband?"

"I don't see him yet, but here—" and she turns up the Empress in the sixth position, "We welcome the great lady, who promises a certain reward in the future, should you choose to act."

"The choice is mine?"

"The cards do not predict, but only instruct."

Just then a piglet wriggled through a gap in its pen and ran under the table. Sarah stooped, cussed and grasped. This broke the uncanny air that had briefly settled around them. All too quickly in Kate's eyes, the woman surrendered the gleam of possibility that had momentarily lit up her chapped face.

On her way home, Kate was two bits richer and twice as heavy of heart. A reading that had gone well always filled her with regret of her own limitations. Before the great, unfathomed abyss of meaning, she was a mere child collecting pebbles on a beach. There were unscrupulous practitioners, to be sure; Almira still believed the cards to be nothing more than a quaint sort of scam. But with every cry of affirmation from a client, with every honest dollar earned, Kate felt more obliged to be worthy of the skill she had developed. Invest nothing in the cards and one profited nothing. But take them as a matter of science, a syntax of pictures and symbols, and the prospect of true clairvoyance glittered, not so far away. Slowly, with due caution, she came to believe herself more worthy of the title she had adopted, Professor Katie Bender.

A man rode toward her. From the cut of his shoulders and the straightness of his back she had an inkling of who it was. At this suspicion she was chilled at the back of her neck and flushed to the cleft of her collarbone. Her pace slowed; she had an urge to flee, but to where, in that immensity? A bitterness filling her mouth, she set her jaw and forced herself forward.

"Good afternoon, Miss Bender," Leroy Dick said, doffing.

"And to you, sir."

Gray eyes looking at her, shining beneath dark, dashing parentheses. Features gently weathered, like battlements of some castle host to great and daring deeds. And oiled boots, shining by the ministrations of a faithful woman. To be that wife, the cherished helpmeet, overcome with devotion at the mere sight of his boots standing in a closet—

"The choir is improved with a genuine contralto."

"I'm pleased to contribute," she replied, voice audible but quavering. Her throat felt suddenly dry, as if she had recently battled a fire. Afraid he would see through her, she would not meet his eyes. His horse, as if aware of her discomfort, stepped backward and fetched to the left, obliging him to rein up.

"Well, good day, then," he said, finger to hat brim.

"Good day."

With that, he continued on his way, and Kate stood for a moment, collecting herself. For there was no question now that she was lost. Like Isaac Newton's key to the Philosopher's Stone, lost. Lost as she was alone and unrecognized in her time.

When she became conscious that she was walking, she was in sight of the Bender cabin. Sometime in the course of her wandering the sky had clouded over, a listless drizzle jeweling the bluestem. She moved on, but in the meandering fashion of a drunk or distracted person, half seeing the cow pies and soggy hoofprints that swallowed her pointed boots. She envisioned Leroy aloft again, riding the prairie, but with her mounted sidesaddle and harbored in his arms. On her finger, a ring, and against his shoulder, her head. She closed her eyes and breathed the vigor about him, the odor of his pure, honest rectitude, the goodness in strength and strength in goodness.

Almira was behind the cabin, washing a shirt in a basin of creek water. She had been working it hard, pressing and abrading until her arms ached and the muscles burned beneath her pendulous breasts. She stepped back, drawing her wet forearm across her mouth until she tasted the soap. And then she saw Kate standing there, watching her.

"*Du.*"

"We're going to have to stop all this," said Kate.

As the lye in the soap burned the scratches on her arms, Almira slung them about to soothe them in the breeze. Her eyes trained on Kate.

"You say I must stop the washing?"

"Don't pretend not to know what I mean."

A short distance away the Bender men worked among the apple trees they had planted in the spring. The grove was not so large as to constitute an orchard, but big enough for their purposes. The trees were young yet, too small for grafting, and the men spent great effort in grooming the soil around them, sculpting it into neat and regular rows. Rows, they figured, that were wide and tall enough to conceal what they needed to conceal.

When Almira looked over, John Senior immediately and wordlessly sensed her distress. Dropping his rake, he summoned Junior and hulked in the women's direction.

"So it stops, and how do we keep ourselves?" said Almira. "We sell apples, maybe?"

"There are other ways. I've advertised my service at the hotel. I had a very good reading this afternoon."

"You and your games. They are good for pocket money, no more."

"You're wrong, as you are often," Kate replied, sounding more of the aggrieved daughter than she intended. As the men came within earshot, she met Junior's eyes, bidding for his support. He responded:

"She's real popular with the ladyfolk, I'd be prepared to swear. They think the world of her and they pay cash money too. I've seen it."

"Free me to do it all the time and I'll show you something. Take me to Independence and let the word get around."

"At fifty cents a mark?" Almira snorted. "A dollar? We came out here for that?"

"It's a level business, so they can't persecute for it. That's something," said Junior, to which Kate added, "The longer we do the other, the more dangerous."

"That is barely nothing! Do you have anything to say about it?"

Almira looked to the old man, who wore an expression like someone who had just lost a lot of money at a game of chance he didn't entirely understand. Confronted with this instance of overt, frank communication between human beings, he became confused, and then annoyed. He turned and went back to his spadework under the trees.

"*Hau ab, Feigling!*" she cried after him. To Kate, she rumbled: "You are crazy. Read too many books, this is what happens."

"You can't do it without me, so this is how it will be."

The old woman, near the end of her resources in English, muttered in German as she attacked her laundry.

The argument not so much won as adjourned, Kate retired to the cabin to remove her dusty walking clothes. As she stripped to her camisole, she rehearsed sotto voce what she would say when the subject was brought up again. Out of the corner of her eye she glimpsed Junior through the window, smoking and watching her. In this instance, she didn't turn away, and she didn't lower the screen.

Outside, Almira approached John Senior as he tortured the soil, watching until he ceased ignoring her.

"*Was?*"

"What is there without her?"

Wiping the sweat from his forehead, he plastered the strands of his unkempt eyebrows across his temples. "Just wait," he said.

IT TOOK ONLY a few days for the first test of Kate's determination to arrive. They knocked without any need for prompting, as the crepe black of a moonless prairie night cloaked the trail—a grown-up man and a boy. She opened the door and found them dressed in similar fashion, in woolen greatcoats and brimmed felt hats, faces expectant and smudged with dust.

"Are we too late?" asked the elder one.

Kate had not expected someone to show up unsolicited. She

stood with her mouth open for a moment, unable to conjure the words that would send them packing. In the interim Almira appeared, hands knotted together, her face cracked by what might have been a reasonable simulation of a smile.

"You are not too late. *Kommen Sie.*"

The strangers came in, glancing about as Junior stood frozen behind the counter, unsure what to do, and the old man took prudent refuge behind the canvas.

The father was gray-skinned and hollow-eyed, but the youthful architecture of his face was reflected in the boy's, which had a sweet and full-lipped femininity. They already looked like victims.

Almira invited the father to the table. "We have a soup savory enough to warm your bones," she said, bidding him to the far seat, by the canvas. His eyes were still on Kate, though, as relief battled with confusion; he seemed to like the words, but was unsure about the music. Kate froze him with her eyes, saying, "It *is* late," until Almira lost her patience and growled *"Warum lässt Du ihn nicht in ruh?"*

Kate laid a hand on the back of the boy's collar and replied, *"Ich lass' dich nicht sterben,"* and then to the father, "Brockman can take you. He's close by."

The father went behind the table, and examining at the dried grease stain on the canvas, shuddered. Then he circled around the far side of the table and took the boy in hand.

"We don't want to be any trouble."

"No trouble! No trouble!" cried Almira. But her tone conveyed emergency instead of reassurance, and had the opposite effect to what she intended. The father shrank toward the door, jabbering apologies as the boy, clinging to him, made low mewing sounds of fright as he stared at the gap between the canvas and the wall.

The old man was standing there, eyes blazing, grasping his hammer. If there was any doubt left in the father's mind, this display solved it.

"If it's all the same, we're leaving," he said. "Good evening."

"Go, then," spat Almira. "And may starvation make you suck your child's bones!"

THUS KATE SACRIFICED on account of her feelings for Leroy, which brightened and ventilated the baroque labyrinth her heart had become. She felt drugged by these purities. The more she thought about them, the less steady she felt. She went about on legs that seemed to belong to someone else, working on principles she had no feeling for. Walking to her appointments, she became so engrossed in her thoughts of him that she stumbled down the wrong cow paths, adding miles to her trips. At the grocery, she started tasks and forgot they were in progress, as when she started to make butter by scalding fresh milk on the stovetop. Almira discovered the brown, feculent substance that remained, letting out a cry of disgust she never showed at a genuine bloodletting. The old woman's rebuke struck her as something far away and amusing, hardly audible under the music of that perfect syllabic couplet, *Leroy, Leroy.*

At the hotel, she made beginner's mistakes—mixing up orders, dropping plates—that she hadn't made while she was a beginner. Her task was made more difficult by the thought that *he* might walk in at any moment, with that carefree jangling gait of a figure sewn together loosely, bound by sinew and strength and the easy grace of a man who attracted women as easily as he stepped and breathed and shone his gray eyes before her desperate, distracted hopelessness. Puzzled, Alice Acres whistled and shouted across the dining room, "Looks like a girl in love, if I don't know better!" On hearing that, Kate's solicitous and heavily armed admirers sunk into their drinks and swore they'd shoot the lucky bastard who dared take her away from them.

Sunday services were the only time she was sure to lay eyes on Leroy. She prepared for church by scrubbing her face, then patting it with a powder laced with arsenic that give her skin a faint metallic glow. She arranged her hair so it tumbled from beneath her hat and across her shoulders in flexuous waves. She kept Junior waiting in the cart for so long he fell asleep, then cursed him for his slowness on the trail. They arrived at Harmony Grove late, rushing into the chapel after the service had begun, causing the congregants to turn in mid-soing. When certain of the men kept staring as Kate took her place in the choir, their sisters and wives swung their elbows to force their eyes back to their hymnals.

After, at choir practice, she had planned to position herself in the front of her section, right where he could see her. But when the moment came she became suddenly shy, thinking perhaps that the time had not come for her to be worthy of him. She stood in the back instead, burying her face in her sheet music, until the urge to peek got the better of her, and she looked up. Leroy was there in his usual majesty, in easy command of the space around him, beating the time with his large, callused, yet graceful hands. The sight of him caused her to feel a hollowing within that was unnerving, thrilling. She planted her eyes back on her music.

Back at the cabin she felt she could postpone no longer: she had to hear what the cards said about her future with Leroy. But she couldn't do something so consequential in front of Almira. After sweeping out the front room, she leaned the straw broom beside the counter, wrapped a shawl around her shoulders, and struck out across the trail with the deck concealed under her apron. The old man was in his usual place on Sabbath afternoons, sitting in the shadow of the cabin with his Bible open on his lap. She gave him a glance as she passed; his eyes flitted up at her, seeming to take her in but blankly, as if unable to focus beyond the distance to his verses.

She went some distance away in the direction of Spill Out Creek. When she was out of sight, she sat down on a patch of soft grass under a willow. She had been pondering which spread to use, as the more elaborate ones she used with her clients, like the Cross, seemed unfitting in this case. The matter at hand was not whether to buy a new combine or how to assure a good crop, but something purer and plainer. The destinies of two souls and their love—two things and the sum of them. Yes, a simple three-card pull.

She shuffled the cards, drew three from the top and laid them in a line on the grass. The first would be about her, the second about him, and the last their future. She turned over the first: the Four of Swords, Minor Arcana. With its appearance she gave a small, gratified cry: swords were the symbols of challenges, of work left to be done. Yet the number 4 betokened stability, stasis, quiescence. The card reflected the challenge of pausing, taking stock. It suggested respite from momentous tasks—a respite that, ironically, might seem more challenging than the work itself. In light of her decision to quit the murdering business, it was a very interesting card to pull. She felt vindicated in this decision, and encouraged in her judgment in making others.

Next, the Knight of Wands. Here was an appealing fellow, brightly dressed, sallying forth on some gallant errand. And yet in her experience his appeal could be deceiving: it could conceal a certain recklessness, activity for its own vain sake. In connection with Leroy Dick, the card's appearance puzzled her—in his natural graveness, he seemed the very opposite of vanity. She considered the discrepancy for a while, staring into the gently swaying tendrils of the willow, until the solution presented itself. And then she slapped herself on the forehead at her obtuseness, for Knight Wands also attended the departure, *iter interrupta*. It was the card of transitions, calling for the resolution to break with the past. With respect to the potential end of Leroy's marriage, this card fairly pulsated with significance.

Finally, the Chariot, Major Arcana. She fell back, right hand over her mouth. It was an odd card to correspond to their future together, the card of triumph through struggle. When it appeared, she usually read it as a call to the kind of narrow, grasping determination that might be taken for selfishness. Selfishness indeed, for a cause worthy of being misunderstood, even reviled. They would be together then, but not easily, and at a price in blood.

The shade of the tree chilled her straight through. The cards had given, but now they had taken away. She had chosen well to stop the killing, but the struggle was not over. She would need an act of courage to reverse herself again.

She gathered the cards and held them in her lap, warming them in her hands.

Chapter Fourteen

Persimmon and Stone

Oh that I was where I would be
Then I would be where I am not
Here I am where I must be
Go where I would, I cannot
Oh, diddle lully day
Oh, de little lioday

—**"Katie Cruel," traditional Scottish folk ballad**

FEBRUARY, 1858

YOUNG KATE COULD tell when the railroad men were about to knock off from the sound of the tamping rods—the ones they used to pack the black powder in the drill holes for blasting—being thrown in a pile. The great metallic *clanks* of heaped iron marked the time of day like the chimes of a clock tower, if the mean little camp of tar and cesspits had any such thing. Instead, the doggeries and brothel tents spontaneously roused when the workday was done, the men filing home with money in their pockets and their brains addled by twelve hours of hammer-swinging and rubble-clearing and fiddling with fuses. Some of them staggered back home with bottles already in hand, from the boys who sold them at the very edges of the work zone. It never ceased to amaze Kate how fast a man could make himself seem drunk when his mind was set on it.

It was six months since Clarrity had left her with Almira. Somewhere in that time her seventh birthday had come and gone. She had not thought to share the date with her new guardian, though it loomed larger than Christmas in her former life. The latter was a public festival, a time she always had to share with other men bellowing for brandied eggnogs and holiday luck and further credit from the house. Her birthday, however, was a celebration she and her father shared in private, for which he saved the best gifts for her alone. He presented Nickers to her on her sixth, the pony led into the hotel lobby and caparisoned in roses for her delight. When she summoned this memory in bed at night, it made her weep. Convincing the lawmen that Kate was her daughter was only the beginning of the association. When Kate was stubborn, Almira was obliged to beat her. If she was in a kind mood, she used a knotted rope on the back of the child's legs; when she was not, or if Kate supplied some pretext, she became more ingenious. After a client had left behind a pair of boot hooks, Almira took them to Kate's hair. As the girl dangled clear of the ground by her unkempt mop, she stared into Almira's eyes, impassive, relentless, until the other cried, *"Kind vom Teufel geboren! Spawn der Hölle!"* and beat her further, leaving bruises upon bruises on her back, her thighs, her rump.

But never her face. For when the drunken railroad men came,

tramping up from the works ankle-deep in mud or snow, Almira made Kate stand outside the tent with her face washed and hair combed out. There was no wrong kind of attention for her to attract: if someone made an indecent remark, she was instructed to smile and say nothing; if they tried to touch, she was to lead them inside, where Almira would be waiting in a censorious lather:

"Is it my daughter you have cast *ungeheuerliche* eyes upon, you dog?" she would cry. The mark would deny it, of course, and Almira would go on not believing him, making him more and more panicked and less drunk until she made her offer: they might fuck Almira if they wished or they might not. But for her silence, they would nonetheless pay her the sum of five dollars.

Most did pay, and a few of them took up the challenge of her parted skirts. While this business was conducted, Kate was trained to retreat across the thoroughfare to a place far enough for propriety's sake but close enough to summon in case of trouble. If Almira cried out the code word, "persimmon," the girl was supposed to run for a local brawler Almira kept on retainer, for special interventions.

One of her more notable customers came to her at an odd hour, just after noon when the sky had turned a queasy, lemon-colored overcast. He was big man, barely taller than he was wide, with neatly combed whiskers and hat pulled down so hard it bowed over the dome of his skull. There was a cigar in his mouth, which he fidgeted and turned in his fingers as he strolled with the deliberate pace of a man too important to be anywhere in particular. Kate watched him go by, glancing and briefly appraising as he picked his way through the ruts with his ivory-handled walking stick. He showed her his suited back, vast and curved like some great woolen cello, until he slowed, stopped, and turned to regard her again. There was a question in his eyes that she could guess but was too young to answer. He spoke:

"*Guten Tag, kleines Mädchen. Ist deine Mutter da?*"

There was something familiar about the man, but also something that broke her nerve. She ran into the tent, coming out again under cover of Almira's broad rear end. She peeked from back there as Almira challenged the man, saying, "Don't you have anything better to do than frighten children?"

To which the visitor twirled and puffed his cigar. "*Ich habe das Glück heute! Zwei Schönheiten zum Preis von einer . . .*"

"You'll have your fill of bad luck if you don't state your business, *aufschneider.*"

It was the first time they laid eyes on John Flickinger. He was at that point just an ordinary poseur, a fairly skilled card cheat and whoremonger out of Illinois whose drinking had not yet jaundiced his skin, pickled his brain, and turned him into the derelict that would one day be known as Pa Bender.

In their tent, they entertained him for several hours simply by listening to him expound—entirely in German—upon himself and his exploits. He had come from the other side after the troubles in '48, having done some sort of mischief there that he hinted at but would not specify. He had worked at meatpacking in Chicago, at every position in the line from splitting the skulls of live steers to shoveling entrails. After tiring of that trade, he drifted west, where he found mixed success at the gaming tables. In St. Louis he was tarred and feathered for staking poker hands with plugged coins—an event he recounted with the sort of humor that came from knowing it could have gone much worse. In Arkansas he came into possession of a teenage squaw, whose services he sold out of a wagon at lumber camps.

As he attested to his skill at this trade he looked pointedly at Kate. But Almira disabused him of this notion: "The girl is fine where she is," she said. "I've invested enough in her." Upon which Flickinger lost interest in their conversation, claiming he was expected at the richest poker table in the camp. He rose, retrieved his walking stick, and plucked a quarter eagle from his purse. Placing the money in Kate's hand, he laid an admiring caress on her cheek. Then he tipped his hat to take his leave.

"You never said what happened to the squaw," Almira said to him.

Flickinger paused at the flap, gave a slight smile, and pushed through.

"*Nichtsnutz*," Almira spat in her chaw bucket. "To imagine we'd need the likes of him." Then she plucked the coin out of Kate's hand and told her, "You, back outside. And don't drag *Kacke* like that in here again."

Even as she cursed Flickinger, pleasure curled Almira's lips as she fingered his money.

For Kate's error, Almira conceived a lesson: after she was finished with her next client, she summoned her and made her stand at attention with the chamber pot. "Go ahead, do the necessary," she bade the fellow. The miner, a six-foot-tall giant with a full growth of beard to his solar plexus, had conducted his business with Almira with his underthings puddled around his booted feet. After regarding the girl for an instant, he fished from his shorts a warty sea creature the color of a day-old bruise.

His water came hesitantly at first, in fits and burbles. But soon it streamed enough to splatter Kate's breast and neck.

"*Stehen und bewegen sich nicht*," Almira warned, regarding her coolly until the task was done. With a parting shake, the miner tucked himself away and gave the corner of Kate's mouth a playful caress with the same fingers.

"Now dump that and wash yourself. I check you do a good job!"

They encountered Flickinger again two years later in Virginia City, Nevada. This mountain town, perched in the lee of the Sierras, leapt into existence in 1859 after the discovery of a massive vein of silver. In a matter of months it was one of the biggest settlements in the swath of continent between Denver and San Francisco. Newcomers were still coming by the thousands when Almira and Kate found their way there, in hopes of either profiting directly from the Comstock lode or indirectly from the men who worked the diggings.

Kate had by this time come into her fullness of girlish beauty. She was tall and ginger-haired, with lips full and cleft like blossoms erupted with fragrance. She was not a woman yet—not in the fundamental sense—but teetered on that precipice. The newly rich placers of Virginia City, strolling past Almira's tent with pockets full of black-veined ore and imaginations pent laden with fantasies, swiveled their heads at her and circled back.

Almira would give them a few minutes to get acquainted with her bait, then charge out in pointed (and pointedly loud) indignation. Soon the miners began to feel their fortunes and their expensive dreams about to slip away. Instead of cash money, Almira received her payoffs in grayish Comstock ore. Soon she had whole wheelbarrows of it, striped with the color of precious metal she'd learned to read as well as the faces of her hapless marks.

They were in the town one afternoon, Almira enjoying a pipeful of tobacco she'd traded for a fat cobble, Kate a fresh apple that cost a dollar because it had been packed in by mule from California. The single road through the camp was jammed with ore wagons. The butt of each backed up under the snouts of the blin-kered teams of the next. Pedestrians maddened by the delay in crossing the town's one street tried to push between the wagons, risking bites from the miserable, ornery horses. Most didn't try, waiting as much as an hour for a break in the traffic. Almira and Kate had been standing for twenty minutes before they recog-nized Flickinger right in the front of them.

He was beside the thoroughfare, leaning on a mine car that had been stripped of its wheels and overturned. The usual cigar was in his mouth, stuck and smoldering as he stared into the ground, but the rest of his appearance suggested he had come down in the world. Instead of a suit, he wore a grease-tracked union suit with suspenders, his denim pants patched in mismatched fashion on both knees. On his feet he wore only socks, which were still clean, as if he had just lost his shoes. Instead of a trimmed and cologned face, he displayed a thatch like a backwoodsman, with bristles sticking from his nose and the caves of his ears. In his sallow skin and the bloated redness around his eyes, Kate recognized the fa-miliar attributes of the well-lubricated man.

She thought him more horrid than ever, but his obvious turn of bad luck seemed to attract Almira. She paused in front of him, waiting for his reverie to break.

"Oh, du bist es . . ."

"Yes, indeed," she replied. "What happened to your shoes?"

He cocked his head and smiled, unfurling a line of suppurat-ing gums. "Lost," he said.

"Best win 'em back before the weather turns."

She clicked open the little leathern purse she kept on a string around her neck. "This will get you started," she said, taking plea-sure in returning the favor he'd once done her. He took the money with the unhesitating matter-of-factness of a man with no pride left to defend.

"*Danke. Ich zahle es zurück.*"

"No need. Just stay away from them antifogmatics!"

A gap opened up in the traffic as an overheated horse collapsed in its traces. Almira gathered Kate's hand in the manner of a dock worker seizing the mooring rope. "*Komm, du . . .*" she ordered, and showed Flickinger a bob of her head—a "see you before too long" parting nod—as she crossed.

"Until next time," he replied. Then he gave her money a close, skeptical look.

Chapter Fifteen

An Interview Concerning Domestic Matters

SEPTEMBER, 1871

THE HIATUS HELD, but at the cost of tranquility at the Bender claim. Almira, impatient that her cracker tin was getting no heavier, took to fits of violent pique—slamming pots on the stove, neglecting the men's washing, casting hateful glances in Kate's direction. Kate contrived to be out of the cabin as much as possible, taking herself off to readings for miles in any direction, allowing Junior drive her in the wagon when she had need to go farther out. For his part, Junior tried to relieve the tension by becoming even more solicitous and chipper. This didn't have its intended effect: his buoyant mood became so galling, Almira swore to cut his throat if he looked at her sideways.

The old man's behavior changed not at all. When he wasn't

working their modest garden or grooming the ground over those other "plantings" in the orchard, he sat in the afternoon shade in front of the cabin, studying his Bible. He would stare long and hard at travelers coming up the trail. But only proper commerce was allowed with them now, so he would sour and look down. This often drove travelers to take their business to the Brockman place. Seeing this, Almira came out and slapped his book in the dust with a wet ladle. Even if they were not currently in the murdering business, they needed to be seen as conducting some legitimate activity.

"Couldn't help but notice," she addressed him, in German, "that you've shown a strong resistance lately to the nose grease. Care to tell how a man so given over to spirits will change? Whence this sudden strength of character?"

He slowly bent and retrieved his book. He made her wait as he thumbed through the pages to find his place again, then replied, "Got a calling."

"By what reasoning do you call what you got a 'calling'?"

" 'Behold, thou hast driven me out this day from the face of the earth,' " he recited, without need to consult the text, " 'and from thy face shall I be hid; and I shall be a fugitive and vagabond in the earth; and it shall come to pass that every one that findeth me shall slay me. And the Lord said unto him, "Therefore whosoever slayeth Cain, vengeance shall be taken on him sevenfold. And the Lord set a mark upon Cain, lest any finding him should kill him." ' "

Almira went inside.

One autumn Saturday a customer arrived not even John Senior could drive away. She came from the southeast, straight across the prairie, mounted legs apart like a man. Her head was covered with a straw sun hat tied with a green silk ribbon, which shadowed her face until she was ready to dismount. Junior, who stood at the window describing her approach to the seated Kate, gave a snort of recognition.

"Who is it?"

"Seems it's Mary Ann Dick."

The name sent a freezing stab through Kate's belly. As she waited for the knock on the door, her thoughts flew to those gatherings on the lawn outside the church, to all those choir practices when she intermittently sought and hid from Leroy Dick. He had never showed a glimmer of reaction. And indeed, Kate would have been disappointed if he had responded like all the others. Those other slavering fools, leering and fishing with their eyes—she despised their desperation, their implicit invitation for her to take advantage of their desire. Indeed, ignoring them was her gift of mercy, as she would not raise their hopes and empty their purses. And in return for this, how they resented her. They would turn to their friends to call her a "peart whore," an "uppish bitch" giving them "the high hat." They said it fully in her hearing so that she would know the real nature of their attention.

No, Leroy Dick would never comport himself in that way. Instead, like some soaring angel, he remained too far above her to see the little torch she'd lit for him.

Mary Ann Dick was another matter. Wives, after all, soar not so high, and tend to notice things like the little tricks other women play to catch their husbands' eyes. In those moments before Mrs. Dick reached the door, as Kate sat in panicked stillness, she was sure that her desire had been noticed, that the other had come to settle her hash.

She rose. Not wanting to open the door disarrayed, she reached back to bun her hair. When the soft knock came, she drifted to the door feeling fifty pounds lighter, as if she had been emptied bodily.

"Kate," her visitor said. She had just removed her hat and was looking at her with a faint bemusement.

"Mrs. Dick! What a surprise."

"Oh, I'm sure not!"

Lightness. Emptiness. Her hair was knotted too loosely and would dislodge around her shoulders.

"Would you like to come in?"

Mary Ann was not a beautiful woman, but a formidable one whose eye level was higher than the crown of Kate's head. With her apron left at home, her solid green frock dominated the color-less room. After taking in the cabin's plain-spun amenities with a single, sweeping glance, her eyes settled on the cards on the table.

"You must know why I've come. It's all over the county."

"What is?"

"You are either very modest or very shrewd, my dear . . ." she said as Kate readied for the accusation to come. She wondered how Junior had managed to disappear so quickly.

"Must I beg?"

Mary Ann gestured at the tarot. Kate, finally understanding, flushed with relief.

"Of course! Sit down! I mean, please . . ."

Unbidden, the other sat with her back against the canvas. Just as she settled in, someone opened the cabin's back door, flooding the kitchen with a glare that back-lit every stain and imperfec-tion in the surface of the partition. Around Mrs. Dick's head there suddenly loomed a stain of bodily fluids, a halo of cranial ejecta. Showing no outward reaction, Kate kept her visitor's attention on the cards, shuffling them with a practiced slowness that lulled clients into a calm receptiveness.

The door shut; she recognized the footsteps.

"Mother, Mrs. Dick is here! Please bring coffee!"

The footsteps paused. There was a clang as Almira transferred the coffeepot to the stove.

"No need for that," Mary Ann said. "I don't want to be trouble . . . I shouldn't have come."

"Not at all."

Settling down to business, Kate learned that her customer's concerns were garden-variety—an issue of household finances, regarding the purchase of some farm equipment. As she turned over the cards she kept a close watch on the other woman, looking for any sign her questions were pretexts. But there was nothing of the jealous wife about Mary Ann Dick. Instead of insecurity, she seemed ennobled in her sturdy plainness. Moreover, there was a subtle air of pity about her, as if she took Kate for some exotic animal that had been lost among God's more viable creatures. Kate had seen this arrogance before, among the respectable women in the towns she'd visited. It rankled; she felt a temptation to read the cards uncharitably, just to get back at the woman. But she refrained, as it would have discredited her craft more than it would have educated her client.

Meanwhile, Junior had returned. He was outside, examining the quality of the tack on Mrs. Dick's horse. What he was thinking was obvious to her, as it was to the old man as he made his way from the apple orchard, wielding his shovel halfway up the shaft like the improvised weapon of some medieval farmer conscripted direct from the fields.

Almira appeared with the coffee, not so much serving the

cups as foisting them. She met Kate's eyes and asked, "*Wird sie gehen weg von hier?*"

Kate gave a single, sharp shake of her head. The very notion was unthinkable—they never took locals who might be missed or tracked to the grocery. But the hiatus had apparently made her partners desperate, and stupid. She dismissed Almira with a flick of her eyes.

As she turned up the latter cards in the spread, Kate's reading became more general. She perceived that money had always been an issue in the Dick marriage. The dispute over buying a reaper was rooted in a deep, abiding sense of mistrust. At this, Mary Ann's eyes widened slightly; planting an elbow on the table, she absently fingered a locket on a chain around her neck. The card of the High Priestess appeared in the ninth position, giving Kate pause.

"What is it?"

"She suggests a hidden element," Kate replied. "A factor hidden in mystery that may be apprehended only in stillness."

The other looked away, enacted stillness by dropping the locket.

Meanwhile, someone else opened and closed the back door. The way the floorboards creaked told Kate it was the old man back there, behind the canvas. Junior came to the front window, peering in with faint expectancy, while Almira came out and crossed her arms. Their hovering made Kate uneasy—could it be that they were set on defying her? Her thoughts raced as she read on, spinning as she considered what she would do. Mrs. Dick sat absorbed in the cards between them, strands of her straw-colored hair clinging as it grazed the partition, while behind it the old man must have been gazing at her shadow, measuring it for final hewing. The others looked on significantly in that manner that filled Kate with trembling anxiety, through which she saw their undoing as Leroy came that evening with a terrible accusation on his face that turned aside all her assurances and put their love forever beyond fulfillment. Oh! Her words became nonsense now as Mary Ann's face creased with puzzlement at this incoherence, and was that a slight rustling of the partition, a flutter in the air as an arm was cocked back?

"We need to go!" Kate exclaimed, jumping to her feet.

"Now? Why?"

"The reading is over. Come now."

Mrs. Dick allowed herself to be led out as she looked down on Kate with part-mouthed astonishment. So intent was she on Kate that she didn't notice the expressions of the other Benders, slinking and glaring back like slighted jackals. None of them followed her out of the cabin.

"There. Git on your horse and go," Kate ordered. She grasped Mary Ann's forearm so hard she left a mark on the skin.

"I feel as if I'm intruding," Mrs. Dick said as she massaged her arm.

"Not at all. If you don't feel the reading was worth my fee, take it back. Here."

And she held up her dollar, holding it contemptuously by the corners.

Mrs. Dick didn't take it. Instead, she asked, "Are you all right, my dear?"

The woman's presumption—that it was Kate who was in danger and not herself—was breathtaking. Even now, in the midst of this sacrifice, this self-abnegation in the face of love, the nobility of her sentiments was not recognized. Rage coursing through her chest, she hissed through tight lips, "I am quite fine."

"If there's something you can't tell me now, come with me. We can send for your things."

The woman was determined to be planted in the garden like a turnip! Kate, at her wit's end at how to get rid of her, laughed in her face. "How shall I convince you?" she asked. "Small minds like yours come here with no respect, like you are getting a horse shod!" She spat on the ground, then regretted it, for it was a habit she'd picked up as a child from Almira, and displayed only when she was upset and not thinking.

"You have no need to be afraid," said the other, and laid a hand on her shoulder.

Kate drew back. She uttered her next words with exaggerated precision: "Do I look like a victim to you, Mrs. Dick? You people—I can't imagine what possesses you to see me the way you do!"

With a tight smile of dismay, Mary Ann Dick turned away and stepped on the mounting block. In the saddle, she gathered her reins and looked down at Kate with an appraising eye.

"The Lord is patient," she said. "He will abide the turn of ages."

"It may take that long."

She stood and watched the other ride away, cantering into an autumn evening that seemed to shut behind her like a curtain. Suddenly the atmosphere felt close, too heavy to be squeezed from her lungs. She turned northwest and with puzzlement noted that she could discern no horizon. Instead, above an indistinct smudging of distance she saw fingers dark as denim bent-knuckled into the air. The tips rose higher, fluttering and fading as they grasped at the nape of the sky.

Junior came out and stood next to her.

"Some kind of storm?" she wondered.

"Fire."

"Brockman came before, talking about it," said Almira, who had appeared behind them. "It's been burning for days. Coming this way."

Brush fires, like locusts and hail, were inevitable hazards of prairie life. She heard tell of it from half-drunk tradesmen at the hotel—conflagrations that spanned whole counties, sheets of flame that reared and spat, burning some claims, sparing others, irrespective of fortune or circumstances. In that footsore, half-conscious state she reached at the end of her shift, it was easy for her to imagine the birth of these blazes, to see the fork of lightning or the tossed cigarette in a tuft of dry grass. She envisioned the men coming with shovels and plows, gouging out firebreaks as the line of flames approached. And she could see their despair as they halted it in one place, only to watch it spark up in ten more places downwind.

"Shall we worry?" asked Junior.

"I won't," said Almira. "My roots hain't deep."

At nightfall they gathered in front of the cabin to watch the show. When it was too dark to read, the old man laid his Bible aside and took out his pipe, packing the tobacco with a methodical grinding. Kate gazed across the weedy black expanse, listening to the peeping of the crickets that—like most humans—were oblivious to the roasting of their fellows just a few miles away. Junior chain-smoked cigarettes, the glowing cherries at their ends flaring as he inhaled. A faint, infernal luminance appeared in the distance. It brightened as she watched, driving the stars from view as it blued the sky around the rampart of smoke.

The clock chimed ten. The glow had become so strong Kate thought she could just see the glimmer of actual, licking flames.

Junior suggested the wagon be hitched; he wondered if certain items should be readied for loading. Almira said, "Well, I'm to bed."

"What, now?" Junior asked.

She laughed. "Anything happens, it won't till morning."

"I wouldn't be so sure when it comes to these things."

"Let her go," said Kate. "If the fire comes, she'll get good practice for the great by-and-by."

"Such a way with words," Almira sneered. "And as shifty as a Philadelphy lawyer."

Kate shifted to confront her. "Before you go—don't do that again." And by *that* she made clear with her eyes the untoward plans they'd all had for Mary Ann Dick. "We had a pact. Put me in that position again and I'll leave you flat. Mark my words."

She'd addressed herself only to Almira, as if the old woman was the font of all treachery and loathsomeness. The latter stood for a moment, then replied with a twist of her lips, "Yes, I believe you would, wouldn't you?"

Around midnight Kate tried to sleep. Through the small hours she got up now and then to look west: the fire seemed to burn no brighter, and faded with the dawn. The fitful night made her sleep late. Wrapping a shawl around her shoulders, she headed outside, where she found Junior talking to Rudolph Brockman. He was reclining in the seat of his wagon with one of Junior's cigarettes in his lips. His clothes were splattered with dry mud, the remains of his hair cowlicked in back and matted in front with the salt of dried sweat. He sat up when he saw her.

"Morning, Kate."

"Good morning, Rudolph."

His unabashed gaze at her morning dishabille made her wrap her shawl more tightly around herself.

"Rudolph's been out at the fire," said Junior.

"I have. Was there most of the night."

"Is that a fact?" she replied, turning northwest. There was still a haze in the distance, but the great plumes of smoke were gone. The receding of the emergency was some kind of relief, she guessed. But she also felt an odd disappointment, a sense of being deprived of an exceptional moment.

"There were fifty souls out there with picks and shovels. They dug a couple of miles of firebreaks, all by torchlight. That must have been a sight in itself, all of us out there in the middle of the devil's own desert. They had four wagons runnin' for water all night, and twenty more men spreadin' it in front of the fire. Damned if any of it did any good, with all those sparks. A fountain like ye never have seen, high than a skylark's fall."

"So how did you stop it?" asked Junior.

"They didn't," Kate interjected.

Brockman looked at her, a smile forming. "*Ja*. The wind changed a few hours before sunup. It blew the devil right back on hemself. By first light it was out."

Kate turned to go inside. "Thank you for stopping to see us, Rudolph."

When she was gone, Brockman stared after her in frank, if ambiguous, wonderment.

"You're asking how she knew about the fire," said Junior.

Brockman looked down on him as if a stone had suddenly broken out in song—and a nonsensical song at that. But Junior was not to be deterred.

"You see, she *sees* things," he declared. "How she sees is not for us to understand. She just does."

Chapter Sixteen

Burned and Breakfasted

THEY WENT OUT late in the afternoon to view the fire's aftermath. Making an excursion of it, they took a picnic lunch of bread, cheese, and smoked pork. Kate wore her church outfit and Junior his felt top hat. The old man took his shoe hammer.

Just beyond the mounds they found a fork stuck in the middle of the road, tines down. Almira had seen this before, in the highlands of Missouri and Arkansas, when someone had wanted to turn a threatening wind from their property. Here, they thought the magic might also be good for diverting fires.

Moving on, the old man drove a cartwheel over the fork, knocking it down.

"What did you do that for?" asked Kate.

The twin humps of his shoulders rose and subsided in a gesture that seemed to say, *Why not?*

Soon they reached a seared expanse, encrusted and issuing little curls of smoke like a pan of scalded milk venting through its skin. Here and there stood the remains of barns and fences the fire had overtaken, their uprights standing black and riblike. Relentless as it had been, the burning came to a sudden, inexplicable stop along a front whose position was as arbitrary as it was vast. Closer, and its smaller casualties became visible: little blackened carcasses of mice and rats who had only just escaped the hot ground, only to crawl a few feet into green grass and die. Where there were no people to deter them, crows fluttered down to pick at the banquet.

Kate sat in the bed of the wagon with her eyes on all of this but not seeing it. Her mind was still on the encounter with Mary Ann Dick. What could have possessed the woman to come to her just then? Why, on that day of all days? If her years with the cards had taught her anything, it was that there were very few coincidences, very few eventualities without some hidden significance. If she were her own client, she would have advised herself to think about how her own conduct had invited near-disaster. For it was a lie that mystics like herself blamed the stars for every turn of ill-fortune. More often, she called not for her clients to resign themselves to Fate, but to strive for self-knowledge.

However mystifying, Kate's encounter with Mary Ann Dick had one lasting consequence. To her mind, in defying Almira in particular, she had shown character, because it was something she had never done before. Scorned her, yes—shown disrespect and circumvented her intentions—of course. But this time she had looked Almira straight in the eye and shown her what's for.

At last, she had exercised the prerogative her position gave her, for the purpose of sparing a life that was, truth to tell, an obstacle to her happiness. When Kate considered her sacrifice, she felt much like a heroine in a novel, handsome and misunderstood and doomed by her nobility to a life of loneliness. It made her want to cry, this splendid gesture of hers. And it made her very pleased, for it meant she had evened the scales with Mrs. Dick. She had proved she was worthy.

Her worth was enhanced further by a remarkable incident at the Cherryvale Hotel. She had delivered a tray to a crew of rowdy railroad surveyors who proceeded to breakfast directly after a night crawling the saloons. Having separated herself from the earthy stink and grasp of the ringleader, she turned to see another patron, sitting upright with his hands around his throat. He sat alone and his face had gone dusky like a wine stain; in his eyes was the kind of panic of a man who had lost his last handhold on his way over a cliff. There was a ham steak on the plate in front of him, covered with onions and gravy and the utensils he had dropped as he began to choke.

Kate went to him at once. No longer having the breath to cough, the man was pounding his napkined chest with his fists. Kate, floating before him like the harbinger of his Maker, took his hands gently in hers. Drawn into the shining blackness of her eyes, he calmed. She laid an open hand on his cheek. As if dazzled by the glare at the threshold of Heaven, he blinked, and seemed to forget he was choking. "Only faith. Only love," she whispered, and beneath her nourishing gaze he attempted a last swallow— and succeeded.

The other diners at the ten o'clock breakfast sitting were silent. But when they saw the man was saved, his head bent forward to savor the breath she had restored, and Kate coolly retrieving her tray on her way to the kitchen, they gave her a polite round of applause. This acclaim carried her through the doors and went on for a few moments more, until she came out and made a curtain call, and the surveyors whooped and whistled, and the rest set down their coffees and cigarettes and gave her a solid ovation.

When she returned to the kitchen she found Alice Acres eyeing her. "I've been serving here since it was bare rafters," Alice remarked, "and I never had occasion to save a man's life."

"I'd just as soon left it to you."

"Didn't seem that way," Alice said, and winked.

On her handbill, Kate had claimed she could "heal all sorts of diseases; can cure blindness, fits, palsies and all such diseases." Most of these conditions, she believed, had no basis in the physical body but were manifestations of maladies of spirit. Treating them lay well within the power of the tarot, which conferred self-knowledge and therefore a power to heal that enlarged and complemented book medicine.

Saving the choking *Frühstücker* in front of witnesses established her fame like no handbill ever could. In the following days she found messages left for her at the hotel desk. At homesteads five, ten, even twenty miles away, there were agues and tremors and pustulations to treat, and colicky babies and mothers with melancholy. Men had pains in their extremities that would not ease or eyes that would not focus. One invitation described a blacksmith who had been kicked in the temple by a horse: when he regained consciousness he seemed fine, but could no longer put names to his tools. Another woman, the mad wife of a farmer beyond the Mounds, had to be tied to her bed because she refused to eat anything but chips of broken lime from the walls of their cabin.

As Kate read these appeals, she shook her head and marveled at the depth and variety of human misery. Meanwhile, Mr. Moore watched her with an impatient twitchiness about him, checking his watch. He too had never seen a waitress with these kinds of extramural skills—and was not sure he liked it.

She took all the business she could. Sometimes she would lay on hands, or recite charms derived from the *Lesser Key*; more often her services lay in simply affirming that her patients were beyond her power to heal. Yet this alone helped some of the afflicted, who revived and brightened in her presence. Desperate wives watched her caress their husbands and were glad. Windows and doors were shut to preserve the fragrance she left behind in rooms.

Though she couldn't know it at the time, this was the zenith of Kate's public regard in Labette County.

So busy did she become that she was obliged to take Junior's help in running her out to her clients. On the trail they sat mostly in silence, with Junior catching her eye when he could and Kate not giving him the opportunity, until their eyes met by accident and Junior would flush and look away. When she was at the cards or visiting sickrooms, Junior hung around outside, watering the horses and talking to the husbands and ranch hands over the trough. "That's money well spent," he would say, indicating Kate with his chin. "She's a genius. She can do some things Jesus could do."

"Is that so?"

"Cross my heart."

"Maybe she could rid my crop of those tarnation beetles, then," ventured the husband, which caused Junior to lower his head and take great interest in his horse's drinking.

Kate encountered the man when she came out. His lips were in a sly twist, his expression so untoward that she thought he was trying to be indecent. But then he said, "Howdy Jesus!" and laughed at her.

She was furious—while she was resigned to be scorned sometimes and misunderstood most, she never, ever suffered being laughed at.

When the wagon was out of earshot of the farm she rounded on Junior. "So what did you say to that man?"

"Nothing. The truth."

"The truth isn't for you to declare!" she cried. "I don't ask you to drive to keep your mouth flapping. Just drive and keep it shut."

He muttered something like "shouldn't be talking that way," but so inarticulately that Kate ignored it.

After choir practice that Sunday, and quite without planning it, Kate found herself alone with Leroy in the church. There was a nervous silence as he put away the hymnals and she pretended to tighten the bun in her hair that supported her hat. When she turned around, he was just out of arm's reach as he closed the shutters. Impulsively, just out of the urgency of her need, she came half a step forward. Her gaze skimming the floor, she felt the gravity of his presence. She raised her eyes. Only a few inches the taller, he seemed equally affected by her, setting and resetting his hat until he held it in front of him, brim curled in his sweating fist. She was affronted by this hat that existed between them—an obstacle that had suddenly sprung up between her and a prize she had not anticipated reaching quite yet but wanted now with a childlike, unreasoning intensity. She grasped the hat, giving it a halfhearted tug. He resisted, and she persisted, keeping hold of it.

The moment matured, ripened, and rotted into awkwardness. He placed his hand on hers, not as a lover, but to disengage it gently, paternally. She blushed, not watching him as he made apologetic murmurs and withdrew.

The door clanked shut. Alone, she cursed herself, flailing her fist against her thigh.

"Fool. You fool. You little fool!" she cried.

LEROY SAID NOTHING about this encounter when he got home. He did behave strangely in Mary Ann's view, however, as he discovered her and Gertrude Dienst conversing over cigarettes at the stove. He apologized and retired to his bedroom—something he never did in the afternoons.

"Odd," said Mary Ann.

"A lot's been odd since the new neighbors," Mrs. Dienst remarked, eyes cast down and away in the posture she usually adopted for passing along stories.

"Well, out with it then."

"Not much to tell, really. The Moneyhon baby has taken colic, I hear. Quite sudden it seems. Never been that way before."

"Well if the county turned on its ear every time a babe had a bad night . . ."

"True, but that's not all. We've ourselves got a clock that won't run. It stopped the other day, right around when *she* did her latest miracle in the hotel. Father's been at the works every night, but nothing's for it. It won't turn."

"Hmm."

"And there's more," Mrs. Dienst said, and coming closer, went on sotto voce: "Billy Toles can't get nothing from his cows. All of 'em are as dry as week-old pats. And you know what he says he saw when he was in sight of the Bender place?"

"What?"

"She was *wringing out rags* over a milking bucket. Wringing the milk from *his* cows." And she leaned back after that as if to enjoy the spectacle of Mary Ann's reaction.

She laughed. "I didn't think anybody believed in that kind of witchery anymore!"

"Call it what you want, but isn't it odd that they always have as many stores as they need, but keep hardly any animals?"

"Maybe they buy their stores."

"On what income? If they get ten paying customers up there a month they get a thousand."

"I don't know."

"That's what I'm trying to tell you."

Mary Ann regarded the ashes at the tip of her smoke before flicking them into the stove. She wasn't one to set stock in stories of charms and curses and necromancy. But nor could she deny that there was a foul air around the Bender claim, which she had experienced herself. Afraid of seeming foolish, she never told her friend about her reading with Kate Bender. After all, believing that cows could be milked at a distance was one thing, but admitting she had personally sought esoteric advice on her personal affairs was quite another. And so she muted her skepticism. Taking Mary Ann's silence as agreement, Gertrude felt entitled to believe her own gossip.

Tales of odd goings-on became as common as buffalo grass in the neighborhood and spread faster. George Mortimer, who had learned of the Bender rumors thirdhand from Mrs. Dienst and his wife, suddenly reported that his rifle wouldn't shoot straight. No matter how much he fiddled with the sight, testing it on targets, his shot would always drift to the left when he shot at anything live. On hearing of this charmed gun, his friends were moved to perceive their own signs, like horseshoes suddenly found arms down, spilling their good fortune from their crooks. When none of the Benders were around, conversation revolved around them; when they were present, it dwelled on such obvious inanities, like the hymn chosen for the Sabbath service, that even Junior wondered if everyone had gone simple.

Or gone mad, as Kate suspected when she got home from church one Sunday to find the train of her skirt crusted with salt. On seeing this, Almira stood back and sucked in her breath.

"I've seen that before in a camp in the *stade* of Kentucky," she said. "You are marked a consort of the devil, *Frau Doktor Professor.*"

Junior held up a polished brass pot lid for Kate to see herself. The salt had been spread on the pew just before she sat down. If it stuck, it was supposed to prove she was a witch—and there was much salt stuck in the folds of her skirt. She had encountered such superstitions before in a hundred mining and logging camps from Appalachia and to the Sierras, the primitive craft of ignoramuses who understood nothing of the subtleties of gnostic science. There was scarcely a tent of a whore and fishwife that didn't have its devices, its evil-turning charms. She pitied them.

And yet, she couldn't allow herself to come under attack without some kind of response. As she was changing out of her soiled clothes, and poured a draught of tepid water over the nape of her neck at the washbasin, she considered her occult options. But there was really only one—the same one as when she prepared the spot on the wall for the "glyphs."

The rest of them were soon gathered in the cabin, watching at a discreet remove as Kate drew on the boards with a piece of charcoal. The figure she rendered was based on a figure from the *Lesser Key*: a hermaphroditic homunculus with big head, gangling limbs, bull's-eyes for breasts, and oversized penis.

Almira and Junior were silent, pupils of a teacher introducing incomprehensible math. But then they heard a strange sound—an odd, rhythmic rasping, as if something had struck a rat funny. All of them, including Kate at the wall, turned to the old man: he was slouching there with legs crossed, pipe in hand and poised as his lips cracked open to show wet, black gums. The way his mouth bent, and the otherworldly sawing that came out of it, indicated something remarkable: he was laughing.

Kate glared at them all in turn, disdaining their coarseness. She couldn't make them understand the technology—some minds were too primitive for such things—but she could still protect them with it. When she was satisfied with the figure, she stepped back, raised hands with palms open to the wall and recited:

"Dullix, ix, ux. Yea, you can't come over Pontio; Pontio is above Pilato . . ."

THE THREAT TO Kate's reputation was followed by word of missing travelers, last seen somewhere on the trail between Independence and Fort Scott. All of them were males, on the trail alone, and most were not important enough for formal inquiries to be made. When private investigators or family members did nose about, blame naturally fell on Indians and road agents and animal attacks. Local inns, like the Benders', were never the first objects of suspicion.

Rumors of lost spirits increased the sense that some malefic air had settled over the county. These were precisely the kinds of things that happened when the wrong types were allowed to ply their trades among God-fearing folk. No one believed at first that Kate Bender had anything directly to do with the disappearances. But the disappearances put everyone on edge, and willing to believe the worst about matters far smaller and meaner. Two days after Gertrude Dienst told Mary Ann Dick about the "bewitched" cows, Billy Toles shot three of them. "I'll be damned if I fill a witch's bucket a day longer!" he declared. The next week, Kate went to church with Almira and Junior. There was something different this time. Her male neighbors had always been wont to sneak her subtle glances or whisper untoward comments just beneath her hearing. But now it seemed all pretense to civility had been dropped. Men made their impertinences directly to her face. Behind the backs of their wives, mothers, and daughters, they gestured acts she couldn't understand but sensed insulted her modesty. Almira noticed them too and was none too happy to explain each outrage in detail.

"The miners used that face when they wanted a cocksucking but could not ask for it," she explained. "Do you know this, cocksucking?"

"Yes, I know," Kate growled, her cheeks flashing red. Despite her convictions, it made her uneasy to hear such a foul word used casually, on consecrated ground.

"You know it only from books, I think!"

After the service, as she strolled the yard to make the customary pleasantries with the women, she was met with glacial coolness. Mrs. Dienst smiled and saluted but her eyes refused to see her; the Moneyhon and Mortimer women offered up nothing but curt nods. Mary Ann Dick, who certainly understood the secret they shared, seemed atypically withholding, and then rushed off to stay by Leroy's side, which she had never done in all the months Kate had attended services.

And so it appeared the rumors of witchcraft had had their usual effect: when a young woman was convicted in the public mind, the respectable ladies of the community shunned her, and the men suddenly felt themselves freed from all scruples. Especially galling were the hardened attitudes of the women who had sought her advice, in some cases just a week before. To her courtesies, to her professional discretion with her secrets, they repaid her with contempt.

It was an occupational hazard of faith healers that their patrons were indebted to them. Indeed, a practitioner's very effectiveness depended on a spiritual potency she had and her patrons lacked. Consulting her made them feel their inadequacy. Kate had seen it all before and took it in stride.

None of this really mattered to her as long as Leroy was there. With relief, she turned away from those small minds, those peasants, the broke-down purple wars. He was standing by the chapel doors, conversing with effortless affability with this or that person as his sculptured, tendoned hands grasped his hymnal. Seeing him, she could not help but love this ideal, this model of effortless virility. For look at him, the calm radiance about his person that charmed and entranced all about him. His physicality beguiled her—it was the perfect complement to the spiritual power she had cultivated within herself. How could she not love him? How could ordinary women not love him, if only in their dull, bovine ways, offering him only those benefactions of the flesh any woman could?

Kate imagined Mary Ann Dick attempting to please him—or imagined it as best she could, for lack of direct experience. For as many times as she had glimpsed Almira in the act, the latter had never sold Kate herself, never let her lure be snatched. And with Almira it was always a brief, stinking, violent act—a shoving, hurried thing, with the two grunting and the adipose waves coursing up varicose, puckered thighs. It disgusted Kate, and it disgusted her still more how much the men enjoyed it. Dogs performed the act with more dignity in the streets.

And so she moved toward him, unconscious of the space between them, the puddle of tobacco spit she strode upon, or her own body. She was aware only of the eyes that beheld him, and her throat burning for lack of the right words. As she approached, she saw him turn, saw his eyes settle on her. It was as if someone had opened an umbrella inside her chest, so fast did her heart swell.

"Good morning, Leroy. Missus Dick," she said, choosing her words deliberately. For him, she offered familiarity, the warmth of open arms and the female bosom; for his wife, a bland formality.

"Miss Bender," replied Leroy. And his eyes did not avert but dwelled on her in a way that thrilled her at first. But as they fixed her for second after silent second, she grew afraid. For there was no response there to her summons, no heat. Only a blankness that felt like a dismissal. That, and a note of incomprehension in the set of his lips. With that glance, she felt totter the entire edifice of her hopes. Her voice shook as she took the hint, saying, "A lovely sermon today from the minister, wasn't it?"

"Yes, lovely," replied Mary Ann, staring.

"Good morning, then."

"Good morning."

Kate turned away and proceeded directly to the wagon. She kept smiling and walked with the unhurried ease expected of the occasion.

He doesn't love me.

Her legs felt alien to her now, foreign mechanisms she was obliged to work. There was some tissue rending in her that ran from her chest to her groin and back again. Junior appeared beside her, offering his hand as she stiffly mounted the seat. She saw his lips move but expected nothing of his words and didn't hear them. He knew enough to drive her home without speaking again.

He doesn't love me.

In the yard beside the cabin, Almira watched from the wash-tub as Kate alighted without waiting for Junior to help her down. She ran inside without saying anything, affliction flashing on her face. If other tantrums from years before were any guide, she expected Kate to fall on her bed and cry into the bedclothes until she tired and fell asleep. In the middle of the night she might wake and start again—lamenting her loneliness, beseeching her father to come and rescue her, until Almira yelled across the room for her to shut up or be strangled by morning.

Chapter Seventeen

I Will Be Reckoned With

KATE WAS TOO ill the next day to go to work. Nor did she show up at the hotel for the next three days. Instead, she lingered in bed from late afternoon to late morning, reading as long as the light lasted, staring at the wall as the gloom rose and Almira lit the lamp. Kate knew what Almira was expecting: an eruption of emotion that would mark her as weak, as defeated by circumstances she was foolish enough to challenge. She perceived her watching from the stove, spitefully anticipating.

But Kate would not gratify Almira. Instead of weeping, she kept a studious, monkish silence. And indeed, a life of penitent devotion appealed to her. Unappreciated by modernity, she came to think she had missed her proper century, that her soul was intended for a better, more profound time. In a nunnery—or better yet as her male counterpart in one of the great monasteries of Europe—she would have been free from the petty preoccupations of shopkeeps and hoteliers. With nothing expected of her but to pray, she could have studied the ancient classics, written masses and cantatas and requiems, become expert in mineralogy or entomology or icon painting. The potential range of her endeavors would have been so limitless, so grand compared to her life in that tiny, miserable cabin, that she felt the impulse to cry over her thwarted career. But this was exactly what she would not do in front of Almira.

And then, of course, there was the object of the praying, to that Nazarene and his entourage of hypocrites. That would not have suited her. But she guessed she wouldn't have been the only one in the rectory who secretly despised that figure on the cross. Everyone made his compromises.

On the fourth day she got up, stripped to her shift, and bathed herself on the back porch. She used the wooden tub in which they mixed water and lye and meat drippings to make soap, still ringed with grease. When she was done, she felt not so much clean as marinaded, the soap leaving an acrid odor and a glossy sheen on her skin. After dressing, she donned her sun hat and walked the seven and a quarter miles to Cherryvale, picking wildflowers along the way to decorate the tables she would wait upon. When she arrived at the hotel, she was tired but in good spirits, glowing with perspiration and soap drippings, and not thinking of Leroy Dick at all.

Mr. Moore looked up, drinking in the image of her as he usually did. But there was a glassy impassivity in his eyes and a reticence about his mouth that she had never seen in him before. She put it down to her unexplained absence.

"Aren't these pretty?" she remarked, presenting the flowers to him. "The lobelia are in bloom, and these are coreopsis."

"Welcome back," he said, in a tone not welcoming at all. Now that she was close she saw the tiny beads of sweat peeking from the pores over his mouth.

"What's this, Jeremiah? I lay up sick for a few days and you don't remember me?"

"Couldn't forget you, Kate," he said, fidgeting, "except—might you step back here for a moment?"

He crooked a thumb toward his office. Kate, still determined to make light of the situation, offered her elbow for him to escort her, saying, "I'm not sure a proper lady would accept such an invitation. Shall I fetch a chaperone?"

Moore gave a perfunctory laugh. But when the door was closed he dropped her arm and retreated behind the bulky bankers' desk he had imported from Chicago. On the day it was delivered, she had swept the road dust off it for him, polished it, and placed a vase of daisies next to the blotter. Now its function was only to keep a safe distance between them.

"What's on your mind?" she said, concealing her unease by unfastening the buttons on her gloves.

"You should know we've had complaints about certain members of our staff. I usually pay no mind to such talk, but when it becomes serious enough to cost us business, any responsible manager is compelled to act."

"Members of your staff . . . such as myself?"

"You should know I consider myself less beholden to petty moralizing than the typical businessman in this camp. I've spent my share of time in Chicago, New York, Philadelphia. But a liberality of mind can never be an excuse for bad business. And any competent proprietor must take account of sentiment in the community."

"What are they saying about me?"

He sat down, laying his hands athwart the crest of his belly.

"It scarcely bears repeating. I don't credit most of it."

"Are they calling me a witch, Jeremiah?"

He fixed her with his eyes. The suggestion had surprised him.

"No, not at all. No—there's talk of certain transactions occurring in the rooms, of a personal nature. The kind of thing that brings down the reputation of an establishment."

So they were calling her a harlot. In a way, she was disappointed by the quality of the lies against her. To traffic in black magic at least conveyed a certain formidability; to be a public whore was to suffer a common, passive sort of disrepute. Any woman could open her legs and ruin herself in that way. It was her impression many did.

"Who is saying these things to you? The wives? Mary Ann Dick?"

"I don't think it proper to say."

"Not proper to say? And yet it's proper to level such demeaning charges? Are these the fruits of your liberality? To insult me and my family? To think what my father would say when he finds out. And my poor mother . . ." And she let her voice catch, her eyes to mist. Moore shot to his feet immediately, kerchief at the ready. To accuse a young woman of public venality was one thing, but to allow her to weep into her bare hand was unthinkable.

"Er, you should also know that I never approved of my employees distributing handbills to guests. The nature of your . . . side concern . . . is none of my business. But I would like to think I control which services are presented at this hotel."

"Do you care if it's true?"

"What is true?"

"What they say about me."

He sat down again and resumed his pensive posture. "It doesn't matter. Things like this take on a life of their own."

"So there's nothing I can say to convince you?"

"I'm sorry. There's nothing you can say."

And there it was: a certain stress he laid on the words *you can say*, as if there was something else she might *do* for him instead. But he was halfhearted, as if the proposition was something he had just thought of on the spot. They stared at each other, she in frank astonishment, he in rising embarrassment, flushing to the crown of his bald head.

"I'm disappointed to hear that, Jeremiah. I know I've allowed myself to be familiar with you, because I felt comfortable doing so. But I see now I've overestimated your quality as a man. Today, you have shown yourself as nothing other than a shit coward—a shit coward who can't even bring himself to make an indecent proposition. Good day."

Moore parted his lips as if to make a rejoinder—but thought better of it. His face was not only flushed now but a deep shade of purple. It was the same color as the flaccid organ of that miner she had seen dead in Almira's tent.

She collected the few items she had left in the pantry—an apron, a book of poems for slow hours on the job, a bonnet for sunny days on the walk home. As she came out, she caught the eyes of Alice Acres; there was a gleam of recognition at first, and a softening as if in sympathy. But then a shadow fell over them, like a crypt walled in for good. Kate didn't speak to her and was hailed by no one as she crossed the lobby and stepped onto the planks of the sidewalk.

Standing there, she noticed that none of the men were giving her the usual eye, the once-over each performed according to his skill. It was a relief and also unnerving, this sudden revulsion she perceived in everyone around her. For the first time she yearned to see Junior's devoted gaze as he waited for her in the wagon. But she had long ago broken him of this courtesy.

She remained impassive as she walked out of town and into the prairie. But when she was alone her face cracked. Unwilling to betray her feelings to the crickets and grass stalks, she clapped her hand over her mouth and gave up a convulsed sob. The trail ahead of her became blurry, and the leathery smell under her nose was redoubled as her tears wet her kid-clad fingers.

It wasn't until she passed the Brockman place and glimpsed the mounds that she felt her mood shift. Instead of wretched, she became determined. For working an inconsequential job in some minor town had never been her purpose. Her horizons had always been wider than other people's, the quality of her ambition grander and finer. If they didn't want her, so much the worse for them! Their petty, ignorant smugness would be repaid in full, in a different coin than they'd ever suspect.

Approaching the door of the Bender cabin, her cheeks dried by the afternoon breeze, she knew for certain that her time was at hand. For her audacity, for her uniqueness among the dullards and rubes and puffed-up moralizers, she had to be destined for renown. They would reckon with her.

She found Almira beside the stove, scouring her stew pot with sand and elbow grease. She looked at Kate in the half-inquiring, half-accusing way she had greeted her for years. Kate responded with her usual weary disdain, turning away to unpin her hat.

"Back early today."

"You miss nothing," said Kate.

"Ready to get back to work?"

Damn her, what does she see in me? Kate wondered. Without looking back, she strode toward the back door and, with the kind of dramatic pause she had seen among hack actors, delivered a line over her shoulder:

"Maybe."

THE DICKS PUT off the purchase of a new reaper for another year. The decision was reached by default, as the couple's communication had become less frequent, more wary. For as long as they'd known each other, they had spoken more profoundly by touch than by words. Though Mary Ann had thought him pretty enough in his youth, she had not truly fallen for him until that moment when he handed her up to her seat in her father's buggy. The sensation of his fingers grasping hers had made her so weak at the knees she could barely manage the climb. For the first time she felt what the other girls saw in Leroy. Embarrassed by these feelings, she turned her face away from him and murmured her farewell so indistinctly that Leroy thought he had somehow offended her.

Standoffish around him, she became ever more an object of fascination to the young Leroy, who was all too used to batted lashes and fans snapped shut in his presence. Needing to pursue a woman seemed to him as absurd a notion as feeding a prairie dog. Yet this new desire appealed to him: where his effortless popularity had given him an air of indolent, almost feminine passivity, the pursuit of a goal focused his energies in a way that made him feel more of a man. Even his father perceived the change in him, and approved.

He wooed Mary Ann in the customary ways, starting with chaste walks around the churchyard after services. Then he moved on to gallant offers to dance at barn-raisings and weddings, and twilight walks among the cornstalks, fingers entwined. As she seemed to yield, Leroy realized that he had not offended her after all. She was, in fact, like all the other girls, flattered by his presence. But she was also different, seeming to take his interest as some bit of undeserved but unnecessary good luck bestowed on her by the universe. She wanted him, but if she couldn't have him, she would survive. Next to the emotional fireworks he had seen in certain other girls, her fatalism was refreshing. The stakes of spending time with her seemed lower, without tension. Before long he came to look forward to this ease in her company. When their conversation inevitably turned to his ultimate intentions, the prospect of marriage didn't appeal to him, exactly. But he couldn't stomach the thought of losing her to someone else either.

They were wed in the same church where both attended Sunday school, wearing the same clothes they were confirmed in. His best man was his brother Temple. Though older, Temple had not yet found a bride. The way he glowered through the service, a frown cracking his features along the latticework of his scars, showed that he was not happy to have been beaten to the altar by his little brother. When the time came for him to deliver the ring to the groom, he fumbled around his breast pocket, pretending he had forgotten it. But when Mary Ann stiffened with disapproval and a stir went through the crowd, Temple forgot his japes and handed over the hardware.

There was a lot Leroy waited to tell her until after they married. He started with the sad tale of Ernest Tubbs and his ill-fated stay at the Dick farm. She was the first person not directly involved in the affair he had ever discussed it with, and he did it with the relief of a man guarding a secret for too long. She listened with the patience requisite for Kansas brides, who had collectively heard almost as many tales of sabotage, murder, and rape done in the Territory as had been committed. And like virtually all her sisters, she forgave her man his trespasses. For lying there in her bridal shift, the bed still stained with the gift of her maidenhood, what else could she possibly do? As much as any gunman coming off the prairie with his weapon drawn, she was committed.

When his confession turned to his jayhawking days in the '60's, though, her mood changed. As Leroy described the moonlight attacks, the chases, the shootouts and the corpses, a hardness came over her face. As he kept talking, her features froze into a pitiless mask, her eyes retreating into their sockets like an idol to some unyielding god.

He plunged on a little longer, describing the sickness that had come over him as he looked on the bodies of the men he had killed. He recounted how he, Fess, and Bannerman had tried to soldier on after the massacre, tangling with Defensives and secessionists all over the county, but the relish had gone out of the enterprise for him. After Quantrill sacked Lawrence in '64, the three of them swore sacred vengeance for the two hundred killed there. They rode hard for four days, pursuing the bushwhackers south, until something almost perceptibly broke in Leroy's heart. Suddenly, he had nightmares that woke him from cold, cadaverous sleeps— woke him in total darkness when the fires in their bivouacs had gone out and the stars were hidden away behind blank overcast. There was a particular terror in that, the plunging from night-mare to total darkness that refused to betray if he was asleep or waking. It got so bad, he confessed, that he stopped embarking on rides that would keep him out overnight on moonless nights. He took a lot of ridicule from his partners on that, his confession of weakness in the face of the enemy. But the enemies he was fighting were no longer the two-legged kind.

As he told her this, the way she drew back from him finally caused him to stop and wait. Into the ensuing silence crept the clicking of a locust outside the window, measuring off the moments in a lazy, chilled cadence. It had almost fallen silent, like a watch coming to the end of its wind, when Mary Ann spoke:

"Why are you telling me this?"

Those six words were enough. In reply to his vulnerability, to the blackest hollows of his heart, they froze him. But she wasn't finished:

"Because I don't want to hear it. It is unworthy of my husband. I don't care who has not the benefit of God's good grace as a result of your actions. I don't care what side you were on. The Negroes can rot under the ground they worked for all I care, and the Union too. But no husband of mine will not show me that kind of weakness again. Do you understand?"

Too humiliated to look at her, he nodded at the bedclothes.

"Good. Now come and put it in me again. Until I get to like it."

Chapter Eighteen

Necessity

I'll dye my petticoats red,
And face them with the yellow
I'll tell the dyster's lad
I follow the Lichtbob fellow

— "Katy Cruel"

PERHAPS OUT OF pity, or perhaps because it seemed too good to be true, none of the other Benders questioned why Kate didn't go into Cherryvale anymore. They made preparations instead. Junior spruced up the front of the grocery, policing trash and nailing loose boards and generally making the establishment plausible again. The old man mounded up more man-sized furrows in the orchard. Almira gathered ingredients for one of her signature stew pots—the kind that smelled good, but she never bothered to sample for taste because no one was ever intended to survive the first spoonful.

The next candidates appeared that very afternoon—another

father and son. They were dressed in identical heavy black woolens, wearing low caps with shallow brims over their eyes. Back on the trail they left their horse, a gray with a sway back and a mountain of impedimenta. Junior's eyes lit up as he imagined the possibilities buried in all that loot; the old man, glad to be confronted with an opportunity to ply his trade, cracked his dry and mollusklike lips, a grin from the bottom of the bilge.

"*Добрый вечер. Можем ли мы приобрести некоторые результаты от вас?*" asked the father.

"What do you say, friend?" Kate asked.

"*Я сказал, мы можем купить коробку спичек?*" And he began to make a stroking motion in the air, as if plucking an invisible harp.

"We speak English. Or German. *Sprechen Sie Deutsch?*"

She shrugged, turned back to Almira as if to turn the problem over to her.

"At least we know they aren't from around here," said Almira.

"Bound to be something worth the freight in all that kit," observed Junior.

"Careful." Kate looked at the boy, who stared back not with his father's expectant incomprehension but something like amusement. It was likely the child knew more English than his paw.

"What are you waiting for?" demanded Almira. "Invite them!"

She looked at them for a long minute, measuring her reluctance against the pair's appealing naiveté. The death of a child was a crime that couldn't be rationalized so easily. And she still suffered a dull, remnant ache in her chest from her recent setbacks.

"No. I won't."

"Kate."

"Figure out what he wants and get rid of them."

As if her command was in the perfectly good Russian, the father stepped tentatively to the counter, reached out and plucked a box of matches from the shelf.

"*Матчи. Сколько это стоит?*"

"Take it. Go."

After checking that there were indeed matches in the box, the visitor flashed an obliged grin, touching a finger to his cap, and left. The boy lingered a moment.

"Wery pleased it's it," he gabbered. "Thanks you. Thanks you!"

When they were gone, Almira stood over Kate as she lay in bed.

"Them boxes cost a nickel each."

Kate turned from her pillow and through the tangle of her hair replied, "More than the lot of us is worth."

Almira snorted and disgorged a bolus of German curse words in the general direction of Junior, who looked back without offense or comprehension. When she was gone, he continued to stare at Kate. Before long the weight of his scrutiny became too much for her.

"John, we've talked about this."

Junior got to his feet, snatched his hat from the table. He took a couple of steps toward the door, then stopped and looked at her again.

"What *can* you be staring at?" she exclaimed.

"You don't have to let it go on like that," he said. "That Dick feller don't deserve you. If you want, I can make him pay."

She regarded him, not entirely sure what he was suggesting but suspecting it might appeal to her if she listened anymore.

"Get out," she said, and turned her face to the pillow.

LATER, THE OLD man gave the signal from outside. Kate went on sitting at the table, idly turning over her cards as the others scurried to their places. She didn't rise until the knock came at the door. Standing, she propped her hands into the small of her back and stretched. Another knock. She crossed to the door slowly, not caring if they waited, not bothering to straighten her hair or her apron.

She opened the door poised to deliver the usual welcome—but felt the words lodge in her throat when she saw the man waiting there. He was older, of course, and shorter, and dressed in a more citified way than last time they met, in knee-length overcoat and shiny square-toed street shoes. He had his saddlebag slung over his shoulder, its fine silver rivets shining in the light pouring from the cabin. His throat was cosseted by a silk scarf the color of new greenbacks; at his hip was a silver-plated pistol with an ivory handle, set in a tooled holster.

This was a man who had certainly come up in the world. In place of the old leanness, the filling out of many years and many good meals. Around hale and shaven cheeks, sideburns of mature, almost professorial gray. But the eyes were unchanged. They were the same chilly blue, that same gleaming pitiless facade. Their bottomlessness still chilled her, the sense that she was staring through a hole in the ice toward an azure lake that could have been mere feet away, or a thousand miles. A surface that reflected nothing, including the woman standing in front of him. He showed no sign of remembering her.

"You've come just in time," she remarked, armored with her smile.

"Don't get any ideas," grumbled Clarrity, "that I'm hard up 'cause it's dark. I can ride just as far as I please."

"I don't doubt it. I meant to say the good luck is ours."

He came in without waiting to be invited. As he looked the place over, the slightest sneer of disapproval came over his face. His pack hit the table with a metallic clang as it slipped off his shoulder—a sound that set Junior's eyes dancing with anticipation. Junior's feet barely seemed to touch the ground as he went out to tend to the rich newcomer's horse.

"Got anything to drink?"

"Some cider, I think. Harder stuff too."

"Good. Funny you haven't asked me my name. Do we know each other?"

In her disquiet, Kate moved like the marionette of a distracted puppeteer. "Why don't you tell me?" she asked.

He narrowed his eyes. "Don't think so. I would of remembered a proper piece of trail bait like you. So what do you serve here?"

"Just a fine meal, and a place by the fire for the night if you're in need."

"I'm in need of more than that. But I'll take the hash for now."

She coped with an unaccustomed tangle of feelings as she faced Clarrity again. Showing him to the table, bidding him take the spot of honor beside the canvas, she felt suddenly deprived of all her accumulated wisdom. Before him, she felt herself shrivel to girlhood. She was in that hallway again, back against her father, confronted again with the man's mulish sneer and arrogant stink—albeit masked this time by some blossomy cologne he might have picked up in the upscale shops in Denver. She felt diminished, but at the same time charged with a kind of anticipation that made each breath seem sweeter, her teeth sharper, her stomach twist amidst the cords of her innards. For he was entering her sphere now, embarked on a path she had designed. He was the hapless one now, tied to a fate whose string trailed into darkness.

"Mother makes the best stew pot in southeastern Kansas," she said.

He fetched up a little laugh that said "the best in southeastern Kansas is as good as the best nowhere at all." That irritated her, but she had the presence of mind to intercept Almira before she rounded the partition with the bowl. Clarrity was nothing at all to Junior or the old man, but Kate knew that Almira had known him longer than she had, in ways she'd had no occasion to experience. He would recognize Almira, and by association he would recognize her too, and the consequences of that she could not foresee.

"What's the matter?" asked Almira, who was loath to give up the stew.

"Just stay back and keep your mouth shut," Kate whispered. She glanced at Flickinger. The old man was in position, smoothing the head of his hammer like a fastidious man tending a cracked fingernail.

She watched Clarrity for a while after she set down the bowl. His wardrobe had improved but not his table manners. He held the spoon with a tweezer-like grip at the base of the handle, so close to the stew it stained his fingertips. The spoonfuls went into his mouth at such a rapid pace he hardly seemed to have time to breathe. When he did exhale, it was to give a deep, rumbling, wet belch, the wind of his eruption striking Kate full in the face.

She smiled. "I'd ask if you like the stew, but I don't think I have to."

He pushed the near-empty bowl away and leaned back as if to rest, until the canvas yielded under his weight and he bolted upright again.

"Anything would do after a day on this damnable desert. Lord what dull country! I'd sooner shoot myself than stake a claim here."

She leaned closer, practically inviting him to recognize her. In the way she'd known to beguile her guests, she shook her hair from her shoulders so it broke in a slow wave around her cheeks. She said, "You must see much finer places on your travels."

"What makes you say that?"

"Oh, see enough travelers comin' through, you get a sense for these things."

"Do you?" he mocked, then bit off the end of an uncut cigar and spat it on the floor. He pinched at his vest pocket for a box of matches; before Kate could summon him, Junior was at his side with the light struck. Clarrity accepted the favor without acknowledgment, like a man used to being waited upon. Instead, he kept his gaze locked on Kate, until a smile broke on his face that revealed a row of green, rot-stripped teeth.

"We *have* met, haven't we?" he said.

"I'm insulted, sir, that you need to ask."

"St. Louis? Chicago? Denver?"

"I couldn't put a name to the camp."

He puffed grandly, "Well, I must have made an impression, if you still remember me."

"You did. There aren't many who would forget the man who kidnapped them."

"Oh, you might be surprised what folks are prepared to forget!" He laughed. "With the proper incentive."

"Is that so? What are you offering?"

He gave her a long look, as if to confirm that she was serious. As he did so, she perceived the instant when he recognized her:

there was a momentary widening of his eyes, a brief unfurling of the whites. Then he vented, hiding behind the smoke as it wrapped around his head. When he came visible again, his sneer was back.

"I must say this is strange hospitality, young lady! Accusing a man of a hangin' crime not ten minutes after he sets at your table . . ."

"By certain measures, we've shown better hospitality to you than most."

"And besides," he went on, as if not hearing her, "I don't recall any kidnapping. It was more in the line of a business arrangement—of relieving a man of unwanted freight in exchange for a debt. It happens every day."

"You lie every day," she retorted. The suggestion that her father was complicit in Clarrity's crime kinked her viscera.

"Careful who you call a liar."

He then showed her what she had been too preoccupied to notice: his unholstered pistol held at gut level, though not yet pointed at her.

It didn't scare her. Instead, that he feared for his safety—feared *her*—gave Kate a definite sense of satisfaction. Raising her hands to where he could see them, she reached for his bowl.

"You seem to like the stew. Want more?"

"I would, if I were the devil's own fool."

"You're kin to the devil, but I wouldn't call you no fool. Besides, if I was going to poison you, wouldn't I have done it already?"

"Maybe. But I'd just as soon be on my way."

"Suit yourself. But just one question before you go . . ."

He snuffed out his cigar against the tabletop and smiled. "You know, even as a nipper you loved the sound of your own voice. Never let it be said I begrudged a lady her due. Ask your question."

Thus invited, she hesitated, as she hadn't anticipated this opportunity. When the words failed to resolve in her mind, she flushed—for so profound was her loathing of this man, and so deep her wound, she could not find a single question worthy of her feelings.

"Come on, then. Or has a life of whoring made you stupid?"

"Did you . . . ever think," she began, measuring out her words, "what it would feel like to suffer what you did to others? Did it ever cross your mind, the harm you caused?"

He seemed to ponder this as he tapped the loose ashes from his cigar and tucked it in his breast pocket. Then he gave her a twisted smile that seemed to cleave his face right up the cheek and through his mocking eye.

"Don't have to think about it. I've only ever done what's been done to me—no more and no less. You think you had it so bad, girl? Let me tell you how my folks celebrated my fifteenth birthday. My pap started with boxing my ears bloody. Then he broke my left wrist twisting my arm back. After that he put a gun in my right hand and told me to go ahead, air out his guts. I couldn't, so he put the muzzle against his breast and screamed in my face to pull the trigger. I dropped it. He called me a woman. Called me a low-down gutless worm for not murdering him. Then he picked up the gun and told me that was all the educatin' I would need in this world. And I was out that day, without two pennies to rub together.

"You had it so bad? At least I gave you somebody other than your own pap to blame. There's a blessing in that, after a fashion."

He paused, gauging her reaction as he scratched under his chin with his gunsight. When the pistol came down, it was still not pointed at her.

"Even so, what's the use in thinking about it? It's the way the world's made. Does the painter hink it over before she puts her claws in a buck deer? Surely not. That's a good way to go hungry, and leave her cubs hungry too. Where would the mercy be in it?

"A painter's an animal," she replied. "You are a man."

"A peculiarity that makes no difference at all."

Now it was her turn to deal him an ambiguous smile. "You declared it," she said. "Not me."

He was opening his mouth to reply when Almira rounded the partition. As the two old acquaintances locked eyes, Almira fetched up short and, in a girlish gesture, crossed her arms as if to insulate herself from him. Momentarily astonished, Clarrity softened his posture, letting his head brush the canvas.

A strange, inhuman cry sounded behind the partition, like the strangling of a vulture. When the blow fell, a fine mist of blood exploded, leaving a Clarrity-shaped outline on the canvas as his head snapped forward. He sat there for a moment, trembling. His expression was less one of agony than puzzlement, like a man who had mislaid his pocket watch. Then, in a slow, twisting swoon, he found his place on the floor.

What followed this, the first Bender murder in four months, was both the same and unlike the others. The old man rounded the partition right away, hammer in hand, to make sure the deed was complete. Junior cleared the table away from the trapdoor. They opened the cellar and rolled Clarrity below as Almira looked on with an expression of dispassionate appraisal. Kate gave her a glance that asked, *Is he anything to you?*

"Make sure to go through *all* of his pockets this time," she said to no one and everyone, and retreated to her post by the hearth.

Clarrity hit the slab with a mixture of hollow thud and metallic clang. Junior rolled up his sleeves to follow, but Kate stopped him. "No. I'll do it this time."

Having spent too long around a laundry pot in her time, she would not risk getting her clothes splattered. She stripped naked in the sight of God and the devil and all the demons in between as Junior, halfway between shock and wonder, bore witness. When her chemise had passed over her head and she stood bare-breasted before him, Junior became desperate to quit the place, wagging his head from side to side as if to avoid staring at her—but with eyes swiveling in their sockets to keep her in view.

She quashed an impulse to laugh at him, as the occasion was serious enough, and even a villain like Clarrity deserved a sober murdering.

"Give me the knife."

He passed her, handle first, one of the ivory-clad table knives they had picked up in Humboldt. She weighed it for a moment, feeling it become slick with the sweat of her palm. Below, there was nothing to see but a man-sized blot of darkness against the somewhat lighter gloom of the sandstone. Was she simply going to leap into the pit? She had never done this before, and she had not thought it through. She stood there, the blade scratching against the stubble of her unshaven leg as she considered the embarrassment of giving the knife back to Junior.

But then she heard a laugh—a derisive, phlegmy cackle that turned up the hairs at the nape of her neck.

"What's the matter, Duchess?" said Almira. "Too good to butcher your own pork?"

"Shut up."

"Then do it. Do it now."

She stepped off. In anger, in spite, in revenge, and in her haste to get away from her companions, she fell through air. And in the instant she floated above the aperture she felt a sensation not of plunging but of belonging, of snapping into place. The other killings were acts of complication, adding more knots of lies to the weft of the universe. John Jesperson and Hiram the Mormon and the others would not be missed here, but they would be missed someplace, the consternation caused by their individual fates adding to the sum of fear and ignorance stalking the land. Necessity had damned them, but their ends had created only more necessity. Grief and rage. Hope and retribution and all the other conceits. And so on it would go, without end, leaving the world a worse place for her passage through it. The prospect squashed her spirit as flat as the frozen prairie beyond the door.

Finishing Clarrity bred no further necessity. On the contrary, his death would answer many questions. Falling into the pit, she anticipated a great unraveling, a smoothing of a fabric whose design would soon be obvious. Somewhere, her father would understand her act, and raise a glass, and grin in that way he did when he made a big score. Curiously, though she could envision his smile, her daydreams would not disclose the particulars of her father's face. It would not center in her mind's eye, and when she made an effort, she imagined only a shadowy ideal, a composite on all the handsome faces she remembered. Forgetting his face left her sad, but not hopeless, because she never doubted that when the time finally came, when he came to rescue her, she would know him at once.

Cutting Clarrity's throat left her exhausted yet enervated. Back above, she rested on the floor, grasping her knees to her chest as she trembled from the raw, crackling energy that coursed through her limbs. At last the blood dried and she shivered from the draft rushing up between the planks. Almira draped a blanket over her shoulders, and the old man performed what he thought to be a similar service by blowing pipe smoke at her. Junior showed up with a bucket of clean water. When she took up the washrag, she had to scrub off the congealed blood, as if Clarrity's veins had been filled with red grease.

Clean and clothed in her other chemise, she staggered to her bed. She was tired now, in that deep way she had after an afternoon beating laundry at some camp stream fouled with lye soap and camp shit, or ten hours on her feet waiting on customers at the hotel. The others showed her the quiet respect owed someone who had faced and conquered some Herculean labor. Almira turned down the lantern, conscientiously muffling the clank of Clarrity's coins and jewelry as she deposited them in the cracker tin. Junior and the old man dealt themselves a quiet game of rummy by the light of one candle, hardly snapping the cards.

And yet—her final thoughts before falling asleep were not ones of satisfaction, of laying an old demon to rest. Again, they were of Leroy. Why was it that her mind always seemed to circle back to that pain, no matter how far it had traveled? It was like that wolf they had seen when she first arrived at the cabin—of all the places for it to prowl, why would the beast venture so close to the habitations of men? Was it the place where it had suffered an injury too deep to forget? Some need to prove to itself it had truly survived? Forever and onward, the beast ranges farther to escape, yet always returns, keeping faith with its wound. She saw Leroy looking down on her, smiling as he once did and never would, and the casual passage of his hand across his brow, clearing his hair from his eyes. And his gaze passed over her then, to another woman, and another, and another after that, each flick of his eye making her lighter, more invisible, until her body faded to a tremulous, unconscious transparency.

Chapter Nineteen

Dispositions

COLONEL ALEXANDER YORK was flushing marmots when they brought him word of his brother's disappearance. The colonel always went out with his work crews to supervise the clearance of pests. They took a tanker pulled by four big percherons and a hundred-foot length of rubber hose he had custom-made in Ohio, which was a particular pride of his. In each infested area, they parked the wagon and ran the line out to. When the yipping creatures dove into their lodges, the crew flooded each one until water poured from the back holes and the prairie dogs washed out, half drowned.

Some of the vermin were more stubborn than others, inspiring a lively betting game on how long they would hold out. Colonel York did not approve of wagering. But during the war he'd learned the value of letting his men keep certain small vices, lest they acquire worse ones. So he kept the stakes in his cigar pocket, and kept the official time with the gold pocket watch he'd received from his regiment when he laid down his commission. Nobody ever argued over a bet after the colonel had certified a winner. He wasn't the kind of man to suffer questioning of his probity.

By sundown the pasture was cleared, a pile of small water-logged carcasses in a mound as high as his gun belt, toothy pink mouths gaping. They didn't need to be arranged this way; they could have been deposited directly into the ditch his men had already prepared and limed. But York liked to have the fruits of his effort laid out clearly before disposal.

It was a preference that had raised eyebrows before, after that small action in Missouri when a company of his men had cornered an enemy column in a ravine outside of Westport. The enemy called themselves Defensives—but they were Confederates, or as close as made no difference—and by the end of the day there were scores of them dead and scattered in the field. The newspapermen liked a clean count, so York had the corpses collected and arranged in as pretty a line of cold bushwhackers as Jim Lane himself could have wished. Each man was laid out in dignified repose, cap stuck on head, weapon by his side. "Fish Market York" they called him, for his flair with display. There was never any need to guess the number of dead and wounded when Colonel Alexander York carried the field.

Today he'd bagged 216 marmots. His crew were halfway through the pile, passing them hand-to-hand to the pit, when a rider came up with a message from his sister-in-law in Fawn Creek, south of Independence. He perused her finely penned note, the letter in his right hand as he clutched a drowned rodent in his left. After he had read it three times, he fixed his eye on the boy who delivered it.

"How long's your pap been gone?"

"Well on three days. Hain't never been this late before."

"Maybe he found himself some diversion in Fort Scott," said the colonel. The joke raised an obsequious laugh from his men, but was of course preposterous. Everyone knew that Dr. William York was not the kind of man who sought "diversions." He was, in fact, just the opposite: the kind of man who seemed impervious to the weaknesses of mere mortals. His brother would never pain his family with an unexcused disappearance. At least not willingly.

In Independence and beyond there had been word of disappearances of wayfarers along the Osage. Farm boys had busied themselves concocting dark rumors of man-eating boars, packs of slavering panthers, ghostly Indian avengers. Gangs of children danced around lone travelers as they rode out of town, telling them they would die. Adults frowned on such fear-mongering. Yet they still advised travelers to go out only in parties and to keep their weapons in easy reach.

The colonel didn't need to ask if his brother had heeded those warnings; his nephew's face told him all he needed to know.
In ordinary times he would have turned the boy away with an admonishment to be patient—his father would turn up. But the times had become extraordinary.

"Come with me to the house," he commanded the boy. Then, with an air of a man forsaking all pleasure, he handed the dead marmot to the man next to him. That man was Evelyn Whistler, who had come out of Philadelphia to serve as the colonel's field adjutant. After the war, he took the job overseeing York's properties. Where the colonel was thin and copiously maned, Whistler was stout and bald, and naturally dour by temperament. He took the drenched carcass with calm forbearance, as if he could expect life to offer him nothing better.

York leaned in. "How many guns can we get on short notice?"

"I don't know." Whistler shrugged. "Half a dozen. Ten."

"Get 'em."

York mounted his horse, rode out a ways, steered it around suddenly. "And damn it, the man who leaves that tarnation hose out overnight will be cold as a wagon tire when I get back!"

His house was a sixteen-room mansion done up in the French provincial style favored by his wife. The hipped roof and arched dormers had offered some interesting challenges in construction, but the finished house embarrassed him. For he accepted he was no country squire, but at his best a competent soldier, and at worst an unapologetic savage. When he was young and came west, he did so without any of the high ideals of "Christianizing the wilderness" or "spreading the boon of civilization." He wanted nothing more than to get away from all that, to leave behind the world of ordinances and obligations, qualifications and courtesies, flounces, follies and cozies, crockeries and foreigners. For men like himself, the move to the Territories was an act of destruction, a sweeping away of all that suffocating excreta. In its place there would ideally arise—nothing.

Yet here he was, living in a house that represented everything he'd fled. His failure was total, for no matter how far he went, everything he loathed would follow as surely as his own shadow. His impotence gave him a permanent sense of being under siege. And indeed, the only part of the house he liked was the second floor gallery. Winding around three sides, bounded by an ornate rail studded with wrought-iron fleurs-de-lis, the balcony made an excellent firing position.

He changed for the trail—knee-length riding boots, jerkin of beaten leather, wide-brimmed hat lined with sealskin. On his way out he paused at a human skull he kept on his desk, flipping the hinged parietal bone to remove a handful of fresh cartridges. He had heard that ammunition stored in the brain case of a man gained special lethality.

When he came out, his search party was assembled. Seven men, all equipped for a long ride, with carbines and bandoliers across their chests. His nephew, innocent of arms, looked as useless as a boy prince in that crew.

"For Lord's sake, someone give that boy a pistol," he ordered. Launching himself off the block like a man half his age, the colonel steadied his mount and addressed his men.

"The doctor was last seen in Fort Scott. We'll start there, and backtrack over every inch of the trail. We will miss no farmhouse, no privy, no dugout. If any man misses a sign, *any single sign*, he will answer to me."

SINCE CLARRITY'S VISIT, so many had died at the "Grocry," Kate lost count of them. Junior and the old man processed their guests with a speed and efficiency that required no comment. The cracker tin was filled and replaced by a hatbox, which was three-quarters full by the turn of '73. The stream of "abandoned" or "bartered" goods they gave to Rudolph Brockman to turn into cash became so copious they didn't bother explaining anymore, and Brockman didn't ask. He simply examined them, took them off to Ottawa or Independence—the farther away, the better—and kept his cut from the proceeds.

Outside, the apple trees grew up straight and strong between the plots. Nourished by what lay below, some even bore good fruit. One autumn Saturday, Almira collected the best and baked them into a pie two feet across and four inches deep. She served it with fresh cream at the next Harmony Grove picnic. Kate watched with perverse fascination at her neighbors tucking into heaping plates of the pale, sickly flesh. Fittingly, the topic of conversation passed to the mystery of the disappearing travelers.

"I won't speak for anyone else, but I've my suspicions about those vanished men," pronounced Gertrude Dienst. Upon attracting the attention of everyone around her, she took a long pull on her lemonade to keep them in suspense. Then she said, "There never was a red Indian clever enough to do such mischief over so long a time. They don't have the . . . *application* for it."

"Oh, don't be so sure o' that," objected Mrs. Moneyhon in the brogue that had not faded after ten years in America. "It's the devil makes 'em devious."

Mary Anne Dick stood by, nursing a cigarette that had burned almost to the fingers. She entertained no illusions about red Indians or wild animals or former Negro slaves out for revenge against the white race. To her mind, this evil had to dwell very close by, in plain sight, in a form innocent enough not to arouse suspicion. Moreover, the fiend must have the benefit of some kind of shelter, to work his crimes without fear of being seen. But, like Kate, she only listened to the others talk and did not share her thoughts.

Mrs. Dienst wasn't ready to surrender her point: "Mark my words, there are white men responsible. Before long they'll have to search every farm between here and Thayer. All of us will be suspected."

"Stuff and applesauce!" retorted Moneyhon. "This isn't Christian doing, I say."

"Let us assign guilt to no single race of men," said Minister Dienst, who approached the women with a spoon and a plate full of Almira's pie. "The devil comes in the form of his choosing. Red, black, white—it matters not to him the form of his instrument. For he is the deceiver of the whole world. Remember Corinthians: 'It is no great thing if his ministers also be transformed as the ministers of righteousness; whose end shall be according to their works.'"

Kate coughed at the sight of the minister quoting chapter and verse as corpuscles of Bender apple shone in his beard. No one else moved to help her as she struggled, so Brockman presented her with his mug of cider.

"From our apples?" she asked, rasping.

"From Iowa."

She drank. The rest of their neighbors did not look at them, but Brockman's gallantry to her was noted, and remembered.

Kate's independent enterprise—her readings and therapeutic consultations—added little to her bankroll. Business had shriveled in most of the farms close in to Parsons and Cherryvale, as malign tongues continued to spread lies about the nature of her services. The good women of Labette County looked on her with contempt, while the men alternated between smug moralism and lusty impudence. Farther out, though, she was still in demand: she once had Junior drive her as far as Thayer to see a farmer about a possessed dog, and to Osage Mission to read the cards to an old woman suffering from ague. These trips, with their opportunities for her to speak to people other than Junior and Almira, kept alive the thinning tendril still connecting her with the rest of the human race. But they never paid enough for her to leave the Bender enterprise behind.

There came a time, she had found, when her loneliness faded, and mere aloneness conferred upon her a certain power. In the language of the mathematical texts she had once studied, she had weight, breadth, extension like every other mortal being, and yet she seemed to move along a unique set of axes. This private world intersected with the public one only in certain places—the shops in Cherryvale, choir practice, the serving table at the grocery— and there only with an increasing air of unreality.

And yet, as she studied these moments, she came to see the un- reality stemmed from that unique perspective. Her axes not only intersected with the rest, they cut them through, like the beams of some hitherto unknown radiation that clarified flesh and exposed the bone. Conversations between strangers displayed their hidden meanings. Smiles transmogrified. The digits of extended hands betrayed their calculation. Patrons at the grocery lay with brains split on the sagittal plane, ugly dispositions pulsing forth. Never so insulated, she never before saw so much.

Time came when Brockman acted on his aspirations with Kate. He had been giving her significant glances for two years, dropping compliments, making clear that she was welcome to visit his claim any time. She would smile, showing him enough attention to flatter him but never enough to be confused with ro- mantic interest. After all, they had come to need Brockman and his contacts among discreet merchants willing to sell the goods left behind by their "guests." Of course, he could know nothing of how all those horses and saddles and shooting kits had really come to be orphaned. He enjoyed the profits too much to dare ask awkward questions. But disappointment in love, Almira warned her, might loosen his tongue in the company of the wrong people. Handling Brockman was her most demanding role—certainly more significant than the simple coquetry she used to distract their short-term visitors.

He paid her an unsolicited visit on an unseasonably warm March day. He stood below the single step of their doorway wearing a freshly laundered shirt and suspenders, examining his hat as if there was something deeply fascinating about it. His boots were caked with spring mud but shone enough around the clumps to show he had polished them that morning.

Men who approached women could be divided into two types: the ones who did so with smiles on their faces because they enjoyed the chase, and the ones without. Brockman was without. Instead, he showed the kind of frown a man wore when he took a steer to auction in a soft market, dubious of his return.

"*Guten Morgen*, Kate."

"Good morning to you, Rudolph."

"Uncommon fine day, isn't it?"

"Indeed it is."

"Well, I thought then that I might disturb ye to ask if ye might come out and walk . . . just out and about. If that's agreeable."

She reached out to tweak him in the breastbone. But he was standing too far away, so she poked the air. Brockman regarded this gesture with alarm—if she actually moved to hug him, he seemed as likely to draw his gun as let himself be touched.

"Of course I would, Rudolph. But Mother has me on the broom just now. Can we take a turn tomorrow, after choir?"

He winced at the complication. "I would be very pleased."

Hat back on head, he retreated along the trail until he dropped into the low ground near his claim. There he paused, with only his head visible to her, standing as if arrested by some momentous thought. He stayed that way for a few moments as he weaved slightly on his feet, hands in his pockets.

Kate shut the door.

Inside, Almira glanced at her sidewise over her sewing. "Best be careful around that one," she advised.

"Listen at you, making noises like a mother."

From time to time Kate would order a new dress from a catalog, which the old man and Junior would fetch from the railhead at Thayer. Almira told her this was a waste of her money, and dangerous too, insofar as it made the family seem wealthier than mere grocery clerks ought to be. She could never wear such nice frocks in public. But it meant something to her to own the trappings of a finer sort of lady—one who belonged in the company of a dapper entrepreneur and cardsharp like her father. When she saw him again, she meant to look every bit as turned-out as the day she had been torn from him.

Next Sabbath, she discarded caution and wore something new to church: a dress of baby blue silk, trimmed in white velvet with mother-of-pearl buttons. On her head, a self-colored cap trimmed with spring wildflowers and a gauze veil. With the veil down, she saw the world as if through a heavenly vapor, pleasantly scattering the sunbeams and draining everything of its ugly details. The men of Harmony Grove preferred not to acknowledge her, but couldn't help themselves, staring into a middle distance that included her in their peripheral vision. The women were better at concealing their envy, looking to each other significantly until their friends signaled it was safe to steal disapproving looks.

She didn't hide herself in the back of the choir this time, but claimed front and center of her section. There, Leroy confronted the scrubbed, shining, full-lipped presence of her. However un-flappable he stood, there was no mistaking the extra color about his neck, the way he contrived to avoid looking directly at the altos. Kate, eyes on the hymnal, permitted herself the merest smile as she enjoyed the disruption around her. Nothing struck her quite as satisfying as exposing hypocrisy.

At the picnic, Brockman lost no time exacting what she had promised. With everyone watching, they went off on their own down the dirt road, Kate behind her veil again and Rudolph scur-rying along beside, holding the hems of her skirts out of the dust.

"Wunderschön," he was saying. "Ye are a visitation, my dear Kate. And don't fear that I've missed the significance of thy timing, on the very day ye promised me thy company."

"You presumptuous devil! To think a man would take such a high opinion of himself!"

They had walked out far enough among the fields not to be overheard. She curled her arm around his like folks in civilized places, as a lady always seeks the protection of her gentleman, and Rudolph gave a small start but did not recoil. The pressure of her gloved hand, and the eyes on him, loosened his tongue.

"It couldn't be a secret how the feelings arose on thy account, Kate. I mean mine."

Smiling, she said nothing. She'd often found that in situations like this, where a gentleman needed rebuffing but could not be written off, the less she said, the better.

"Ye must have thought, 'That's a man who has spent all his years with tar in his shit, what he got to offer me? Just busting sod and the doggeries of Parsons is all he knows.' But thy be wrong about that, *mein Liebling.* I've seen something of the world. Before Kansas, I was in Baltimore, and before that the great city of Dresden, in the kingdom of Saxony. My grandfather kept the seals for the royal elector at the Zwinger. I have seen the setting sun blaze on the shoulder of the Semper Opera. I have heard Schiller float on the Elbe at dusk . . ."

She had once read a geography book that described the splendors of Dresden, Florence of the East. Intrigued, she grasped him closer.

" . . . After the troubles of 'forty-eight, we went west. I knew no English when I took ship in Hamburg. When we landed in Baltimore six weeks later, I spoke it better than the Americans who worked the dock."

"From what I've seen of the pitiful creatures they let into this country, that's not much of a boast."

"What I want to say," he flared, "is that I'm not a stupid man. I can see your purpose."

"Can you? What is my purpose, then?"

He offered up a smile that seemed in service of some private joke. It froze her, for while she granted that he had some vague notion of how they'd come into all that "lost" property, she didn't want to believe he knew everything.

"Ye want to get out. Ye are not made for this place. Thy enemies can see it, and thy friends."

"My enemies? Goodness!"

"Ye would go, but ye want a man who'd be willing to serve thy need—if any man be worthy."

"Do I?"

"Ye can use me if you want to, Kate. Let me be thy faithful instrument."

He stopped then, and stared into her eyes as he grasped her skirt with one hand and his hat with the other. The wind was rising and the clouds crowding in from the west. The sudden chill raised goose bumps on her neck as Rudolph's forwardness made her blush and her lips feel dry and pent and ready to peel apart like a thistle blossom.

"I see ye. You're the only one who's alive here. *Alle anderen sind tot.* They are just going through the motions of living. Can ye see me?"

For a moment she was anxious, and speechless. To endure her loneliness, she had to believe she was exceptional, uniquely gifted among clods and drudges. But what to do with a sign like this, that someone out there was looking back at her not only with interest, but with perception?

It was more discomfiting than comforting—at first. But when she looked into his eyes, and saw there the simple animal need she had seen so often before, in all the others, she steadied.

"I don't say you're wrong," she said carefully. "I'm happy to hear you say it. I have to tell you I've always felt I'm supposed to be somewhere else, fulfilling greater purposes. Does that sound mad?"

"Thee may always share thy madness with me."

"I tell you sincerely that I intend to see oceans."

"As you shall. As you shall."

"I'm so very miserable here, Rudolph. Can I trust you with that secret?"

"*Ja.* And more."

She grasped the end of her veil and tugged it closer to her face, as if it would make their exchange more confidential. "There may be a time when I'll call upon you. It may not be soon, but it won't be long. Will you be ready?"

"I will."

"Good. Now walk me back."

They turned about as the first raindrops began to fall, the church picnickers scattering before them like lies before a single powerful truth.

That pleasant Sunday was chased away by a final blast of winter. Frigid winds coursed over the plains, pushing so hard against the cabin that the joists popped and draughts spun among the rafters. Outside, the sky was a translucent, milk-glass vault that let all warmth drain from the earth. Under Junior's boot heels, the newly sprouted grass was crisp with frost. He found the Benders' small stock of animals hunkered down in their pens, the chickens loath to leave their roosts, the pigs curled up and steaming in their little circles of frosted shit.

As he did every morning, the old man ambled to the orchard to groom the furrows, hatless head lost in a cloud of condensed breath as he slashed the frozen ground. He was doing no practical good, and Kate would have told him so if the man acknowledged a word she said. But Flickinger had long since ceased exchanging articulate speech with her. Instead, he would listen to her voice with a quizzical look on his face, as if some bird or insect had spoken. His expression around her was usually one of bemusement, whatever she did or said seeming to confirm some secret expectation. Surpassingly strange, he filled her with dread of what he might ultimately do to betray them all. She suspected the last body to be planted in his beloved orchard might have to be his.

The posse appeared around noon. It came up between the mounds like any party of travelers, but instead of proceeding along the trail to the grocery, it struck straight across the prairie to Spill Out Creek. The riders split into details, a few sweeping the creek bottom, others bushwhacking among the cottonwoods and brambles, beating off the blackberry thorns with rifle butts. They proceeded this way, as if searching for something, across half a dozen neighboring farms and onto the Bender claim. In no case did they ask permission to cross property lines. Nor did any of the owners dare challenge the seven heavily armed strangers as they grimly scoured the creek.

Only when the riders were done searching did they approach the cabin. All four Benders stood at the back window, dumb with apprehension. Every man in the posse was armed to the teeth, trail-splattered, horses foamed and gleaming. All showed signs of hard riding except for the man leading them, in his knee-high boots and leathers, who was spotless and carried no arms except for a single revolver holstered under his left armpit. His expression was not exactly grim, but darkly expectant, as if he was closing in on some reward half sought and half dreaded.

"Them boys is up to no good," said Almira.

Under the circumstances, it made more sense to let Junior greet them. Despite the cold, he went out the back door in his shirtsleeves and suspenders, boots half fastened. The posse pulled up in a semicircle around him, horses spewing a wall of vapor through which a voice demanded:

"*You* the proprietor here . . . ?"

Through the single pane of glass, the leader's voice boomed like God's own flatulence. From behind, Almira clutched Kate's shoulder. Kate heard an odd sound, like small bones being shaken in a cup; turning, she saw Almira trembling so violently her teeth chattered.

"You all right now?"

"Our fate is plighted," replied Almira, "the Furies are nigh."

"Been at the jug cider?" Kate asked, glancing at the old man for a trace of cleansing mirth. But of course he didn't laugh.

Outside, the interview was not going well. None of the visitors had climbed down from their horses, and Junior was lapsing into that hangdog posture he assumed when despair got the better of him. Kate seized the old man's wool greatcoat off a nail in the wall—a tentlike thing, oil-stained and smelling of his unwashed self—and threw it around her shoulders.

"I'm going out."

"Don't get us hung," advised Almira.

The air outside seemed heavier than the fabric draped around her, laden with a frigid, clinging kind of wet. All dozen heads turned to her as she emerged, and a good number of the horses too; Junior, when he saw her, rose perceptibly in height.

"And this is my sister, Kate . . ." he said.

The leader regarded her, his eyes as black as the clipped moustache at this lip. His gaze was narrow, analyzing her as if he were a gem-cutter trying to ascertain the best angle to split a stone. Then, a brief nod.

She said, "I would wish you a good day, gentlemen, if the climate were more salubrious. But we must make do with what Providence intends for us. Can we interest you in a hot fire and a meal?"

"Thank you, no," he replied in a voice straight from some patriarch's dais. "As I was telling your young man here, I am Colonel Alexander York—retired. This here is Mr. Evelyn Whistler, my associate, and the rest of my party . . ." He indicated the others in a gesture that was less an introduction than a show of force. "We are here from Independence on a matter of life and death. My brother was seen in these parts before he went astray. His name was Dr. William York, and he was on his way back from Fort Scott when he disappeared . . ."

At the name of the missing man, Junior stiffened. The reaction was involuntary, and almost imperceptible, but to Kate it seemed the next worst thing to a confession. She glared at him, and in his regret, he became argumentative:

"How do you know he disappeared coming back from Fort Scott, instead of on the way?"

York turned on Junior, eyes igniting. This, perceived Kate, was the look of a man who relished the chance to vanquish a challenger.

"Because, *sir*, he was seen there before he started back this way. In Fort Scott, a man matching his description bought cigars, and supplies for his practice."

To show weakness before this man would make him bolder, she thought. She crossed her arms and said, as tartly as she dared, "We are always eager to help travelers in need, whether it profits us or not. But we are not accustomed to being interrogated by our guests. Especially ones without the courtesy to come down from their mounts."

A smile cracked the colonel's face. Then, lashing his reins around his saddle horn, he swung over a leg and dismounted. Whistler followed suit, then the rest.

"Thank you," she said. "And now I bid you come inside out of this cold, so we might discuss your problem. As much as I would like to accommodate all of your men, our lodgings are rather small, as you can see."

"Yes, I indeed see. Can we trouble you for some water, for the horses?"

"Of course. My brother will show you."

Inside, Almira had the oven stoked up so high the windows were fogged. York came in, lip slightly curled at the evident meanness of the place. When Kate invited him to sit at the table, he perched at the very edge of the chair, as if expecting to be ejected. Whistler declined her invitation, preferring to hover on the periphery.

"Would either of you care for some coffee? Or something more fortifying, perhaps?"

York shook his head, gingerly planted an elbow on the table. He removed his hat, revealing a sabre scar that snaked up his high forehead to notch his hairline.

"Well then," said Kate, taking up the chair opposite. "Tell me again what happened to your brother."

"He took a runabout and sorrel mare up to Fort Scott last week, on business. It's a trip he's done well on a dozen times, without incident. He was expected back five days ago. Without a doubt he took this trail when he started back last Friday. He ought to have passed this very cabin—if he made it this far."

"What did he—*does* he—look like?"

York shrugged. "He rode out in a buff-colored trail suit, checked waistcoat, black hat. White linen shirt with European-made cuffs. He was well turned-out. He has a successful practice."

Kate looked to Almira. "Do we remember anyone like that?"

Almira shook her head.

"Could it be some professional duty detained him along the way?" Kate asked.

"For five days? Without sending word he'd been delayed?"

"Some of these outclaims are isolated. I've had occasion to have my own skills summoned at short notice, from quite a distance."

"Young miss, your skills notwithstanding, I know my own brother. This is not conduct we have ever seen from him before. It's possible something foul has befallen him."

The colonel turned to regard Junior as he returned from showing the posse to water. He was clearly measuring Junior up and down, appraising his capacity for mischief.

"There are reports of disappearances traced to this area," he continued. "Quite a number of disappearances, in fact. You are aware of that?"

"We are. Please understand, sir, that it is our practice never to turn away a traveler in need, no matter what hour they may reach our door. These are quiet parts. But what acts dark of night might conceal, no one may be sure."

"I'll ask again," York pronounced, eyes closed like the effigy of Justice herself. "Do you remember someone matching his description?"

Kate, by contrast, was unblinking. "I believe I do. Perhaps a week ago. I was alone here—my family was in Parsons, on business—and I'm not in habit of entertaining gentleman guests on my own. He took some water and offered to sell us some paregorics from his kit. Said he had too much of the stuff. I declined. Then he climbed back on his rig and went on his way."

"East or west?"

"East."

"Was this exactly a week ago, or more or less?"

"More or less. I couldn't tell you the day."

"You can't remember the day your family all went into town and left you alone?"

Kate looked to Almira. "Can you recall?" Almira shook her head mechanically, and to Kate's mind, unconvincingly. But before she could speak, Junior blurted—

"I was nearly waylaid myself not long ago, close by here."

Kate had not expected any such story but managed to keep a

smile on her face. Almira, however, would have swallowed her fist if her mouth had been big enough. Unable to control her unease, she retreated behind the canvas.

"Explain yourself, son," demanded York.

"I was coming back with supplies last week when someone made a run at me. I heard the shot and the bullet miss my ear, but I couldn't tell from where. So I lowered my head and drove out of there at a gallop."

"Where, exactly?" asked Whistler. He had been so silent, Kate had forgotten he was there.

"It was a few miles outside of Cherryvale, where the trail winds around the Dreyer place. There's a creek and some trees."

York rose. "You'll show us the spot, now . . ." he commanded. Then he added with threadbare courtesy, "Won't you?"

Junior lowered his head. "I will."

Kate followed the colonel to the front door, where he turned on her.

"What's wrong with that one?" he indicated behind the canvas.

She shrugged. "What mother wouldn't be upset to relive an attack on her only son?"

"Yes, what mother wouldn't?" he replied, that smile brushing his lips again. He tipped his hat. "Good afternoon, miss."

Chapter Twenty

The Bitch of Justice

JUNIOR WAS AWAY for the rest of the afternoon. The others scattered to their separate tasks: Almira to her laundry pot, Flickinger to the orchard, Kate to her tarot. There was no discussion of what York's visit meant for their enterprise. There was nothing to conceal, no telltale signs to erase, because they never left any. All that the colonel left in his wake was a sense of unease—an odor of imminent threat that festered as if he'd left one of his drowned marmots on the floor.

Kate laid out her cards in various patterns but found her vision blocked by anger. Almira's performance in front of the colonel was hapless, infuriating. And while she had long ceased to expect anything from Junior, his strange story of being ambushed on the trail was sure to make matters worse. She always thought of herself as the outsider in their partnership, the one anyone could tell didn't belong there. She had never wanted to swing the hammer.

Yet there she was, forced time and time again to use her wits to save them all.

She had always hoped she could exact her share of the profits without really being of them. Her suffering had purchased that much at least, to pull her weight by dint of her presence, of the smile she sent into the world as easily as mailing a letter. And when the time came, and her funds were right, she would leave them all flat, without consequences or regret. Yet now circumstances were casting her in the role of the leader. The more her acts determined their collective fate, the less she felt in control of her own.

They returned Junior an hour before dusk. As the old man watched from his usual vantage outside, the riders collected themselves and resumed their journey to Fort Scott. They bid no goodbyes, made no pleasantries as they set off. The old man waited until they were out of sight, shut his Bible, and angled his watching chair against the wall to keep the snow off the seat.

He walked in as Kate confronted Junior. The latter was sitting with his coat undone, prying off a boot and most of the sock with it.

"So the fool returns from his errand. Tell us—was it a true catastrophe, or just a waste of time?"

"You do me no justice. It all went as I expected. I took them to the spot, and the lieutenant—Whistler—even said it was a pretty place for an ambuscade. I gave them no reason to doubt me."

"Were they impressed with the evidence you showed them? The tracks and casings and bullet holes and such?"

Junior's boot slipped free, launching across the store. He slouched back against the wall, spent.

"Well, I wouldn't say that."

"That colonel is not the kind to take the word of a stranger.

He's empirical—he's going to want to see proof. Isn't that right?" Kate asked, swiveling toward Almira.

The other scowled, as if unpleasantly surprised to be included in the conversation. "*Das sind schlechte Menschen*. Them boys is up to no good."

"Is that all you have to say? Is anyone else prepared to be of use here? If not, we'd better light out now, or resign ourselves to stretched necks."

Junior shook his head. "He's got no evidence to suspect us, neither."

"He already does, though he may not be aware of it yet himself. Any fool can see it."

"Oh, aren't you the smart one?" Almira mocked.

"It's not smarts but the sense the Lord gave any mule."

"He had no reason to doubt me," insisted Junior. And with a contrite grimace, he held up his dirty sock for her to take away. For even then, at the sharp edge of their crisis, there were certain verities to honor.

Kate felt like snatching the sock and stuffing it in his fool face. Or she could have wound it around Almira's neck and strangled her misery at its source. But instead she took the foul garment, fingered its stains, and took it to her laundry basket.

"You see what your glyphs and magic do for us now, I think," derided the old woman. Kate didn't rise to the bait, but turned the thought over in her mind, and rejected it. The colonel was not a man to be affected by fear of invisible forces. It was an advantage of modernity, she found, that obliviousness amounted to a powerful defense. She would need other skills to cope with the likes of him.

The posse returned two days later. Spying them from a long

way off, the old man muttered an archaic curse and went on spreading manure around the apple seedlings. Wicker switch in hand, sweat plastering her brow, Kate paused from beating their freshly laundered linens. So much for believing in Junior's road agents, she thought. Then she beat the blankets so hard she split the calluses on her fingers.

The colonel's crew was at half strength this time—just four riders, including himself and Whistler. York alighted and tipped his hat at Kate, but otherwise continued his interrogation as if no time had passed since his last visit.

"You said he was heading east," he stated.

"Did I?"

"You best not lawyer with us, miss. My brother's rig was found in some woods ten miles west of here. *West,* I said. Horse is gone, but it's his property, all right. Anything to say about that?"

She shrugged. "What would you have me say? I saw him go east, but maybe he turned around and went west the next day. Maybe he had foul weather. Maybe he forgot something."

"And if you believe that . . ." chimed Whistler.

"Let me understand, Colonel: are you accusing me of something? I told you my family was gone the day Dr. York called. Is it your intention to impeach my name by suggesting I have something to hide?"

"Yes, we won't have that," interjected Junior, taking his cue for once. "No one has ever had occasion to speak about my sister's honor."

"No, you mistake me . . ." said York, momentarily flummoxed by the turn in their interview.

"For all our time here," Kate said, "I've kept my good name, though the men of this county have behaved in far from gentlemanly fashion! And to have strangers come into our home and make such insinuations . . . it is disgraceful! Unspeakable!"

"*Unerwünscht*," suggested Almira.

"Exactly."

"Understand me: I accuse no one of nothing. It is my entire purpose to learn my brother's movements in the last week. Nothing more."

"It's easy to think otherwise, the way you lord it about."

"The last thing I think myself to be, miss, is a 'lord,' " he said.

"I'm relieved to hear it." Then, nudging him gently by the arm, she took him aside for a discreet conference that, because the cabin was so small, everyone else could hear anyway.

"You and your family must be suffering the unendurable. Believe that we wish nothing more than for you to see his safe return. Trust me when I tell you that your visit here is not just happenstance. There is a larger purpose to it . . ."

She presented him with a folded piece of paper. Opening it, he read the words PROF. MISS KATIE BENDER. It was one of the handbills she had distributed at the hotel.

"A *perfessor*, you say," he said, eyes parenthesized by mirth. "A formidable title. And what skills might we expect of you, young lady?"

"Sympathetic gnosticism. Revised Lurianic theosophy. The art and science of telling."

"My, what a passel of syllables."

"You will be more impressed by the application."

He searched her face. Perceiving she was serious, he glanced at his assistant.

"Do you go to school for that kind of learning?" asked Whistler.

"It cannot be an accident that fate has brought us together," she said, again ignoring Whistler. It took no theosophy to know he was mocking her. Coping with such ignorance was distasteful, but if she had to deal with it, it would not be with an underling.

"How can we deny the fortuitous correspondence between need and means?" she asked. "You pose a question, I have the means to an answer. An adept is measured by the magnitude of the questions she treats. Come back here this evening after sunset. Come alone. Bring an item that once belonged to him—a piece of jewelry, an article of clothing, anything. I guarantee to you, be he alive or dead, the cards will relieve your uncertainty."

York was no longer smiling. To be caught laughing at something not meant as a joke was an unfamiliar experience for him. It made him feel duped, and not a little frivolous, and inclined to react with surliness. Whistler knew what was coming:

"The colonel will be glad to take help in any form," he interceded. "After the more conventional forms of investigation are exhausted . . . he may well hold you to your offer."

"I can ask for no more," she replied, "than faith and an open heart."

The party mounted up and struck west. When they were out of earshot of the cabin, Whistler steered his horse beside York's.

"You make anything out of that?"

"A queer family is what I make of it," replied the colonel. "The father looks to be a low-grade imbecile. And the mother . . ."

"Hardly better. But I'd bet my last two bits they know more than they're saying."

"They know something. Something useful, I don't know. Better we turn up that mare. Find her, and we got the party that sold her."

The moon rose full over freshly sown fields, gilding the furrows with silver. The colonel did not return for his reading—as

Kate had expected he would not—but she sat up anyway, in Flick-inger's watching chair, stockingless and clad only in her cami-sole. The brush of evening breeze against her bare shoulders was unfamiliar to her, as was the feel of fabric against her bare legs. She concentrated on these sensations, eyes closed lightly, opening them now and again at some rustling in the grass or the turn of a bat's wing above her head.

DR. WILLIAM YORK had indeed come to them ten days before. He rode a fancy conveyance, buckle and watch chain shining and smelling of fancy soap. He stood at their door with the black bag that marked him as a professional. Not some upjumped yarb or purveyor of quack nostrums, but a genuine book doctor.

"Evening," he hailed her.

"Good evening," she replied, eyeing him up and down. In time, she would realize he had something of his brother's ravening lean-ness about him. But there was a fullness to his mouth, a sensuous-ness to its curves, that distinguished him.

"Might I trouble you for a drink and perhaps a bite to eat . . . before I push on to Cherryvale?"

"There's nothing in Cherryvale, sir, that cannot be bettered here. Come in."

He had come on that rare day when they'd taken down the canvas partition, thinking to clean the unsightly spot in the middle. Unlike their other guests, he could see straight across the cabin to the back door and Almira glowering at her stove. The old man was seated at the table, shoe hammer already in hand. Not a welcoming spectacle, but no worse than other tableaux a doctor might see on house calls to remote claims.

The doctor needed no encouragement to set himself down at

the table. His manner with a spoon and knife were worlds better than any visitor they had seen in those parts. Kate seated herself across from him, enjoying his display of gentility. She had barely finished questioning him about his destination, his means, his contacts in the area, before Flickinger rose from his chair. York looked at him with an expression of pleasant anticipation on his face, as if expecting to converse about the prize turnip at the county fair. He still looked that way when the old man, with almost nothing of a backswing, struck him flush in the face with his hammer.

Kate felt a scream crawl from the pit of her throat. York did not open his mouth but merely gushed blood from the hole where his nose had been—an aperture in the shape of an upside-down horseshoe, the kind that let the good luck run out. Then he crumpled to the planks like a balloon figure whose pin had been pulled.

She rounded on Flickinger. "Fool, you didn't let me talk to him!"

He fidgeted with the head of his hammer, mixing York's blood with the dirt and nose grease that were as always at the ends of his fingers. "He sounded like he needed fixin'," he said. Then he withdrew to his seat, picked up his Bible and resumed his study.

That was the last traveler they entertained until the elder York showed up at their door. It was the smoothest of any of their disposals, with hardly a misstep. No missteps, except for that small piece of missing intelligence, that he was a successful physician from a nearby town.

Now, under the sowing moon, she became conscious of a faint whistling, out in the darkness, becoming more insistent. Staring ahead, she glimpsed something white crouching in the grass fifty yards from the cabin. She rose, and padding onto the stubbly turf, came upon a kneeling figure.

"Took ye a while to come," said Brockman. He spoke softly, but in the wake of her reverie, his voice boomed like cannon shot.

"Shush, you fool! What are you doing here?"

"I think ye must know. It's all over the county."

"I know that if my parents catch you here . . ." she replied, searching over her shoulder. Whatever the legitimacy of his pretext, the notion that a man would take it upon himself to imperil her position in this way infuriated her. Never before had such a big and empty place seemed so small, so crowded with spying eyes. Becoming conscious of how flimsily she was dressed, she crossed her arms over herself.

"That colonel," whispered the other, "came by our store twice, asking the kinds of questions ought not be asked. He has it from somewhere that there is something between us."

"Something?"

"He spoke around it. He *suggested*. I wanted ye to know it didn't come from me."

"The man is distraught from the loss of his brother," she replied. "We should pity him, and help him in any way we can."

"Pity a snake and suffer his fangs."

Alone with Brockman, she felt more compromised with every moment that passed. It was a quality of certain men, an artifact of their earnestness, that they could not conceal their need. And Brockman was very needy.

"It seems to me that you barely know anything, Rudolph."

"I know that rig was known in every town from here to Fort Scott. It could not be sold safely."

"So you just left it?"

"I had no choice."

"And the mare?"

"I hired a man to take it down to Indian territory. I've use him before—he can be trusted."

"Seems you've done your level best, then. What would you have of me?"

He shifted. Though it was too dark for her to see his features, she knew he had that beset, dyspeptic look on his face, the one he wore when the occasion called for him to declare his devotion.

"I think—ye are displeased with me—though I do only what may serve ye—"

Approaching him, she laid a hand on his left cheek and bent to kiss him on the right. His unshaven mug bristled like a flank of a boar. But there was also an earthly, surprisingly sweet smell to it, like roasted sweet corn. If not actual affection, she suddenly felt a sense of responsibility for him.

"You should not come here. Trust me—be patient. That is how you may serve."

"I will be patient," he attested.

The colonel came a third time two days later. Mounted, he rode at a walk with Whistler at his side. Ahead of them was a man on foot with a leashed dog. The latter was some kind of hound. Its white fur was ticked with red, its pendant ears sweeping the ground as it slung its snout back and forth across the turf. Kate watched them approach from ten minutes away. They sometimes veered off the thoroughfare, but came back as the hound dug its hind legs into the earth, standing almost erect in its frenzy to get back on the trail.

They were more or less at the door when Kate opened up.

"Pleasant afternoon, Colonel! I see you've finally come back to see me."

York's adamantine glare begrudged no pleasantries. His gaze

shifted from her to the dog and back as the animal leapt and snaked forward, straining to follow the scent into the Bender cabin. The colonel presented his gaze as if it was its own indictment. She met it squarely, signifying nothing, a bottomless void to swallow whatever shot from his eyes.

"You understand what this hound is tracking?" Whistler asked.

She presented an open hand to the dog, thinking she might distract it. But the animal only gave her palm a perfunctory sniff.

"I never denied your brother was here. It is fortunate for you that he was. His presence should make it easier to account for his movements. Have you considered my offer?"

York's mouth twisted with repugnance. "I am too occupied presently," he said, "to avail myself of such methods."

"May we bring the dog within?" asked Whistler, indicating the cabin.

"You may not. For it will only tell you what you already know."

Whistler eyes widened, flitted in the colonel's direction.

"You should think hard on that answer."

"Gentlemen, this is pointless. I have already availed you a source many times more valuable—"

"I ask you again: will you step aside?"

"No. Not without speaking with my parents first."

"That is reasonable," opined Whistler, to which the colonel was about to say something, changed his mind, and looked away in smoldering sufferance.

"My brother and father are away in Parsons until this evening. Come back tomorrow—if good sense has not persuaded you otherwise."

York, with a click of his tongue, reversed his horse. The dog had other intentions: so reluctant was it to abandon the search that its handler had to sling it over his shoulder. As it was carried away it gazed back at Kate, letting out piteous, yelping barks.

"My offer stands, Colonel!" she called out to him. "I'll find your brother for you, even if he's in Hell."

When York heard those words, *even if he's in Hell*, an alarming sensation seized him. All the color drained from his face, and the back of his neck became sensitive to every stirring of the breeze. He was a man comfortable in his certainties, but they did not usually come to him this way, in the tone of a woman's voice. For the way she said the words—that she could even imagine such a mild man could be in Hell—convinced him his brother had suffered the worst. Death, by misadventure or some darker means.

The sensation wrung his gut. The mechanisms of intuition, after all, were as mysterious to him as any other kind of divination. Such things usually struck him as womanly, and embarrassed him. But this one burned and froze him, as if he had been shot with a bullet carved of ice.

He rode on and didn't look back. He went all the way back to Cherryvale, to the livery, where he didn't meet the eyes of the man who accepted his horse. Without a word to Whistler, he proceeded straight to his hotel. In his room, he tossed his hat on the bed and filled his wash basin to the brim.

Even if he's in Hell, she'd said.

Justice would come in its course, but it would keep for now. Instead, he plunged his face deep into the basin until the water overtopped his ears and his nose rested against the porcelain. Then, with a freedom he would never otherwise indulge, the colonel loosed a cry of grief.

Chapter Twenty-One

Resolved

SUNDAY

THE PARISHIONERS AT Harmony Grove were startled to discover that regular choir practice had been canceled. Instead, a community-wide meeting was convened in the schoolhouse. To accommodate the greatest number of citizens, no chairs or desks were left in the classroom. The people gathered on their feet, muslin frocks brushing woolen sleeves, fans and hats beating the stuffy air in rhythms that became synchronized as the congregants became more and more absorbed in the grim business laid before them.

Minister Dienst stood aside, arms crossed, wearing the expression of a man waiting for a train he doubted would ever come. Seated beside him was an entirely bald man in a saloon keep's apron, absently manipulated the ends of his moustache. To his left was George Majors, justice of the peace, leaning in to whisper to Leroy Dick. The latter was dressed in a suit of white linen that gleamed incandescent yellow in the full sunlight of the window. Dick cast a worried glance at George Mortimer, who stood with his wife as she kept up a monologue of barely audible commentary. Mortimer looked to John Moneyhon, standing in front of him with an obvious bulge in the small of his back. The Irishman, sensing someone watching him back there, turned, smiled, and flashed the pistol he had stashed in his waistband, flouting the convention that firearms were not to be carried in town halls. Moneyhon winked; Mortimer frowned.

Among the last of the attendees to arrive were Old Man Bender and John Junior. Entering with heads down, they greeted no one and took up position along the back wall. Their presence was not as notable as the absence of Katie Bender. The nonappearance of the "witch" relieved some but disappointed most.

When it seemed to Leroy Dick that most households of northwest Labette County were represented, he nodded to the man in the chair. The latter tapped the desktop with an ink pot to hush the assembly.

"I, Amboise A. Tarn, my turn being up at chair, hereby call this meeting of the citizens of Osage Township to order. Who will serve as secretary?"

"I will," quavered Daniel Lindsay, the blacksmith. Looking ill-at-ease, he folded and unfolded a single sheet of white paper with his sooty fingers.

"Any old business?"

"In the m-m-matter of the school board elections for District 30, the votes have been counted and duly recorded by the town clerk."

"So noted. Please read the tally."

Lindsay raised the paper to within six inches of his nose and squinted. "For the first position, Mr. C.G. Groen, forty-two votes, Mr. A. Fairleigh, fifteen votes. For the second position, Mr. H.H. Reid, twenty-eight votes, Mr. J. Sawforth, twenty-one—I mean twenty-seven—votes. And for the third, unopposed position, Mr. Leroy Dick, seventy-two votes. Those are the results."

Lindsay folded the paper. There was little reaction to news of the election among the people: Charlie Groen, the first designee, stood front and center, but merely frowned.

"Any other old business? No? So resolved without objection." Tarn tapped his ink pot again, continued, "On to new business, then. Leroy, you have something to present?"

"I do," said Leroy as he stepped in front of the blackboard. Some of the onlookers had vaguely pleasured looks on their faces just to see him fill their field of view. Before the chalk clouds on the slate, his white suit cut a striking figure, like a gleaming sail against a stormy horizon.

"Kindly proceed."

"Good morning, friends. It's good to see so many of you have come today, on short notice. I promise you this won't take long. You should know that we wouldn't have called this meeting without good cause. I'm guessing some of you have already figured what that cause might be. Even so, I ask you all to give this matter your utmost consideration, because it affects us all and likely will continue to do so until it is dealt with, once and for all.

"Putting it to you straight: the disappearances that have lately occurred on the Osage have not only raised concern in these parts, but have alarmed the entire state. The parties concerned have been almost entirely from other places, bound for territories outside our borders. But I think you all must see that a reputation for lawlessness is not in our interest. *Especially* not in our interest, given certain tragic events in the recent past. It also goes without saying, but I'll say it anyway, that even if you don't care a fig for any of that, even if you believe it has nothing to do with you, the prospect of mortal danger on our thoroughfares has concrete consequences. There have been reports from some of our merchants—only reports, so I cannot vouch for their accuracy—that parties transiting west have begun to bypass this part of our state, and even Kansas entirely, by using trails through Nebraska. I believe Mr. Bohlander of the Parsons Mercantile Association has much to say about that situation, as well as Mr. Watts in Thayer, should you wish to talk to them.

"I reckon we can all agree, then, that regardless of how you see the nature of the threat, it is something we must deal with. Short of apprehending those responsible, just showing our good faith by eliminating our community from suspicion would be of positive benefit. Therefore, as your trustee, it is my duty to lay before you the following proposal—"

"Hold on right there, Leroy!" George Mortimer called out. "What gives anyone reason to believe we have something to do with this business? These are good people here."

A murmur of agreement swept the gathered, moving others to shout, "Good people!" The groundswell rolled on to the back wall until it broke against the promontory of Flickinger's disdain. Instead of joining his neighbors in their civic pride, he impulsively kicked his legs out, screwing up his lips into a sneer of contempt.

Leroy replied: "I believe that goes without saying, George. Our problem is that some of the vanished were tracked to this area and, it appears, went no farther. I believe we have a special speaker this morning to tell us more about that. With the permission of the chair . . . ?"

"No objection."

Leroy looked to the figure standing at the back door. For the occasion, Colonel York had doffed his riding clothes and put on a proper black suit, with starched cuffs and a blood red cravat. Stepping into the classroom, he removed his hat. But instead of standing by Leroy Dick's side, he stood a good distance away, as if his *auctoritas* could not be shared.

"This is Alexander M. York, out of Independence. Some of you may know him from the War, when he led the Twelfth Kansas Volunteers. Last November he was elected state senator, representing Montgomery County. He must shortly leave for the capital to take up his duties. But before he goes, he requested the opportunity to make a direct appeal to the people of this township. Senator?"

York surveyed the audience before he spoke, an appraising grimace on his face. Far from playing the supplicant, he wore an expression that challenged them all, as if it was they who were about to be tested.

"Morning to you. As your trustee has said, I have been entrusted with the office of senator. But the honor came as a reward for my service in the late war. I ain't no campaigner, and the appeal of the hustings is quite beyond me. I am a soldier, and as such will speak plainly, hoping you will understand the circumstances that cause any indelicacy on my part.

"It has been near on two weeks ago that my brother, Dr. William York, went missing. If you don't know him, he is like unto me in coloring and build, though he favors a more genteel style of dress. He was returning from Fort Scott in the runabout he has often used for such trips. Four days ago his buggy was found abandoned near the Verdigris River. There was nothing in the traces. Upon further inquiries, my agents have found a man in Parsons, a shopkeep, who sold cigars to a man matching my brother's description. He reports that the customer got back on a runabout and headed west, in the direction of Cherryvale.

"There's no reason to believe he ever made it there. In the last few days, myself and a few volunteers swept all the stream bottoms between the Verdigris and the Neosho. I have sent representatives as far as Ottawa in the north and the borders of Indian territory in the south, posting inquiries. None of the railroad agents up there remember seeing him buy a ticket or board a train. For these reasons, I strongly believe that whatever befell my brother must have happened in this area—perhaps no more than a few miles from this very spot."

He paused to observe the effect of his words. Despite his disavowals, his military experience had given him ample experience in compelling listeners. Yet the general sentiment was not positive: an air of indefinite skepticism, even hostility, was palpable in the room. Minister Dienst cleared his throat.

"You should know, Colonel York, that there has been talk hereabouts regarding the manner in which your men have conducted your search. Reports of armed men trespassing, trampling fences. We'd all sure appreciate you treating that subject."

"I'd be delighted," the colonel replied. "And I'd so do by saying categorically that anything like that was done despite my expressed orders to respect property lines. Fences were never supposed to be crossed except between streambeds. It is sure regrettable, and if anyone would come to me and show cause for restitution, he will get no argument from me. That is my pledge as a gentleman and an officer.

"You should all be aware, though, that the disappearance of my brother has caused a great amount of distress among your neighbors in Independence. He was a good man—a good family man—who gave of his time and his skill without regard to his convenience. Many of the men who rode with me here have been fixed up by Billy—Dr. York—personally, whenever they've had the need. They all have an attachment to the man, and in their zeal to find him, they may have crossed certain lines . . ."

York paused, continued in a lower, confidential tone: "His wife and daughters fear the worst. They are obviously distraught. They should be here themselves, to beseech your patience, but they could not come. They just could not.

"I could sit here and appeal to you in the name of our common humanity, and for justice. Now that I'm here, it's hard to speak as anything more than a man facing as great a loss as a brother can bear. We already lost our eldest at Spotsylvania. After that, we both learned a lesson about what is truly important in this world. We swore to look after each other throughout the years the Lord vouchsafed us.

"I'm a man of some means. I have resources—but there is nothing more I can do without the help of the good people of this township. We need to search every inch of every farm. We need to eliminate possibilities, and hopefully drive those responsible into the open. For that, I humbly beg your sufferance. And I thank you for your kind attention today."

As Colonel York had reached the end of his request, involuntary cries of sympathy went up from some of the women. Gone were thoughts of busted fences. Every citizen of Osage Township who had lost a husband, a brother, or a cousin fighting back East felt compelled by his misfortune. The colonel rose, and with a stiff-legged gait that betokened his pain, left out the back. His men were gathered outside, chewing on tobacco and stalks of bluestem. None of them met York's eyes. He went to his horse, reached into his pack, and pulled out a fifth of whiskey. He uncorked it—but thinking better of it, covered it again. He would not drink until business was completed inside.

Amboise Tarn called for a vote on the proposition to devote the community's resources to York's quest, but none was necessary. The measure was approved by acclamation, and a committee comprised of Leroy Dick, Daniel Lindsay, and Minister Dienst appointed to draw up a release for the local newspapers. The announcement was drafted over oatcakes, jam, and coffee at the Dicks' kitchen table.

At a meeting of the citizens of Osage Township, Labette County, Kansas, held at the schoolhouse in District #30, April 13, 1873

A.A. Tarn was called to the chair, D.D. Lindsay appointed Secretary and the following preamble and resolutions were unanimously adopted:

Whereas, Several persons from adjoining counties are missing, and supposed to have been murdered; and,

Whereas, Suspicion appears to rest upon the citizens of this community, and believing ourselves to be unjustly accused, therefore

Resolved, That we heartily sympathize with the friends of those who have been slain, and that the citizens of Osage Township will make every effort in our power to detect and bring to justice the murderers,

Resolved, That the Independence, Parsons, Chetopa, Thayer,

and Osage Mission newspapers be requested to publish the
foregoing resolutions.

To the resolution—which amounted to a townshipwide war-
rant to search every property—the Bender men had joined the
overwhelming consensus. John Junior raised not just one hand
but both, making it appear that the old man had joined the acclamation.

Last to arrive, Flickinger and John Junior were also the first to
leave. When they'd mounted the army wagon and wobbled some
distance down the road, the old man turned to Junior.

"*Es ist vorbei.*"

THE PROPERTY SEARCHES began the next afternoon, but without Colonel York. An important vote had come up in the State
Senate, for which the Republican party required every member
of its caucus. With an escort of three, York reluctantly set out for
the LL&G railhead, then located at Thayer. He sent two of his
men back with instructions that occurred to him on the trail. One
of them was to delay sweeping the Bender place until after the
legislative session. It was the only search he wanted to conduct
personally.

Harmony Grove was visited first, under Whistler's close super-
vision. Men were sent into every room and cellar and corncrib.
Teams tested the ground, probing for soft spots in the soil with
iron tamping rods. Trash piles were sifted and burn pits examined for unusual remains. The investigators were meticulous and
grim—except when Mary Ann Dick surprised them with a table
of savories and lemonade. The search of the Dick place therefore
took longer than any other.

At the Tom Mortimers', beside the vegetable garden, the rod men discovered signs of a recent burial. Mortimer explained that a puppy, the favorite of his youngest daughter, had been planted there after being stepped on by a horse. Whistler insisted on digging up the grave anyway. As the girl wept and protested, the men exposed the articulated skeleton of a dog, still fur-draped. Whistler ordered them to probe for anything hidden underneath. When they were done, they tossed the jumbled bones back in the hole. By that time the girl had lapsed into a gibbering reverie that disturbed her parents more than her sobbing.

"Now was that really necessary?" asked a perturbed Tom.

"Yes, it was," replied Whistler.

Spring surrendered to a premature summer. Sodden winds arrived from the south, summoning prairie grasses that stemmed an inch a day. The sultry conditions tempted livestock to range far from their feeding troughs. It was not unusual for small-time ranchers like Billy Toles to find calves had slipped through loose fence rails, goats absconded to the streams to browse on fresh brambles. Retrieving them became a seasonal pastime; Toles wandered the fields with a lead rope in one hand and cigarette in the other, his quest becoming a sort of walking meditation as he smoked and felt the spring sap rise.

He felt it rise especially when he contemplated the lovely Kate living just a short distance away. Kate in her domestic dishabille, hair overflowing her shoulders, a smile or a manly cussword on her lips. Her closeness was the inspiration for many encounters he imagined over the long winter, fantasies that excited and shamed and confronted him with the dilemmas of manhood. Eventualities—circumstances that would make him the gentleman savior or the conquering rogue—pursued each other around his brain. Ideally, he would be both, savoring her helpless beauty and honoring it with his chivalry, his tenderness. He carved her name on the inside of his privy to contemplate as he relieved himself.

On that fateful day he found himself on the perimeter of the Bender claim, looking for a heifer that had pushed down a fence post. The cabin was quiet: there was nothing rising from the stovepipe, and the front door was shut. Old Man Bender's chair was empty, turned and leaning against the wall, and there was no one in the orchard. Are the Bender men away? Toles wondered. Have they left the women alone?

He waited, pretending to examine his cigarette in case they were observing him. But after five minutes it seemed clear to him that the place was entirely empty. He took a few steps onto the property, thinking he would quickly withdraw if someone appeared at the window. No one did. He ventured closer—and that's when he heard the moaning.

It was not human, but contained too much despair to be animal. The lowing came from the rude corral the Benders had set up out of barked wood and thatch. Walking casually, hand in pockets as if he was perfectly entitled to be there, he went to the corral, snubbed out his cigarette, and peeped inside.

What he saw was something he had never encountered in a lifetime around livestock. A calf was lying inside the shelter, tied by the neck. From the number of flies on it, and slow undulation of masses of maggots under the skin, it must have died days earlier, maybe a week. Its mouth was open in that way he'd seen dehydrated cattle on open range, the tongue blue and extruded. Even in death it was still pointed in the direction it had strained to go in its last moments.

The cow was still standing there, just out reach of her calf. On seeing Toles, she cast a soft brown-eyed gaze on him, shook her head and loosed a long, groaning utterance that seemed to invite her own death. Between her legs hung the entrails of her burst udders. These were fibrous and pink and peppered with flies planting their young in her living flesh. Abruptly the breeze shifted, and he was struck in the face by the smell—the dank stench of the calf and the putrid emanations from the mother as she rotted from within.

Before Billy Toles was quite sure of what he was doing, he was running. Quite forgetting his horse, he ran all the way to Harmony Grove, not stopping for wondering passersby but jabbering about corruption and the Benders and the inhumanity he had seen. He ran to the house of Leroy Dick and pounded on the door with two hands, frightening Mary Ann Dick half to death when she opened up.

"Goodness, is there a fire?"

Called to speak, his tongue had gone too dry to utter a word. He bent over, hands on his knees, collecting himself as Leroy's boot steps sounded across the boards. And then he was there, breakfast napkin stuck in his collar.

"What's on your mind, Billy?"

"The Benders . . ." he rasped. "The Benders is gone."

Chapter Twenty-Two

Hell's Half-Acre

APRIL 23, 1873

"MEN, GET YOUR shovels!" Leroy cried. "I think I see a grave."

The searchers ran en masse to the orchard, their heels churning up the soil Pa Bender had so frequently groomed. The oblong patch of ground was so difficult to see that Dick lost sight of it from ground level.

"Billy, fetch that rig over here!" he ordered. Mounting the runabout again, he saw the outlines of the grave, its backfill less shrunk from the rain because it was packed tighter than the seed mounds around it. By gestures, he directed George Mortimer to the spot. Mortimer looked at his feet for a few moments until, with a rueful nod, he perceived what Dick meant.

"Bring me a spade."

The Mortimer brothers, George and Tom, made short work of the digging. Just a few feet down the edge of George's shovel struck something half solid. He eased the soil aside, exposing a surface that was at first impossible to read. With another nudge, some of the caked soil fell away, revealing a human scalp.

"Sweet Jesus!"

"The Lord spare us!"

The Mortimers dropped their shovels and exposed the body with bare hands. The victim was a white man, facedown and naked, his knees bent at shallow, awkwardly opposed angles. By evidence of the light gray of his hair he was about forty years old. The dirt made it difficult to assess the condition of the skin, but Leroy could tell this was not an old burial. Forced to guess, he'd have said he died within the week.

"Was he *mahrdered*?" asked John Moneyhon, his brogue manifesting a combination of "murdered" and "martyred."

Kneeling beside the body, Tom Mortimer worked to expose the face. The neck was stiff; turning the head was a struggle, until something seemed to crack within and the neck became an elastic stalk, free to turn beyond any natural angle.

As sunlight fell on the dead man's features they saw the eyelids were parted, the eyeballs purplish and protruding. The nose was entirely missing, leaving a chambered cleft. The neck itself was split open, the flesh rippling grotesquely, like crumpled paper. It didn't take a coroner to tell that the victim's face had been smashed with some blunt object, his throat carved from ear to ear.

The body's discovery electrified the crowd. A tumult of explanations expanded concentrically as witnesses in front turned to explain what they saw to those behind them. After that, cries of outrage, grief, and—here and there—an incongruous sprinkling of laughter from those who couldn't take their tragedy without a dose of humor.

That was when Leroy Dick finally became aware of the size of the throng. There were already more people gathered around the grave than had attended Sunday's Harmony Grove meeting. Another mob swarmed around the Bender cabin. Still more people—people he didn't recognize, people he never saw at church—converged from every direction. He had no idea that many folk lived in this quarter of the state, much less Labette County.

Some came mounted and some on wheeled conveyances, but most seemed to go on foot. How had they known to start this way in time? he wondered. How had they known there would be something to see? For he was used to uncovering acts of violence in his jayhawking days, and during the war, but this time felt different. In wartime, civilians stayed clear, lest they become casualties. Here, the carnage exerted an attraction that seemed as irresistible as it was ghastly. Some of the newcomers brought their children. Some bore picnic baskets.

One useful arrival was Dr. Erasmus Keebles of Thayer. An older gentleman on the edge of retirement, he took a fast, fortifying swallow of rotgut before easing down from his buckboard. The crowd parted for him as he shambled over the uneven ground, one leg dragging from an old war wound. At the grave, he knelt and went through the formality of feeling for a pulse.

"Is this your missing doctor?" he asked.

The question drew blank faces. Though William York had lately become the most discussed man in Labette County, no one knew what he looked like in life. There was no photograph, and the only man nearby who knew him personally, Whistler, had honored his boss's instructions not to approach the Bender claim.

"He sort of looks like his brother," said Minister Dienst, tilting his head sidewise.

Now that they knew what to look for, the men trampled the apple saplings in search of more graves. There weren't enough shovels to go around, so they tore the earth with boards pried from the Benders' fence. Soon they turned up another body— again male, again naked. This one had several large holes punched through the back of his skull. On seeing these, a certain corre- spondence occurred to Leroy.

"Billy, please fetch those hammers from the cabin."

He returned with the three they'd discovered under the stove. Hefting each in turn, Leroy selected the largest hammer and knelt over the remains. The head precisely fit the wounds in the back of the victim's skull.

"It's the devil's work!" someone cried.

Leroy felt a fit of light-headedness. The quality of this body's decay, its reduction to a bag of bones, was too close to that other corpse he had helped bury on the prairie years before. It was a memory he had succeeded in repressing for a half his lifetime, but was all the more powerful now that it had stirred. He shot upright, trying to settle his stomach with a deliberate effort of will. But he had to walk away for the moment, retiring some distance from the orchard to find his calm.

Looking back, he considered the frenzied nest of activity around the Bender claim as if he were peering through a telescope. With this remoteness came another wave of emotion—this time dismay. He was no detective, but he knew that such a disorga- nized search, no matter how righteously intended, would destroy as much evidence as it would recover.

The stir over the discovery of the murder weapon lasted only a moment before the throng's attention was compelled by the next outrage. The third burial was a collection of severed human limbs. These were more corrupted than the whole bodies, blackened by what appeared to be a halfhearted attempt to incinerate them. As George Mortimer probed the remains with his wagon rod, he uncovered a small leather-bound book. Fishing out the half-rotted thing, he read the spine:

"It's *The Book of Mormon*."

The sun climbed and the temperature rose and more bodies came to light. The exposed burials and the churning of hundreds of feet turned the trim little orchard into a blasted moonscape. Someone showed up with unused rafters from a barn-raising. A gang of men positioned the wood under the Bender cabin and levered it off its foundations, exposing the tiny cellar and crawl space. As sunlight fell on those fetid spaces for the first time, the crowd of onlookers pressed in close, as if expecting to see a fully equipped dungeon. All they got, however, was a sandstone slab smeared with an indefinite brown substance, and a face full of stink. Most of them soon turned away, handkerchiefs at their noses. Not a few were temporarily put off their picnics.

A thorough search of the cabin turned up a miscellany of objects—lengths of broken watch chain, money clips empty of money, eyeglasses, assorted buttons from a dozen different garments. For lack of clear evidence connecting these to any of the bodies, they were piled on a barrelhead in the yard. Passersby pocketed them as souvenirs. And when they ran out of compelling mementoes, they started to work on the cabin itself, tearing off wallboards, sashes, roof shingles. Most of these, the genuine remains of the notorious Butchers' Inn of Labette County, ended up as conversation pieces in parlors all over the state of Kansas.

Certain of these objects became the focus of private rituals. Some were burned, to ritually punish the Benders through the things close to them. Still others were thought of in a different way: according to certain contrarians, anything the Benders touched had protective power, capable of warding off fell influences because they were imbued with such powerful evil. Horseshoes from the Bender corral were kept as talismans for years, falling ultimately to children and grandchildren never informed of their history. The last corroded remains of a Bender horseshoe was tossed in a slag heap by a descendant of the blacksmith Daniel Lindsay in 1932, after hanging over the door of his shop for almost sixty years.

Dr. Keebles approached Leroy, unlit smoke in mouth and patting himself in search of a match. Leroy struck one of his own.

"Obliged," the doctor mouthed around his cigarette. After a long drag, he said, "I understand you're the man to talk to about the disposition of the bodies."

"I can't claim any such thing."

"Who's the coroner in these parts, then?"

"It's Dr. Bender—no relation—up in Iola."

"Well, we need to get these bodies under cover soon or there won't be much left to identify."

There were a half-dozen open graves in and around the orchard. None of the bodies were of local people, so there had yet been no identifications. A message had been sent to Whistler for his help, but neither he nor the messenger had returned yet.

There was a commotion as more remains surfaced. The diggers around the grave seemed compelled to gaze longer at this one, until their faces all seemed to orient in Leroy's direction.

"Aren't they calling you?" Keebles asked.

"Appears so."

They walked together with little urgency. Or more accurately, with all the urgency drained from them, for as the full scale of the calamity sank in, a few more bodies could do nothing to make it worse. As they approached, most of the diggers seemed to wander away, as if realizing some prior engagement. When he and Keebles got there, only Minister Dienst was left. He had an expression on his face, a look of empathic sufferance, that Leroy saw him wear at funerals for infants who'd died too young to have names.

"I'm sorry, Leroy," Dienst said, laying a dirty hand on his shoulder.

"We're all sorry . . ." Leroy began as he looked into the hole.

This one was dumped faceup. The features didn't register to Leroy's eyes at first, as he regarded the gash across the throat and the fingertip-sized bruises at the jaw. It occurred to him that he had finally achieved the kind of clinical gaze necessary for this kind of work. But then he allowed himself to look at the victim's face—to look at it as one would a living person, instead of a body of perishable evidence. That's when its familiarity dawned on him.

"Heavens no . . ." he began, then choked. He said: "God help me, what will I tell Mary Ann? What will I tell her?"

He removed his hat, because he could think of nothing else to do. And then, alternately holding the hat at his side and in front of him, he despaired of his composure once more and walked away.

Keebles studied the poor soul in the pit for a few moments, then tossed his cigarette.

"Is this someone he knows?" he asked Minister Dienst.

"His cousin. A rootless soul, as I recall. I don't believe they even knew he was missing."

"*His* cousin? And his first thought was for his wife's feelings. Remarkable."

"It is not remarkable," replied the other, "if you know anything about our Leroy Dick."

The Benders' horse and rig were gone. After the rain, the wheel ruts of the old army wagon, with its mismatched axles, were only faintly visible. Some diligent souls took it upon themselves to track it off the property and onto the Osage. At least initially, they seemed to have gone northeast, in the direction of Fort Scott. But the rush of onlookers soon turned the trail into an indecipherable mess. New arrivals from that direction were asked if they'd met a party of two men and two women along the way. No one had.

There was talk of launching a posse that very day. But Leroy had no hope a blind search would turn up the Benders. They had at least several days' head start, and there was no reason to expect they had stuck to the trail. In that time the fugitives could have reached any of several railheads, each of which could have taken them in several directions. The best hope for justice lay in wiring out an alert, hoping for further information.

But as the bodies piled up and the mood of the crowd grew uglier, it became less content simply to wait around, taking in the Benders' handiwork. The searchers dug into an old well, discovering a pair of corpses disposed haphazardly together. A bit of velvet ribbon in the hair of one body suggested they'd found their first woman of the day. The victims apparently were a couple, traveling together when they made the fateful mistake of visiting the grocery. Minister Dienst remembered hearing of a missing couple when he was in Humboldt the previous year: they were newlyweds—she from Missouri, he bringing her back to a claim he'd staked in California. The girl was only fifteen.

Then someone noticed that Rudolph Brockman was among the gawkers. He was walking from grave to grave, a peculiar expression on his face—not so much shock or disgust, but rueful, as if some suspicion of his had been confirmed.

"Brockman! Tell us where your friends are!" shouted Tom Mortimer.

"Weren't you with that witch after church the other day?" someone else chimed.

"The nerve of him coming back here!"

A look of slow, heavy-eyed surprise, like a cow at the end of the slaughter chute, came over Brockman's face. He had not anticipated this kind of trouble. If he had, he wouldn't have tied his horse so far away. With unconvincing nonchalance, he reversed course.

"Get that man!" shouted a picnicker.

A mass of grasping avengers closed around Brockman. They secured him by arms, legs, shirtfront. Someone plucked the slouch-rimmed cap off his head and tossed it into the crowd, triggering a scrum over its possession.

"*Lass mich in Ruhe! Ich bin unschuldig!*"

"You shut that squarehead talk!"

"*Ich kannte sie nicht! Lassen Sie mich gehen!*"

"I warned you . . ." said Mortimer, and after measuring the distance with outstretched arm, slugged Brockman across the mouth. His hand had a rock in it. The force of the blow drove one of the German's half-rotted eyeteeth into his mouth.

"Take him inside!"

They all understood what this meant. With Brockman half staggering among them, a dozen men pushed their way into the Bender cabin. Keebles followed with Leroy, who shouted, "This is unlawful, boys! He should be taken to the marshal for questioning."

"Every minute those bastards get further away!" replied Billy

Toles, and then added—because he was still haunted by the starved calf, "Right before her eyes, it was!"

"There's a way to do this properly. Tell them, Minister."

Dienst looked at Leroy with practiced compassion, then shook his head. "I'm sorry, Leroy, but I agree with them."

When the searchers lifted the cabin they left it slightly askew on the ground. Some of the men stood uphill of the others as they tore down the canvas partition. By the pitiless light of a naked oil lamp, they looped a rope around a rafter. John Moneyhon tied the noose, looking up from his work now and then to give Brockman a black look. The latter went on in German, bemoaning his fate, cursing his tormentors, but at that moment none of them would acknowledge understanding his language, much less take sympathy.

They noosed him and held him as three men took hold of the other end of the rope. Then, with the same collective "*Ho!*" they voiced at barn-raisings, they lifted Brockman three feet off the floor. Their one concession to mercy was to leave his hands free. As he dangled, he struggled for purchase on the rope as he sputtered and spat blood from his bloody gums.

"Still sounds like his *jarman*," joked Moneyhon.

They studied him as his face went from white to pink to red to blue. When his eyes had bugged so far that their roots were exposed and his movements seemed drunken, they released the rope. He dropped to the floorboards too weak to break his fall with his hands.

George Mortimer stood over him. "Where are the Benders?" he asked. "They couldn't have done all this alone. They had help. Where did they go?"

He only gasped and wheezed, so they hung him again. Another

lamp was lit and placed on the table, casting an enlarged, twisting shadow of Brockman against the roof.

This time they waited until his tongue poked out like a blue-headed snake from its hole, and Minister Dienst spoke up.

"That's enough."

They dropped him. Mortimer knelt and asked again, "Where are the Benders?"

Too exhausted to struggle for breath, Brockman simply stared back.

"Up."

Their neighbor was pulled aloft again. By now Leroy was furious. He was not only embarrassed to be part of such crude proceedings, he was conscious of the crowd of witnesses gathered around the open doors and windows. Pairs of unflinching eyes shined through the holes in the walls left where the souvenir hunters had peeled away the boards.

At the back window there was a stranger in a herringbone suit. Engrossed, the man struggled to drink in everything with his eyes as he scribbled furiously in a notebook.

"There are going to be murder charges if this goes much further!" Leroy warned.

They ignored him, observing as Brockman kicked and swung. Soon his eyes turned back in their sockets and he lost consciousness.

"Can't you tell he didn't know?" Leroy said. "Why would he show up here if he was part of it?"

"He knows somethin'."

Leroy pushed Mortimer aside and hugged Brockman's legs.

"Let him go!"

They dropped the rope, letting the twitching body fall on

Leroy, who teetered for a moment as he tried to keep his balance, then collapsed.

No one moved as Leroy disentangled himself. All of them seemed in a state of moral suspension—waiting, like the third parties outside, to see if events would brand them just or damned.

Keebles came forward and laid a finger athwart Brockman's neck. He seemed about to declare something, then paused as he kept his hand there.

"He's alive," he granted.

The men's faces were impassive. By the time Brockman's eyes were open, most of them had already skulked away. Later, few of them, except for Leroy Dick, would ever acknowledge they were in the room that night.

Leroy sat beside Brockman as the latter recovered his wits. After ten minutes he turned on his side and begged for a drink; Leroy found a tin cup on the stove and some more or less fresh water in a cask. Tasting it, Brockman spat it out and said, "I said a *drink*."

"Sounds like your English is back."

The other man rolled to his knees and treaded the empty air behind him as he tried to gain purchase on the floor. It took him several fruitless minutes to become reacquainted with his extremities. Leroy stood up with him, a steadying hand on his elbow, until Brockman bent over again to fetch a hat—not his own, which was long before claimed by the crowd, but someone else's, abandoned in the tumult. It was too small for him, so he mashed it down over his chapped pate. If it had a decent brim he would have covered his face, but the narrow shade concealed only his eyes.

As he turned to leave, he turned up his collar to hide the rope burns around his neck. Leroy held his arm.

"It would sure be a service if you told us what you know. About those Benders."

Brockman faced him, eyes hidden but lips pressed thin. It looked to Leroy like regret but was something else. The trustee, after all, had no experience in common with the unrequited. For even as they were hoisting Rudolph Brockman by his neck, even as his windpipe closed and the gallery of his tormentors receded to a dull smudge of light at the center of his vision, it was *her* words he heard, making him promises as empty as the air he clutched.

"She never called on me," he said, voice dry. Then he pulled away from Leroy's grasp and headed into the night.

Eight whole bodies had been recovered that day, along with partial remains of three more. By the end of the day, with no more graves appearing, the casual onlookers began to drain away, leaving only a few figures to cast divided shadows by the light of scattered torches.

It was late, nearly midnight, when Colonel York arrived with a small entourage and a wagon. Whistler jumped down, and after examining the first body recovered that morning, gave York a grim nod. The latter didn't dismount, but only turned his face into the night. The coffin was off-loaded, opened, and filled with the doctor's remains. When it was lashed in the bed of the wagon, York approached Leroy.

"Know where they went?"

"Nobody knows."

"How many others, besides our Bill?"

"Eight. Ten. Hard to say."

York chewed this over. "I suppose you'll all be moving on, then."

"Moving on? Why?"

"A town can't survive something like this. They murdered it, along with these poor souls."

Leroy considered this. Clearly, this was the grimmest day in the short history of the township, even counting the war and the troubles that preceded it. But the thought that the homes they had built, the schoolhouse they had raised with their own hands, were to be condemned by the acts of a few itinerant maniacs, struck him as unjust beyond measure. By some chance, he thought of the little blackboard in the classroom, where every Sunday he would write chapter and verse in his most careful hand. He knew that little blackboard, with its maplewood frame and the chip in the upper right corner the size of a half-dollar, as thoroughly as any stretch of real estate in the vicinity. Losing it suddenly seemed the most tragic thing in the world to him.

"I don't think that's right," he said.

"Better move on," replied York as he turned his horse around. "This place will go back to desert, mark my words."

The colonel and his party left immediately, not stopping for the night in any of the surrounding towns. For his part, Leroy haunted the site until his watch chimed once. Then he finally climbed on his runabout, hoping to snatch a few hours' rest before returning in the morning. His prospects for sleep, alas, were dim.

As he left, one of the other lingering figures darted toward him. "Twelve men have already promised," said a breathless George Majors. "More guns may come on later, when the posse meets. At sunup."

Though he was justice of the peace, magisterial distance was not Majors's style; he was in among the grave diggers from the first hours of the search. "Can we count on you?" he pressed.

"I can't make no promises. There are duties for me here."

"You can come when you can. But hurry up. We'll have them sons of bitches before long."

As Leroy pulled out he sighted something new on the edge of the Bender property. Closer, he found a sign, newly painted and erected in a pile of dirt. It read:

THIS CLAIM TAKEN, APRIL 1873, BY R. ELDER

Chapter Twenty-Three

The Benders Divide

A WEEK EARLIER the four Benders woke in the dark. Silently, they went about their morning ablutions, dressed, and made their last survey of the cabin's contents. When they mounted the wagon, the crickets had hushed, the sky entwined in the purple fingers of dawn.

The outlines of the cabin were just becoming discernible as Kate regarded it for the last time. She had lived in it for nearly two and a half years, longer than in any single place in her life. At that moment it was empty, but also crowded, for they'd left faces permanently etched in its nail heads and knotholes. They gaped at her as she sat with Almira and Flickinger. The latter glanced at the fine gold watch he had taken from Clarrity, and cursed Junior's soul. When the younger man joined them on the wagon, he had a look of accomplishment on this face. "Almost forgot to wind the clock," he explained.

"Why?" asked Almira, in that way that promised no answer would suffice.

They took the trail for as long as they dared, fearing with every turn of the wheels they would meet someone they knew. Two miles out they could no more afford to go east; the old man, making liberal use of the switch, turned the horse due north, directly over the prairie. The ride off the trail was smoother, with no grounding and bouncing through ruts. The only sound—other than the creaking of the ancient springs—was the hiss of tall grass as it caressed the underside of the wagon. Looking back, Kate could see four lines of flattened grass unspooling behind them.

"We're leaving a track," she said.

"It won't last the day," replied Junior.

"That might be too long."

By mid-afternoon they approached Thayer. The LL&G line, bound for Parsons, lanced straight southeast before dead-ending a few miles beyond the town. Following the new tracks, they reached the railroad station but stopped well away from any other soul. Junior stood in the wagon bed, tossing their baggage down to the old man, as Kate and Almira attended to their tickets.

Kate suffered a stab of anxiety when she found the window unattended. Pressing her face against the bars, she could just see the agent seated to her right, napkin tucked into his collar as he slurped from a bowl. She knocked on the window frame, and failing to get his attention, rapped harder. He looked up, frowned.

"You're acting like you're on the run," Almira whispered in her ear.

Kate waved her off as if bothered by a fly.

"Help you, miss?" asked the agent through potato-crusted teeth.

"Four to go as far as Humboldt."

"Round-trip?"

"One way."

"She means round-trip," Almira interjected. And to forestall any argument, she discreetly jabbed a fingernail into the flesh of Kate's arm.

The agent looked at them. "Which is it, ladies? One-way or round-trip?"

"Round-trip, sorry," replied Kate.

Tickets in hand, they returned to find their baggage piled on the rude plank road that served as a platform. Having abandoned the cabin sooner than they expected, they'd had no time to purchase proper luggage. Their belongings were stuffed instead in the kind of random containers seen among destitute souls fleeing a few steps ahead of their creditors: an apple crate roped in a bedspread, a canvas feed bag lashed with wire, a trunk clad in spotted dog hide, so old and worn it gleamed in the sun.

Junior stood nearby, smoking. When he turned, he gave Kate a look of simple, unabashed delight, as if he expected never to see her again. The look worried her, as it seemed to suggest that he saw some future in their collaboration.

"Where is himself?" Almira asked him.

"Tending to the wagon."

"And the bank?"

He smiled, dragged on his cigar, rolled it from his lips. "You know he won't let it out of his sight."

"You let him go alone?"

He shrugged. "Where's he gonna go?" Then he opened his jacket, exposing the pistol he kept holstered there.

There had been few times in the last two years when their hatbox full of cash was out of Almira's direct control. If she had been a locomotive, she would have had to bleed off steam to keep from exploding. "Well, he'd better hurry up," she grumbled. "Train's almost in."

On the theory that a wagon abandoned at the station would attract attention more quickly, Flickinger drove it out of town. A half mile west he found a stream shaded by a copse of cottonwoods. He left the wagon there, the horse tied to the wheel to keep it from attracting attention. He didn't bother to check if everything was removed from the bed. The only thing he retrieved was the precious hatbox, tucked under his arm.

Shading her eyes with a gloved hand, Kate recognized him a long way off by his stooped, simian shuffle.

THE TRAIN—A GILT-EDGED American with the broad-mouthed funnel of a wood-burner—pulled in before Flickinger was quite there. With only a few passengers getting off and only the Benders waiting to board, the stop was destined to be brief. Junior tossed their bundles up to the porter in the baggage car as the women watched the old man. He was doing his impression of a man running, arms and legs moving but not seeming to propel him any faster than his gouty usual.

Fortunately there was a delay as the engineer came down from his cab. Ignoring the privy house that was right beside the station, the engineer stepped beside the driving wheels and—after checking there were no ladies about—urinated on a squeaky leaf spring. He gave it a good soaking, spraying it until the hot metal ceased steaming and the stock was marked with his particular odor. Fastening his flap, he looked up and discovered a ten year-old girl with her head out a carriage window, watching. He tipped his cap to her.

As Flickinger ran, the hatbox rang and crunched under his arm, sounding to Kate exactly like it was—a load of ill-gotten loot. Mounting the track, he stumbled, hitting the roadbed with a metallic clang that caused Kate and Almira to gasp in unison. The "bank," fortunately, did not spill its contents. He collected himself and rose just as the engine gave its last whistle.

There weren't many passengers originating in Thayer, a small town at the end of the line. The last car was empty except for a sleeping drunk who had come from the direction of Humboldt and was now slumbering his way back. The Benders took the middle, opposing seats in the center of the car. They sat in silence, avoiding each other's eyes as the train picked up speed, and Kate began to feel—not just hope—that she was leaving Kansas behind for good. Glancing out the window, she imagined a lone, heroic figure on horseback, pacing the train, his face at once featureless and turned lovingly in her direction.

The conductor, working his way from the back of the train to the front, came by to check their tickets. Almira handed them over without exposing her face to him. The old man made no acknowledgment at all, but Junior offered a wide, over earnest grin that seemed more than the occasion demanded. Fortunately, the conductor was nearly as indifferent to them as the empty seats around them. Glancing up as he punched their tickets, Kate searched his blue eyes and saw nothing reflected there.

The stop at Chanute had come and gone when it finally seemed safe to speak aloud.

"Much as I'm enjoying this journey, am I alone in thinking we should discuss our split?"

Almira turned to her, then the drunk down the carriage, then back to Kate. "Split? What split? We stay together."

"I say that's the stupidest thing we could do, considering they're looking for a party of four, two women and two men."

"If you think you're going to put something over on us by taking more than your fair share . . ."

"She's right," declared Junior. "Four together is conspicuous, but two couples might get away, no trouble."

"Nobody asked you," Almira snapped, and glared at Kate. It was a face Kate had seen before, whenever the possibility of parting from her long-term had been raised. A more naive soul might have mistaken this for affection, but Kate took it only as fear of losing her meal ticket.

Then, with a prefatory rumble, the old man spoke: "We split. Soon as we can."

There was a brief silence as they all absorbed this eruption.

"If we must, then it's by sex," Almira said. "You and the boy go south, me and the girl north."

"What's to draw a body south?" asked Junior.

"If you paid half a goddamn mind when we talked about this before, you wouldn't ask fool questions."

"You take it to the end of the line and keep going south and west," Kate explained. "Down near the border there are places with no law. The whites stay north, and the Mexicans keep south, and they try to forget what's in the middle."

"Sounds like no place for a woman," he replied. "Almira, you go."

"Like I said—the men go south, the women have no trouble hiding out back East. In some city or other."

Kate made her play: "Husbands and wives would be just as good. Better maybe, because nobody hardly wonders about a couple traveling together."

Almira dealt her a look hotter than the embers flying by their carriage window. Junior, by contrast, fairly gleamed with pleasure.

"Don't think I don't know what you're about," Almira grumbled. "You still think you're the smart one, don't you?"

"I think the proposition should at least be put up for a vote."

"Seconded. And I vote to divide by couples," Junior declared.

"And I say by sex!"

"Then it's two to one so far," said Kate, and turning to Flickinger, "Declare yourself."

The old man seemed not to hear. She was about to repeat the demand when he suddenly threw his head back, exposing the thatches of thick gray hairs ringing his nostrils.

"*Kein Zweifel*, the witch is right," he said. "It's no place for a girl."

The other three looked at each other, confused.

"So how do you vote?"

"*Ich will nicht.*"

"An abstention, then!" chirped Junior. "Two to one, the motion carries."

Almira jabbed him in the side with her elbow. "I say, like hell it does! This isn't the damned Territorial Congress!"

"It's decided," Kate growled. "I won't go another step with you, and that's it."

Almira stared at her with rage barely contained. But when Kate did not relent, and the matter seemed to drop, her rheumy eyes softened into something like tender wounds. When she spoke again, there was a quaver in her voice.

"So it is over, then? For all my trouble over you, it ends just like that?"

Kate, unmoved: "If you expect anything more, you're as stupid as you are low."

Almira turned to the window, lashing them all with her silence. Or so she thought.

For her part, Kate could hardly contain the happy pounding of her heart. If she was truly free of Almira, she was one step closer to reunion with her father, and out from the shadow of Clarrity at last.

The Negro porter removed their motley belongings from the train at Humboldt and hung around with open palm. The old man, still clutching the hatbox full of money, merely stared at him until the porter gave up. Kate, taking pity on him, opened her little embroidered purse and gave him two bits.

The four of them stared at each other as the train pulled out and everyone else on the platform receded out of earshot. As much as they were tired of each other, they were the only close company each had known for many months. Kate's imminent independence excited her, but also filed her with a sick-making apprehension. The chin ribbon securing her hat suddenly felt too tight. Loosening it, she found her gloves bothered her too, so she tore those off.

"So who goes south?" asked Junior.

Almira, who observed Kate's discomfort with a certain satisfaction, wagged her head. "You *Kinder* would never make those outlaw camps."

"I won't argue with that."

The women got tickets: two one-way trips to Lawrence for Kate and Junior, and two for Vinita, in Oklahoma Indian Territory, for

Flickinger and Almira. The men, meanwhile, retired to a privy to divide the bank. The process took a while. There was a line at the door by the time they came out, with some—but not all—puzzled to see two men come out of a piss-house together.

As Junior came back she interrogated him with her eyes. He nodded: the old man had offered no trouble on the division.

"How much?" she asked.

"Forty-nine thousand six hundred and fifty two."

So there was something more than twelve thousand dollars coming to her. She turned the sum over in her mind, relishing the prospect of impressing her father with such a bankroll. She envisioned his approval as he saw what an earner his little girl had become. There were many games she could stake him with that kind of fortune—which wouldn't be strictly necessary, of course, because such a successful gambler would not need her help.

More immediately, it would be enough to establish "Professor Katie Bender" in a style appropriate to her skills. She could purchase property in any of the better neighborhoods in Chicago, Buffalo, New York. Instead of cheap handbills, she could afford to advertise in the weekly magazines. When she'd worked at the Cherryvale Hotel, she had taken copies of *Harper's Bazaar* that had been left in the dining room. Often, she'd lost track of time leafing through its pages, imagining her skills extolled there in fancy type, until Jeremiah Moore or Alice Acres reminded her to get back to work.

Thinking this way, she hadn't noticed Almira sidling up to her.

"I was a girl once, when me and my mother worked the Alte Brücke in Frankfurt. Did you know I had a pet?" she asked. "It was a little white hound, white all over with a black tail and black—

how are they called—*socken.* That's what I called her, after those paws. I loved that dog, from his pink nose to his pointy tail, so much that I would steal food to feed it. You see these scars on my hands? I earned them back then, when I was caught with a bit of *wurst* from a cart. The butcher did me with a horsewhip, and though they bled and I made tears from the pain, I took my punishment, *willens,* for this hound, because he went to sleep satisfied that night, with his little belly full."

Kate sucked in her breath and released it slowly as she endured the inescapable.

"Until the day I woke up under the bridge, and Socken was not there. I looked on every street and down every alley. I took more beatings from my mother because I would not bring the men to her, I would look for this dog. I went to sleep the first day with wet eyes. And the second night. Until the third night, when I knew he would not come back. In those days, small animals were eaten by the rats if they were not guarded. That's what I think happened to my sweet little Socken, when I was not watching.

"But you see I was wrong, because on the seventh day he did come back. He was dirty, but plump, because he'd found some dumping somewhere, some offal, and had spent his time eating himself fat. He came back to my arms happy, moving his tail. And I made tears when I picked him up, and tears when I took him to the Main. I could hardly see him as I pushed him into the water, and held him under as he fought me. Until he shook and stopped moving. Then I let him go, to float down the river, with all the other things people threw from the bridge. And that was the last pet in my life, my Socken. Did you know that?"

She found Kate's eyes, and in the manner of her gaze drove

home her meaning. Kate, for her part, would not begrudge her the satisfaction of a response. For if circumstances ever tempted her to go back to Almira, she would certainly drown herself first.

"Better get ready," she said. "Train'll come soon."

It was the southbound, for Indian territory. Now that they had voted to separate, neither party wanted the burden of luggage. Almira and Flickinger took the apple crate and feed bag, on the theory that they would attract less notice in the rougher parts they were bound to; Kate and Junior were left with the steamer trunk clad in hideous dog hide. They would have abandoned it, if it meant all that potential evidence was forever beyond discovery. But of course it did not. For their transgressions, the pursuit would come, and would find every bit of material left behind. Each step in their journey would be reconstructed to the limits of the memories of everyone they met. For their safety, they could presume nothing less than Pinkertons on their trail, or what was marginally worse, God Himself.

The train was bell-less and black and unadorned like a cast-iron stove. No passengers got off, and the conductor had his watch out as soon as he hit the ground—the universal symbol of the short stop. Just like that, the moment of separation came. The men exchanged a handshake of two parties contractually satisfied. Leaving her bags to the old man, Almira pulled up her skirts and mounted the carriage. She refused to look at Kate or Junior, keeping her eyes fixed forward as she took her seat.

"She's blood-addled," explained Flickinger as he grasped Kate's hand. Kate had never touched him before, and as much as she expected that to be a disagreeable sensation, she was surprised: the hand was warm and mostly greaseless. He did not overpress. And there was unwonted softness in the way his eyes peered through his dangling brows, meeting hers.

"It won't last," she finally said.

"The worst things never do."

It was as if she had dropped a glove at the zoo and seen it gallantly returned by an ape. With a parting squeeze that was, again, surprisingly human, the old man let her go. Bewildered, she watched him loft his bags on his shoulder and scale the steps with a supple, youthful ease. She looked to Junior, who was equally astonished.

"You really don't know some people." He shrugged.

With a shove that seemed to come from behind, the engine engaged. Kate watched, half disbelieving, as Almira slid away with an ease so much in contrast with her barnaclelike purchase on the rest of her life. As the train rolled away under its fan of gray smoke, she expected Almira to tumble forth at any moment. But no one appeared, and as the train receded to a faint parenthesis on the horizon, she finally allowed herself to contemplate her next step. She turned to Junior.

"Thank God, alone at last," she said, wrapping her arm around his.

His eyes met hers as she cast the old familiar spell—the charm of possibility. He raised his eyebrows: "Yes?"

"Yes," she replied. "After all, aren't we husband and wife?"

To this, he feigned a nonreaction, like a man who would neither believe his luck nor endanger it by asking questions.

The northbound Southern Kansas Railroad train pulled in next, bound for Iola, Lawrence, and points east. Aboard, she took a spot beside him, not across, and kept their bodies in contact. The train accelerated, adopting a slow, loping motion as the roadbed rose and fell upon the shallow undulations of the plain.

They passed Ottawa, where the four of them had started their wagon trip to the cabin in '70; the town seemed larger and fouler than she remembered, with columns of coal smoke rising from a dozen stacks. Roads reached out from the settled area deep into the prairie, ready to serve homesteads yet to be built. Kate glimpsed a farmer behind his plow, flicking his horse with the switch as the steel blades of the sodbuster curled back the turf. He paused, wiped his forehead with his arm, and swiveled his head slowly as he tracked the train into the distance.

An hour later they were in Lawrence. The station serving points south was on the eastern edge of town, at the end of a swooping curve that gave passengers a clear appreciation for the new downtown. This had been rapidly restored after Quantrill's raid during the war. For those who would look, however, lingering evidence of that disaster was not hard to miss: blackened joists of burned buildings and mounds of charred brick were piled roof-high in the bog beyond the tracks.

There were tented carioles waiting at the station to take passengers into town. They hired one to take them to the best hotel in Lawrence, the Eldridge House. They checked in as "Mr. and Mrs. Hancock" of Kansas City.

The act of writing their aliases in the register seemed to propel Junior into paroxysms of anticipation. On the stairs toward what he took to be their nuptial bed, she could sense the excitement in the way he took the steps. She encouraged him, proceeding up before him, rocking her hips before his eyes. Halfway up, she glanced down at him, lashes shining auburn in the lamplight, edges of her lips suggestively curled.

Their room was on the third floor, with a canopied bed lined with ruffled skirts, chinoiserie washbowl, and lacquered commodes trimmed with ivory-colored doilies. She noted a sickly sweet odor, like the scent of dried flowers, but found no bouquet—what she perceived as sweetness was merely the absence of mildew, dust, and horseshit. The refined surrounds, so clearly superior to the squatters' camps and frontier quarters of her adult years, roused long-dormant tastes in her. Though she no longer remembered details of the places she stayed with her father, she felt them, in the place that assured her who she was. It warmed her to think this would be her new life.

The bellhop had only just gone when Junior grabbed her. She countenanced it, suffering his lips on her face as her hat tumbled from her head. He was engrossed in this kissing for some time before he realized she was not kissing him back. Pulling away, he looked at her uncertainly.

"Have I misconstrued what you said before, about being husband and wife?"

"Of course not. It's that *thing*. I can't look at it any longer."

She inclined her head at the dog-hair trunk, which sat cheap and incongruous in the splendor of their room. Releasing her, he stood over the trunk as if to menace it, declaring, "Yes, what an ugly impression must this thing make when our purpose is to make a better one! It should be removed from your sight—the sight of anyone of taste."

As he bent to lift it by the handles, she laughed.

"Best salvage what we can from inside, before it meets its fitting end."

There was not much to save: Almira had packed some of their threadbare bedding and some of the more costly patent medicines. Kate removed a bottle of the latter and put it aside while Junior was not looking. She also rescued the pink hemp ribbon they had taken after Jesperson's murder two years ago—his memento of his lady love. She had meant to dispose of it, but never seemed to find an appropriate place. Fetching about, she failed to find one just then either. She rolled it into a ball and stuffed it in her purse. The rest of the contents she waved for him to take away.

"Be sure it's never to be found."

"No other soul will ever see it."

He was away for half an hour. She contemplated a bath—which she desperately needed—but decided there would be time enough for that later, when she was free. For now, she had to make herself ready for him.

He found her lying on the bed in just her camisole and knee-length drawers, hair flowing down her shoulders like molten bronze from the crucible. For lack of proper rouge, she had colored her cheeks with drops of her own blood. Seeing her, he stared, blinked, swallowed—he forgot to close the door. She angled her torso to the wall, permitting him a glimpse of breast that, despite malicious tongues, no other man had yet seen. He shut the door.

Before getting to cases, she offered him a drink from a cut-glass goblet. He took the glass without looking at its contents, draining it in a single gulp. This made her laugh; bringing him up short, she raised her glass and sipped from it with pointed slowness. He could stand no more. Snatching her goblet, he tossed it across the room and pitched himself on her.

One chiming of the clock later, Kate's camisole and drawers were still on, but Junior was sprawled across the bed in a medicated stupor. His rest was thanks to approximately fifteen doses of Tott's Teething Cordial, "a salubrious Preparation of the most wholesome ingredients Formulated to soothe Baby's nocturnal discomfort." The actual ingredients were not listed on the label, but judging by Junior's drooling on the bedspread, he found them more than "salubrious." He snored with the clicking sound particular to infants.

She dressed, and packed what little she wished to take in a small valise. The case was, in fact, pitifully small—she was leaving all her clothes, shoes, and most of her toilette. Abandoning them was troubling in a small way, but also liberating. She was sloughing away her old skin, shedding the blood and spunk and guilt she had accumulated in all the lost years. The charge of sorcery was there too, and the salt of the witch test, and the residue of shame from Leroy Dick's rejection. For this trip, she wore just a traveling dress of plain linen and a featherless bonnet. If she could have fled to her next career with face veiled completely, faceless like a refugee from the seraglio, she would have. But that would attract its own kind of attention.

There were some $25,000 in banknotes and coin in their joint share of the bank. Gazing at this pile, she contemplated taking it all—but did not. Theft would only oblige him to hunt her down. And whatever one might say about Junior, he had earned his share of the Bender windfall.

She kept the sack, transferring Junior's portion to an empty pillowcase. Then, with a final check in the mirror, she cracked the door. She took a last look at Junior, sparing him a trace sentimental fondness—for she hoped this would be the last time she would lay eyes on him.

When she reached the bottom of the stairs, the desk clerk peeked from behind his newspaper, cocked an eyebrow.

"Checking out already, Mrs. Hancock? Anything amiss with your room?"

"No. Can you arrange a cab for me, please?"

He glanced from her valise to the stairs, as if expecting Mr. Hancock to follow. "Be needing help with your bags?"

"Just a cab to the station, please."

"East- or westbound? There are two stations."

"That, sir, is no one's business but the driver."

"All right."

He tilted himself off his stool to go outside.

"One more thing . . ." she said, holding a fifty dollar banknote so he could see the denomination. He halted. "If Mr. Hancock should inquire where I might have gone, could you see that he doesn't find out from you?"

The clerk smiled.

Chapter Twenty-Four

Bounties

REPORTERS WERE ON the abandoned Bender property right on the heels of the neighbors. Christening it "Hell's Half-Acre," they competed to cast an atmosphere most worthy of Edgar Allan Poe. "What follows in its facts may read like the recital of some horrible dream," began the *Kansas City Times,* "wherein nightmare mirrors upon the distempered brain a countless number of monsters and unnatural things, yet what is set down in the narrative is as true as the sun." The *Times* went on to enliven its readers' breakfasts with the following: "[Dr. York's] . . . skull had been driven into the brain, and from the broken and battered crevices a dull stream of blood had oozed, plastering his hair with a kind of clammy paste, and running down upon his shoulders." In a similar vein the Cincinnati *Commercial* reported, "The excavation beneath the house in which the murderers had allowed their victims to bleed before burial still bore the horrid signs. The scant rains of summer had not washed away the blood from the margin; it was half full of purple water."

As the coexistence of good looks and bad deeds was hard for many to rationalize, one of the few sure things known about the Benders—that Kate was a handsome woman—came in for hasty revision. Her "very high cheekbones, very sharp chin, resemble a wolf," reported the *Southern Kansas Advance,* which went on to describe her as "round or stoop-shouldered, and rather hollow-breasted." In the *Walnut Valley Times* she was "quite young, [with] red hair, and a person of rather repulsive appearance." *Harper's Weekly* had her "a repulsive-looking creature . . . with a vicious and cruel eye." By the time she appeared in the New York *Sun,* she was just "slatternly."

Inquiries went by wire in a widening circle that reached Chicago by the twenty-fourth. They described a family of four, all adults, traveling together and speaking German, with the warning that the youngest and most cunning, the notorious Kate, could for all intents and purposes pass for a real American. From Topeka, Governor Osborne issued a proclamation noting "the atrocious murders recently committed in Labette County, under circumstances which fasten, beyond doubt, the commissions of these crimes upon a family known as the 'Bender family,'" and establishing five hundred dollar bounties for the "apprehension and delivery" of each suspect. Whether they were to be "apprehended and delivered" dead or alive was left ambiguous. The handbills, which bore no illustrations of the suspects, were posted in freight offices and railroad stations. Most of them soon disappeared into the pockets of certain passersby, who supposed they might have a better shot at the Benders if no one else was looking.

Rudolph Brockman wasn't the last immigrant to suffer the suspicions of his neighbors. German-speakers all over state suddenly came in for close, and possibly profitable, scrutiny. The entire Roach family of Ladore, just seven miles from the Bender place, was detained for questioning—until the fact that the family consisted of five people, not four, and that the Roaches were known residents of their town going back to before Benders came to Kansas, convinced cooler heads to free them. The brief description of Old Man Bender in the governor's proclamation ("about sixty years of age, five feet eight or nine inches, German, speaks little English, dark complexion, no whiskers, sparely built") was vague enough to apply widely; lovers of justice all over Kansas were inspired to parade their "Dutch" vagrants and drunks, trophylike, through the streets of their towns. None of them turned out to be Pa Bender. Scores of red-haired Janes were likewise roused from their hovels in work camps and mines, hauled before their local peace officers, and held on suspicion not just of prostitution, but serial murder. None of them panned out as Kate.

Among the good people of southeast Kansas, the Benders' temerity to escape provoked intense frustration. Posses, hastily convened and poorly instructed, hit the trails mere hours after the bodies appeared, heading more or less in random directions. One from Parsons combed the wooded shores of the Verdigris River. A party from Cherryvale went south, into Oklahoma Indian territory. A third out of Thayer, believing the Benders had gone to ground somewhere nearby, left no stone unturned in the countryside around their town. The Thayer posse was so thorough that they halted a party of Minnesota Norwegians on their way to settlement in Colorado. The foreigners were forced out of their wagon at gunpoint, and compelled to unload all their belongings for inspection. Emptying the wagon was a two-hour process that only made the members of the posse more ornery. No suspicious articles were found, and when one of the Norwegians—a sixteen-year-old boy—made the mistake of mouthing off to them in English, he got a pistol-whipping. Asked later why he had accosted Norwegians when the Benders were known to be German, the leader of the posse explained, "Them Norweggers are roundheads, and a roundhead is a roundhead, and nobody can tell me any different!"

The first real break in the case came with a headline in the Thayer *Head-Light*. Down in a nearby draw, a man named Charles Nelson had stumbled on what looked like an old lumber wagon, abandoned with its horse. The horse, a mare, was not in its harness but tied alongside. The harness itself was found under the wagon, as if hastily disposed. The famished animal had been left for so long that she had licked away the wagon's paint and chewed up its rail.

Upon reporting his find, Nelson and a sheriff's deputy returned to examine the wagon more closely. In the box they found some dried, unhusked ears of corn and an old shotgun with one barrel loaded. A wooden board was nailed below that, apparently to patch a hole in the bed. On the board was written the word "Grocery." Prying it loose, they found another word on the reverse, painted in a more clumsy hand: "Grocry."

When Leroy Dick heard about the recovered wagon, he rushed north with Whistler and George Majors. By that time it had been taken to Thayer for safekeeping. The instant the livery doors were opened, Leroy recognized the Benders' old army wagon, with its mismatched front and rear axles. He had seen it parked often enough at Harmony Grove on Sabbath mornings.

"You know for a fact that this belonged to the Benders?" Whistler asked him.

"To a certainty."

"Then I'll be to Independence today. Good day to you, gentlemen."

And with that, Whistler was off to launch the posse outfitted by State Senator York. As Leroy had suspected, the Benders had made for Thayer, the closest railhead. The connection between the wagon mystery and the murders moved the sheriff at Thayer to inquire at the train station. There, he found a ticket agent who remembered a pair of "Dutch" women who had purchased four tickets.

"Would you say these women match the descriptions in the governor's proclamation?" George Majors asked.

Though the bill had been hanging on a post in sight of his window for days, the agent regarded it as if seeing it for the first time. Tugging a lip, he shrugged.

"I suppose they do. To look at them, there wasn't nothing funny about 'em. It was just that they were confused about the kind of ticket they wanted—one-way or round-trip—and that don't happen every day."

"They bought a round-trip?"

"They did."

"The low, crafty bastards."

As Leroy and Majors rode home, the latter was full of plans for the constitution and direction of the party they would launch the next day.

"But the agent says they left by train," Leroy objected. "They're likely a hundred miles from here."

"Maybe they are. Or maybe that's just what they want us to think. Nobody saw them get on that train."

"Well, I guess . . ."

"We have to be sure. And there must be a posse," Majors said, almost plaintively. And of course there had to be one from their town, because it was the place most foully tainted by the Benders' career. In saloons and upon kitchen tables throughout Kansas, the question was still asked how such brazen atrocity could go on in one place for so long without someone sniffing it out somehow. All the adults in the area were confounded by two equally disturbing possibilities: either their moral sense had become nearly as corrupt as the Benders', or they were too stupid to suspect what was going on right under their noses.

One of their defenses was to remark on the "cunning" of the Benders, on the preternatural cleverness they had displayed in duping everyone around them. Of course no one had suspected anything, this defense ran—what decent mind could plumb the depths of the Benders' wiles, especially that of she-wolf Kate, who beguiled men's loins even as she lied to their faces? It wasn't the fault of decent folk to fail to imagine the worst in people. She might even have been a witch.

As Majors went on about the posse, Leroy was quiet. The prospect of riding out stirred up memories he sooner have never confronted again. For despite proclamations from Topeka and talk of bringing the monsters to "justice," he knew what any posse of righteous avengers would do if they caught up with the Benders. A shot behind the ear and a shallow grave for each was the most humane fate that awaited them. If he rode out, he would be jayhawking again—plain and simple.

He kept his misgivings to himself when they reached Har-

mony Grove. He continued to nurse them as a party consisting
of Majors, Billy Toles and his brother Silas, Moneyhon, Mortimer,
Starr, and Lindsay agreed to meet before sunup the next morning,
each bringing as many additional volunteers as he could.

Leroy remained quiet as he went home, took his favorite chair
in the parlor, and picked up an old newspaper—one that thank-
fully did not discuss the Benders. When he failed to concentrate
on the news from Europe, he laid the paper aside, interleaved his
fingers and gazed into the cold fire grate. Have I turned coward?
he wondered. When the conscience quails so violently, how can a
man not suspect his courage? For the sense of inadequacy he felt
was not a vague one, but rooted in true and datable events, palpable as the bump on a bone once broken and poorly set. It ached
anew every time someone gazed on him with that damnable ad-
miration. The esteem that mocked him for being both unworthy
and a fraud for pretending otherwise.

By chance, his eye rested on a swath of blue silk Mary Ann
had left in her embroidering basket. The color took him back to
a certain Sunday morning, when Kate Bender had showed up in
a dress the same color. Though he never made it his business to
notice such things, the robin's-egg vision of her would not quit
his memory. Nor the twist of auburn against her neck, nor her
black eyes turned in his direction, beseeching him from out of
their depths. The voids attracted him despite himself; he felt the
influence of some planet too shadowy and distant to see.

The room was darker when he came out of his reverie. Mary
Ann was standing there, deep within the room and arms crossed
as if she'd been watching him for some time.

"I never told you the truth," she said. "I went to see them once."

Leroy was surprised. "The Benders?"

"It was a while back . . . more than a year. I made them a welcome visit, seeing that they were always off on their own. I brought them a pie."

"You risked your life for a pie."

"Nobody had an inkling of that business then," she replied, irritated with his masculine obtuseness. "Nothing untoward happened . . . at first . . ."

He leaned forward in his seat.

"She showed me all due courtesy, but I could feel there was something amiss," she said. "The girl was afraid of something in that cabin. So I told her she might always seek refuge here, if need be."

"And what reply did she make?"

"She pretended to take offense. But her true feelings were not hard to feature."

"So you'll have no truck with her being a witch?"

"I am not Gertrude Dienst."

Leroy rose and took her in his arms. Being several inches shorter, he had to straighten his spine to kiss her on the cheek.

"You credit that girl too much," he said.

She smiled. "I say she was afraid, but that doesn't make her innocent."

"I'd not think what might have happened to you in that place. You were reckless, madam."

She disarmed him with a smile and pecked him on the nose. Then she left him alone to ruminate in the fading light.

He never thought of himself as a man liable to flights of imagination. But the idea of his Mary Ann alone in that cabin, with the creatures that dwelled there, made him shudder. It was almost as frightening as the thought of the Benders free to continue their predations on other husbands and wives and children, merely by outrunning the consequences of their crimes.

Taking a match from the box in the writing desk, he lit the lamp. It flared, throwing off an infernal glare until he turned the wick lower. When the lamp was set the way he liked it, the parlor was wrapped in warm twilight, its walls remote in the shadows. He could imagine the limits of his sanctum stretching away to a great distance, the mantel clock ticking like the unwinding of the Lord's celestial mechanism. Filled with the calm of domestic repose, he sat back, wanting no more than to watch the ring of oil smoke collect at the mouth of the glass.

What horrors existed in the world without his knowledge, he could do nothing. Running down the Benders, however, was an opportunity to make a difference that could be measured in lives. Confronted with that choice, his conscience could permit him none of his weaknesses.

He found his wife in the kitchen, sitting with a catalog.

"Majors wants us out before the sun. Can't say how long we'll be gone."

She searched his face, measuring the depth of his purpose. She shut the catalog.

"I'll have the coffee on."

THE POSSE RODE the course of the Neosho, watering their horses in the river as the temperature rose to summery heights. They figured the watercourses were a good bet to find the Benders, because the woods along them offered a good place to hide out during the daylight hours. When they were in rifle range, they proceeded in single file, with a good distance between the riders in case of ambush. At night they bivouacked under cover, with regular watches set.

Over coffee and grub they debated what might be in the minds of their quarry. Considering their modus operandi, Junior and the old man were clearly cowards, not willing to risk a fair fight with their victims. It took a fair stretch of imagination to think of them as skilled gunfighters.

"Even a bad shooter can be dangerous notwithstanding—if he's close enough," averred George Majors.

"They didn't just leave their hammers, they left their shotgun," added Billy Toles.

"Yar daft," Moneyhon declared. "With all those souls they planted, you think they didn't come by a few weapons? They're ahrmed to the teeth, I say."

"Small good it'll do 'em if they can't hit a cow from the milking stool," insisted Billy.

Leroy was too keyed up to listen to petty squabbles. "There's merit to all your arguments," he said, "but no sense in trusting to chance. We'll take them as if they shoot like the James gang, and that's that."

They proceeded up the Neosho to Iola, and made inquiries there. No one had seen a party matching the Benders' description, but there was great general interest in recent events in Labette County. Retiring to the local saloon for drinks before heading out, the posse was peppered with questions.

"Is Kate Bender as comely they say?" the barkeep asked Leroy.

"Isn't that a matter of opinion?"

He poured Leroy another drink, unsolicited. "Sure. But is she?"

"Would you like her to be?"

He grinned. "Yes, I would."

"Suit yourself, then," said Leroy, and slapped his empty glass on the bar.

The twelve of them headed out as the sun peeked over the trees. The sensations of a dawn ride, in force and far from home, transposed Leroy a decade in time. The smell of early morning fires from strange hearths likewise took him back; the wary glances of passersby, wondering at his purposes, were no different than those given before the war. He saw the bodies of the dead Defensives on the prairie. He saw fingers in the grass, scattered like worms from the rain, and the desiccated husk of Ernest Tubbs Junior, reciting Latin nouns of the second declension. He sucked in breath. His horse half turned toward him, perceiving his unease. He leaned down, gave him a pat on the neck. The horse laid back his ears.

The farms north of Iola were better established than the ones in southern Kansas. There were proper horse fences and consolidation of claims as the first, dilettante stakeholders had sold out to the successful ones. Here and there rose a church with a proper steeple. Though he felt as if riding into his personal past, he was in fact glimpsing the future of his community. The example was steadying, a tonic after too many hints that his home was beyond the pale of civilization. It may well be rude now, he thought, but soon it would not be. It was in the nature of things.

They reached the railroad, rode along it for a while, then meandered west to rejoin the river. A couple of days out from Harmony Grove, their objective hadn't changed, but their enthusiasm had. Hour after hour in the saddle began to tell on rear ends used to buggy travel. Where the idea of riding down the Benders had seemed a practical possibility from the comfort of their armchairs, reacquaintance with that vast stretch of country cooled their ambitions. What started as a purposeful gallop became a steady walk, then a desultory trudge. For most posses, that was in the nature of things too.

They turned north as they approached the belt of greenery around the riverbed. The Toles boys posted themselves as sweepers on their left, riding as close to the trees as they dared, as the rest of the group observed from within pistol shot. Leroy watched them close, not adverse to the possibility of finding their quarry at last, finally getting the damned thing over with. But they had no such luck: for mile after mile, the sweepers stared between the trees at a river in spring spate, streaming over empty banks. In one spot a few runaway cows sheltered, leaning against the cottonwood trunks. In another they found an abandoned campsite, its patch of ash neatly ringed by cobbles fetched from the river. Billy Toles stuck a finger in it. The ashes were cold.

They went on, thoughts turning to the prospect of lunch. It was therefore with some air of unreality that they saw Billy's brother, Silas, shout and point downstream. Out came the pistols and rifles from their holsters; gone was good order and discipline. Leroy felt his heart scaling his rib cage as the posse converged on the spot where Silas spun his horse and whooped. Was it to be as easy as this?

They had found a camp of one tent, with a small fire burning. Two men were sitting as their biscuits baked in a pan greased with bacon. Their gun belts were hanging from a branch, pistols still in their holsters. Neither moved to retrieve them as the posse approached.

"Morning!" said the one.

"Howdy do, boys!" said the other.

Reining up, Leroy had a good look at them. They didn't have the look of tramps: both were lean of face and more or less clean-shaven, and their equipment was in reasonable shape. Their mounts were fine quarter horses, well-cared-for. There were two men in sight, but three horses.

"Good morning," replied George Majors. "Pardon us for dusting up your camp."

"Not at all," said the one, waving an absolving hand. "I am Mr. Morris, and this is Mr. Crane."

"Pleased to meet you. We're up from Labette Township on peace business. Have you seen four Dutch traveling together, two men and two women? One of the men would be hirsute and ugly, one of the females young and handsome. They are most definitely dangerous."

The men looked at each other.

"Can't say we have, sorry."

"Well, if you happen upon them, here are the particulars . . ."

Majors held out a copy of the governor's proclamation. Rising to take it, Morris glanced at the reward and whistled.

"Two thousand! What'd they do, blow up a train?"

"Read on and you'll see. Good day now."

"Would you like to break your trip with us? We got enough coffee."

"Much obliged, but we have outlaws in our sights."

Majors was turning away when Leroy asked, "I see you've got three horses. Someone else with you?"

Messrs. Morris and Crane smiled at each other in a manner Leroy found disturbing.

"Well, that depends on your definition of 'someone,' " replied the former.

"Can't see that's our business, Leroy, when these gentleman aren't the Benders . . ." said George carefully.

But it was too late: Leroy caught sight of a face peering from between the tent flap. As he stared, the face gathered substance as it found the light, manifesting at last as a girl's.

"Well hello there!" said Mr. Crane. "You've decided to join us, I see . . ."

The newcomer was a Chinese. Leroy could not confidently discern her age, but by her slimness she seemed no more than fifteen. Her face was pale, her features fine, with her nose slightly turned up at the tip. Her long hair, tied off at the end with a piece of burlap, was the kind of gleaming black that shone blue. In those coarse circumstances, he would have called her pleasing to look at—if not for the unhealed cut at the left corner of her mouth, and the bruises around her neck.

"Gentlemen, this is Ah Quim. A partner of ours."

"That really her name?"

"She answers to it for sure. Show the boys, Crane."

Mr. Crane nuzzled the fire with the toe of his boot and kicked out a smoking branch.

"Ah Quim! Fetchee!"

Regarding her companions and the posse with equal wariness, she crawled through the flap. Rising to her bare feet, she revealed she was wearing nothing but a threadbare chemise and an incongruously ornate set of petticoats, like something stolen from a French bordello. Messrs. Morris and Crane watched her with almost parental fondness as she bent, plucked up the branch by the not-glowing end, and brought it back to the fire. From her grimace Leroy could see the wood burned her fingers, but she delivered it without a making a sound. When she was done she turned to go back to the tent, but Mr. Morris held her by the arm.

"Gentlemen, our partner is most dexterous. Now that you've seen her, would any of you care to partake?"

Leroy forced himself to be civil. "Are we to believe this young woman is here by choice?"

"Why don't we ask her? Ah Quim, are you restrained here in any way?"

The girl looked down, muttered something in Chinese.

"What's that prove?" Leroy demanded.

Mr. Crane raised his arms in a gesture intended to indicate the entire world. "As you can see, she is not tied up, and there are no walls around our camp."

"That was not my goddamned question."

"Mr. Dick, a word please!" Majors interjected.

Leroy leaned over in his saddle, spat, and steered his horse next to him.

"What are you doing, Leroy?" Majors whispered. "What business is this of yours?"

"If that girl is anything other than a kidnap, I'd go home right now."

"So what? Throw a chip and you'll hit a chink whore in any of these camps. You think they're all here by choice?"

"Can you see the bruises? On her neck?"

"Every minute we stay here the Benders get farther away. Remember them, the Benders?"

"George—"

"Keep this up and maybe you should go home. Explain it to Mary Ann, your particular interest in 'Ah Quim.'"

Majors looked to Morris and Crane. "We'll be on our way now," he told them. "If you see the party we're looking for, be sure to get word to a peace officer."

"Are you sure you won't take coffee? Something else?" Mr. Morris said.

They continued north. When they had ridden fifteen minutes, and the curl of smoke from Morris and Crane's campfire was no longer visible, Billy Toles shook his head.

"Can't say I like those sons of bitches."

"None of us do," said George. "But we can't stop to correct every shitheel we see, can we?"

Leroy and his horse issued simultaneous snorts, though for different reasons.

They made fifteen miles by the time the night chill crept into the hollows and their stomachs growled for a respite. Hobbling the horses, they let them loose to browse on fresh grass by the river. Leroy stretched his bedroll the farthest away he dared without triggering suspicion. He also made sure he was close to the stream, where the horses would doze.

The men spent a few hours after sunset sitting around camp as they usually did, envisioning the fate of the Benders. Their revenge fantasies took on an increasingly baroque cast the longer the murderers evaded them, with punishments that would make Torquemada blush. Leroy had never taken part in this talk. As much as he despised the Benders, he'd had some direct dealings with them—especially Kate—and found it hard to connect those living persons with evidence of their acts. Taking pleasure in loping off their body parts, or burying them alive, or "giving that witch the one-fer she deserves," could never sit well with someone who had actually seen such acts performed, not so many years before.

"I'll take the first watch," said Silas Toles, a light sleeper who was often seen wandering the camp in the small hours anyway.

"I'm for the second," Leroy volunteered.

The camp settled and the moon rose. After the usual chorus of bodily orifices, Leroy and Silas were left the only ones awake. It seemed only moments to Leroy before he heard the soft chiming of Toles's watch from his breast pocket. Leroy sat up, signaling the other man that he was ready to take over.

Silas Toles was under the blankets only a few moments before he too sawed wood. Leroy went into the bushes and retrieved his horse. Packing his things, he mounted and, from that height, scrutinized the camp again, assuring himself that no one was pretending to be asleep. Then, at a pace deliberate enough for his tack not to jangle, he headed southeast, toward the moon.

Chapter Twenty-Five

Where Leroy's Foolish Act Prompts a Detour

HE REACHED THE camp of Messrs. Morris and Crane just after dawn. They were exactly where the posse had left them. Dismounting some distance away, Leroy tied his horse and proceeded with gun drawn.

Just rekindled, their fire was still smoky. Morris was bent over a cook stand, fiddling with its chain; Crane was leaning against a tree in his underwear, flap open, emptying his bladder. The latter left his gun belt hanging on a branch. Leroy walked up without announcing himself and waited for them to notice him.

"Hello again," said Mr. Morris, eyes finding at Leroy's weapon. "Come to take us up on our offer? Where are your friends?"

"Here presently. Stand away from that fire. And you"—he indicated Mr. Crane—"move away from that belt."

"Might I complete my task?" the latter asked over his shoulder, in a tone that grated him. Leroy let off a shot that shattered the bark a foot from Crane's head. Crane performed a sort of reverse broad jump, irrigating his leg.

Leroy tossed a rope to Morris's feet.

"Tie him to that tree."

"Tend this first?" asked the moistened Crane.

"Please do."

Mr. Crane holstered his johnson. As he presented his arms for his partner to tie, Mr. Morris looked at Leroy with a pitying expression on his face.

"Would it be imprudent to say that this kind of theater is hardly necessary, given that we'd gladly have bargained for the girl?"

"That would imply she was your property to negotiate," replied Leroy.

"We bought her square off a pimp in Denver."

"Then someone needs to have a word with that pimp."

He glanced at the tent to find the girl halfway out, an inquiring curve to her brow. Her hair was pinned high on her head, revealing fresh red marks on her neck.

When Morris had Crane secured, Leroy shoved the former against a different tree and tied him himself. The man kept up a constant, derisive patter as he worked, inquiring whether Leroy would like a turn with Ah Quim in the privacy of their tent, hinting that he'd better tie a good knot because he'd have a company on the trail soon enough. Leroy suffered him for as long as he could.

"Keep talking if you want a blown kneecap for your trouble."

With words and gestures, Leroy invited the girl to collect her things to leave. Ducking within, she came out with only a single item: a handful of bronze coins that were holed in the middle and tied with a piece of red ribbon.

"That all you got to take?"

She replied in Chinese.

"You speakee no English at all?"

Messrs. Morris and Crane laughed. "Isn't it obvious she's fresh from finishing school?" the latter mocked. "A regular doctor of philosophy!"

Leroy spied a canteen by the fire. Bringing it to Morris, he said, "Better drink now. Liable to be a long time before you can again."

He fixed Leroy with a look of refreshingly genuine hostility. After he'd downed half the canteen, Leroy took it to Crane, made to tilt to his lips—but then closed the cap.

"This is for that smart mouth," he said, and hung the shut canteen over his neck.

"God damn you, sir," said Crane.

"He may yet."

The girl sat a horse like someone who had never encountered one before. Unable to gallop, they made slow progress west, toward the headwaters of the Verdigris River, as Leroy considered what he might do next. The girl kept a guarded eye on him the whole way, evidently expecting some fresh humiliation. No temptation of that kind crossed Leroy's mind, but he tried to reassure her by keeping his eyes to himself. Whether he felt more guilt for his race or his sex, he couldn't say.

They paused to drink, and Leroy ventured to try speaking with her again:

"You know where they bought you?"

She stared, answered unintelligibly.

"Was it Denver?"

Her eyes widened. "Den *war*," she said.

"Yes, in Colorado. Is that where you're from?"

More Chinese. Denver was too far away to ride in anything like the time he could spare, but it was a plausible destination. He would have to take her straight north, overland to the Kansas-Pacific road. They could have doubled back to the LL&G, which joined the Kansas-Pacific at Lawrence, but that would have been the obvious choice to Morris and Crane too. More worrying, he was more likely to run into someone he knew—some merchant or preacher or paper-pusher out of Topeka—riding the LL&G. And he would soon as not avoid explaining why he was not with the Bender posse, but riding the rails with a celestial whore.

"Better get your ass under you," he said, confident she could not understand. "We got a ways to go."

To that, she fetched up a sound that sounded like *humpf,* as if she did understand. Leroy, confused, kept his peace for the rest of their ride.

BACK IN LAWRENCE, the natives were puzzled by the behavior of a certain newcomer. The young man who had checked into the hotel under the name "Hancock" was seen wandering the thoroughfare, asking if anyone had seen his wife. The spectacle caused much amusement; more than once he was invited to try his luck at the whorehouse.

But Junior was in no state for jokes. When he woke up alone in the room, he immediately had an inkling that the worst had happened, for part of him had never believed Kate's change of heart. He checked the privy, outraging a woman in midstream. He checked the restaurant, accosting diners at their meals with such persistence that one man threw a heel of bread at him.

He interrogated the hotel clerk, who said nothing at first. Junior offered him cash. The clerk declined, and continued to do so until offered the sum of fifty dollars. Then he abruptly recalled that a woman matching her description had come down several hours before and gone out.

"Did she say where she was going?"

"It is not in the habit of this establishment," the clerk bristled, "to importune its guests."

Though it was a sizable town, Junior covered it all in the first day of Kate's disappearance. It was dark before it occurred to him to check if he still had his bankroll. Sprinting back to his room, he found that he did. This further convinced him that some terrible thing must have befallen Kate, for if she had run out on him, she would have taken his share too.

He started over again the next day, stalking the place with his hair wild and his shirttails hanging out. Crawling under buildings, he came out covered with dirt. He bought a shovel at the hardware and commenced digging up suspicious piles on the edge of town. The owner of an apple orchard had to chase him away at gunpoint.

When he got around to attacking fresh graves in the churchyard, the good people of Lawrence had had enough. The sheriff ordered him to collect his things from the hotel and be on his way. Junior, who was in the middle of reversing the burial of a child, begged to continue. He said, "This is something I know. She may be buried alive!"

The sheriff marched him back to the Eldridge and waited outside his door until he'd packed his things. Then, after Junior had paid his bill, he demanded, "Which station?"

"I don't know."

"You got someplace to be? Any friends or relatives to get to?"

He blinked. "No."

In the end Junior told him he'd rather just walk. The sheriff, who was by this time ready to toss him in the Kansas River, escorted him some way down the trail and turned him loose.

"If you need supplies, the next town is Sibley. See you go there and not come back."

Junior nodded like a man bearing a full load of guilt. The sheriff watched him proceed west until he was out of sight, hoping the episode would end there.

He was right—with one exception. Two days later a posse of fifteen riders thundered into town. The sheriff, who was sitting and smoking in front of the town jail, watched them come up the street, their carbines gleaming and their faces hard. Evelyn Whistler dismounted.

"You the sheriff?"

The other glanced down at his badge. "Appears so."

Whistler unfolded a paper and gave it to him.

After carefully placing his lit cigar on the arm of his chair, the sheriff withdrew his reading spectacles from his breast pocket. He wiped the lenses with his shirtfront and perched them carefully at the end of his nose as Whistler, fidgeting, governed his impatience.

The letter was lengthy. Bearing the letterhead of "Senator A.M. York, & Colonel, ret.," it identified the bearer as leader of a duly deputized peace force in pursuit of the notorious Bender clan. Its descriptions were more detailed than in the governor's proclamation, but it likewise did not anticipate the clan would separate, more or less assuming that family ties would keep them together.

The sheriff returned the letter. "Haven't seen a party like that here, sorry."

"We would make inquiries around your town, if that doesn't presume on your position."

"My position is how you see."

The sheriff didn't move a muscle. If he were pressed on the matter, he would grant he didn't like gangs of self-appointed avengers invading his town, be they well-connected or not.

Whistler pulled out a kerchief to mop the sweat from his bald head. His search had forced him into some of the hardest riding he had done in years. He was dusty and exhausted and had no time to indulge the vanities of provincial lawmen.

"Then we'll try the livery first," he said, mounting. The sheriff watched him over the top of his reading glasses, waiting until the last moment to say, "There was one fellow a couple of days ago."

Whistler turned his horse around.

"Tell me."

"It was one man, not four. A young man, sort of dim. Spoke with a touch of Dutch accent. Matches the description of the younger man."

"Where is he now?"

The sheriff grimaced, tossed his head. "Couldn't say now. He was making himself a public nuisance, so I sent him packing over the Sibley road. That was two days ago."

"You didn't hold him?"

"Had no reason to. He was a fool, not an outlaw."

Whistler grimaced. "Which way?"

The sheriff stuck his thumb east.

"Let's go, boys!" Whistler cried.

The posse rode out of Lawrence without watering their horses or taking some grub, but not soon enough for the sheriff, who pocketed his glasses and resumed his smoke.

Colonel York sat at his desk on the floor of the Senate chamber in Topeka and stared across the aisle at his fellow senator from Pottawatomie County. Dressed in his governing duds, with fine shirt of French silk and a watch chain of twenty-four-carat gold stretched across his belly, Senator Spruance Halls was engrossed in picking his nose. He had made a habit of it since York had arrived at his post, never showing any awareness he was anywhere but his own privy. Once, York had tried to remind him of their august surrounds by clearing his throat. Halls, alas, had the statesman's gift of selective deafness.

The time came for a procedural vote. When the H's came around, Hall instantly recorded "Aye!" His eyes were down, his finger was in his nose, but his ear was never less than superbly tuned to parliamentary procedure. Thereafter, York held a begrudging respect for his neighbor on the Senate floor. However much his colleagues had their fingers in unsavory places, their legislating skills were never to be underestimated.

The day was given to consideration of further land grants to the Kansas-Pacific Railroad, which sought titles beyond the nearly one-quarter of the state already granted by Congress. It was a prospect York looked dimly upon, suspecting a plot to enrich eastern investors. He was not likely to support state grants no matter what arguments were advanced, but he listened to them all, bearing in mind that gracious sufferance was the portion of all elected representatives.

He was poised to fall asleep when his secretary grasped his shoulder.

"Mr. Whistler is here."

It took a moment for York to realize what this meant. Coming out, he found Whistler alone in the gallery, still in his riding clothes. At his feet was a package about the size of a hat box, clad in burlap. York gave his secretary the look that caused him to disappear. Neither he nor Whistler spoke until they were alone.

"Which one is it?"

"The son. Junior. Outside of Lawrence."

"Figure he'd be halfway to Montezuma by now."

"If you ask me, he wasn't in his right mind."

York knelt, examined the package. The bottom was moist with a black, viscous substance. At its contents, the colonel showed neither expression nor comment. Truth to tell, he barely recognized the face—he would have preferred that she-wolf, Kate.

"There's the matter of certain funds that were recovered from the body . . ." Whistler was saying.

"Which are of no concern in this quarter," said York, raising a hand. "Should there be any expenses beyond what you have anticipated, you may square them. Otherwise, let there be an anonymous donation to the widows and orphans."

"Understood."

York weighed the package. It was heavier than he would have thought, but just a weight. A thing of mass and extension that had once embodied its own universe, now merely an object.

"You know what to do. Fetch me the others."

"We will."

He returned to the Senate chamber with his trophy slung over his shoulder. After all the days and weeks of fruitless searching, and the bitter harvest of his grief, he was not quite ready to let John Bender Junior go to his rest.

None of his fellow legislators took particular notice of his burden. Reaching his desk, and heedless of the congealed blood, he dropped it among his papers on the leather blotter. The thud distracted Spruance Halls from his excavations.

"You been huntin', Senator?"

"After a fashion," York replied. "After a fashion."

Chapter Twenty-Six

Pests

FROM ELDRIDGE HOUSE, Kate proceeded to the Kansas-Pacific station on the east-west line. The alternatives discussed back in Thayer—to go back east or to the outlaw colonies in the South—inspired her to take neither. She opted instead to go west, to try her luck in the Colorado Territory. A city like Denver, only recently linked to the transcontinental railroad and growing fast on mining and timber, would have a large pent-up demand for the kind of extraordinary services she could provide. And even if it didn't, she could always try her luck further west, in Salt Lake, Virginia City, or San Francisco. At the very least, she could take solace in the fact that every mile she went was another mile between her and Almira.

Her train was a few miles out of Salina when, weary of hearing her voice in her head, she picked up the little volume of Horace she could never seem to get through. She was particularly struck by a line from Book 1: "Pale Death with impartial tread beats at the poor man's cottage door and at the palaces of kings."

She became aware of the steady pinging of raindrops against the roof of the carriage. The noise became so loud she raised the window shade and peeked out. There she saw what she first took to be a storm of soot swirling around the train, as if the contents of a coal hopper had become airborne. The true nature of the "storm" became clear when one of the swirling black projectiles struck the pane, leaving a smudge of green innards.

So we witness the plague, she thought. She had heard the stories of the locusts—of onslaughts so fierce they stripped the paint from fences, lifted shingles from roofs, ate the leather from buggy seats. Farmers found the flesh of unpicked fruit consumed, leaving only the pits hanging from the trees. Travelers caught on open ground were thrown when their horses panicked; cattle were left bloodied and blind as the pests attacked their eyeballs. It was one of the most dreaded hazards of the Great American Desert.

By some chance, the swarms had not appeared in the years the Benders operated the grocery. Her first impulse, then, was to think herself fortunate to have her curiosity satisfied now, in her last hours on the prairie. That impulse did not last.

A wing of the swarm withdrew, gathering into an enormous coil. It towered and tumbled and rolled beside the train for a while, dipping now and again toward the ground to taste its prospects, until it rose, contracting. The passengers at the windows pressed their noses to the glass, waiting to see what would happen next.

The cloud exploded, pouring forth fleshy missiles that slammed against the panes. She heard the tinkle of broken glass from somewhere; women screamed, and a man took out his pistol to brandish at the swarm. Kate reflexively covered her eyes. When she peeked through her fingers, she found her window still intact. But the swarm was not done with them.

Outside, the black cloud was suddenly gone. She looked skyward, expecting to see it scud away like a departing thunderstorm. Yet above there was nothing but blue. Then she dropped her gaze to the ground—and discovered there was no ground.

Instead of grass and ties and soil, there was a living carpet of locusts. Their armored bodies shined like splatters of grease in the sun. Their legs and wings and antennae bristled, resolving into chitinous eddies as the creatures flailed against each other. Now and again she saw a bump on the landscape that might have been a recognizable object—a buggy inundated as if the insects had collectively decided to mock the shape of a human conveyance. One of the bumps kicked, lifted its head. The horse got its eyes open for only an instant before the swarm closed over its face.

The train was losing speed. Two cars and a tender ahead, the engine huffed and churned with steam that should have sent it hurtling at sixty miles per hour. Yet it was doing only half that and slowing down. Puzzled, the engineer leaned from his cab to peer down the track. The right-of-way was so solidly covered, the wheels of the engine's fore truck carved a wake of insects. The engine was stalling due to a phenomenon not unheard of in plains railroading: the driving wheels had lost adhesion to the track because it was slick with the crushed bodies of locusts.

The engineer closed the throttle, hoping less steam would enable the drivers to engage better. Instead, the train lurched as if he'd pulled the brake. Leaning out, he saw the drivers spin, catch, and slip again. He whistled. Bowing to necessity, he closed the throttle, saw the train to a safe halt, and—because the cab had no door to close against the swarm—took refuge in the first passenger carriage. As he traversed the aisle in his greasy overalls and sweaty stink, he tugged his cap at the startled passengers. Taking the first empty seat, he stretched out and threw a forearm over his eyes. In five minutes he was catching up on his sleep.

And so for the second time in her life, Kate found herself marooned on a train. The predicament depressed her, and not only because she faced an unknowable number of hours stuck there while being sought by the law. The very idea of being back in that same position made some unreasoning part of her despondent, fearing that her career was also stuck. Tempted to cry, she bent over and buried her face in her book. But for the moment she didn't cry, for she reminded herself that at least Almira wasn't there, and she had $12,413 in banknotes in a purse hung by a string under her skirts.

Half the day later the pests had shown no inclination to leave. As the hours wore heavy on the passengers, they idled away the time at the windows, tossing lit cigars and cigarettes. Where they landed, the insects parted, forming holes around which they would spiral, as if they were draining underground.

The women took out their knitting, their pocket Bibles, or if they were particularly bold, their penny romances. Kate was tempted to offer them impromptu tarot readings but decided against it. Under the circumstances, advertising her expertise would probably not be wise.

The ordeal mercifully ended before sunset. A boy who had no cigars or cigarettes to fling at the locusts decided instead to try his precious India rubber ball. Bouncing, the ball disturbed so many of the tiny monsters that some invisible threshold was crossed. The entire swarm began to ascend, and the passengers, at first pleased but then panicked, rushed to shut the windows. The black blizzard swirled around the train and then rose, manifesting into a dome that distant observers took for some enormous explosion. The train was momentarily thrown into darkness as the sun was blotted out.

And then the light returned. The swarm had vanished as abruptly as it had arrived, leaving a clear sky. But the consequences of its stay were scattered on the ground all around them. The buggy parked beside the tracks had been stripped of its upholstery. The grass as far as she could see had been trampled down by millions of tiny feet, the taller plants stripped of leaves. The horse that had been overwhelmed struggled to get back to its feet, its eyes and nostrils bloody.

The sun's return had a rejuvenating effect on the engineer. He yawned, stretched, and scratched the thatch under his arms. Then he went forward again, making small pleasantries at the passengers before he passed through the door to the tender.

Ten minutes later they were under way. Kate returned to her Horace, skimming over the last of the pages before the train made its scheduled stop at Salina. She had just closed the book when she looked up and found a man staring at her.

He was seated in one of the opposing seats across the aisle. Dressed fairly well in a suit of blue and black plaid, he nevertheless had the look of a man not used to city clothes. In the creases of his deeply lined face was the grime of a thousand days on the trail; in his eyes was the glint of a gaze that had spanned miles of empty space. Those eyes were on her now, concentrated across the mere feet separating their seats. Kate paled.

He rose, leaned into her space and said, "You're Kate Bender."

His voice was like a load of ore dumped from a mining car.

He paused to watch her reaction—which she made as minimal as possible—and added, "I'm sure of it."

Kate smiled a smile that was frayed and mirthless.

"Do I know you, sir?"

"I'm the feller who's going to bring you in, that's who I am."

"Is this a joke?" she asked. "Or is it customary in these parts for men to accost solitary women?"

He smiled. "Clever, aren't you? They said that. But it won't do you no good."

Their eyes locked. Kate was reeling from her discovery, but still fortunate in one respect: if this was a lawman, he surely would have identified himself as such. He was likely just a freelancer, a civilian who made a career of perusing bounty notices in post offices and railway stations. Most likely he was as shocked by his good luck as she was by her bad.

"Help! Somebody please help me!" she cried, rising a little in her seat. All eyes in the carriage turned to her; the plaid suit didn't retreat, but his lips lost their cocksure twist.

"Is this man disturbing you, miss?"

Another passenger, an ordinary workman traveling with his family, stood up. The bounty hunter kept his eyes on her as if she'd somehow contrive to vanish if he turned his head. But the workman insisted:

"You better play your game somewhere else, friend. There are families here."

"Yes, this man has been bothering me since Lawrence," said Kate. "He won't take no for an answer."

"This here is a wanted criminal," the other man said. "She murdered a dozen men in Labette County."

"Did she now?" the workman laughed. "I bet the pretty lady is an anarchist to boot!"

"Listen friend, why don't you just sit down, shut up, and mind your business?" And with that, the bounty hunter parted his jacket to reveal the worn wooden grip of a Remington 1858.

"Are you a constable, sir?" asked another male passenger, rising. This one spoke with a British accent, and was dressed in a seersucker suit that was severely wrinkled from hours tucked in his seat.

That she had attracted two such disparate defenders struck Kate as absurd; fearing she'd laugh, she covered her face in her hands and cried, "He won't leave me alone! I'm at my wits' end!"

"I'm telling you rubes this girl is a murderess. Don't you read the papers?"

"Murdered them all with her bare skinny hands, I bet," the workman said, and looked to the seersucker, who approved the joke.

A third man rose—this one much broader in the beam, with a knife the length of a rolling pin on his belt. His odds deteriorating, the bounty hunter closed his jacket.

"This isn't over, Miss Kate Bender."

"This is just what he did before. He'll wait for me at the station and try again on the next train!"

"Well he won't this time," declared the third man as he bellied the bounty hunter down the aisle. The latter gave way as the others joined in, pushing him the length of the carriage and through the door.

A moment later she heard a commotion in the next car. Male voices yelled, and there was a bang as if a body had struck a wall. Then she saw a dark figure fly from the train, arcing like a diver into the sea of short grass. There was just time for her to see the bounty hunter carve a furrow among the stems. His gun followed, disappearing in the morass.

Her benefactors returned. With a slight bow of his head, the seersucker reclaimed his seat. Kate, obliged, returned a shy smile.

At Salina, she exited the train and, to confuse any possible pursuit, bought a new ticket and reboarded. Now she had two tickets, her first one to Denver and a second as far as Hays City. If the Salina ticket agent was questioned, he could only honestly report that she had debarked far short of her real destination.

She took a window seat in the darkest corner of the car and cracked the window to smoke. The pleasant familiarity of cigarette smoke was soon overwhelmed by the concentrated stench of dung, which wafted through the train from the cattle pens windward of the station. She suffered it as long as she could until suspecting that the odor was permeating her clothes and hair.

She turned to shut the window—and saw something that stopped her. There was a man standing on the platform with a newspaper. He was middle-aged and still handsome, his fine silvery hairline converging to a widow's peak, his brow lined with the character of a fine oaken chest. Hands on the window frame, she stared at him with her cigarette drooping from her lips. His hair was long, brushing the top of his starched collar. His black suit was free of dust, his pleated shirtfront crowned with a cravat of blue silk. He was every inch the quality of man she imagined her father had become in the years of their separation. He was wealthy, worldly, and—from the lack of a ring on his left hand—unencumbered by some clinging mediocrity of a spouse.

Seeing this man both thrilled and frightened her, for as much as she liked to imagine meeting her father by blind luck, the fact remained that she didn't know him. Of his appearance, she had only the slightest of memories. She had tried to conjure up his face in her mind for months after joining Almira, lying awake at night with the effort of it. By pure will she had managed at first to cobble together some impression, mostly regarding how he smelled of cigars and rosewater, and the contour of his hands, which she used to lace among her tiny fingers. She remembered the peculiar calluses he got from holding the cards. But the years and the beatings had stripped her of her memories of her father's face, his voice. She liked to believe that some hidden power, some imperative of their shared blood, would tear away her ignorance the moment she laid eyes on him again. But the fact was that she wasn't sure—just as she wasn't sure if this gentleman, with his newspaper on the platform at Salina, Kansas—should mean as much to her as she hoped.

The man noticed the unfamiliar woman staring at him. Meeting her eyes, he gave a brief nod. In his eyes was a flicker of lust, and Kate knew it must not be him. She shut the window.

FOR THE SAME reasons he avoided the trains, Leroy did his best to skirt the property lines and stay out of sight of homesteads. The exercise made him feel like a transgressor, even as he did what was manifestly the right thing.

His companion did nothing to make him feel better. On the trail and at the campfire, she kept her eyes down, as if the slightest provocation would set him off. Though she had been treated like chattel much of her life, she had a superior way about her that made him feel like some unwashed brute, a barbarian from the steppes who slept in his saddle and gargled with urine. When he offered her perfectly decent trail food, like a stale biscuit or a piece of roasted snake, she would take it, examine it, and look at him as if asking, "Do you expect me to eat *this*?" And yet, she lacked the instinct for what he took to be obvious courtesy. When she had the need, she would hike up her overfancy petticoats and relieve herself right in front of him and his horse. Appalled, Leroy looked away—and felt sorry for the horse.

It occurred to him to learn her real name. He tried to learn it by pointing to himself and saying, "I am Leroy Dick. Dick. *Dick* . . ." To that, she widened her eyes and folded her arms across her chest.

He persisted, naming himself and then pointing at her, until she laid a hand on her breast and said "Biyu." He repeated the word, Biyu, but the sound displeased her coming from his mouth. Assuming a sour expression, she shook her head. "Ah *kim*," she insisted, and refused to answer to any other name out of what, to him, seemed sheer bloody-mindedness.

At last they approached Salina. This was a growing town tucked in the confluence of the Salina and Smoky Hill rivers, its profile dogtoothed with steeples. After asking around, he learned there was a small Chinese population. They occupied what turned out to be half a street, with three laundries, a butcher, and a cobbler. He chose the cobbler to make further inquiries.

The shop was a former saloon, with empty whiskey bottles still on the shelves and a bar converted to a cluttered workbench. The only light in the place was from a single lamp and the daylight leaking through the gaps in its slapdash construction. When the proprietor stepped out from behind his work he turned out to have enough English for his business. On seeing him, Biyu uncorked a torrent of furious Cantonese that took the man by surprise. Her outburst pasted his ears back until, after some minutes, it subsided like spent anger. The cobbler shifted his eyes at Leroy in a way that made Leroy nervous—there was no way of knowing if she was making wild accusations about him.

"You understand her?" he asked.

The cobbler frowned. "She speaks in dialect. Hard for me."

"I took her from a pair of procurers round Iola. She says she knows Denver, so I thought I might send her over there. I would take her myself, but I'm on peace business . . ."

The cobbler raised a hand to indicate he had no use for details. He called out, and a woman appeared from behind a curtain. Biyu commenced speaking again, and the woman—presumably the wife—listened with what seemed like comprehension. As she interpreted Biyu's story back to her husband, he nodded, rubbing his chin.

"She say you save her life," he told Leroy. "You need reward, but she sad to have nothing to give . . ."

"No need," replied Leroy. "Ask her how we can get her back to her people."

The cobbler asked his wife, who questioned Biyu.

"She not from Denver. She say she have no family there."

Now it was Leroy's turn to rub his chin problematically. It appeared the girl's rescue might divert him even further from his purpose. Or worse, he would have to explain what he had done to Mary Ann.

The cobbler and his wife conversed in a way that seemed to have great consequence, as Biyu listened with widening eyes. After a final affirmation, he turned again to Leroy.

"She stay here for now. Maybe she go home, to China. We see."

Leroy was astonished. He looked to Biyu, who looked back with an expression that said *If not this, what?*

"Are you in earnest?"

The cobbler jerked his head, not understanding.

"I mean, is this what you want to do?"

"This is what we do."

Turning back to his bench, he selected a pair of men's boots. It was a fine set in brown leather, not for riding but for strutting about town.

"Your reward. For her."

Leroy gazed at the shoes, disconcerted. "No, I can't," he said.

The cobbler shook the boots under his nose. "You take. *Reward.*"

Clearly, to refuse the gift would be a serious insult. He took the boots. As the cobbler's wife led Biyu through the curtain, Biyu looked back at him with the frank gratitude she had denied him on the trail.

The proprietor retired behind the bar again, abruptly losing interest in him. Leroy moved to leave, but hesitated.

"How old is she? Might you ask?"

The cobbler shouted the question. After some murmuring, the answer came back.

"Twelve years," he said.

Leroy wandered Salina for some time. Feeling he needed food, though not particularly hungry, he drifted to the Pacific House dining room and examined the board of offerings. The prix fixe meal was a steak of undeclared cut, boiled cabbage, and baked potato, for seventy-five cents. Sitting alone at the table farthest from anyone else, he ate deliberately and without pleasure, requesting three refills of his shot glass until his waiter brought him a whole bottle. He was almost finished when he noticed that his unspecified steak was sirloin and that it was well-done, not medium as he had requested.

He sat for a while with a toothpick and his evening smoke. In one crystal clear moment he saw that there was indeed something more he could do for the girl. He tossed a dollar on the table and went straight out to retrieve the horses from the cobbler's.

The livery was east of town, opposite the mills on the bank of the Smoky Hill. After securing his own mount, he led Morris and Crane's horse—the one Biyu had ridden—into the barn. There were two men inside, talking and in no particular hurry to serve him. As he waited, he made some mental calculations of the cost of getting the girl to San Francisco. And though he had no clue how much passage on a freighter to Asia would cost, he hoped the sale of one good chestnut mare would cover most of it.

He had been turning these thoughts over for some time when he began to attend to what the men were saying. Seems that there was an unusual arrest made at the train station the day before. The person apprehended caused the men some amusement; this was not the usual run of fugitive, but a woman. And not just any woman, but a fine, handsome one, of the caliber rarely seen among Kansas wives or prostitutes. From the way they marveled, Leroy would have guessed the exotic spy of some foreign power had been caught—the kind that could pass for a countess or the concubine of a king. One of the men was quite sure she was the mistress of a German baron who had disappeared on a bison-shooting expedition in Nebraska.

"She killed him?" asked the livery's owner.

"There's talk of murder."

"Go right to hell."

"I'm only telling you what I heard. Not a word more."

Leroy's curiosity got the better of his patience:

"Any of you know what this woman looked like?"

The owner eyed him through the gloom and dust. "Sorry for my language, mister. Didn't see you standing there."

"Got a horse to sell."

The man's examination was quick, composed merely of leading the horse in and out of the barn and slapping its flesh in various places. He looked the animal in the eye, as if asking it what a fair price might be for itself. Then he said "A hundred dollars, including the tack."

"I was hoping for a hundred and fifty, and twenty for the saddle."

"What a splendid thing is hope."

"A hundred twenty. Including tack."

"I'll give you a hundred and ten."

"Done."

An hour later he had the liveryman's signature on a note to the bank, payable to "Leroy Dirk." Fingering it by the edges, he turned it around and around as he contemplated making the liveryman write it again—but opted not to.

"So this girl that got clapped yesterday. Did you see it happen?"

"Not while I got a business to run," came the frosty reply.

"Would it be a good bet they'd be keeping her in the town jail?"

"I never tell a man how to bet. But you'd not be far wrong."

The streets of Salina were dirt, but lined with boardwalks neatly carpentered and painted white. Clopping around, Leroy found the jail just a couple of blocks from the hotel where he'd had his supper. The wood frame structure looked much like a small office, except for the two cells in the back. His eyes swept the spaces behind the riveted meshwork. There were no prisoners there.

"Afternoon," said the suited man behind the desk. A mature

gentleman, his pale dome shined where his hair receded. A pair of gray handlebars descended from his ears, bowed along his jawline and met under his nose. There was ink on his lips where the wet his fingers to turn the pages of his newspaper.

"Good day," he replied, his position awkward. "I am Leroy Dick, trustee for Labette Township."

"Labette? That's a ways off, Mr. Dick."

Extending a hand, the man introduced himself as Luke Parsons, the sheriff.

At length Leroy learned he was the very Luke Parsons who had joined the John Brown gang during the troubles before the war. He was with Brown at Palymra, and in the fight at Osawatomie, trading fire with a superior force of proslavery Missourians. But when Brown went east to build up his war chest, Parsons chose to settle permanently in Kansas. Like most of Brown's compatriots, the great man's reflected notoriety had made him a minor celebrity. That he'd taken up a badge in remote Salina was news to Leroy.

Parsons was nothing if not instantly obliging to a former jayhawker. On hearing Leroy sought the Benders, Parsons promised to set him up with the best lodgings, a good meal. He regretted the poor deal he had gotten for his horse—if he'd asked at the jailhouse first, he would have gotten his price or better. He was more than amiable—until Leroy brought up the subject of the "countess" arrested at the train station.

"Oh, *that*. She's not here."

"I can see that. Is there anything to the story?"

"Well, she ain't no countess. Or a Bender, for that matter," he said, face purpling. "There's a man who *thinks* she is, I'll give you. When I came by to make sure it was all done under the flag of law, he waved a *document* under my nose." And Parsons tore off the syllables of that word, *document*, like it was the devil's own alibi.

"The governor's proclamation?"

"A letter from a certain senator in Topeka, the gist being I should go hang myself. So what was I supposed to do? Go against the interests of senators and congressmen and all the king's men, for this little confection of a girl? So he's got her."

"Got her?"

"At the courthouse. If he hasn't set out with her already. What business is it of mine, anyway? I'm only the sheriff of the whole fucking county."

They sat for a moment as Parsons simmered and Leroy pensively chewed his lip.

"So this man. He's a Pinkerton?"

Regaining his humor, Parsons laughed. "You said it, my friend! Though I'd sooner call him a dandy. Say it to his face, in fact, if I didn't have duties a fair man must place above his pride."

The courthouse was a new-built, two-story affair made out of native stone, with arched windows and a cupola. It was the kind of grand structure they could only dream of building in Harmony Grove, though Salina was not a much older community. Confronted by a line of chambers off the main corridor, he was directed first upstairs, then to the back of the building, and finally to the most remote room, a small office used by the town surveyor to store the county plats.

Inside sat two people: a man he didn't know, and Kate Bender. She wore an unadorned traveling dress, her hat and gloves lying on the table before her, beside a half-drunk cup of tea. As they looked at each other, a smile gathered on her face, as if some private promise had been redeemed. He had to tear his eyes from her.

The Pinkerton was a real sharper—a gentleman in a silk suit, with gold cuffs and a mane of silver hair. He also had a cup of tea, and deck of cards laid out for solitaire. Though he only worked for Colonel York, he seemed more a senator than his employer.

"Something you need?" he asked.

Leroy explained himself and how he found his way there. As he listened, the Pinkerton leaned back, interlacing his fingers as if he were a critic evaluating a show. When Leroy was done, he kicked his way back to an upright position. Something about the way he did this made Leroy think he would not get a good review.

"Well, I'm pleased to meet you, Mr. Dick, but all I can tell you is what I told the sheriff. I represent certain interests in Topeka that supersede local authority. I'm to deliver this suspect to those interests without distraction or delay, and I intend to do just that."

"With respect, sir, as trustee of the jurisdiction where the crimes were committed, I would say I represent more than 'local authority.' "

"Alleged crimes," interjected Kate.

"That may well be," the sharper replied to Leroy, ignoring Kate. "But my orders make no such distinction. If you want, you can take it up with the senator."

He held up York's letter for him to read. Leroy didn't take it.

"I think you know this is irregular as hell. This woman is a fugitive from justice, not the object of some private vendetta."

"You're wasting your time with this fool, Leroy," said Kate. "Don't you think I've been telling him the same thing since yesterday?"

"You shut up, cunt, or I'll shove those gloves down your cocksucking hole," snarled the Pinkerton.

Then he turned back to Leroy and continued as if their exchange had never been anything but a pleasant chat: "You are at liberty to take the matter to Topeka, sir. For now, I must ask you to leave, before you overexcite the prisoner."

Vexed now, Leroy turned slowly to the door, then stopped with his hand on the knob.

"I never caught your name, friend."

"Maybe if you read the letter, you would have."

He was through the door when Kate called after him, "Don't let them do me this way, Leroy! If I must answer to the law, let it be by your side!"

Chapter Twenty-Seven

Dispatches

WHAT WAS HAPPENING, and the obviousness of its impropriety, put Leroy in a writing mood. He went to the train station to send wires. His first telegram went to the governor's office, protesting this flagrant obstruction of justice. As he did not know the whereabouts of Justice Majors and the Labette Township posse, he sent messages to every station in eastern Kansas, imploring them to come at once to Salina, or if delayed, direct to Topeka. Finally, he dispatched an appeal to all the sheriffs in a hundred mile radius, posing them the question: "Are we men of the Law to surrender our duties entirely to men from private concerns, whose first obligation is not to justice, but the settling of petty scores?" One of these went to the attention of Wild Bill Hickok, who was marshal in Abilene, just twenty miles east. Leroy was fixing his hat on his head to leave when an answer came back—Hickok, alas, had left his post in Abilene more than a year previous.

He found Sheriff Parsons in a saloon on Santa Fe Avenue. Parsons seemed glad to see him again, at first—until Leroy appealed to him to do what was clearly the right thing.

"It ain't about what's right," he said. "It's about what's already fixed to happen. As long as that girl finds her proper end, what's it matter who ties the noose?"

"That's the whole distinction, isn't it? Whether it's done under flag of law or some other way."

"Maybe most times, but not this time."

"I don't think you believe that."

Parsons drank, barked for another round. He sat there looking agitated for some moments, with Leroy silently looking on, not drinking and not leaving, until at last he pounded the bar with his fist.

"Come on, then." The sheriff rose, tightening his gun belt a notch.

Back at the courthouse, the sharper was bent over his dinner. Kate ignored hers, preferring to lose herself in another book, *Ivanhoe* by Walter Scott. The Pinkerton had found it in the bookshelf that served at the town lending library. He'd picked it for Kate at random, but the sudden appearance of Leroy Dick made a tale of medieval knights and chivalry seem more than apt to her. When Leroy returned with the sheriff, she felt like singing with joy. He has not given up, she thought. He means to redeem me.

"Something *else* I can do for you gentlemen?" asked the Pinkerton, who was not liable to sing at all.

"You can relax," said Leroy. "We don't need to see your paper again . . ."

Parsons stuck an arm around Leroy's shoulder to shut him

up. He said, "As far as I can recollect, there's nothing in your orders that says we can't speak to the prisoner. Why don't you and I get a drink while you let Mr. Dick here interview the young lady?"

"Have a drink yourself. I'm not letting her out of my sight."

"Suit yourself."

To prove he meant business, Parsons locked eyes on the man and didn't waver until the other put down his fork.

"I see you two will plague me until you get your way. He gets five minutes, then."

The sheriff and the Pinkerton retired to the corridor, where the latter crossed his arms and refused to go any further. Parsons took out his rolling papers. "Want one?" he asked.

The other shook his head. "I don't smoke those."

" 'Course you don't."

Inside, Kate closed her book, laid it aside, and turned a pair of soft, wondering eyes on Leroy. She no longer felt the anger that had supplanted her devotion. Instead, there was a sense of vindication, for he was there, all alone, waging war for her rescue. But knowing Leroy and his paladin-like modesty, she would not embarrass him by pronouncing such feelings out loud.

"I'm happy to see you, Leroy," she said.

"Are you? Why would that be?"

"I see you have some mistaken notions about me that do no credit to your broadness of mind."

Leroy would have laughed at her, but he didn't want the Pinkerton to hear that. Instead, he kept his distance, his back against the opposite wall.

"What makes you think my mind is broad?"

"I can see it. Just as I foresaw that you would come for me now.

The signs are written of our fates, in letters made of rubies on the golden door. They were there to read, and always have been."

He shook his head. "You're talking nonsense. All I know is what we found buried your claim. All those men. The child."

"What child?"

"The one you threw alive into the pit, to suffocate under her dead father. Remember?"

She frowned. "Now it's you speaking nonsense. I remember nothing like that. Who would be capable of such a thing, Leroy? A crazy person?"

"So you deny any knowledge of the killings?"

Kate rose and approached him. Her skirts rustled in the quiet of the room. The sound of his own breathing seemed as loud as the trumpets at Jericho. He caught his breath just before she came within arm's length. She paused.

"You're afraid of me, Leroy," she stated, with a plaintive strain.

"Will you tell me where the others are?"

From her heart's very core, she yearned to reach out to him. Even some article of clothing, like when she seized his hat at Harmony Grove, would have been enough. But she dared not.

"I won't lie to you, or try to bargain with knowledge I don't have. The Lord's truth is, I don't know. We figured you were looking for a party of four. So we separated at the station in Humboldt, and never told which direction each was headed."

"None of them rode north with you, for even a short while?"

"Wouldn't that just defeat the purpose, Leroy?"

"Who waited in Humboldt for the others to be gone?"

"I left first. I don't know who waited the longest."

He shifted his feet. What she said had the ring of truth, but he had heard the legends of Bender guile. He sensed he was being served lies wrapped in truth to make them more palatable—or perhaps truth and falsity cleverly layered. He was out of his depth. But if the Pinkerton got his way, there might never be the chance for a professional lawman to question her.

He persisted: "And the money?"

"You might ask the party outside about that. His name is McDonnaugh, by the way. He styles himself 'Captain McDonnaugh'—a rank I do believe he gave himself."

"How much are we talking about?"

She withdrew to the window to weigh her answer. Beyond the tar-paper rooftops a train chugged with antlike slowness on the edge of town. Beyond that, the expanse of prairie with its oceanic swells, heaving and rising to meet fleets of cloud. "It's something more than twelve thousand dollars," she finally said.

Leroy was impressed by this sum—but not surprised.

"More than you'd expect from selling patent medicines. Are you sure you'd rather not confess?"

His tone struck her as mocking. She turned, flaring: "You presume too much. You and people like you, all snug and safe in your warm houses and your arrogance—have you seen what I've seen? Do you know what suffering is? If you'd been ripped from the bosom of your family, reduced to petty criminality against your nature . . . maybe then you'd understand. To be just another sheep among the flock is no trick. Try keeping your easy virtue when you're forced to consort with monsters! Until you know the answer to those questions, who are you to judge me?"

"So your answer is no?"

"Go to hell, Leroy Dick."

She shifted back to the window. As he could think of nothing more to ask her, he moved to leave. He was halfway through the door when he suddenly reversed himself. McDonnaugh, who was standing with Parsons not five feet away, called out to him as he closed the door: "Two minutes left!"

Kate didn't expect him to stay but didn't betray her surprise. Then he surprised her further by sitting down for the first time, laying his hat on the desk next to him.

"Sit," he ordered.

She obeyed. When she was settled, Leroy leaned forward in his seat, resting his forearms on his knees as he fixed her with his eyes—a gaze so harsh she would never have suspected him capable of it.

"They came from where we didn't expect them, down the Oregon Trail, over Hogsback Ridge in the southwest. We never knew how many until after, when they said more than four hundred men rode into Lawrence that morning. To a man, they were professional bushwhackers—men who'd killed and maimed and burned through three years of war, and a decade before that, when men did their killing freelance, without need of a flag.

"First thing they did was block all the roads, so nobody could get in or out of the town. The people were driven off the street, into their homes. Then the searches began. They had a list of men they definitely needed to kill—Jim Lane, for one, and Mayor Collamore, and some newspapermen—and were determined to hold the town until their errand was done.

"Their first victim was a minister of the cloth, picked right off his milking stool. They went on, house to house, demanding the male members of each family come out and face justice. When the fathers and brothers came out, they shot them through the head. If they didn't come out, the bushwhackers broke in, fetched them, and shot them through the head. Some of the young ones they shot while still in their mothers' arms. They shot another man while he was holding an infant daughter. They saved ammunition by having their victims stand back-to-back, shooting through the forehead of one and out the forehead of the other. Some, they just kicked over and over, knowing from experience that there's only so much kicking a skull can take. In four hours they killed near two hundred men and boys. After, there were deep red puddles in the mud of Massachusetts Street, like it had rained blood.

"I came to Lawrence that morning to buy oats and coffee. When the shooting started, the shopkeeper ran out of the general store. He left me and another customer—a boy no older than thirteen—hiding out in the storeroom. We listened to them shooting people for more than two hours. We heard the women and children screaming, and the bushwhackers laughing, enjoying how the victims begged for their lives. I heard of a young wife who pleaded with Quantrill to spare her husband, a man she claimed had proslavery sympathies and had no use for Jim Lane and his jayhawkers. To that, Quantrill promised he, personally, would not harm a hair on the man's head. Then he walked away and let one of his lieutenants blow the man's brains all over his wife's dress.

"Soon they came into the general store, looking for men in hiding. I heard them ransacking the stock—men with Missouri accents, others from Kentucky and Tennessee and Texas. They broke glass display cases. They busted open the storeroom door, though it wasn't locked. Then they started going through the boxes, looking for loot.

"I was sure I was about to buy a bullet; I wasn't sure what the boy hiding in the room with me felt, but I could guess. They were coming closer. I was armed with an old Colt that was good for only four shots. It was enough to take a few with me, if was lucky. But I just wasn't one for futile gestures.

"I could see where the boy was hiding behind a cask about ten feet away. Slipping a spare bullet from my belt, I tossed it at him, letting it skip along the boards in his direction. The bushwhackers heard the noise, followed it, and found the boy. Without so much as a single question, the leader took out his gun, cocked it, and shot him between the eyes.

"They left the body where it lay. Thinking the room was cleared, they never looked for anyone else. I stayed in that spot for two more hours as the boy's blood pumped out of him, covering the floor. I can tell you exactly when his heart stopped, to the very second: it was when the flow became a slow leak, like a pot of ink dumped on a blotter. It took longer than you'd think, considering how piecemeal his head was.

"Half a day after they came, Quantrill's gang withdrew. They left all of Massachusetts Street in flames, except for a saloon—and the general store I was hiding in. Turns out Jim Lane got away, running half naked through a cornfield. And I came through without a scratch. I came out to join the survivors as they stood on the street, too struck with their survival to do more than stare at the fires. My knees were bull's-eyes of gore, from crouching in the puddle of blood of that boy. The boy I'd deliberately given up to save myself.

"I've never told anyone else that story, not even my wife. What I did, I've had to live with for ten years. I've had to live with it, explain it to myself, try and fail to come to terms with it. Sometimes, when I dream, I still see the boy's face—though I can barely remember the faces of old friends I rode and fought with. I have no doubt his will be the face I see when I close my eyes for the last time. And the shame I'll feel for the rest of my days, at what I did."

After being still for the duration of his story, Leroy sat up straight.

"Sheep among the flock, you say? That's the man you've playing at love with. And that's who I am to judge you."

When he came out, the Pinkerton asked, "You get what you came for?"

"I might ask that of you."

McDonnaugh raised an eyebrow.

"Better tell your employer," Leroy continued, "whatever you stole from that girl is owed the families of the dead men. Every penny will be accounted for."

"What makes you think anything was taken? The word of a murderer?"

"Why not? She's been more cooperative to this investigation than you."

The Pinkerton fetched up the kind of easy smile brawlers do at the prospect of a fine, clarifying fight.

"That's enough, boys," said Parsons, interposing. "This ain't the way."

There was a surprise waiting for Leroy at the telegraph office: an answer from George Majors. The posse turned out not to be far away at all, having paused to rest and resupply at Junction City. Majors wired back: "Will make the fifty miles by tomorrow P.M." Majors, of course, would not give a fig for whatever letter Captain McDonnaugh waved about. Backed up by the judge of the relevant jurisdiction, Leroy was sure they would have no trouble taking custody of the suspect from the Pinkerton.

"Just to see the look on that dandy's face will be satisfaction enough," Parsons said.

"We may never get to see it if he catches the first train out tomorrow."

"That's what I got deputies for," the other replied with a wink.

That night, thanks to the sheriff, Leroy slept for free in the finest room in the Pacific House. The room was finer and grander than his bedroom at home, but its size only made him feel the absence of Mary Ann more keenly. Nor did he sleep much, with the face of that dead boy in the storeroom in Lawrence refreshed in his mind. Lying awake, staring at the plaster medallion on the ceiling, he regretted he disliked gambling. Poker players always had an alternative to suffering through insomnia.

In case McDonnaugh tried to slip the prisoner out of town early, Parsons had his deputies posted at the courthouse and the train station. The Pinkerton wasn't on the first train east, nor on the second, around ten. By early afternoon they had watched seven trains come and go, without McDonnaugh showing his face.

The Harmony Grove posse pulled up in front of the jail shortly before 5:00 P.M. Leroy was glad to see them, but tension hung heavy on the reunion. George Majors seemed unable to look at him without showing disapproval. Acidly, he remarked, "Good to catch up with you, Leroy. Though you might have told us you planning to strike it freelance . . ."

Leroy caught the eyes of all the riders in turn—Billy Toles, looking exhausted but also excited; Moneyhon, who was standing up in his stirrups, looking for a saloon; Silas Toles, whom Leroy didn't know very well, looking back with faint curiosity. No doubt they all had heard his disagreement with Majors over what do to about Biyu. Nor would it have taken a genius to figure out where he had gone.

"Did you happen on those two skeezicks on your way, Morris and Crane?" Leroy asked.

"We most certainly did. They seemed mighty chaffed when we found 'em. Seems they was robbed of certain of their property, including a girl and a horse."

"Is that a fact?"

"It is indeed."

"If it's all the same to you two pards," said the sheriff, "I think it might be time to head to the courthouse."

"You don't need to ask me twice," replied Leroy, and shot George Majors a look that said, *I may have struck it freelance, but it was me who found her.*

THEY RODE LINE-ABREAST to the courthouse, forcing other traffic aside as they blocked the street. Tying up, they gathered in silence and seriousness, as if they were about to hang Kate Bender, not take custody of her. Parsons and George Majors engaged in a subtle struggle to march at the head of the party, walking fast but not fast enough to seem eager for the distinction. Parsons managed to be first through the door and first up the stairs. For his part, Leroy Dick thought he had as good a claim on the lead as anybody, but had no taste for petty jockeying.

Bringing up the rear, Leroy was last to see that the office where McDonnaugh had kept his prisoner was empty.

Parsons circled the room like a lunging horse, as if he could conjure up the two by wearing a circle in the floor. Majors crossed his arms, pushed his hat up on his head and guffawed.

"Seems the she-wolf grew wings!"

"Never figured you for the spiteful type, George," said Leroy.

"They ain't gone yet," growled the sheriff, and shoved the others aside as he went out.

They rushed to the train station, where Parsons's deputy—a slight, pin-striped banker type whose badge seemed too big for him—was posted.

"How long you been here?"

"Going on three hours," said the deputy.

"And you're sure the Pinkerton and the girl didn't come through?"

"I'm not much for shootin' and ridin', Luke, but I can keep my eyes open."

Still not satisfied, Parsons interrogated the ticket agent. The latter had been at his desk since eight in the morning, but he'd seen no one resembling the description of the dandified McDonnaugh and Kate.

Parsons had one more stop to make. He had a man outside the livery too, who had likewise seen nothing. But the man in the barn had indeed met a silver-haired man—not that morning, but the previous evening, before Parsons had posted his watch. McDonnaugh had retrieved his own horse and purchased one other. In fact, he bought the very same chestnut mare Leroy had sold after bringing in Biyu.

"Well, they're somewhere out there, and they got a day's head start," said George. He indicated the prairie beyond the town limits with the resignation of a man referring to the contents of a sunken ship.

"We know they're headed to Topeka," Leroy began. "If we don't stop—"

"He's not likely to take a direct line. If you know where to start, I'm glad to hear it," replied Parsons. In a gesture that signaled his defeat, he removed his hat and laid it at his side.

Chapter Twenty-Eight

Saline

What is life? It is the flash of a firefly in the night. It is the breath of a buffalo in the wintertime. It is the little shadow which runs across the grass and loses itself in the sunset.

**—Attributed to Chief Crowfoot, Siksika First Nation (Canada)
Also quoted by Perry Edward Smith, multiple
murderer, in Truman Capote's *In Cold Blood***

May 7

THE FIRST DAY out of Salina they struck northwest along the course of the Saline River, following Indian trails where possible, deer trails when necessary. The Pinkerton's head was covered by a hat with a brim the diameter of a barrel lid, shielding him from the elements and covering his telltale silver locks from distant observers. Its gray color made Kate wonder if she was wrong about his captaincy. It might have been earned after all, and not necessarily in the army that won the war.

"You ride in service of old Jeff Davis?" she asked him, by way of conversation.

"Shut up."

"Not hard to feature why you wouldn't want to advertise that fact. The Pinks weren't precisely friends of the Confederacy, is my understanding. Not that anyone would who signed your commission, with so many cheats and frauds around . . ."

No answer. Observing the sun for a moment, she remarked, "I suppose you know we're headed west, away from Topeka."

"Will you shut up?" he repeated, steering his horse closer to hers. "Or do I need to gag you?"

Under ordinary conditions, conversation would help keep her warm as the clouds massed and the wind picked up before the rainstorm. Before they left Salina he had put a cattleman's duster around her shoulders that protected her from the dust but held little heat. The intention, she gathered, was much like the hat he wore: to obscure her figure from a distance. Warm or not, she sank her head into the canvas as far as she could as the shadows deepened and the trail stretched for mile upon dreary mile before them. In short, though she preferred to talk, conditions were not ordinary.

The clouds soon opened, casting down heavy drops that slapped the ground. The storm became a deluge, obscuring the atmosphere like a fog, turning the wool traveling bonnet on her head to a supine, sluglike thing. She went on like this for some time, drenched, until McDonnaugh looked back through the plunging sheets and took pity. Coming up beside her, he gave her his hat and donned his usual one. Her bonnet he crumpled and stuffed in his coat pocket.

They trudged onward for several hours more as the storm climaxed, then moderated into a steady downpour. Her horse ambled with eyes half closed, ears folded back to keep the water out. Fatigue made Kate slump and struggle to keep her sidesaddle position. She wanted to excoriate McDonnaugh for rushing her out of town, for disposing of all her clothes to "save weight." But she didn't, for he would only tell her to shut up, and possibly stuff a handkerchief in her mouth.

Late in the afternoon the sun ducked beneath the layer of cloud and shone through the drizzle with a brief, golden radiance. By some obscure process of decision-making, the Pinkerton elected to take them under some trees by the river and camp for the evening. He helped her down from her mount with unwonted—likely habitual—courtesy, but ignored her thereafter as he hobbled the horses and laid out his bedroll in the only dry spot. He did not gather kindling.

"Are we to have a fire? My clothes are wet."

"There'll be no fire."

"I'll have to lay them out."

"Suit yourself. But keep in mind that if I shoot you for running off, I still get paid."

So much for courtesy. She proceeded through the bushes, to the riverbank and disrobed. There was no doubt that he was watching. She thought, in a merely theoretical way, that she might turn this exposure to her advantage, to use his desire to put him off his guard. As she stepped out of her petticoats, she was tempted not to stop at her chemise—which was dry—but to offer herself naked to him. After all, wasn't that what a true she-wolf would do?

Alas, although she saw the use in it, she couldn't play that kind of temptress. It had too much of an odor of Almira about it, the crude stripping and posing, as she had seen her do a thousand times for her johns in the work camps. The memory filled her with a disgust that banished all capacity for deception.

She returned with a blanket around her shoulders. McDonnaugh, who was sitting with a hand mirror and some scissors, looked at her and fetched up a grunt. "Thought you'd try to use your cunny to beguile me. It wouldn't have mattered, I'm almost disappointed you didn't try."

"You've got the gun. Do your worst."

"I decline. You're not to my taste with them small titties. And the murderin' and all."

He went back to his mirror, angling the sun's last rays as he trimmed his moustache. She watched him at this for a while, then closed her eyes and began to shiver. This gradually became more violent until spasms coursed through her body. Her teeth chattered. The sound drew the attention of the Pinkerton, who put down his mirror and watched, bemused.

"If you're trying to tell me you're cold, I got another blanket."

She opened her eyes. Still shaking, she raised her arm, and with a crooked finger pointing, rasped, *"You will die ugly. I foresee it."*

He shrugged. "If I die, I die. But I won't leave an ugly corpse. And why don't you tell me this, Professor Kate: if you can truly see the future, how is it you didn't see me coming to get you on that train?"

"The gift is not given to serve us. We are given to serve it."

"Seems to me your time of service is almost done."

Overnight, the temperature dropped to near freezing. Sometime after they retired—it could have been thirty minutes, or three hours—a half-moon rose. In its weak light she slipped out of her bedroll and went to the bushes to pee. When she came back she could see the glint of the captain's open eyes as he waited for her to come back. His held his pistol cocked on his chest.

After an exhausting sleep, Kate was back on her horse with her dress still half wet. At least the sun was shining, driving away the mists from the hollows as it mounted higher and hotter. Cursed by awareness, she filled the empty hours with pointless observations—the color of a mantis perched on a stalk, so vivid green it almost glowed, and the number of objects made by the hand of man that floated on the Saline. She noted an old fence post and a cracker tin like the one Almira kept their stash. The money, she was reminded, that had disappeared when the Pinkerton yanked up her skirts to search for a weapon. At either act, assaulting a woman or stealing her money, he showed no particular pleasure. She found herself thinking fondly of John Junior's good-natured simplicity. Junior, who still had his share, and was probably five hundred miles away. Who was sorry now, she thought, that she had left him behind?

"I'm hungry," she declared.

He reached into his pack and came out with a round, flesh-colored object. When she reached for it, he withheld it until he could say, "Odd that you didn't *foresee* eating this stale biscuit!"

Whatever warmth the sun cast by day was gone by sundown. The cold, her damp clothes, and the hunger began to tell on Kate's body. It started with a headache that engirded the base of her skull, squeezing it until she felt as if her brains were leaking down her neck. Her shoulders began to ache and a sweat stood on her brow that never seemed to dry no matter how often she wiped it with her sleeve. When the wind blew across her face, she became conscious of the fever, rising in intensity until her head seemed to blaze. The hopelessness of it all—the knowledge that she faced not only a long trail but a noose at the end of it—affected her like some poison she had swallowed, making her decline steeper.

By the third evening McDonnaugh noticed that his prisoner was not well. "You aren't fixin' to tell my fortune again, are you?" he mocked. From his pack, he produced a hunk of salt pork wrapped in burlap. She took it, but in her weakened condition the meat was too tough for her to tear off the bone.

Now the captain began to worry. He stripped some pork with his knife and fed her by hand. The salt only made her throat feel worse, but she felt a rueful sort of victory in seeing him forced to feed her, like a mother. At last, she'd hit on a way to pierce his callous hide.

He didn't make her stumble in the dark to drink from the river, but shared his canteen. When it was time to bed down, he fetched the extra blanket and threw the duster on top of that for good measure. The next morning he let her sleep until an hour after sunrise. When she awoke, he had fresh coffee waiting.

But it did no good. She sickened in the saddle, her head drooping lower and lower. The mare, perceiving her distress, had the courtesy to slow down, and the Pinkerton was left to circle them both, cursing his misfortune.

"Ain't it my luck to pay good money for a horse? I could have brought your head in a sack."

"To hell with you, Clarrity, if you won't let me speak to her first," she said, eyes half lidded.

"What?"

"He's my pony don't you dare sell him. Ain't no deal you can make that won't get you shot in the face. My paw, he bought Nickers. Ain't no deal . . . nothing to do with me. My paw is watching, sure as you won't live to spend those winnings."

"You're deleterious, girl," said McDonnaugh.

"What're you offering?" she said, looking straight at him but not seeing him. "To forget the harm you caused? Air out his guts, you might of. He's watching for sure."

Bad as she sounded, the Pinkerton wasn't quite ready to quit the trail. Coming alongside, he lifted her chin to look into her eyes. The rims were the color of strawberry bruises, and her skin had gone sallow.

"Broke down," she said, smiling.

"That's the truth," he said. He figured they were sixty miles from Salina, in a direction no one was likely to seek them. Was that enough for him to keep his prize? There was no way to be sure. But he could be sure that she would not survive another week on the run, sleeping outside, without recovering her strength.

He led her to a covered place to rest for the day. As she rested on a felled log, he collected kindling, produced a box of matches, and lit their first evening campfire. The spectacle served to crack her delirium—as the flames rose, she leaned in as close as she dared, staring into them. The light, so long withheld, was the point of a knife cutting through the bleary tangle of her sick.

"Damn you, you'll roast yourself to death . . ." said the dandy as he stamped at the hem of her dress. Upon dousing the little flames with his heel, McDonnaugh tugged her backward by her elbows, then emptied his canteen on the smoking threads. Kate watched with remote interest, never raising a hand to save herself. Seems he preferred to deliver her alive after all.

"Now look what you've done to my skirt, just when I got it to dry," she remarked.

"Funny. Fancy seeing you laugh as you go up in flames."

"You'd have to get in line."

After she was safely situated, he disappeared into the brush, the crunch of his footsteps fading into the distance. He was away for a time she didn't care to measure in the fire's exquisite influence. When he reappeared in the light, he had a gray rabbit in his fist.

"Hallo! Salt horse is off the menu for now."

He cleaned and spitted the carcass, and laid it across the fire in two forked sticks he hacked from a cottonwood bough. He was fussing with the fire, nudging the wood as if he had some perfect arrangement in mind, when he suddenly stopped and stood up. Peering into the trees, he kept an ear cocked. His hand lay loosely on the grip of his pistol.

"What is it?" she asked.

He raised his free hand for her to be silent. They stayed that way long enough for one side of their dinner to cook through; as if direly inconvenienced, he bent to turn the spit, begrudging any sound the procedure made. Then he was back to interrogating the dark.

It was never the absence of light that spooked Kate. To her mind, darkness connoted nothing more than absence. Lying in the hotel rooms of her childhood, she grew to appreciate the deep darkness that didn't include the veiled lamps of soiled doves plying their trade or the muzzle flashes of angry gamblers. Unbroken dark hid her from harm. Nothing bad ever happened to her there. When she arrived at the Bender cabin for the first time, she did so without fear—until that wolf had stared into Flickinger's lamp. The light of its eyes terrified her more than gazing into the deepest of inky-black pits. It was that light, that unexpected gleam from the eyes of monsters lying in wait, that she dreaded—as she dreaded what might appear among the trees as McDonnaugh stood there, listening.

At length he gave up. Fetching his pack, he produced a small leather pouch, poked two fingers in, and sprinkled salt on the rabbit. By then the meat smelled good enough for her to forget McDonnaugh's vigil and her illness. He held the spit for her to tear off a piece, which she did like a ravening animal. For his part, the Pinkerton didn't touch the meat until he had stuffed a napkin down the front of his ruffled shirt.

"My, you're a fastidious one," she said, her mouth rimmed with grease.

He took a tentative bite, staring at her as he swallowed. "And I've never seen a 'professor' eat like a freight-car bum."

She gnawed her piece down to the bones, then sucked the marrow. He held out a flask. She found this contained not water, but an odd-tasting liquor.

"It's sloe gin," he said when she regarded the flask. "Not stuff I usually pass around."

She tipped it again. As she drank, she saw a figure rush from behind the Pinkerton.

The newcomer moved swiftly, soundlessly, as if it were floating above the ground. McDonnaugh hadn't moved when a heavy object crumpled him from behind. The figure stood over him, stark in the firelight, and lifted the mallet to strike again. This time the Pinkerton's skull cracked, making a sound like the splitting of a fence rail. Blood spattered through the camp, wetting the assailant, the horses, Kate's face. The disassembly of his skull had exposed an artery that spasmed in the dirt.

"By the blood ye are sanctified," said Flickinger as he stood over the mess he had made.

Kate was too stunned to speak. She stared at the hash of bone and brain on the ground as the disembodied vessel spurted, wilted, and went still. Yet for all the blood, the napkin under McDonnaugh's chin was hardly stained.

"Nothing to say?" the old man said to her. "After all the trouble I went through tracking you down?"

"I . . . I . . ." she stammered, the cords in her throat wound too tight. This was clearly Flickinger that stood before her, but he was not quite the same. He was no longer a stranger to comb and razor. He had acquired a better tailor, with breeches and a collared shirt with a checked vest. Gore notwithstanding, he seemed half civilized. And yet—clean-shaven cheeks did nothing to soften those vaguely simian proportions of that brow, that nose, that almost nonexistent chin. The way he hulked over McDonnaugh, he could reach the ground without stooping.

"Hell's bells, after those first few nights I thought he'd never set a fire. So I featured, it's either now or never."

"You've been following us?"

"When have I not looked after you, gumdrop?"

That word. She watched him as he bent in the dirt, extracted the spit from the dead man's fingers and tested the meat.

"Es ist noch warm . . ." he said.

"Why did you call me that?"

"What? Doesn't every father have a special name for his little girl?"

Kate felt a vast chasm open in her abdomen. Cool at first, but with rising anger, she regarded Flickinger as he settled on his haunches to finish his meal.

"You're a liar," she said. "You know nothing about my father."

He frowned. "You were young, but don't you remember our time doing the poker rounds together? You don't remember all the things I bought for you? The books? Nickers?"

"Shut your mouth! I don't know how you know all that, but you aren't him. He's nothing like you."

"The day of that business with Clarrity . . . I sure am sorry about that. Never had a day since I didn't regret it. Drove me to years of drink—until I ran into you at that shithole camp in Colorado. Figured if I let on who I was to Almira, I'd never get you away from her for decent money. So I had to be patient . . ."

"Please, stop . . . I don't want to hear it!" she cried, covering her ears.

"Suit yourself. I'll grant you I never planned to wait so long to take you away. But after we lucked into that little business with the grocery, I figured, what was the bleedin' rush? You were so good at running that show, you did me proud. Now we got enough bankroll to hit the circuit again. We're together for good now, gumdrop. And we got the world at our feet."

She wiped the blood from her face with the crook of her arm. At least with Flickinger's mouth full of rabbit, she didn't have to listen to his lies. If he was father to anything, it was just that—father of lies. Was this all some trick to enlist her services? She felt herself calm; she didn't know how he'd learned details of her childhood, but she sensed Almira's malign hand. Putting her name to this evil made it easier to endure.

Kate let their eyes meet. Still engrossed, the old man gave a satisfied grunt. She had never swung the hammer before, but she expected she might, in due time.

Acknowledgments

THIS WORK OF fiction sticks close to the history as far as it is known. In fact, no one is sure what happened to the Benders after they fled Labette County. There was a court case brought in 1889 against two Michigan women said to be Kate and Almira. But their physical identification was never secure, and the woman said to be Kate, one Sarah Eliza Davis, had none of the real Kate's lively intelligence. The case was dropped in 1890 for lack of evidence.

There is also a tradition of deathbed confessions by men claiming to have been part of posses that caught the Benders. In most of these "confessions," such as that of Jacob S. Frazee, the Benders were dealt summary justice and the participants sworn to secrecy. Unfortunately, none of them led to a shred of physical evidence proving that the murderers were, in fact, caught. For these reasons, I have indulged artistic license in envisioning what happened after the Benders' disappearance.

The published histories I consulted included Fern Morrow Wood's *The Benders: Keepers of the Devil's Inn*, Phyllis de la

Garza's *Death for Dinner*, and John T. James's *The Benders in Kansas*. I also wish to thank Wayne E. Hallowell of Cherryvale, Kansas, for giving me access to his voluminous collection of Bender material—as well as an after-hours look at the notorious Bender hammers in the Cherryvale Museum. His help with my research was not a given: many of Cherryvale's residents despise the legacy of the Benders, preferring that their town be remembered as the birthplace of actress Vivian Vance ("Ethel" on *I Love Lucy*). The town's "Bender Museum," a recreation of the inn and grocery, was closed down in 1978 and never reopened.

I am also indebted to those who supported this project on Kickstarter, including (but not limited to) Nina Faust, David Hollander, Wayne Hughes, Tawny Martin, Robert Newton, Paul Noffsinger, Pamela Reichert, and Todd Yellin. Thanks to Robert Pohl for looking over the German, and James Warner for his comments on an early draft. All writers depend on the kindness of others, whether they be benefactors, editors, or readers.

About the Author

NICHOLAS NICASTRO was born in Astoria, New York in 1963. He has earned a B.A. in English from Cornell University (1985), an M.F.A. in filmmaking from New York University (1991), an M.A. in archaeology and a Ph.D. in psychology from Cornell (1996 and 2003). He has worked as a film critic, a hospital orderly, a newspaper reporter, a library archivist, a college lecturer in anthropology and psychology, an animal behaviorist, and an advertising salesman. His writings include short fiction, travel, and science articles in such publications as *The New York Times, The New York Observer, Film Comment,* and *The International Herald Tribune.*

Discover great authors, exclusive offers, and more at hc.com